KEY WEST

WHERE IT GETS HOTTER THAN YOU THINK.
WHERE EVERYTHING UNDER THE SUN CAN
HAPPEN. AND DOES.
WHERE THE HEARTBREAKERS AND THE
HEARTBROKEN KNOW PLEASURE IS THE KEY.
AND NOTHING IS IMPOSSIBLE . . .

KEY
WEST

Burt Hirschfeld

BANTAM BOOKS
TORONTO · NEW YORK · LONDON

KEY WEST
A Bantam Book

PRINTING HISTORY

*William Morrow edition published January 1979
2nd printing .... February 1979
Playboy Book Club edition January 1979*

Bantam edition / October 1979

*Bantam Books are published by Bantam Books, Inc. Its trade-
mark, consisting of the words "Bantam Books" and the por-
trayal of a bantam, is Registered in U.S. Patent and Trademark
Office and in other countries. Marca Registrada. Bantam
Books, Inc., 666 Fifth Avenue, New York, New York 10019.*

PRINTED IN THE UNITED STATES OF AMERICA

Norma Inez Hayman was born in Key West and raised there. Eighty-four years later—after good times and hard times—she died in North Carolina.

She was a tiny, feisty woman with a fierce passion for life and Key West was her natural habitat, no matter where she went or where she lived. A true Conch, she was hard-shelled and crusty on the outside, pink and substantial inside.

This one, with affection, is for Norma Inez . . .

Author's Note

Key West is a sandy gem in the blue sea on the edge of the continental United States. Latitude: 24 degrees north. Longitude: 81 degrees, 48 minutes west.

Psychologically, historically and geographically remote, it is strongly influenced by and very much a part of mainstream America.

But the Key West described herein is a writer's fancy. An essence, an invention, the Emerald City afloat in the warm ocean. The people of this book—Dutch, Paco, Annie, John Roy Iversen, Welles, Sam Dickey, Grant, Louise, Maribelle, the others—are not real. They were never real. They never breathed the sweet air of Key West, or fished the Gulf Stream for billfish, or sipped a cold brew at Sloppy Joe's or Captain Tony's. They belong only in the story told in these pages.

Key West is a fiction, a tale delivered with affection and an author's fervent wish that it will entertain and divert and be generously received.

B.H.

PART

I

1

There's a South Street, of course. A southernmost beach. And, inevitably, a house which the guides on the passing Conch trains point out as the southernmost occupied structure in the nation. All of the houses look out at the Atlantic Ocean, as if anticipating the appearance of the new explorers, the new saviors.

Most new arrivals come by car across the Overseas Highway—Route 1—from the mainland. Or by air, putting down at Key West International Airport aboard ancient Air Sunshine DC-3's, a slow, somewhat uncertain flight from Miami.

For them, the view toward the old continent revives textbook memories of Conquistadores, of pirates and galleons laden with gold; wreckers still seek treasure out of Key West. Also, out of the east, comes the threat of killer storms that sometimes lash the Old Islands.

The Keely house had been erected to survive the fiercest of hurricanes, built on steel-reinforced pilings with thick concrete walls and small windows. The low roof was fastened to laminated beams by great black bolts: six inches of concrete topped with a double layer of black tar and finished off with Mexican terra cotta tile.

The house was situated on a canal, off Sunshine Lane. Secluded and safe, or so Arthur Keely wanted to believe. A sixty-three-foot aluminum cruiser, complete with a luxurious master stateroom and space for a crew and four guests, was moored in the canal. It was trimmed in varnished teakwood and the aluminum deck had a nonskid finish. It had been built to Arthur Keely's specifications as a gift for his new and young wife, to celebrate their relocation to Key West. During the three years they had lived in the house on Sunshine Lane, the boat had been at sea only five times.

Carefully tended lawns sloped down to the canal, spotted with trees and shrubbery bent by the sea winds. Beyond the flagstone terrace, a swimming pool under the shade of a blue-and-white canvas awning, fringes trembling in the sunlight. Bettyjane Keely preferred not to put her body into salt water, convinced it accelerated the aging process.

Inside the house, original Warhols and Rauschenbergs, a half-dozen Jasper Johnses. Also Barcelona chairs and soft-leather sofas, zebra-skin rugs scattered on the tile floors. African wood sculptures were clustered along one white wall of the living room like a tribal gathering. Corkscrews, bottle openers and egg slicers had made Arthur Keely rich; he manufactured them. Being rich mattered to Arthur since it allowed him a wide area of self-indulgence. Arthur bought whatever he wanted. Or whomever.

Which was how he came to acquire Bettyjane. Clothes, jewels, automobiles; they went to Bettyjane in the weeks after they first met until the investment returned a dividend; eventually Arthur was permitted limited access to her long and lovely body. In due course they were married, and Arthur cut back considerably on the gifts. He firmly believed in not spoiling his relatives. Bettyjane matched him move for move. Their sex life was uninspired, routinized and infrequent.

That worried Arthur. But then Arthur worried a great deal about a lot of things. About the state of the world, for example. The economy. The Youth of America. War in the Middle East. Peace in the Middle East. The health of your average American. The national failure to exercise properly. And lungs. And hearts. And legs.

Arthur felt strongly about legs. "Good wheels," as he put it, "are vital to a person's health." In his private gym Arthur had a stationary bicycle, a treadmill for running in place, exercise machines, weights, a rubbing table, a sauna. Four times a week a masseur labored over Arthur's body. It was a lean body that managed to disguise the fact that it had lived over half a century. Arthur was handsome, with bright eyes and a white smile. There was not a gray hair in his head. His voice was vibrant and firm. His handshake was strong. His breath sweet. Arthur had, however, one serious problem. Bettyjane was his problem. Bettyjane gave Arthur nightmares.

Bad dreams. Really bad. Almost every morning he woke washed by cold sweat, and craving his wife's beautiful body. Half asleep, lonely and afraid, Arthur would reach for her, yearning for a loving response. Forget it.

"You woke me" was her usual complaint.

"I need you."

"Keep your hands off."

"You're my wife."

"So's half the world."

Arthur had been married seven times before Bettyjane. "I love you."

"Hah."

So once again Arthur was forced to confront the truth about himself. Despite his great good looks, his great smile, his terrific physique, very few women actually liked him. Not for what he was deep inside. The delicate and sensitive man he knew himself to be. His money was all they wanted, as witness the unconscionable divorce settlements he had been forced to make. Arthur concluded that he was unlikable, unlovable; but why?

"I'll buy you anything you want," he told Bettyjane one morning, the exact words he had used with his other wives.

"I've got everything I want."

"Nobody's got everything they want."

She thought about it. "You're right, there is one more thing."

His desire rose, his hopes rose. "Name it. Anything."

"I want you out."

"What?"

"Out of the house. For good."

That upset Arthur a lot. However, being a man who had always catered to women, he did what he was told. He left.

"I'm leaving," he announced, a soft Mark Cross leather bag hanging from each hand.

"Good riddance." Bettyjane grinned triumphantly in

the direction of Livia, the Cuban maid. Livia, possessed of a face and a shape that made strong men quiver and weak men grow strong, grinned back.

Two of a kind, Arthur concluded gloomily. "I'll be back," Arthur threatened.

"Over my dead body."

"You can't live without me. We are one, now and forever."

"Hah!" Bettyjane gloated.

Livia giggled.

"I love you," Arthur declared. "I need you. I will have you."

"Agh," Bettyjane said with regal disdain, "go and fuck yourself."

When a week passed and Arthur did not return, Bettyjane's boldness increased. She contacted a lawyer—Walter Bergson—and instructed him to begin divorce proceedings, making it clear that she wanted at least fifty cents on every dollar Arthur had. Bergson said he'd get back to her.

In celebration, Bettyjane phoned Ken Davis at the Slim & Gym. Davis was pretty to look at, strong and stocky, and enjoyed an almost continuous erection of the penis. Davis boasted he could make love for twenty-four hours with neither sleep nor food. Once a barroom bouncer, he pushed grass and took part in an occasional burglary for profit, sharing the proceeds with his brother-in-law, a uniformed member of the local police force. Davis greeted Bettyjane's call with indifference; women were always coming to him for physical attention of one kind or another.

"How you doing?" he said, trying to place the name.

"Why don't you come over, take a swim in the pool."

Davis recognized a sexual invitation when he heard one. "What about your husband?" All of them had husbands.

"I put him out."

"Righteous."

"Can you come now?"

"This minute?"

Bettyjane purred into the phone.

Davis checked his calendar. He was free for the next two hours. "What's the address again?"

Bettyjane took a hot shower, during which she shaped

her pubic hair with a cuticle scissors. She painted her toenails a lustrous pink and later brushed her hair until it shone. She was applying makeup with concentrated concern when a soft popping noise drew her attention to the bedroom. There was a second pop.

"Damn," she muttered, thinking Livia had broken something again. Servants had scant respect for the value of their mistresses' possessions. Bettyjane opened the bathroom door. "What in hell was that, Livia?"

Livia gave no answer. She was lying face up on Bettyjane's king-size bed. "Up!" Bettyjane commanded. "This is no time to goof off. I told you, I'm expecting a guest. Finish your work and beat it back to your own room."

When Livia didn't respond, Bettyjane moved closer. Anguish was permanently frozen on Livia's lovely face. "Livia!" she called. "Please get up." A pool of blood had formed between Livia's breasts, bubbling with diminishing force. "Livia," Bettyjane mumbled almost reproachfully.

Newly made dead, Livia did not respond.

The man in the doorway did. "Looking good, lady."

She came around slowly, as if providing time for him to go away. But shen she looked, there he was, complete with the long-barreled .22-caliber pistol in his hand. "No," she said, and stepped backward. She held out her hand as if to push away the inevitable. "Don't do it. Don't do that to me."

He shrugged a little and shot her in the chest. The impact was surprisingly slight and when she fell there was no shock, no great pain. Still, she was unable to move, unable to get up. He came over to where she lay and put the pistol to her temple and finished the job.

Bill Vail had disappeared ten days before Bettyjane Keely was shot. There was no connection apparent between the two events.

However, Vail's absence was noted almost at once. He was a methodical man who acted in an entirely predictable manner. He rose at the same time each morning, did things in the same order and in the same way so that if clocked there would have been no more than a second or two's variation from day to day. This quality made him good at his work; he was thorough, cautious, dependable.

He was a man of habit. Each day he ate lunch at the restaurant atop the La Concha Motor Inn. Some local fish, broiled, with broccoli or spinach, a little lemon. Tea with honey and no dessert. He would smoke a cigaret afterward and exchange a few words with the bartender before returning to his desk at City Hall.

Twice a month he had his hair trimmed at Ralph's shop and every Saturday Ralph shaved him. He bathed once a day and his nails were manicured and lightly polished. He wore a class ring from Rollins College and it was generally known that he had started out in life to become a Methodist preacher, until he turned to police work for a career.

It was Bill Vail's boast that he had never been out of the state of Florida, only reluctantly left Key West and possessed no desire to visit any other place. Bill Vail enjoyed his life, hungered for no other way, for no greater rewards. He was, he liked to say, a satisfied man.

His disappearance disturbed a great many people. After all, it was so unlike Vail to simply go off without telling anyone. Foul play was immediately suspected, since it is generally supposed that policemen live dangerous lives. The detectives went right to work, spent a succession of eighteen-hour days and came up empty.

Vail's small remodeled Conch house was undisturbed, the closets and drawers in order, shoes lined up with military precision and carefully shined. His new Oldsmobile was parked on the street where it was always parked, showing no signs of forced entry. And there was no corpus delecti.

Rumors went around. Vail had been taken to sea by some bad guys and fed to the sharks in the Gulf of Mexico. Or buried with an anchor chain around his waist. Or he absconded with money from the Policemen's Retirement Fund. Or off to live in the south of France with the Barracuda, a local lady of reputation. But the Barracuda turned up after a three-day holiday in New Orleans claiming no knowledge of Bill Vail.

The mystery deepened and anxiety diminished in direct proportion. Life in Key West went on as before. After a week, most people ceased talking about Bill Vail. The police maintained an open file on the case and every rumor was checked out. But nothing came of it and Wilbur

Huntoon was moved over to be acting assistant chief and he instructed John Roy Iversen to handle the remainder of Bill Vail's responsibilities. As a result, there was an immediate increase in efficiency in all areas, to the great satisfaction of Police Chief Henry C. Watson, who informed everybody who would listen that new blood always produced results.

2

From Miami to Key West on the Overseas Highway. Two lanes, hopping from key to key past construction sites, slowing for ramshackle towns, past diners closed in the night, past marinas offering boats for hire and shacks peddling light tackle and cut bait and grubby motels used only by day fishermen or couples in a hurry.

Sam Dickey had seen it all before, and the trip bored him. He slept fitfully most of the way, awakened periodically by nasty, insinuating dreams that he dared not consider for very long.

Once the trip had been neither boring nor easy. In the beginning of the century, Key West could be reached only by boat. But in January of 1912, Henry M. Flagler arrived in Key West on the first train, the guiding genius and force behind the construction of the Overseas Railroad, sometimes called "Flagler's Folly." Cheering crowds welcomed the eighty-two-year-old Flagler and he walked into Key West on a solid path of roses. Subsequently Flagler established a fleet of seagoing ferries to transport his railroad cars to Cuba.

Nature proved to be too much for Flagler's railroad. On Labor Day, 1935, a hurricane with two-hundred-mile-an-hour winds tore up some seventeen miles of roadbed. High winds and angry seas destroyed workers' camps along the keys, and tracks were ripped from their ties and twisted into impressionistic shapes, railroad cars were heaved around like toys, ending up hundreds of feet from where they had stood originally. Five hundred people perished in the storm.

Travel between Key West and the mainland resumed by boat and by air. But that was not satisfactory and work was begun on the Overseas Highway, which was formally opened in 1938. From Miami to Key West, 167 driving miles.

It was at Marathon that Sam Dickey finally forced himself fully awake and took a couple of slow hits on a joint as the bus rolled across Seven Mile Bridge. He tried to work the cramp out of his right leg and waited for the grass to do its part. After a while the tension drained away and he was able to doze some more. By the time they reached Key West, the sun was already over the horizon and hot, but Sam slept on, peaceful and unaware.

In New York, the ticket seller had vowed that the trip would end within minutes of the E.T.A. "Estimated time of arrival," the ticket seller had said. "Part of the service, see. Otherwise, what the hell, you could fly, right?"

"Ever taken the trip?" Sam had talked himself into believing that contact with strangers was a rich human experience which made life meaningful and noble.

The ticket seller was alarmed by the question. "Whataya, crazy! What I wanna leave here for, y'know."

The bus arrived three hours behind schedule. Not that Sam cared. Time, he believed, was an artificial construct designed to entrap the working class in a never-ending swamp of production and consumption. Sam did not own a watch.

"Go with the flow," he said often. And when he could, he did.

But now, back in Key West, uncertainty surfaced in him again and he wished he hadn't allowed Tandy to talk him into the job. Tandy McWilliams was editor, publisher and founder of *Rock-the-World*, a weekly journal of pop music that had, in the space of three years, become very successful. Thus inspired, Tandy allowed his ambition free rein and was steering his brainchild into other areas: theater, literature, politics.

"I want to broaden its appeal," he told Sam. "First step, the arts. I want to begin a series of profiles, or interviews in depth, of important performers, artists, writers. I mean to penetrate the psyche of the American artist, if you catch my drift. You're a literary freak, Sam, I want you to kick things off for me. Pick a writer, anybody you want, and do a piece on him."

The idea had stimulated all Sam's conflicting ambitions and fantasies. He grinned at Tandy. "Grant," he said, a hint of maliciousness in his manner.

Tandy made a face. "Lawrence Grant. Who cares about that old fart any more? All that macho bullshit. Just a cheap adventure writer. How about one of the gay writers? Gay is in these days. We'd pick up a hundred thou in circulation going with some prominent gay."

Sam felt the bad feelings coming back, but let nothing show. "Get another boy."

"It's gotta be Grant?"

"Yeah."

"I don't suppose you know him?"

"I met him once. In Corsica, actually. Spent a couple of days together. Nights as well. Boozing, going from bar to bar. Quite a scene, my man, complete with entourage. Men, women, God-knows-what, mostly young. Everybody cadging drinks and vicarious thrills off the Great Man."

"But he loved that, all those chicks."

"He turns on to women. But his wife was along."

"Which one?"

"Hilda."

"Number seven, isn't she?"

"Five, I think. Used to be an actress."

"That right? Flicks?"

"A few, I think. Most beautiful creature you ever saw. Fascinating."

"You make it sound good. Okay, we go with Grant. But where the hell is he? The man could be shooting tigers in India."

"He's in Key West."

"How do you know that?"

Because, Sam didn't say, I keep track of Lawrence Grant. Because I'm hooked on him and his entire way of living. Because I'm a Conch, a native-born Key Wester,

and my father lives there and I want to go back. And am
terrified to do so. He said only, "Grant moved down a few
years ago."

So Sam had accepted the assignment and now, strid-
ing along Duval Street, he wished he hadn't, wished he had
stayed away, wished he didn't feel compelled to confront
his past. And his present. A tall lean man with high bony
shoulders and hair that hung down the back of his neck,
he looked too young to be out alone after dark. His cheeks
were smooth and he could go for days without shaving. His
mouth was wide, sensual, his nose narrow and flared slightly at the nostrils, his eyes wary, pale, checking out the pe-
riphery. He liked to think that he missed very little, understood a great deal, could express in words everything;
the eternal conceit of the young writer.

He went into the Fisherman's Cafe and had a Cuban
coffee, very strong, very sweet, and examined the pay phone
on the wall as if it were a dangerous beast. Finally he made
the call. To his surprise, a woman answered.

"May I talk to Dr. Dickey, please."

"Not here." She spoke in a flat uniform voice, layered
with preoccupation.

Her presence—whoever she was—startled Sam and
shook his expectations, his prejudices. He felt unfocused.
"Who's this?" he said.

"Ellen." She spoke as if she belonged.

He grew increasingly uncomfortable, sought for the
right words to say.

"Any message?" she pressed.

"No, I don't think so." Why so cautious? He intended
to see Charles, wanted to, and there was no reason to be
resentful because he wasn't at home waiting for this call.
And the girl—the girl didn't matter. Not at all.

"Call him at his office. I can give you the number . . ."

"Forget it."

"Who—?" she said as he hung up.

He wondered what the girl looked like. Ellen. The
name didn't fit the sound of her. She sounded wispy, im-
permanent, about to take off for distant climes. Ellen was a
solid handle, the name of a person well centered and
anchored in place.

He hit the street going rapidly past a line of small

houses ·that looked the way they had always looked. But all were shops now: a leather worker, a silversmith, a souvenir store. The Old Island had changed, yet managed to retain its essential nature despite the changes.

In Sloppy Joe's, he ordered a beer, and another, then called Charles's office. The receptionist said, "Dr. Dickey, may I help you?" Sam hung up and headed for the men's room.

A burly tourist in plaid Bermudas worked his way up to the urinal. He grinned back at Sam. "Old Hemingway used to hang out in this place. It's a strange feeling, like you're a part of history. Sort of a magic, metaphysical moment, as if Old Ernie was still here."

"I know what you mean."

"You do?"

"Sure, there you are from Peoria, pissing on old Ernie. Gives a man a real thrill."

"Yes, sir," the tourist grinned, shaking off the last drops. "It does, doesn't it?"

City Hall squatted on Angela Street where it crossed Simonton, wide stone steps leading up to the double glass doors of the front entrance. A buff-colored two-story structure, it possessed little architectural interest, a design intended to camouflage the stuffy mediocrity which infects municipal governments everywhere. Politicians discovered scant glory in their lofty positions since most Key Westers gazed upon them with suspicion, distrust and downright loathing. Lying was deemed endemic to the political trade and every officeholder was judged guilty of crimes against the people until proven otherwise. Few are ever found innocent, as most Americans readily concede. Having accepted that point of view as a political truism, the average Key Wester, being tradition-bound, goes about his private enterprise treading lightly lest he spoil the other guy's hustle.

On the street floor, the city clerk, the courtroom, the squad room and various offices of the uniformed police force. Also the office of Police Chief Henry C. Watson, the public service room, rest rooms for men (2) and women (1), et cetera, et cetera, not to mention the candy machine. Any big-city mayor or councilman would have felt right at home on Angela Street.

Up one flight, at the end of the hallway abutting the firemen's kitchen, the Detective Division. The Detectives, as it was generally called, gazed down on the municipal parking lot, to the rear of City Hall. It was rumored that despite this surveillance, two cars a day were lifted out of the lot, at least one of them belonging to a policeman. But no accurate figures were kept to substantiate this and Chief Watson insisted privately that it was all a dirty canard concocted by left-leaning liberal anticop elements in the community. Currently, the lot was being savaged by giant machines, torn up to make space for a parking garage. Until then, cops and municipal employees alike parked behind the First Federal Savings & Loan or in no-parking areas in the streets. A number of cops were settling personal disputes with other cops by ticketing their cars. There had been two fistfights as a result and one officer had actually drawn his service revolver in an effort to end the harassment. He'd been roughly disarmed and muscled into a holding cell until good sense prevailed, the incident never officially reported.

The Detectives was a rectangular chamber containing the requisite number of institutional metal desks, file cabinets and hard-bottomed chairs. The chairs provided scant support and minimum comfort and were blamed for the high number of detectives taking early retirement. All citing lower back trouble.

There were ten detectives: eight sergeants and two lieutenants. They worked two shifts, but the nature of the job frequently caused a man to labor extended hours and so detectives were not expected to report in at any particular time. Days often went by with only one or two of the men making an appearance. No one seemed to mind. No one thought it unusual. It was, it was pointed out when anyone made mention of it, the way things worked in Key West. Taped to one wall in the Detectives was a hand-lettered sign:

NOTHING IS BETTER THAN IT SHOULD BE

No one argued the point.

Behind his desk on the window wall, Dutch Hollinger massaged his strong chin, ran his fingers through his thick, still-brown hair, knuckled his tired eyes. A cop; Hollinger looked the part. His face chipped and craggy, with a wide body that seemed desperately uncomfortable in the too-small chair. Add an almost furtive cast, as if one eye were fixed on the exit, ready to go. There were those who took him to be soft, too willing to compromise; they were wrong. Others viewed him as hard and unbending, angry; they too were wrong. Still, a portion of each of these qualities existed in Hollinger, and more. A careful observer noted that his voice, sibilant and low, owned a serrated edge that made clear this was a man not to trifle with.

Dutch Hollinger had been a cop for a long time. For so long that there were moments when he could not remember having been anything else, or done anything else. But other experiences, other jobs, seemed to matter very little now.

He sipped watery coffee out of a Styrofoam cup and studied the crime report. Seven cars had been reported stolen during the night, three burglaries had taken place, fourteen bar fights, one knifing (a minor but embarrassing wound), plus some random property destruction. An old man named Templeton had been jumped by a couple of thugs, beaten and robbed. Templeton had been hospitalized. One tough guy had been charged for brandishing a loaded pistol in a public place, the Cock and Bull Bar & Grill, but since he had not fired the weapon it was likely he would be released in his own recognizance sometime during the morning. In the winter, during the tourist season, there would be a marked increase in muggings, fights, pickpockets and hustles of one sort or another, most involving middle-aged men on holiday without their wives. They needed keepers, not cops, Hollinger believed, and told himself for the first time that day that he was wasted in the job. He was trained, competent and smart; he should be fighting crime in some big city up north. Instead he was putting in his time, waiting for retirement to roll around. Hell of a way to go . . .

"Read anything good lately?"

Hollinger hadn't heard Iversen enter the room. There was that about Iversen, an ability to materialize, as if from nowhere. It was a surprising quality in a man so large, so designed by nature to attract attention. He moved with a cock-of-the-walk swagger, and was quick to

produce an engaging smile that made him seem even
more attractive than he was. He had China-blue eyes that
actually twinkled and sunburned cheeks and neatly cut
straight blond hair. It was the open face of a Texas
Ranger, friendly, luminous, and slightly askew, as if Iversen were mocking those not in on the private joke.

"No Melvilles in this store, Acting Lieutenant," Hollinger said.

"Moby Dick," Iversen said. "Never was able to finish
it. Too heavy going for me. You see the movie, Dutch?"

Hollinger shook his head.

"Gregory Peck with a beard and a pegleg. I prefer
my movie stars straight."

Hollinger avoided looking at the other man. All his
life he'd been dissatisfied with himself. All those shining
athletes back in high school. The tall, graceful boys
with the well-formed limbs and clear eyes, squared-off jaws.
The kind who looked good even when they did badly. Hollinger had played guard on the football team, had broken
his nose three times. He had been a plugger, and even
when he played well, nobody noticed. At guard, you did
the job, finding what satisfaction you could, not expecting
applause, or recognition. It seemed to Hollinger that all of
his life had been that way.

He rubbed his eyes again. "Three times," he said.

"What?"

"Moby Dick. I read it three times."

"Jesus, Dutch. You sure do punish yourself. You look
awful, do you know?"

"Up late last night. Working."

"Me too. Only I was out killing snakes. What were
you onto, Dutch?"

"The Seabreeze Motel, all night. Stuck away in the
fire stairway. Christ, what a life!"

"Ah, you love it, being a cop. Make a good collar?"

"A hooker and a thief."

Iversen appeared interested. "Sounds okay."

"They set up some character out of Jacksonville.
Dumb bastard, going to sleep on Inez."

"Inez Gavilan? Word I had was she'd moved on to
Philadelphia or New York for some big-time hustling."

"She's still around."

"Neat little ass on that one, fine boobs."

"She's finessed a book salesman."

"The town's loaded with hookers, gives the place a bad name." Iversen looked as if he meant it. He was a Conch, an original Key Wester born and bred. His great-grandfather had come over from the Bahamas and passed his name along. Acting Lieutenant John Roy Iversen IV was the full name. If Iversen had had a son he would have been the Fifth. Those old-line Conchs, Hollinger told himself, often took a proprietary view of Key West, as if the small island belonged to them, a legal and moral inheritance. John Roy, at least, was not stuffy about it, did not make speeches or voice his resentment of newcomers. Hollinger smiled to himself; he'd lived in Key West for nearly twenty-five years and to some people he remained an outsider still.

"Yes," he said. "Lots of hookers."

"Got to give the tourists what they want, I suppose. A wild and wooly Key West."

"I suppose."

"A spot of cooz never damaged any man, Dutch. Remember that."

"That goes in my memory book, Acting Lieutenant," Hollinger said in that mild way of his. "Any way you look at it, Inez did a job on that book man. Put him right to sleep."

"Sweet loving will do it every time."

"That's when she split, leaving the door unlocked. And thirty seconds later who goes strolling in but Ralph Sedly."

"That poor-ass Conch! Busted him twice in the last six months, and treated him most kindly. Next time I claim his ass."

"The book salesman woke up and started yelling and Ralph came down on him a couple or three times."

"So you went in?"

"Sedly fussed a bit until he realized who it was and went limp."

"Never had spine, ole Ralph. That ought to get rid of him for a few years."

"Except for one small detail."

"What's that?"

"The book salesman is married and means to remain so, doesn't want his wife to find out he diddles hookers when he's on the road. He won't press charges."

"Oh, no, my chile—"

"Believe it."

"And Inez?"

"She'll be out by noon."

Iversen rocked back and forth as if working himself up to leave. "Seems like the bad guys are gaining on us, Dutch."

Hollinger grinned in agreement. The grin stopped when the sinewy man with the big hands of a heavy hitter appeared. He cocked his head as if requesting permission to enter the detective bureau, but kept coming on with a long stride, tilted awkwardly by a perceptible limp.

"Morning, Dutch." He spoke in a gentle voice, halting, as if unsure of himself. Hollinger knew better.

"Look what walked in," he said flatly. "You know this character, Acting Lieutenant?"

Iversen inspected the other man and shook his head.

"Shake hands with Isaac Ben-Ezra, ex-cop, sometime head-hunter and a man who comes around only when he wants to share his troubles."

"Now, Dutch," Ben-Ezra said in an apologetic voice. He was smiling.

Iversen offered his hand and they executed a brief handshake.

"What are you selling, Izzy?" Hollinger wanted to know.

"Dutch, Dutch, just a friendly call."

"You happened to be passing through?"

"Something like that."

"You got to understand, Acting Lieutenant, Izzy here lives in Los Angeles these days."

"San Diego." Ezra lowered his eyes shyly. "Dutch and me, we go back a long time."

"Izzy is a P.I."

Iversen seemed interested. "You on a job, Mr. Ben-Ezra?"

"Nothing worth talking about, Lieutenant."

Iversen nodded. "Well, work to tend to. Wilbur Huntoon awaits without. The man says he's going to flop a new boy over to us, Dutch. Any day now, is what he says. Good meeting you, Izzy. Any help I can give, just say the word."

"Nice guy," Ben-Ezra said to Hollinger.

"You always were big on first impressions, Izzy."

"Does that mean he's not a nice guy?"

"John Roy's been around a long time. Experienced. Good at what he does. Probably be chief some day."

"You see," Izzy said. "I was right. A man's got to trust his instincts."

"Not when his instincts are as often wrong as yours are, Izzy."

"Ah, Dutch, are you mad at me, or something?"

"Why are you here, Izzy?"

"Just a small job is all."

Hollinger looked away. "Whatever it is, the answer is no."

"Not nice to talk to your old friend that way, Dutch. How've you been?"

"Forget it, Izzy."

"A friend comes all this way to see a pal and he says forget it. You're looking good, Dutch."

"No more projects, Izzy. These days all I do is police work."

He turned up his hands. "Used to be one myself, Dutch, remember?"

"I'm off the adventure kick. Go back to San Diego. Find yourself another boy."

"Nobody turns 'em out like Dutch Hollinger any more. Besides, I'm just looking for one particular lady."

"No trouble there, Key West's full of ladies."

Ben-Ezra laughed, a thin staccato lacking all humor. It occurred to Hollinger that Izzy had never been easily entertained.

"The name is Janet Quint."

"What's she done wrong?"

"She split on her husband. He misses her. He loves her."

"Nobody believes in love any more, Izzy."

"You've become a cynic, Dutch. Where'd you go wrong? Mr. Quint wants his wife back and I'm here to accomplish that little chore for him."

"Leave me out of it."

"Just checking in is all, Dutch. Make sure the law knows what I'm up to is all."

Hollinger grunted softly.

"Let me buy you dinner, Dutch."

"I'm not hungry."

"You will be by tonight. Still an early eater?"

"Seven o'clock. The Pier House. It's expensive, but you're paying."

"Mr. Quint is a very liberal employer. See you at seven."

Hollinger watched the other man leave. How long had it been—three, no, four years—since he had seen Izzy Ben-Ezra. The private detective seemed altered in ways that were submerged, meant to deceive. He found himself concerned about Ben-Ezra, about his well-being, about his happiness.

Happiness! What a strange word to use. He almost never thought about happiness; certainly not his own. He made himself out to be one of life's mechanics, keeping the wiring intact, the plumbing in order, oiling the noisy hinges of the implicit social contact by which people existed. He made collars, got his share of solves, tried not to do damage to innocent people, tried not to rock the boat. But happiness; that was not a condition he expected to attain, nor deliver anyone else to. Least of all Izzy Ben-Ezra.

The phone interrupted, John Roy Iversen on the other end. "Hey, Dutch, I'm in with Acting Assistant Chief Huntoon. You ready for an honest-to-God genuine crime?"

"What've you got?" A man waiting it out didn't need any hard cases on his back.

"Murder, Dutch."

"No, thanks, bubba. I got me some stolen cars to look out for."

"Actually two murders, Dutch. Chief Huntoon says two killings rate the attention of his two crack detectives, namely you and me. We'll take your car, mine is in the shop again . . ."

Graham and Louise Welles lived in a large house on Petronia Street, not far from the old Naval Base, now closed down and in the care of the civilian government.

Graham suffered a certain antipathy toward civilians, especially in matters military. He took much pleasure in being within sight of the base, as if its once impressive power and population provided a residual luster to his present activities.

Graham was a student of history. He remembered that Key West had once been known as the Gibraltar of the Gulf, that its history as a naval base went back to the days when pirates roamed the Straits of Florida, preying on American shipping. The buccaneers paid tribute to the Spanish government and left its galleons alone, receiving tacit approval in exchange. Until the U.S. Navy put an end to piracy in the area.

As far back as the Civil War, Key West had been a major military base, the only southern city to remain under Union control for the whole war. During the Spanish-American War Key West was a garrison and communications center, supplying the war effort in Cuba. In World Wars I and II, Key West played a heavy role, thanks to its strategic location and fine harbor.

But no more. Smug little men in Washington had, in their limited wisdom, shut down the base, the buildings and submarine pens empty and wasting away. Another move to weaken the nation, and leave it more vulnerable to foreign attack.

These days Graham seldom went near the base, for it evoked bitter memories of peer through these high black iron gates and see the deserted streets and empty buildings. He did take a certain satisfaction in the knowledge that the Little White House, once so favored as a vacation home by Harry Truman, was shuttered and of no further use. Graham had never forgiven Truman for not letting Douglas MacArthur win in Korea. That was the ultimate sin—not winning. As if war were a game meant to build character and to hell with the outcome. Too bad those Puerto Rican nationalists had failed to get to Truman in Blair House back in the forties. Of course, Graham never uttered such thoughts aloud, being a good and most patriotic American.

Always careful in his choice of words, he was especially judicious in what he said to Louise, his second wife. Louise was twenty-five years younger than Welles, a woman of dramatic, almost painful beauty: slender, graceful, with fine black hair and large eyes to match. Her skin was a pale wash, her cheeks falling smoothly to a delicate jaw. She spoke in slow, honeyed tones, as if she knew something special and wished to keep it secret.

She was an ideal wife for Graham. An organized housekeeper, she managed servants easily and with kindness. Her dinner parties were well planned and always a social success. She managed to make every man desire her and yet gave no offense to their wives, most of whom were older than Louise and saw her as a sweet child, so good for Graham.

She lived within the budget Graham set out for her and though she dressed well—but conservatively—she spent very little on clothing, showed only a minor interest in jewelry. She was neat in her person, clean and private in those matters that Graham believed should be kept private, such as her toilet requirements and the disposal of garbage.

Whenever Graham went off on one of his business trips, he felt secure leaving Louise behind by herself. He knew she would attend her work for the Women's Club, the Garden Club, the Historical Society. And never, never, would do anything to displease or embarrass her husband. In short, she was a perfect wife, satisfying most of Graham's marital needs, though he couldn't say that he really liked her. But then, Graham hadn't ever met a woman he actually liked.

Louise understood that. Had learned it early in their marriage. Had deciphered the restraints Graham put on her socially and sexually. He limited her freedom in bed and elsewhere, cataloging conduct he considered proper in a spouse, listing those activities he described as unladylike, un-Christian and disgusting.

"Rules matter," Graham told her on their wedding night. "Right and wrong ways of doing things. Is that clear?"

This much soon was: Graham was a man of high principles, unshakable morality and an immense store of practical knowledge. There was just one thing wrong; he didn't know a damned thing about women.

After the honeymoon, on her second day back in Key West, Louise began to consider the possibility of taking a lover. The idea startled her, shocked and alarmed her. It also was titillating and made her wonder what kind of man would most please her. Someone young and strong, sexually daring, imaginative. Someone less clean and not as plucked as Graham was.

Such a lover never came along. All the men on Key West who fit the fantasy were either gay or hopelessly outside her social orbit; she never met them. She came in contact with retired businessmen—G.M., G.E., A.M.F.— or pensioned generals and naval commanders. They reminisced incessantly about their wartime exploits of their big deals, and treated her like a blood relative. Their wives talked about the mahogany furniture they'd bought in Hong Kong, the handwoven carpets from Iran, the unique paintings done by starving artists in Brazil. They all played bridge and golf and every Friday afternoon one of them gave a cocktail party to which all the others were invited. They lamented the changes that had taken place in America, how ill-mannered young people had become, pointing out that morality no longer counted for anything. They remembered how it used to be.

They had been, Louise knew, the True Imperialists, serving the old Robber Barons. Out there conquering the natives for God, country and the Almighty Dollar. But she never spoke those words aloud, keeping a pleasant smile on her porcelainlike face and always remembering to keep her knees locked together when she sat down.

In time she grew to hate the life she was leading. She loathed the hot island sun. Hated the endless sea. Hated the people she knew and the new ones she met and, most of all, hated Graham. The future she perceived for herself was evident and empty. It terrified and depressed her. Unfortunately, there seemed no way out, no way to alter her existence, no way to make it better.

Until she met Lawrence Grant.

3

"Divorce is an extremely serious matter."

Hilda Grant stared out of bright dark eyes at the small man in the white suit. He had the pinched features and the thin voice of a midget. She was disappointed with this appearance but his reputation far outstripped his stature.

"They say you're the best divorce lawyer in the state of Florida." There was authority in every word she spoke, without gestures or body movement. Hilda Grant was not always comfortable in her own skin, but she seldom let anyone in on the secret.

"South of Atlanta, I'd say." Terence McNally looked her over with obvious approval.

Deliberately, she crossed her legs and put on her most dazzling smile. She was an imposing woman, her dark hair drawn tightly back against her skull setting off an intelligent, smooth brow. Her skin was tawny and umblemished, her mouth wide, the lower lip almost too heavy, but lush and blood-red. She did not look forty years old.

"You were an actress?" he said. He'd read that she had made a dozen or so unimportant movies before she married Lawrence Grant.

"Spare the small talk, McNally." She gave him a quick smile to show she intended no harm. "Let's get down to business."

"Tell me exactly what it is you want from me, Mrs. Grant." It was a struggle not to look again at those legs, those fantastic legs. He had a powerful urge to bite her thighs. Lucky man, Grant.

"I flew up to Miami for this meeting. What I want is

. . . a divorce, Mr. McNally. Get me out from under that big, hairy sonofabitch, that's what I want."

"I was referring to a settlement, Hilda. May I call you Hilda? What do you want in the way of a settlement?"

She faced him without any change of facial expression. "Call me Mrs. Grant. I want everything."

"Everything?" He was disappointed. A good proportion of his sex life came from business. Women in the throes of divorce seemed only too happy to bed down with their lawyer. It was, obviously, the handiest way to pin horns on the soon-to-be-departed husband. Revenge, McNally had learned early in his legal life, was everything.

"Grant, the bastard, cost me my career, my youth, a good part of my life. I want to be paid back. In full."

McNally had heard it all before. Divorce brought out the worst in people. Or maybe it was marriage. Man and woman were not created for one-to-one cohabitation. Variety was essential for sanity and full satisfaction. McNally rubbed his hands together and shot a glance across Hilda's bosom. Neat little titties. Perky. Sweet and round. He blinked his way back up to her marvelous face.

"I am obliged to say this. Is there any chance of effecting a reconciliation?"

A flood of memories almost brought tears to her eyes. A vision of the young woman she had been when she first had seen Grant. So young, so vulnerable, so willing to risk everything for that man, for her love for him. What an incredible jolt it had been to meet him—awesomely large, those great powerful shoulders, a handsome head that might have been sculpted by an ancient Greek, his strong, even features. How beautiful he'd been! How she had craved him, how she had come to love him, to depend on him.

She shook her head as if to clear it. "No chance," she murmured; then louder. "No chance at all."

"You have no more feelings for Mr. Grant?"

She stared at McNally as if seeing him for the first time; the man was obviously a fool. "Feelings? I love him, don't you understand? I've always loved him and I suppose I always will. There's never been a man like Grant, no one —at least not for me. There never will be. But the bastard, he's destroying me, if he hasn't already done it."

"Then you mean to obtain a divorce?"

"Divorce, yes. That's my only chance. He taught me that, Grant did. Survive, whatever the cost. Live and go on. It's the ultimate triumph. Yes," she ended bitterly. "Get me a divorce."

McNally busied himself with some legal documents on the desk. "Sometimes this can be a very distressing business. Sometimes I think I ought to give it up."

"But not for long," she said, without malice.

"No, not for long. It pays awfully well."

She filled her lungs with air. "Back to business, then." Her face firmed up, her mouth tightened, all vulnerability was wiped away. In its place a brittle and shining veneer behind which she concealed the frightened little girl she felt herself to be.

"Mr. Grant is one of the world's greatest novelists."

"Spare me the literary criticism, McNally. Just get me loose and get me rich."

"Nevertheless, I remain an admirer of your husband's work. He is a fine stylist, a writer of truth in fiction, his characters live in my head."

She snarled. "The man writes about fishing, fucking and French food. He can't bait a hook, he's a lousy lay, and he steals all his recipes from Julia Child. Dammit, McNally, get on with it! You're going to need grounds, right?"

"Right. Grounds are always necessary."

"He's screwing around."

"And who is he having an affair with?"

"An affair! Are you kidding? That raunchy bull would dip his stick in any handy pot. Spends most of his time getting it on with groupies."

"Groupies?"

"Yes. Horny little girls who turn on to writers. The bars in Key West are full of them, ever since Hemingway. They clutter up the place, underfoot wherever you go. Literary name-fuckers, ask anybody."

"You made this discovery recently—about your husband's infidelity?"

"It's been going on for years—"

"But now—?"

"I've had enough. I want out."

"With an equitable settlement."

"All I can get."

"The whole ball of wax, if possible."

"Is it possible?"

"I'll need an accounting of his assets."

That sobered her up. There was the house in Catherine Street; a fine old two-story structure with galleries rimmed with black wrought iron and wooden shutters and in the front yard two traveler's palms and a superb royal poinciana near the gate. The house had been put up in 1910 by Henry Vance, one of the engineers at work on the Overseas Railroad. The rooms were spacious, the ceilings high, with slow-moving fans in every room. Grant had bought it two weeks after moving to Key West. He loved that house more than anything he owned.

"I must have the house," Hilda said sweetly.

"And everything in it," McNally added.

"Everything . . ."

"What else?"

She shook her head.

"Another dwelling, a car, his own boat. He's a noted fisherman and—"

"He doesn't believe in owning things, not Grant. Says it ties a man down, inhibits him, makes him vulnerable. Writers," she ended scornfully.

"I see. What about stocks? Bonds? Land?"

"Nothing. Grant says it's immoral for money to make money. Says it separates people, social classes."

"All right," McNally gloated. "That means cash. He must have it socked away. Switzerland or the Bahamas. Safe-deposit boxes. Under the bed. Where?"

"There isn't enough money to get through the year. Grant spends money as if it's going out of style. Nothing sticks. Those safaris in Africa. The trips to Asia. Up the Amazon. Those years in Europe. My God! We've lived like kings and queens and bought drinks for every rummy on the loose. Grant hates to drink alone, hates to do anything alone. Says he's by himself most of the time, anyway. Writing, that is. Says loneliness is a writer's greatest asset and deadliest curse. Then there are the other four."

"Four?"

"Wives. The old bull's been to the well before me.

He's got nine children and supports them all. Wives, kids, and a number of their relatives. I've never been able to decide whether it's generosity or ego. Money is for Grant to piss away."

"Royalties?"

"Some, not much. Checks come in every six months, smaller and smaller amounts. Grant's got the reputation but he's no backlist giant. His readership fell off years ago."

"What's he working on now?"

"Who knows? He doesn't talk about work in progress. Says it's bad luck. Whatever it is, he's been at it for nearly five years. That means five years without any substantial income."

McNally sat back and worried for a moment or two. There had to be some way of exploiting this situation. Of copping a substantial fee. Lawrence Grant had to pay—somehow.

He said, "Letters?"

"Letters?"

"To famous people. Or even unknowns. Surely he wrote letters."

She began to laugh. "Not a one. Not that I know of. But I can compile a hell of a lot of old and very large telephone bills. Grant hated to write, said he got his fill working. Said that's why they invented the goddamn telephone, so writers could talk and not write. Sure, he knew them all, Shaw, years ago, Gertrude Stein, Hemingway, Faulkner, Joyce, Fitzgerald, Steinbeck, even Charlie Chaplin, Dietrich, some of the other Hollywood types. But letters, no way."

"Well," McNally said, as if he had some dramatic and secret plot in mind. "We'll squeeze him for whatever he's worth and just a little extra."

"Tell me how."

"With your help. A private investigator may be in order. We'll do a double check on his assets—"

"If that bastard's been holding out on me . . . !"

"And those little escapades. Evidence, not accusations, is what makes a good case."

"Then you'll take the case?"

McNally leaned toward her, eyes chilly and mean. "I'll murder the bastard . . ."

She felt very small suddenly, very sad, and all alone.

Graham Welles saw himself as a survivor. A highly adaptable member of an adaptable species. A species that had survived, yes, but more importantly had prevailed over all other species. Over the environment itself. Welles looked upon mankind as a wondrous creation of the Divine Creator, graced by His inspiration, a breed without limits, able to acomplish wondrous effects in this world.

And some men were clearly superior to others. Able to accomplish more, do better, willing to try to move mountains and in many blessed instances able to pull it off. Welles viewed himself as one of these superior beings. Whatever the circumstances, wherever he might find himself, whatever demands were placed upon him, Welles knew, *knew*, that he was equipped for the job. With dispatch. With a high degree of competence, and with style. Welles believed that style was a necessary aspect of any leader of men. Style separated the man out front from his followers. Style and imagination, he would amend. And the degree of personal courage involved.

Welles believed that his life—that every life—had a purpose, known or not. And it was incumbent upon each man to fulfill that purpose, or be forgotten forever. Treasure was only part of the reward Welles sought. More important, more gratifying to him, was personal Honor. Duty. And Country. Welles had dedicated himself to his Country, to the Right Way of Life, to righting the wrongs that some men inflicted on their fellows. Welles saw himself as a White Knight in mortal conflict with the Forces of Evil.

Cemented into the immutable truth of his beliefs, Welles was a man at home wherever he happened to be. In the Miami Airport, for example. Air Sunshine put him down at 12:45, only a few minutes late, but in plenty of time for his appointment. Without luggage to wait for, he strode off at once, making his way toward the hotel lobby. Everywhere he heard the melodic sounds of spoken Spanish, clusters of people coming from or flying out to Latin America. That sweet language washed over him and he began almost at once to think in Spanish and he knew that he was doing the right thing. The only thing.

Persky was waiting in the hotel lobby. He was a slight man with wispy gray hair in a linen jacket and an open-collared white shirt. He looked ineffective and ordinary, but Welles knew better. Jacob Persky was a man to admire, to defer to, to avoid offending.

They shook hands briefly. "There's a car outside."

It was a shining black Cadillac with a thick-necked driver who, after seeing them seated in the back, went around to his place and drove off without a word.

"It's been a long time, Jake."

"Time passes."

"Not too much more time for our side, I believe."

"One lives in hope."

Welles sat back and made no effort to say more. Persky was a man who spoke only when necessary. He was a man of action, a doer, a shaker, a mover. One of the great men.

They turned onto Interstate 95 and headed north, keeping to the new speed limit. Soon the vistas opened up and the country seemed larger, flatter, less populated.

"Cows," Persky said. "All this is Forester's. About ten thousand acres, all cattle ranch. Cowboys in Florida, imagine it?"

"He's a big man."

"Big enough," Persky said, putting an abrupt end to that exchange.

Welles took no offense. Important men had important things to think about.

Almost as an afterthought, Persky handed Welles a rectangular package wrapped in plain brown paper. "You'll appreciate this."

Welles stared at the package.

"Open it later," Persky said, looking at the passing terrain. "You still railroading?"

"Nearly two thousand feet of track. I'm making my own turntable. Multilevel layout, six tracks, eighty-five turnouts."

"Maybe you'll show me someday." Persky tapped the package. "It's a pretty good model of the Heisler logging and mining loco. You ain't got it already?"

Welles shook his head. "That's very kind of you, Jake."

"It's a beauty. I got myself one, too. A real brute, they say. Could climb a fourteen percent grade and still make it on the sharpest turns. You'll like it."

"That's thoughtful of you, Jake. I remember very well the layout you built in the house in Havana—"

"The railroad room—Esther used to tease me about playing with toys, may she rest in peace."

"You have a feel for model railroading denied to most men. You do splendid work."

The small man looked away as if embarrassed and nearly thirty minutes passed before he spoke again. "Baseball," he muttered, with a shake of his narrow head. "American boys playing baseball in Cuba."

"Exhibitions," Welles said.

"Exactly. Setting us up for bigger and worse things. It just isn't right."

"Not like in the old days, Jake."

"Sure not like in the old days. That fucking Castro, I'd like to take him out, once and for all."

"Is that why I'm here?"

Persky turned his flat cold eyes to Welles. "Why you're here you'll find out from Forester and me when we get into the compound." He clamped his mouth shut and they made the rest of the trip in silence, giving Welles a chance to reflect on what he knew about Spencer Forester.

The ranch had been created by Spencer's grandfather, when Florida acreage was cheap and available. Using it as a base, Grandfather Forester had built a financial empire that included oil fields in Louisiana, a shipping company which sailed under foreign flags, an import-export firm with offices in New York City, and the Forester Florida Bank.

By the time Spencer's father finished running the family business, he had tripled its worth, pushing the operation deep into South and Central America. Automobile assembly plants. Coffee plantations. Railroads. Two chains of retail outlets for American manufactured goods.

Spencer was only twenty-three when his father died. He took over the business himself and in ten years doubled the size of the empire. Now forty years old, he ran things with a cool arrogance that comes only from being born into wealth and power, and knowing that you deserve all you own.

The Forester Compound was in the northeast corner of the ranch, established on a rise that overlooked a sandy beach and the ocean beyond. A ten-foot-high wall of stone and cement and topped with shards of broken glass surrounded the buildings and armed guards patrolled the perimeter with attack dogs, day and night.

Two guards examined Jacob Persky and Graham Welles with tough competence, checking their names against a roster of expected visitors, before passing them through the black iron gates. Inside, another guard escorted them from the parking area to the main house where a Philippine houseboy in a white jacket took over, put them in a sunlit room that opened to the sea. There were two large oil paintings on the walls: a very good Matisse and a Cézanne that was brilliant. Welles was impressed; Persky ignored the paintings.

When Forester appeared, he placed himself in an old leather chair, crossed his legs and folded his hands in his lap. He had the compact look of a tournament handball player. Pale eyes dominated a small face. He motioned the two men to a long white sofa and inspected Welles clinically.

"I know a great deal about you," he said at last. "Jake says you're a good man."

Welles knew better than to reply.

"Onetime navy commander. Destroyers during the war and later naval intelligence. Very good. You retired after twenty. Why so young?"

Welles allowed himself a small smile. "I imagine you know that as well."

"Oh, yes, State Department. Cultural attaché in Guatemala and later Mexico City." He waited and Welles let him wait. The faded, wolfish eyes glinted as if in pleasurable anticipation. "I nearly forgot—you were CIA, weren't you, Welles? A case officer."

"Now you have it all," Welles uttered softly. "Almost."

Forester sat back. "I read your book—*Search for the Superman* . . . You published it when you were quite young."

"Twenty-one. A year after I finished at Yale."

"*The Twentieth-Century Quest* you subtitled it. Very provocative. How goes the quest, Welles?"

"As all worthwhile journeys, never-ending."

"I like that. We see life in the same way. The search. The struggle. The accomplishment and the victory that allows one to launch the quest all over again. You're right, Jake, he's a good man."

"Best man at the Bay of Pigs, Mr. Forester," Persky said. There was no deference in his voice. He merely stated facts. "More like Welles here and I'd be back in Havana with my boys, running the casinos, everything else."

"One day, Jake, one day."

"We got common interests, you and me, Mr. Forester. We work good together."

Forester accepted the compliment, attended Graham Welles again. "You're wondering why you're here . . ."

"You'll tell me."

"Indeed. But first a dollop of recent Florida history, for background. The state is best known as a playground for the idle rich, and for the tourist trade. Nouveau riche in Miami, old money in Palm Beach and so on. Old money ran the state, of course. But fluctuating land values and an uneven economy provide an impoverished psychological condition in which to operate a financial marketplace. Very few people were willing to take Florida seriously."

"I always did well in Florida," Persky said, as if dealing in long-ago memories.

Forester ignored him. "Nothing remains static. Efforts to bring the state to financial maturity have been made, are being made. Bankers, industrialists, businessmen of various stripe, have joined in the common effort. Men of stature, responsibility—"

"Men like yourself?" Welles said.

Forester measured him at length. "Not . . . quite . . . like . . . me. But similar. Our mutual endeavors have been successful, though we have done nothing to publicize our triumphs. We function in the shadows."

"I believe in quiet work."

"I expect you do. Are you aware that the airport in Miami ranks just behind New York, Los Angeles, San Francisco and Chicago in volume of goods? Or that the growth rate is twenty-five percent?"

"I'm impressed."

"No you're not," Forester said quickly but uncritically. "You are not a capitalist with a capitalist's overriding concern for profits. You are, however, a creature of the system, and that is enough for us today."

"Which brings us to the question of my presence here."

"You are here in order to join us in a venture that will appeal to your ideological set and nourish your love of adventure."

"I'm listening."

"South Florida, Miami in particular, is growing. Some of the nation's largest banks have opened branches in Miami. More than half a hundred major corporations have located their Latin American divisions in the area. Certain Latin countries do all—repeat, *all*—their banking in Miami. Are you familiar with the Edge Act, Mr. Welles?"

"Two laws enacted by the state legislature that allow foreign banking institutions to conduct international operations in the state." Welles was dismayed to discover that he wanted to please Spencer Forester, and prove to him that Graham Welles was a knowledgeable, trustworthy man.

"Very good." It was the automatic compliment of a teacher to a student. "And also to allow *branch* banking, an aspect of the business not yet fully exploited. All of this adds up to one vital fact: Florida is swiftly turning into a major financial center. Clients need not go elsewhere for their banking needs. Consulting services, technical assistance, computers, accounting, communications with the entire international banking and business community are offered right at home. I hope all this doesn't bore you, Mr. Welles."

"I am far from bored, Mr. Forester." It was all beginning to come together for Welles and he began to understand why he had been summoned. "You're talking about Latin American clients, I take it?"

"Yes, exactly. For too long we Americans have ignored Latin America. Politically, socially and in business, as well. We have barely scratched the surface of a market which is extremely rich potentially and always expanding. It could be, it should be, it must be, our peculiar and private province." Forester stared into space, not moving for nearly a minute. "Nobody can be permitted to interfere."

"That rotten Castro," Persky growled.

"Jake is right," Forester said.

"That's why I'm here," Welles said. "You want me to do something about Castro?"

"You were a case officer at the Bay of Pigs. You are and have been very much involved with the veterans of that ill-starred mission. You are retired from CIA, Mr. Welles, yet sub-rosa work occupies your attention much of the time. No one else is in quite the same position as you are. One could say you are unique."

Welles suppressed an emotional response. Anger was easy. Blind retaliation was for lesser men. Insults and arrogance could be tolerated when one knew one was right, when one knew one's time always came. He had never enjoyed being patronized, now less than ever. But people like Spencer Forester always underestimated a man like Graham Welles, saw him merely as an adventurer, a tool, a weapon, an operative for hire, to be used and subsequently discarded. Welles knew what he was doing, where he was headed, what the future held for him. He spoke in a mild, discursive way. "Permit me to quote from Security Action Memorandum Number 31, dated March 11, 1961: 'Every effort should be made to assist patriotic Cubans in forming a new and strong political organization.' That memorandum encouraged those who were willing to risk everything in order to rescue Cuba from Fidel Castro and communism. We were betrayed again. We are being betrayed again. All this talk of normal relations with Castro, of trade, of tourism. Castro has not changed. He means to infiltrate and corrupt all of Latin America. My friends and I oppose this whenever we can."

"And my friends and I agree with your attitudes. Your general approach to the problem. It is our most profound desire to prevent Castro from succeeding in his aims. We intend to put an end to this false and treasonous friendship with Fidel now cropping up. We will terminate Castro, and Castroism."

"In order to protect that rich marketplace you mentioned?"

For the first time, a hint of annoyance seeped into Forester's manner. He uncrossed his slender legs and crossed them again. His eyes swept Welles's face as if seeking some suggestion of a fundamental character flaw. Satisfied, the tension eased out of his joints.

"Surely you don't object to that, Mr. Welles?"

"Not a bit."

"Profits can accrue to us all."

Persky jabbed a finger at the air. "As long as I get the gambling concession, and a few other exclusive rights. You won't have trouble with me or my people."

Forester acknowledged Persky with a nod. "Jake can supply people, hardware, and a good working knowledge of Cuba, should such assistance be in order."

Persky straightened up. "I got people on the island still. Good men, Cubans. They can't wait for the old days to come back."

"I have my own people—"

"Pride goeth—"

"Pride has nothing to do with it. If I need help, I'll ask for it. Castro," Welles said, as if seeing the man. "There have been at least a couple of dozen attempts on his life. He always lands on his feet. He's smart, tough, and well guarded."

Persky snorted. "Anybody can be hit, you give the contract to the right guys."

Forester asked for silence with a gesture, and got what he asked for. "Don't burden me with details. Somehow, this movement toward reconciliation between Cuba and the United States must be terminated."

"A bullet in Castro's brain," Persky said.

"Whatever it takes," Forester said. He stood up. "My friends and I have no interest in Pyrrhic victories." He crossed over to the huge picture window in one wall and stared out at the horizon. Without turning, he said, "Are you the man for the job, Mr. Welles?"

"That depends."

"On what?"

"On the parameters set forth."

Forester came around. There was an almost beatific expression on his face. "The right man will define the job for himself."

"Strategy. Operations. Recruiting."

"All in your province."

"You will expect reports?"

"I expect results."

"The kind of tactics that are required can be dangerous and good men can lose their lives. Such risks are understood, but the men must know that their families will be—"

"Financially cared for for the rest of their lives. I guarantee it."

"Good. Budgetary considerations will be high."

"We'll establish a secure communications network between us. Send your needs along, I'll see to it that they are fulfilled. A drop should be set up where funds can be deposited and retrieved."

Persky said, "I'll work it out."

"Very good, Jake."

"You want some of my people?" Persky said.

"Later perhaps. I had intended to return to Key West this evening. I'll go to Miami instead. Consult with my people for a day or so. Preliminary plans have to be made. A campaign is in order, not just an occasional strike."

"Exactly," Forester said. "We want to completely disrupt this diplomatic move toward normal relations."

"My friends and I will work on the problem."

"Then you accept the assignment?"

"With one thing understood from the start—"

"And what is that?"

"If I am betrayed, my men betrayed, I'll come after you myself. Kill you myself."

Persky clucked proudly. "I told you he was the only man for the job . . ."

Charles Dickey stood naked at the window, the soft night air cooling his skin. Beyond the bougainvillaea, beyond the protective row of palm trees, he heard the intimate laughter of the couple in the pool. After a while the laughter ceased and the splashing about and he could not keep a vision of them embracing and kissing out of his mind. Presently there was more laughing and splashing and he supposed they were chasing each other around the pool. He longed to join them, to romp in the water, to play in a childlike fashion with neither guilt nor shame.

He mocked himself in silence. Charles Dickey was no innocent, nor were the people in the pool. They all knew what they were doing, what they wanted to do, what was permitted and what was forbidden.

The nocturnal swimmers lived in number 8; Charles in number 2. Eight houses made up the compound. Each had once sheltered a Cuban cigar maker and his family. But all of the cigar makers were dead, or moved on to Tampa to grow old in the service of a good smoke. Anglos lived in each of the houses now. All comparative newcomers to the island. There was the businessman and his wife of twenty years, always fighting, always threatening divorce; there was the playwright, whose one Broadway hit would support him until death separated him from those precious royalties; the two fashion models who existed in lesbian bliss; a dentist and his dog, a pug who looked very much like his master; an automobile salesman; an English clothing designer, seldom on the scene; a retired actors' agent, given to recollection of his glory days in Hollywood; and Dr. Charles Dickey.

The back yards of the houses had been joined into a common semitropical garden growing around the shared swimming pool. Gravel paths led from the high wooden gate to each of the houses. The houses were owned separately, but the common areas were maintained by equal contributions from each owner.

Occasionally there was a problem. The actors' agent had once withheld his share for pool maintenance since he didn't swim. And the lesbians had threatened a lawsuit against the dentist because his dog had ripped up their garden. The dentist had once constructed a high wire mesh fench to keep the two women out, "not to keep poor little Kissinger in." But most of the time they lived in peace, if not harmony.

Dickey heard the couple in the pool leave. Whispering to each other. He did not wonder who they were, didn't want to know. He made a point of not allowing himself to be drawn into his neighbors' lives. Polite interest was the most effort he would make. He remained casual, cordial, never encouraging.

The night grew still and quiet. The quick movements or one of those small lizards that inhabited almost every house on the island caught his eye. He reached for the wall as if to touch the creature and it scurried higher. They were welcome since they kept the insect life in check and in no way threatened human beings.

Key West, he told himself, was an agreeable place to live. An easy and open social life that gave free rein to his

unpredictable moods and desires. He could spend a great
deal of time by himself and no one thought it odd; at least
no one commented on it. He swam on impulse, day or
night, winter or summer. He fished out in the Gulf or in the
Straits whenever he felt like it. He could indulge any tastes
he had, at his pleasure, go and come without notice. If
anyone judged anyone else, he hardly noticed. Key Westers
were very good at not noticing.

He heard Corinne stir behing him, let out a small
sound of satisfaction. She was a lovely women, long of
limb and heavy in the bosom, her flesh sensuous and soft.
Her mouth was a marvelous orifice, offering infinite pleasures. Corinne was a giving woman, who made certain
she received equal rewards in return.

"Ah, Doctor," she uttered in a contralto meant to
provoke. "I believe I need another treatment."

"I prescribe a great deal of rest, Corinne," he said,
not turning. "Lots of sleep."

"Corinne wants her sleeping medicine."

He laughed shortly. "Insatiable woman."

"With you, lover."

"I'll bet you say that to all the boys." He tried to keep
it light.

A defensive undertone slid into her voice. "How
many do you think there are?"

He began to feel uneasy. He wanted no conflict. No
confessions. Corinne was lovely and loving, lively, with a
sense of humor about most things. She was bright and
responsive, and he enjoyed her company. Yet he was always sorry when he brought her back to number 2. For
him, always, there was that nagging need to be by himself. Outside most normal avenues of human activity. To
close off all human contact. To nurse his uncertainties and
seek answers to the questions that plagued him and give his
wounds time to heal. Not to think so much; trying to feel
his way through life. To allow his unconscious to work
out the twists and turns, to bring him back to daylight.
He went over to the bed and kissed that full, mobile
mouth.

She stiffened. "I'm not screwing everybody, you
know."

"I know."

"It's important that people are kind to each other."

He didn't know how to apologize directly; it was something he'd never learned, or had forgotten years before. "Things come out—"

She stroked his chest. "In all of us, I guess. Don't worry about it, Charles."

"You are a lovely woman."

"But you'd like me to go."

"There are times I have to be alone."

"Oh, I can understand that. I know all the signs. Some men fall in love right away. Others can't tolerate a woman getting close . . ."

"I've been married."

"Married is not necessarily close." She found her clothes in the dark.

"You don't have to go."

"It's better." The fact of dressing for her was sexual beyond any word she could speak, or action she could take. A leg flexed, a breast descending in gentle profile, the soft round of her bottom.

"Please stay."

"Always leave 'em wanting." She laughed at herself. "Call me, lover, before I have to call you."

"It's always very good with you."

"I get the best of you, Charles. You're a beautiful man. Ta ta." And she left.

He stretched out on the bed, smelling her perfume and her sex, wide awake now and longing for the possible, for the ultimate pleasure. And he set himself against it as if to consider such joy was to give it a dirty name.

Because he had been a petty officer, Edward Templeton was admitted to the Naval Hospital. When Dutch Hollinger entered his room, Templeton was lying on his back staring at the white ceiling. His sunken cheeks were bristling with gray beard and his eyes were tinted yellow and glistening, as if he'd been crying. His hands were extraordinarily large, spotted with liver marks, the knuckles massive, the fingers long. They were the hands of a man who had once been very strong, but now that strength was gone and he was just another sick old man, afraid and alone. In a glass on the table next to the bed, his false teeth.

Hollinger showed his badge to the battered man and identified himself.

The old man lifted one hand, let it fall back. "Look what they did to me."

"I wanted to ask you a few questions."

Templeton closed his eyes and opened them again. "There's no peace anywhere any more."

"Would you rather I came back another time?"

"Ask, mister."

"I understand they took fourteen dollars out of your wallet."

"Out of my pocket. I don't own a wallet. All the money I had."

"Did you see them?"

"There were two of them."

"Two men?"

"Boys."

"Boys? About what age?"

"Not tall, not rough-looking."

"In their twenties, would you say?"

"Skinny, both of them. You wouldn't think such skinny boys could hit so hard."

"Race, Mr. Templeton?"

"Huh?"

"White, black, Hispanics?"

"Oh, yeah. White, I think."

"Good, that's good. Two Caucasians."

"Very fast. It happened so fast."

"Young people are usually very quick, Mr. Templeton."

The old man said wearily, "You get old so fast. Where's the time go?"

"Did you get a good look at their faces?"

"Faces?"

"You think you could identify them?"

The old man closed his eyes.

"From our mug book, Mr. Templeton."

"I'm tired."

"We need your help, to catch them."

"My help?" His eyes fluttered and opened.

"When you get out of here, in a day or so, the doctor said. Suppose I give you a call, ride you down to the station house. Let you look over the mug book."

"Right on my own porch. Came up on my own porch. No respect for people, you know."

"I'll give you a ring, Mr. Templeton."

"No peace anywhere . . ."

"That sun's going to blind me," Ben-Ezra complained.

Dutch had arranged for a table by the window, looking out at the Gulf of Mexico. He had placed his back to the westering sun and now grinned with friendly malevolence at his companion.

"People come to Key West just for the sunset, Izzy. Enjoy, enjoy."

"Sometimes I forget what a pal you are."

The waiter brought drinks and they made small talk, as if to do otherwise were to cause damage, revive old hurts. Yet neither could avoid the past, and each of them knew it.

"You're looking good, Izzy."

"I'm getting old, Dutch."

"Everybody is."

"I got fifteen years on you, close to twenty."

"But you're skinny. Skinny guys go on forever."

"Yeah," Ben-Ezra said. He glanced down at his big hands. "Those jobs we did together—we were a good team. You're the gutsiest character I ever came across."

"Next to you, Izzy."

Ben-Ezra allowed himself a quick, pleased smile. It faded almost at once. "No more. I was always too gullible, trusted people. I made mistakes."

"You were great, Izzy. Once, maybe the genuine article, James Bond and Mike Hammer rolled up in one. Meanest Jewish cop on the West Coast. And still ornery."

"Things happen, Dutch. A man grows older, not so mean, not so brave. I lost a lot, Dutch."

"Everybody loses something. When there's rough work, there was no one better."

"I took a couple of slugs one time and a knife another. Came close to dying."

"You're still around."

"I took my pension, a little extra for disability. Now it's strictly P.I. Better safe than sorry."

"I'll be glad when my time is up."

"You can say that, but it ain't that way, Dutch. You

miss it. The action. The other guys. Belonging. Being a cop is a good thing. I miss it."

"You could've stayed on . . ."

"I lost it, I told you. The reflexes were slower, I wasn't as strong or quick any more. On the range, not such a straight shooter."

"You could've stayed . . ."

"To do what? Shuffle papers while other guys were out in the street? It didn't matter after Esther walked out on me."

"I never understood that, Izzy."

"Who understands anything?"

"After twenty years of marriage."

"Twenty-two years, and she walks. Ridiculous, I tell you. Another man, you see."

"Don't tell me, Izzy."

"It's true. A younger guy, some stud. I told you, I lost a lot."

"Not you, Izzy."

"What the hell did she expect? What did she want? What was she thinking, a woman like that?"

"Ah, Izzy, who understands women?"

"A cop should never get married." Ben-Ezra finished off his drink. "Jesus, Dutch. I miss that woman a lot."

Hollinger searched for words, for emotional balm to comfort his friend. "They come and go," he said.

Ben-Ezra stared at him. "You're like a brother to me, Dutch. But you're a man frozen in place. You don't let people close, inside, you don't let them love you. I was never that way. But I understand, it's okay with me. I'm your pal. But a woman needs more, affection, emotion, understanding."

Hollinger wanted to touch the other man, to reassure him, to express his own feelings, to confess; there was so much to confess. Instead he called for another drink and ordered dinner. "Still flying, Izzy?" he said when the drinks came.

"Not in years. What about you?"

"No more."

"Remember the last one, Dutch?"

"Still shake when I think of it."

Ben-Ezra laughed, a nervous staccato. "Not you. You were very good on the job."

Hollinger struggled to suppress a mounting resentment. "That was ten years ago, Izzy. Ten goddamn long years."

"Ten years? I guess I am getting old."

"I swore off all that shit after that."

"We were the first, Dutch."

"Like Jackie Robinson."

"I never thought of it that way. Nobody'd snatched a gringo out of a Mexican jail before us."

"It was a work farm, bubba."

"Land the plane—you remember that old crate, Dutch?"

"A Piper J-3."

"Right. Put her down, make the contact, load up and take off. Nine minutes in and out."

"You paid off every Mexican in sight."

"Yeah, jailers, guards, even the warden, the head man of that village. But we got our boy."

"The Mounties to the rescue."

"You made it happen, Dutch. You did."

Dutch remembered and remembering, the old fears returned, a cold spot at the base of his spine, a thin layer of sweat along his upper lip, and the awful hard clarity that allowed him to see men and events exactly as they were. Not as they wished them to be. Not as he—Dutch—would have liked them to be. As they were.

"You almost blew it, Izzy." His voice was low and chilling.

Ben-Ezra ducked his head. "It was so long ago."

"You took those banditos at their word—"

"They were lawmen, Dutch, like us."

"They had their hands out, they were crooks. You trusted them and that was wrong. You're on a job, you trust nobody. Nobody. And then you turned your back—"

"Yeah, I did it. It happened, all right. If not for you, I'd've been a goner. You saved my hide, Dutch, don't think I don't know it. I never forgot. I owe you, really I owe you."

Hollinger's manner softened. He liked the other man, respected him; but would never do a job with him again. "Forget it, Izzy. Only keep your back to a wall, or a friend."

"Or a friend . . ."

"On a job, you've got no friends."

"How could I know those Mexicans would double-cross me? I paid them, everyone. I paid them good. Jesus, Dutch, a regular war . . ."

"Not nearly."

"We must've shot it out for ten minutes."

"More like ten seconds."

"You saved my skin that day, Dutch."

"You did your part, once it started."

"I goofed, I admit it. Like you say, too trusting, I don't think things through. I've changed, Dutch. I really have, those days are gone."

"Just as well, Izzy."

Ben-Ezra stared admiringly at Hollinger. "Best damn backup I ever had. Best damn man I ever worked with, Dutch."

"Oh, shut up, Izzy. Just be quiet."

The waiter brought their dinner. Poached salmon for Hollinger and fried prawns out of the Gulf with mustard and horseradish for Ben-Ezra. They ate slowly, washed it back with ice-cold beer, and watched the sun go down.

Ben-Ezra stopped squinting. "Conway's dead, y'know."

"I got word."

"That man feared nothing, and hated everything. Everybody—guineas, spics, yids, micks, the works . . ."

"His own partner . . . ?"

"That was different. Conway always said a partner was a partner for life. Once I went on retreat with him, Father Cahill's monastery up in the mountains near Lake Tahoe. Can you believe it—all those Irish Catholic cops on their knees saying their rosaries and there's Conway mumbling like he's in a hurry to get it over. And there I am, next to him. I said, 'What the hell are you doing, Conway? You really praying?' He must have thought I was nuts. He was a real Believer, y'know.

"Anyway, comes ten o'clock at night and Father Cahill makes the rounds yelling 'Lights out! Into the beds. Sleep well and dream about God, Jesus and the Holy Mother.' Soon everybody quiets down. That's it for the night, I tell myself, and zero in on my beauty rest. All at once, there are all these guys tiptoeing around, glasses clinking, out in the hallway knocking off the booze they've brought along.

"There's Conway cursing spics and niggers and whoever comes to mind and somebody else is singing the Notre Dame fight song and somebody else is talking about all the women he's getting it from, getting louder and louder. That's when Father Cahill, barefoot and wearing an old bathrobe, without a tooth in his head, comes shuffling along with a wooden cane in his hand, beating all those drunken cops over the head. 'Go to bed, y' heathen bastards! Go to sleep and be quiet so's a man can get his rest! Pray for forgiveness or I'll crack your skulls bloody. I will . . .' "

They laughed until the tears began to run.

"Conway was a good cop," Ben-Ezra said presently.

"Crooked as a screw, he was, and we all knew about it. But nobody said anything."

"I guess we were not good cops either, Dutch." Ben-Ezra drew a four-by-five photograph out of his pocket, handed it over. "Is that something special, Dutch?"

"Beautiful."

"Janet Quint. Used to dance on Broadway. That face, that figure. No wonder her husband wants her back."

Hollinger returned the picture.

"She's here in Key West. With a guy named Meléndez. Juan Meléndez Gonzáles."

"Cuban?"

"From Colombia. Meléndez is a bad guy, Dutch. He enjoys hurting people. From what I hear, he leaves a bloody trail wherever he goes."

"I'll nose around for you, Izzy."

"Appreciate any help you can give. You see, the Quint dame don't want to go back to Mr. Quint. Hillary Quint, the supermarket king."

"Big money man."

"She never wants to go back, but she goes. One way or another."

"It's a habit, this thing with Meléndez?"

"Or other dudes like him. Meléndez is the genuine article, however, he's in the dope business."

"For a fact?"

"I can't prove it, not in a court of law."

"Proving is always the hard part."

"I thought I'd nose around, Dutch. Find a little something that might help us both. A good bust for you and Mrs. Quint for me."

"Be careful, Izzy. This is a funny place. Don't rock anybody's boat."

"Never, never. Safe and sensible, that's me these days. There's some extra cash available, Dutch . . ."

"No, thanks."

"Same stiff-necked cop, ain't you?"

"Free lunch once in a while, a haircut on the arm, but that's it for me."

"Matter of degree, isn't it?"

"Don't argue with me, Izzy. My mind's made up."

"Near as I can remember, it always has been."

4

Paco Valentín worked *La Florida* through the blue waters of the Straits of Florida, out into the Gulf Stream. Except for an occasional pelican diving for fish, or some gulls floating on the swells, the sea seemed vast, empty, his alone. To be at sea was to be fully alive in Valentín's mind. The smell of the salt air, the crump of the waves against the side of the boat, the warm sun and the cool breeze, all seemed to him natural and inevitable to the good life.

La Florida was Valentín's pride, his pleasure, and his sole source of income. She was a fifty-three-foot Hatteras, with luxury appointments, with every safety device, tenderly used and cared for since her launching a decade earlier. He had purchased her at a good price, borrowing almost all the money from the bank, and had tuned and polished her to a thing of beauty.

He guided her along at three-quarter speed, the vibra-

tion of the twin diesels below decks providing a sense of
security, the powerful hum of efficiency. Valentín knew
those engines as well as he knew his own body, could strip
them down and put them together again in the dark, kept
them polished and in fine running order out of pride and
necessity. In a world that was careless and incompetent,
Paco Valentín admired people and objects that worked
well. Like himself, the diesels were doing precisely what
they were designed to do.

A few feet to the rear, Tody Ellis was preparing the
chum—chunks of fish, entrails, blood and all, dropped into
a bucket for later use. Tody had earlier set the rigs in
place, lines trailing over the outriggers and behind *La
Florida*, slicing through the wake. Valentín paid little attention to the lines, aware that Tody kept checking them in
case of an early strike. Tody—with Valentín for over a
year—was the most reliable and hardworking mate he'd
ever had. A small black man with a wispy goatee, Tody
labored without complaint, and never sneaked a drink
while on board.

"Hey, *amigo!*"

That would be Lawrence Grant shouting from his
place on the rear deck. Valentín motioned Tody to the
wheel and went back to where his clients warmed themselves in the morning sunlight. Grant was a regular, always
taking a whole-day charter. He might curse and storm at
himself for losing a fish, but he never gave the captain a
hard time. Whatever else he might be, Grant was a fisherman.

"Yes, Mr. Grant?"

Grant swung around in the Pompanette RM fighting
chair. "Two hours, Paco, and not a nibble." Despite the
chill, Grant wore only thin khakis and a short-sleeved
shirt. He was a huge man, even taller than Valentín, with
over-sized hands and feet and a great round stomach. His
arms and chest were black with thick, curly hair and on
his immense head graying curls shimmered in the wind.
Grant had long ago convinced himself that a hairy man
was a living aphrodisiac that very few women could resist.
He held that barbers, politicians, churchmen and editors
were the cause of most of the world's troubles. There was
a bite in his voice. "Losing your touch, Paco?"

There was only a hint of an accent in the Cuban's

speech. "Once we're in the Gulf Stream, we'll catch something. Maybe, maybe not. You know how it is."

"I want to give my young friends here an exciting day."

"I'll go up on the fly bridge, keep an eye out. You want anything, ask Tody."

They watched Valentín climb aloft. "A good man," Grant said.

"And so handsome," Louise Welles said. "All that iron-gray hair against his dark skin."

"Cuban?" Sam Dickey said. A pervasive queasiness had taken hold of his middle and he was afraid he might become sick. It was vital that he not show any weakness: Lawrence Grant was not the kind of man to tolerate weakness in another. And there was Louise. What a beautiful creature she was. He wondered why her husband wasn't along. If she had been his wife, he would never allow her out with a man as vital as Lawrence Grant.

Was there anything between them? The big writer acted as if she belonged to him, a shiny bauble to display and enjoy. He looked up and met Louise's forthright glance, turned quickly away.

"Born and bred," Grant was saying. "Used to be with Castro up in the mountains in the early days, Paco was. Good too, I bet. Decided Fidel was not all he seemed to be and got out. Having a good time, pretty lady?" he said to Louise.

"Are we going to catch a fish?"

He patted her knee and his hand remained in place. If she was troubled by the intimacy, she gave no indication. "For you, we'll clean out the damned ocean." He took a long pull on the can of beer in his hand. It was his fourth beer of the morning and Louise wondered how he could drink so much of the vile stuff.

"I'm so glad you invited me, Larry. You don't think I'll get seasick, do you?"

"Just keep breathing deep, my dear. And think positive thoughts. This is what life is supposed to be like."

"It's better than Petronia Street."

"Make Graham buy you another house."

"Oh, he'd never do that. He likes it, near the Naval Base."

"Your husband is a fool, like all retired military types.

Spend too damned much time obeying orders, they lose all flexibility." His hand was on her thigh now, softly kneading.

Louise felt wicked, excited by the touch of a man's hand not her husband's. "Graham believes you're too indulgent, too easygoing."

"Your husband likes to play bridge with me because I'm a killer and good, a challenge for him. He thinks I'm coarse and vulgar, and too damned fat." He laughed loudly. "After the way the critics have savaged me, it'll take more than a retired sailor to shake my confidence."

Her eyes went briefly to Sam Dickey, taking a quick pleasure in the youthful look of him. Lean and vulnerable, she thought, and barely older than she was. He looked as if he needed caring for. And in contrast, Larry Grant; monumental of belly with weathered cheeks and a toothsome grin reminiscent of Teddy Roosevelt.

"You're right," she said, with feigned insouciance, "Graham doesn't really like you, Larry. Coarse and vulgar, yes. That's what he says."

"Graham won't deal with emotional sturdiness, pretty lady. Your husband finds directness offensive and toughness in another man a dangerous quality. He dares not confront me directly."

Louise considered her reply. Graham Welles—what an odd man he was. Those exquisite manners, his eternal navy discipline, the ease with which he faced every new situation, every new person, as if he and he alone were worthy and correct.

"He's crazy to leave you alone," Grant was saying. "You're much too good to look at. Don't you agree, young Mr. Dickey?"

Sam said, "Louise is beautiful."

She smiled her thanks.

Grant gave him a penetrating glance. "You're a first-class dame, Louise . . ."

"It's getting quite warm," Louise said, standing. She took off her sweater and slacks, aware that both men were watching every move she made. "I think I'll sunbathe for a while . . ."

They watched her go up past the cabin to the forward deck.

"No way Graham Welles can do right by that juicy little piece," Grant muttered. "That man has got a stiff stick up his ass, right up to the chin."

"Good of you to ask me along," Sam said.

"Do a story, do it right."

"Well, thanks."

"*De nada.*"

"What if we don't find any fish?" Sam Dickey said after a while.

"Skunked? Me, never happen."

Sam felt obliged to make conversation, as if in debt to the big writer. "When you hook one of the big ones, Larry, do you ever get tired?"

"Tired? Not this old man. Boy, I do my fifty laps a day, no matter the weather. Don't you believe this beer gut of mine, I am in prime fighting trim. What I hook, I bring in." He stared gloomily out at the cobalt sea. "There ain't no guarantees ever. Could be we'll have to make do with some smaller fish—yellowtails, groupers, maybe a dolphin or two." Grant laughed at the dubious expression on Sam's face. "The fish, my boy. Dolphins are a school fish that run about five pounds. Maybe we'll come up with some mutton snapper. Now that will provide a man with one goddamn fine meal, I tell you so."

At that moment one of the outrigger lines snapped free and pulled taut, peeling swiftly off the 6/0 reel. From up on the fly bridge, Paco cried out: "Sailfish!"

"Get hold of your rod!" Grant yelled. "That's your fish out there."

"Oh, my God, what am I supposed to do?"

Tody Ellis hurried up to help strap Sam into the fighting chair. "You get yourself a good grip on the rod and maneuver the butt end down into the gimbal."

"The gimbal?" Sam's eyes were wide with fright and he cast about for answers.

"The rod holder on the chair between your legs."

He got the pole in place and held on with all the strength he could muster, aware of the pull of the fish as it fought to free itself.

"What do I do now?"

"Just grab hold and play him," Tody said in a soft, caressing voice. "That's just fine, the way you're doing.

Kind of nurse yourself along, boy. Conserve your strength, you understand what I'm saying to you? Let that fish wear hisself out on you 'stead of the other way round."

"You're doing good, Sam," Grant said, eyes out to sea. "Here he comes!"

A silver flash lifted out of the water and hung suspended in the morning sunlight.

"He's beautiful," Louise, come back to see, offered. One of her hands fell lightly on Grant's big shoulder, fingers working steadily.

It took nearly an hour to crank the sailfish on the double line of 60-test close to *La Florida*. Paco, down from the flying bridge, took hold of the heavy mono leader and expertly tagged the big fish.

"He's huge," Louise said.

Grant covered her hand with his own. "A modest catch."

"He's good," Paco said. "But no record. You wanna mount him, young fella?"

Sam shook his head. He was pale, glistening with perspiration, exhilarated by the fight he'd just won. "No," he mumbled.

"Then whataya say we turn him loose, okay? Give him back his life."

Sam looked from Louise to Grant. The writer shrugged. "Your choice, kiddo."

"Let him go," Sam said.

Paco removed the hook and they watched the weary fish move slowly away.

Louise let her breath out. Disappointment mingled with relief; she had wanted the fish dead and at the same time hated the destruction of so beautiful an animal.

Grant heaved himself erect. "Anybody want a cold beer?" He went to the locker and returned, a can in hand. He took a long swallow and belched. "Tell you truly, Paco. When I get my marlin don't hand down any of that ecological crap to me."

Paco returned to his place on the fly bridge without answering. Louise went back to the forward deck and lay down on her back, eyes closed to the sun. The beer finished, Grant tossed the can overboard, and went after Louise. He lowered himself to the deck and placed the tip of one finger just below her navel.

"You," he said in a low growl, "were invented to wear a bikini."

"Aren't you afraid you'll miss your marlin?" Her eyes remained closed.

"The luck is better down toward Cuba. Paco wasn't having any."

"Wouldn't it be dangerous?"

"Life is dangerous." His face was close to her cheek.

"I guess being a Cuban Paco is afraid to get too near to his homeland?"

"Paco afraid?" Grant had tried to comprehend the nature of fear for so many years, struggled to know why some men were able to dominate their fears, while others succumbed with a whimper. He'd thought about it, tested himself against it in war, in back alleys, in front of his typewriter. And knew as little now as when he began. "Sure, Paco's afraid."

She shivered as if she had just exchanged a forbidden intimacy with Grant; but what was it? She almost reached out to him. Her eyes opened to see him hovering over her.

"Know what I am thinking?" he murmured.

"Better not say it."

He wasn't convinced. He placed one big hand on her stomach, massaged lightly. "I have been married five times and known a thousand women . . ."

"I don't want to hear."

"I'll come to see you," he said in her ear.

"At home?" She was startled, delighted, and made to quiver with mixed desires.

"Your husband's away."

"You are a terrible man."

"When we get back to shore."

"No."

"I've longed for you for a long time."

"We hardly know each other."

"I'll make you know me."

"No, please."

He put his finger to her full lips and they spread and admitted him. Abruptly, she averted her head. "Go away, Larry."

He laughed softly, sure of himself now. He stood up. "Shall I tell you what it means, when a woman does that?"

"I don't want to listen any more."

He was laughing as he went back to the fantail, his words trailing back. "I'll visit you, Louise. When we get back."

"Big fish! Coming fast! Big one this time!" Grant's head jerked up to where Valentín was stationed on the fly bridge, shouting, pointing astern. Grant hurried back to the Pompanette. Far back in the wake of *La Florida*, something was closing fast on one of the lures. Grant put himself into the chair and buckled up. He jammed the rod into the gimbal. He braced himself and seconds later the big fish struck.

"Hit him!" Paco yelled.

"Now!" Tody cried. "Get him now!"

Sam cried excitedly, "What is it?" No one answered; no one had heard. He was caught up in the excitement and made mental notes, trying to observe everything, to feel everything, so as to be able later to include it all in his interview.

"Marlin azul!" Paco shouted. He cut the diesels. "Tody, the wheel! Take the wheel!"

"Catch him," Louise urged Grant, from close behind. Her hands were on his shoulders and he shook them off with one great heave.

"Later," he gritted. "This time belongs to the fish and me."

It sounded, to Louise, like a line out of one of his books. She watched the great muscles of his hairy arms flex and define themselves, veined and sinewy, his neck swelling with effort.

The big fish began his run and Grant played out line, gradually tightened up. The fish, as if joining in the contest, allowed himself to be drawn in close to the boat, once in a while drifting up to the surface so they could clearly see what a work of art nature had wrought.

Sam Dickey spoke in awe. "I've never seen anything so beautiful."

"The bastard is evil," Grant replied, struggling to breathe evenly, trying to slow the wild pounding of his heart. There was a tingling in his arms and he felt his strength ebbing, but he braced himself against it. Weakness was a condition Lawrence Grant refused to succumb to. "The dirty bastard!"

"There he goes!" Paco called. "Play him, Grant. Play

him and he is yours." For Valentín, this was a great moment. Since he had come to Key West, had acquired *La Florida*, dozens of marlin had struck his lines. But not one of them had he or his fishermen ever landed. Every time, *always*, the big fish had escaped. Always he had been left with that pervading sense of incompleteness, of a job not done well. This time would be different. Between them—Grant and him—this fish would be caught. Gaffed. Boarded. Hung up to weigh and stuff and brag about. The fish was his as much as Grant's and he intended to have it. "Smart," he urged. "Play it smart and he is ours."

Grant heard nothing. Sweat bathed his massive body and he began to itch in every crease and crevice, with no way to alleviate the annoyance. He commanded himself to concentrate, to focus on the fish, to ignore the insidious weariness that trickled out to the extremities of his arms. He braced himself and resisted the drag of the line. Thirty-three minutes later, the battle ceased. The world grew still.

"What is it?" Louise cried out.

"He's sounding," Paco said.

Grant was glad for the respite. He sucked air into his lungs and gave himself a rest.

"Will he come back?" Sam wanted to know.

Paco crooned lovingly at Grant's shoulder. "Patience, *mi amigo*. Patience. This fish is very smart, very strong. He has lived a long time. He knows everything. Every trick. You must be more patient. Wiser. Trickier. You must be braver and more powerful."

"Soon?" Grant said.

"Soon," said Paco.

"God, he's big," Sam said.

"Two hundred kilos, maybe," Paco answered, eyes fixed on the still blue water.

"That big?" Grant said, fear flushing out his guts.

"More, maybe."

"My God," Sam said. "That's about four hundred and fifty pounds."

The minutes passed with excruciating slowness. Nothing happened. The test line swayed gracefully off the tip of the pole, arching down to where it split the Gulf Stream. And at the end of it, the hook firmly impaled in the marlin's massive mouth.

"Come on," Grant said.

"Patience . . ."

"Goddamn fish . . ."

Louise rested her hands on Grant's shoulder and this time he made no move when she began to work her fingers into the big muscle that went up into his neck. "Good," he told her. She smiled to herself and moved closer to him, bosom pressed against the back of his head. The marlin and the girl, it was almost too much to bear. His crotch began to swell.

Time passed and Grant grew irritable, angry at the fish, angry at his companion. He shifted around in the fighting chair and, sensing his unrest, Louise stepped to one side. Grant blinked into the sun, seeking out the slightest stirring of the surface of the Gulf Stream, some signal that the great fish was about to rejoin the battle. Nothing moved.

"Patience," Paco intoned.

"He got away," Grant complained.

"He waits. You wait."

"For how fucking long?"

"For as long as it takes."

The line jerked and whipped into motion. "There he goes!" Tody cried from the fly bridge.

Grant struggled to keep the rod in its holder, to maintain his grip. His huge belly seemed to expand, an imposed encumbrance, in his way, causing his movements to be clumsy and less effective. He swore at his own body and wished himself slender and tight-skinned once again. He braced himself against the footrest and called up fresh energy, additional strength.

"He is circling," Paco warned.

Grant took in the slack in the line.

The fish leaped skyward. A massive, frozen slice of color. Gone suddenly into the deep and once again the silence. The eerie stillness returned.

Louise mopped Grant's brow and his cheeks. Paco brought him some orange juice.

"That is one smart fish," Paco said.

"I want him."

"We all want him now. We must have him."

"I'll get him."

"Nurture your strength, *amigo*. The fish is resting

now, floating, plotting his next move. He is very clever, that fish. You must be equally clever, when the fight begins again."

The sun had begun to drop below the horizon when the marlin made his next move. An incredible vertical leap, a glint of power and magnificence, a wide white splash. He headed straight out to sea. Grant gave line grudgingly.

"Let up!" Paco cried. "Give him more play. The line is too—"

A sharp crack split the air and made everything quiet.

Paco swore. "*Ay cono su madre . . .*"

Grant leaned back and shut his eyes, exhaled heavily. "I am so damned tired . . ."

Louise seemed puzzled. "What happened?"

"Where'd he go?" Sam said.

"The rod broke."

Grant still held on to the lower end of the rod as line whipped off the reel in a swift discordant whine. The fish leaped again, a final display, as if to taunt the pathetic creatures aboard *La Florida,* then dove straight down. The line snapped to signal the end of the battle.

"He's won," Grant said simply.

Paco took up the broken rod, examined it with professional interest. "That one, he is some fish."

"Maybe he'll come back," Sam said.

Grant stared at the slender youth. "Not that fish." He stood up and went after a beer. "I never had one like him before." He began to cough and when the fit passed, he was red in the face, but laughing silently. He swallowed half the beer in the can. "How about this? I don't feel so bad. Not as bad as I thought I would."

"Maybe we can find another one," Louise offered.

"Not like him," Paco said. "You want another try?" he said to Grant.

The writer grimaced. "Another one would finish me off for good. Let's go back, Paco."

"Take us home!" Paco yelled to Tody on the fly bridge. "You did well, *amigo.*"

"Okay for an old man."

"To lose to a champion, that's not so bad," Paco said.

"Ah," Louise said. "You aren't old, Larry."

"For that fish, I'm old," he said, killing off the beer. "For you, pretty lady, I'm just right. Now be a good girl and fetch me another brew . . ."

She went, as if it were his right and her duty.

5

Iversen lived in a two-story wood frame house on Southard Street, a little more than a block away from City Hall. Not that the big detective ever made the walk. He almost never walked anywhere, attached by emotion and by what he considered necessity to his two automobiles. His particular favorite was a white 300 SL Gull-wing Mercedes-Benz, circa 1955. Iversen had bought it from a retired stockbroker four years before and done it over completely himself since. It was, of course, the only one of its kind on Key West, and perhaps in the state of Florida, and Iversen used it only when he didn't mind being noticed and recognized. When he wanted to remain inconspicuous, he rode in what he called his Detective's Wheels: a blue Plymouth Valiant. Though it appeared battered and commonplace, its engine was powerful and reliable and constantly in tune. Iversen was not a man to take unnecessary chances.

Like the cars, the house in Southard Street had been renovated with taste and care. The old moldings had been stripped away and the walls replastered and painted, the floors scraped and stained dark. There was new wiring to accommodate air conditioning and all new equipment in the kitchen. The upstairs bedrooms had been enlarged and each had its private bath, a concession to Ellen's gender.

Iversen, already shaved and showered, chose his clothes carefully. French jeans, properly faded and fitting over his lean legs tightly, a black lisle sport shirt and a summer-weight houndstooth jacket. He snapped a holstered .32 Beretta onto his belt at the small of his back and went downstairs to the darkened living room. He was about to turn on the lights when his attention was drawn to the front porch. At the window, he moved the lace curtains only enough to permit him to see outside.

They were holding each other. His daughter, Ellen, and Marc. He was soft and pale, with hair to his shoulders and a mouth not at all to Iversen's liking. There was no accounting for his daughter's taste in companions. He shifted the Beretta around to a more comfortable position, making sure it was concealed by the drape of his jacket.

They kissed. A long passionate embrace and Iversen imagined he could see the boy's tongue in his daughter's mouth. He shuddered and his fingers curled up into large, tight fists. He blamed Clarice for the inadequacies in Ellen. Clarice, who had failed him as a wife and had never been a proper mother. Clarice, who had hated being a cop's wife. Who had hated him, had left him and Ellen all those years ago.

The boy's hand went from Ellen's ass under her skirt. A cry of revulsion lodged back in Iversen's throat and he almost choked on it. He listened as his daughter spoke.

"Ah, Marc, take me somewhere, please."

"I can't, not tonight. I'll call you tomorrow."

"Tomorrow night?"

"Yes."

They kissed again and Iversen became aware of his body. It was locked into place, hard and unyielding. Limb by limb, joint by joint, he forced the tension away, breathing deeply, reestablishing control over himself. He put himself in the wing chair in front of the fireplace and crossed his legs. And waited.

More than twenty minutes later, Ellen came through front door. She headed for the stairs, but Iversen said her name.

"Daddy?" She showed no surprise that he was there. No alarm. No guilt.

"Turn on the lamp," he said.

A soft yellow light filled the room. Ellen, her blouse disordered, her hair in disarray, lowered herself to the floor and smiled up at him as if expecting him to praise her.

"I thought you'd gone out, Daddy."

For an extended, terrifying moment she looked like Clarice in that dim light. Clarice come back to taunt and torture him. But Clarice was gone forever, to live a life in Chicago with a tie salesman, a life he couldn't understand, a life he didn't want to think about.

"That was Marc you were with?"

"Yes, Daddy. He's very sweet."

"Davidson, isn't it?"

"Yes, Daddy." Her face seemed to twist out of shape briefly, as if in pain. She was a tall girl, slender, with a narrow face and large round eyes that made her seem bird-like and wary. She had never felt entirely at ease with her father, and since her mother had gone away, that unease had increased, transformed into a vague fear that she felt helpless to isolate or define.

"I have never cared much for Jews," he said, with a charming smile.

"Oh, Daddy."

"Not that I want to incinerate them all. But I have never met one I respected."

She wanted to object, to defend Marc, to defend anyone her father attacked, but the words stumbled across her tongue and never came out. "Marc is so nice," she did say.

"He doesn't respect you, Ellen."

"Oh, he does. He loves me, Daddy."

"I doubt it. I suppose you believe you love him?"

"I do. I think I do."

"I saw what happened on the porch. The way he mauled you."

She found it impossible to assimilate his meaning. His anger was clear, though his manner was mild and his demeanor controlled as always. But something else came through, something she was unable to give a name to. Sometimes it was difficult to find the right words to express what she felt, and without the words there was no coherence to her thoughts. She wished she were as quick as her father, as smart and as confident. He was able always to grasp obscure meanings, able to decipher complex problems.

"I do not want you to see that young man any more."

Her brain seemed to spin, to tip and topple around in empty space. "But we're going out tomorrow . . . we—"

"No. Don't force me to take action against him. He wouldn't care for that, and neither would you, Ellen. Please, do as I say."

She wet her lips and avoided her father's eyes. A mix of resentment and excitement flooded her head and made it impossible to sort out what she felt, what she wanted. She remembered another young man. Tall and fair, not unlike her father. He too had been ordered to stay away from her and when he persisted everything had gone wrong. Something secret and very bad had happened to him; he had simply disappeared. Never heard of again. Ellen thought of him now as the kind of phantom figure who occasionally inhabited her dreams.

"But Marc is expecting me . . ."

"You will not see him again. You will never see him again. Is that understood?"

"Yes, Daddy."

"And there is one more thing, this work of yours."

"I like it."

"You will give it up immediately."

She chewed her lips as if considering her next move.

He didn't wait. "I won't have my daughter cleaning other people's houses."

"I enjoy it, taking care of nice things. It makes me feel good, needed."

"You must remember who your father is. Consider what my friends will say if they discover you work as a cleaning woman. In the fall, you'll go back to school."

"I am not very good in school."

"Trust me, Ellen. I know what's best for you. You'll return to school, do good work, make me proud of you. Now, I have to meet someone on business. It's getting late, you must be tired. Go to bed. You'll be asleep when I return." He kissed her on the cheek and went to the door, paused. "I have only your interests at heart, Ellen. Your future is my primary concern. You are my responsibility, you know." He smiled charmingly and left.

She waited until she heard him drive away before she made the call. Marc answered.

"Can you come over right away?" she said. "No, I'm all alone. He won't be back until late."

"Give me five minutes," he said.

She went out on the porch to wait.

Iversen drove the Valiant without haste. It did not matter if he was late; he knew his man. Benny Skaggs would wait.

The night air was soft and refreshing against his cheeks, but did little to lessen his resentment and bitterness. All these acts of defiance by Ellen, why? That ongoing inability to comprehend his natural concern for her welfare, her future. Her refusal to heed and obey. The underside of life was his business. He was a professional, he dealt day and night with the dark side of human activity. That stubbornness, her willful opposition, could only bring pain and disaster to her. And to him.

She must learn discipline.

Ellen's mother had been the same. Even to the proud shape of her head, the tilt of her elegant chin, those almond-shaped eyes. Even their breasts were alike: high, modest, taut. They, too, would be exhilarating beyond any other woman's, unloosing a soaring passion in him, make him wild. He shuddered behind the wheel of the Valiant, afraid of what he felt, of what he still craved. Clarice. Clarice's flesh. The sweet unsettling scent of her was rekindled in his nostrils. His throat swelled and his anger drew down to a raging pinpoint of overheated light. Men lusted after a girl like Ellen. Would say and do anything to possess her, if only for a moment. To root around on that beautiful young flesh, to violate her, to soil and use her. Iversen knew all about such men. He vowed to save her from the animals, no matter how much she protested.

He turned into Vernon Street, killed his headlights and rolled silently along, parking behind a Pinto wagon. He lit a cigaret and waited for his emotions to subside.

When again in control, he snuffed out the cigaret and went down to the beach. The gentle splash of the small night waves comforted Iversen and he advanced along the sand without urgency, looking neither left nor right. He expected here and there he might find couples locked in a loving embrace, or trios, or more. He had no desire to see them or be noticed by them. Anyone out on South Beach at this hour would be minding his own business.

He paused behind the structure that used to be Louis' Backyard and searched for Skaggs. Benny was habitually early for all meets, which Iversen saw as a show of weakness. Skaggs was a frightened man, though to a less astute observer he might appear hard and strong, tough.

How easy to eliminate a man like Skaggs, a man of caution and easily read habits. How easy to snuff him and never regret his passing. Iversen lamented the passing of Louis' Backyard much more, for it had once been among Key West's premier restaurants and he had always appreciated good food. Quality failed to survive long in this world, he assured himself; most of life was tawdry, ordinary, seldom worth the effort

A shadow shifted slightly, almost defensively, beneath a palm tree: Skaggs. He moved closer.

"Good evening, Benny."

Skaggs appeared, shaking his head. "I don't know, John Roy, there's a lot of trade to be done. Duval Street is jumping."

"Call me Mr. Iversen, Benny." He wanted to set the tone of the meeting early.

Skaggs was a big man, taller and broader than Iversen, but there was a suggestion of uncertainty in him that was clearly evident to the detective. "Bill Vail and me, we were always on a first-name basis."

"Bill Vail is no longer among us. You deal with me from now on."

Skaggs shrugged and shuffled, retreated a step. "Makes no never mind to me. I run my business and that's all there is to that."

"Your business, Benny?"

"Sure. Well, okay." He grinned broadly, placatingly. He hadn't come in search of conflict. Any problems that came up could be settled; that's how it had been with Bill Vail. But Bill Vail was no longer around. *"Our* business," he amended.

"Ah," Iversen said approvingly. "I've been looking forward to this little talk, Benny."

"Me, too. Gives us a chance to understand one another."

"You are easy to understand, Benny. But can you try and understand me? Those girls of yours, how many on your string?"

"Right now—ten, eleven maybe."

"Aren't you sure?"

"All right—ten."

"My colleagues and I take the position that you are under-staffed."

"It's hard to find good girls."

"For forty percent, try harder. Find ten more girls."

Benny's voice rose. "What are you talking about? Our deal is seventy-thirty. I get seventy percent—"

"Starting this week it's forty percent."

"There are expenses, medical bills, transportation—"

"If the partnership is not financially feasible, Benny . . . ?"

"Make it fifty-fifty."

"Forty."

"Goddamn! It ain't right."

"Say yes or no, Benny. No, and the meeting is terminated. Yes, and we continue."

"I don't have much of a choice."

"How clever of you to perceive that. It's yes, then?" Skaggs nodded. "You will at once step up your recruiting procedures, here and up in Miami."

"Here?"

"The town is loaded with young girls anxious to remain. They smoke dope, they drink, they enjoy a good time. Give them a chance to make some money at the same time . . ."

"We always went up north. Bill Vail used to say—"

"Bill Vail isn't here, you seem to forget."

Skaggs bit down hard, the muscles in his massive jaw bulging with contained anger. "What else?" he muttered.

Iversen smiled agreeably. "These girls of yours, you've trained them thoroughly, I assume."

"What do you mean? Sure, they do as they're told. Any of them cross me they know what will happen."

"In other words, you trust them?"

"They're hookers. I watch them. I hold back on some of their dough. Once in a while I belt them around, as a reminder. That builds up trust."

"Tell me about Inez."

"Inez?"

"Inez Gavilan, Benny."

Skaggs grew wary. "What about her?"

"Inez is still with you?" Skaggs nodded slowly.

"Would she go into business for herself, a touch of private enterprise?"

"Not a chance. Inez is reliable, she knows the rules, knows the way I handle trouble."

"Funny. You see, she was just busted along with a small-time thief named Ralph Sedly. Seems that Inez ran a game on a traveling book salesman out of Jacksonville. You acquainted with the Seabreeze Motel, Benny? That's where it took place. Inez set the man up and Sedly finished the job."

"I'll take care of Inez," Skaggs said quickly. "Leave her to me."

Iversen appeared to float closer in the darkness and Skaggs, who longed to flee, didn't dare move. The smaller man took on ominous, threatening proportions.

"Consider the situation, Benny. I'm new in this job. It's important that I do well. I have to be able to depend on my people—"

"You can depend on me, Mr. Iversen."

"I must be convinced. What we have here is an unusual employer-employee relationship, no hidden clauses. Everything's out front, Benny. You get yours, I get mine, and no questions asked. No hassles. No union shop. However, when matters take a wrong turn—"

"You can't blame Inez on me. I—"

Skaggs never saw the punch that caused him so much pain. It caught him low in the groin and he doubled up retching and moaning. Another blow, this one behind the ear, put him down on the sand. Iversen kicked him in the ribs. Skaggs covered up.

"Law and order, Benny. Rules. Otherwise there is anarchy. And that won't do. Inez and Sedly, a little sideline of *yours*. The disease is called greed. Untreated it will spread and our relationship will worsen and grow sick. Commitments must be honored, you understand that, Benny? Be smart, stay smart. Render unto me what is mine and unto Internal Revenue a fair share so that Uncle stays off your back.

"Mistakes happen, you would say. Agreed, and a certain tolerance exists for them. However, you used up your quota in this affair. Now, stand up like a man."

It took some time and considerable effort for Skaggs

to make it to his feet. He held his middle and kept his distance.

"It won't happen again."

"I hope not, Benny. Get rid of Inez and Sedly."

For a moment, it didn't penetrate. When it did, Skaggs grew cold and afraid. "That's not what I do, Mr. Iversen. A little muscle here and there, okay. But no wet work. I never do wet work."

"From now on, Benny, the individual is responsible for his own mess. Clean it up soon. Bail will be set for those two by morning. See that they're sprung, then act."

"How? I never—"

"Off the key, you understand. Somewhere else. Fifty miles away. Perhaps a bath in the Gulf. Do it before they speak your name to Dutch Hollinger."

"Ah, no, Mr. Iversen. I know those two. They would never talk."

"Do it, Benny, and we'll be sure they'll never talk. Manage it soon, Benny."

"Yes, sir."

"Good." Iversen turned to go. "I knew you'd come through for me, Benny. One more thing: I'll be heading over to the Motel-by-the-Sea. Room 202. It's on reserve for me, Benny. I'll watch a little television, kill a six-pack, and enjoy some female companionship."

"Sounds nice."

"I'm sure you know someone suitable . . . ?"

For a long beat Skaggs failed to understand. Then a big, smug grin broke across his face. "I got just the girl for you, Mr. Iversen. A real beauty—"

"That's enough. Someone agreeable, someone adaptable, someone who can harmonize with the complexities of a man's needs."

"Yes, yes, I'll take care of everything."

Her name was Maribelle Trillo. She owned a beauty salon in the Searstown shopping center, alongside Winn Dixie. She employed ten stylists, plus two girls who did nothing but shampoos and two specialists in rinses and bleach jobs. There were two manicurists, two receptionists to make appointments, and the old woman who cleaned up.

There was always Latin music on the stereo and

Cuban coffee and small sandwiches and pastries for customers and staff alike. It was all low-key and leisurely, very friendly. But few women walked out of Maribelle's before running up a bill close to a hundred dollars, though with a sense of getting their money's worth.

Maribelle styled only. Very often she turned the cutting itself over to Oscar, who was willowy and graceful and was a lover of boys, but talented and extremely polite.

Maribelle was a walking advertisement for her shop. She was a tall woman, with more flesh on her bones than some *norteamericanos* found fashionable, though she was well formed and firm, with a graceful walk. Her black hair curled around her head in a modified afro and her black eyes were immense and glinting with deep and private thoughts. She was convinced that her mouth was too wide, her lower lip too heavy, but it was a mouth that men were drawn to, a mouth that smiled easily. But it was the only part of Maribelle's face that did smile; the black eyes were always still and veiled, wise and watchful.

In the small closet at the back of the shop, to which Maribelle alone possessed a key, there was a Remington pump-action twelve-gauge. In her bedroom at home, alongside the bed, was its twin. Maribelle was an expert skeet shot and both weapons were kept clean, oiled and loaded. She pitied the man who would cause her to use either weapon.

In her purse she carried a nickel-plated .32 automatic. And on those days that she felt specially apprehensive, Maribelle strapped a stiletto to the inside of her thigh. The cool steel felt strange and exotic against her warm flesh and caused her to entertain obscene and perverted visions. But she was not going to change her ways. Abroad were enemies known and unknown and only a fool took unnecessary chances.

She was at the shop late that day overseeing Oscar as he worked on Mrs. Whitmore's hair, bored with the process and the babbling of the old lady, wishing Oscar would go faster. The cleaning woman had begun to do her work and the place was uncharacteristically quiet. An authoritative knock drew Maribelle to the front door. Paco Valentín stood there, solemn, expectant, and better-looking than was right for a man.

"Ay! You stink of fish, old man."

He looked her over with obvious approval. "You smell like a woman."

"No me jordas," she said dryly. Then she spoke in English. "Such an old man to think of such matters."

"Oye. If I am too old for you, there are those who believe otherwise."

"Always men boast about their prowess. No, you are not too old for me, Paco. Not nearly. There is something I can do for you, I think?"

"A man puts in a full day fishing, he gets hungry."

"So, you wish to invite me to dine with you. Some fancy restaurant, perhaps."

"It was in my mind that you would enjoy making a hungry man a good dinner."

"I too have worked all day. I too am tired."

"Your picadillo á la criolla. *¡Ay, caramba!* Nobody does it as good as you, Maribelle."

"Liar." She laughed softly. "To cook for you, you think it is easy? You eat enough for three ordinary men."

"Make something *fácil de hacer.*"

"Easy to do, eh! All right, the picadillo. But you will do the shopping. Some ground meat, olives, raisins. Can you keep it all in your head, old man?"

"I will try. And some guava paste . . ."

"And queso blanco."

"I am very weary. It was a difficult day out there today."

"So?" She pursed her full lips.

"There is something . . ."

"And you are too shy to ask?"

"I do not think of myself as shy."

"Then you will ask."

"Must I ask?"

"You think I cannot read your mind, *cabrón?* Old goat. All men are the same."

"That is not a nice way to speak."

"I have not seen you in a week."

He grinned. "Tonight you will see all of me there is to see."

"Such pleasures you offer me."

"You have never objected before."

"Nor will I tonight," she said, before returning to Mrs. Whitmore's hair.

6

It rained during the night. Not for long, but hard, the drops fat and heavy, beating a noisy tattoo on the tin hurricane roof. Long enough and loud enough to wake Hollinger. He lay in bed and smoked and listened to the rain and wondered if this storm would become a gale, then a hurricane. Hurricanes were of concen to all Key Westers, though the Old Island had suffered only a few.

The first hurricane of intensity on record struck Key West in September, 1835, doing considerable damage to the light-ship *Florida,* and stranding a number of vessels on the reefs nearby. One schooner was driven up on a bank and when the storm ended and the waters receded, it stood high and dry. At the time there were no more than eight hundred people living on the key and they were without communication of any kind with the mainland.

A year later, another hurricane hit from the northeast. Trees were uprooted, fences downed and roofs ripped off houses. The lighthouse was washed away and seven people were killed. One house, at the corner of William and Caroline Streets, was washed to sea with a male servant still inside. Neither house nor servant was ever found.

In 1909, another big storm ripped the island, winds gusting up to one hundred miles per hour. Two people were killed and a number of buildings were completely destroyed, including: the Ruy Lopez Company, cigar makers; St. Paul's Episcopal Church; Wolfson's building at Greene and Simonton Streets; the city bell tower; the condensing plant and pumping station of the U.S. Army post; Markovitz' Five and Ten Cent store; plus other structures.

A number of lesser storms have hit Key West since,

but except for the 1935 hurricane, none did much damage. The timing of West Indian hurricanes was best described in the early part of the century by Father Benito Vines, a Jesuit, who directed the meteorological observatory in Havana. He said: "The ecclesiastical authorities from time immemorial wisely ordained that priests in Puerto Rico should recite the prayer *Ad Repellendat Tempestates* during the months of August and September, but not in October, and that in Cuba it should be recited in September and October, but not in August. The ecclesiastical authorities knew from experience that the cyclones of September and October are much to be feared in the vicinity of Cuba, but that those of August were not of a nature to cause apprehension."

The rain stopped as suddenly as it had started and Hollinger put on a seersucker robe and went out onto the tiny terrace that he called his back porch. Everywhere was glistening night-blooming cereus, and rainwater dripped off the tall palms that grew close by. It made him remember that beautiful and very special summer he had spent in Spain with Laura, his first wife. So many years ago. He had still believed in the future then, a future with Laura, and a future in a world made better because he was a policeman.

Too much had happened since. Now he was a middle-aging detective going through the motions on a sandspit at the edge of the ocean, marking time mostly, trying not to remember how it used to be, how it might have been, trying not to make waves.

It seemed to Hollinger that he had given up major and minor parts of himself. His once driving ambition to be the best of cops, to get good things done; all shed like excess baggage too heavy to carry. And the fierce energy that had once fueled his days and nights: in him now the fires sparked only occasionally, giving off little heat. He went with the flow these days, obeyed orders, acted in the expected, approved manner and gave no trouble to anyone. He had taught himself to turn a blank eye to sights he chose not to see; and tried not to imagine what Laura would have thought of him, and how different he had become from those best of times.

Provocative, professional questions swarmed through his head. He went back inside to the small desk in his small bedroom and switched on an old brass lamp that had once served some Spanish privateer—or so said the dealer, who had sold it to him as authentic. He plucked the questions out of his brain and in an antique script taught him by the sisters at Mary Immaculate Convent school wrote them down, leaving room for answers.

The questions—with eyes closed, he could see again the corpses of Bettyjane Keely and Livia Olvera. He smoked a cigarette and reread what he had written.

Why had they been killed?

If he knew that answer, he might very well be able to respond to every other question. Had robbery been the motive, had the intruder been interrupted at his work, panicked at the enormity of his crime and run? Both women were exceptionally attractive; had lust brought the killer to the house? If so, he had departed without satisfaction. Revenge? Jealousy? Perhaps it had all been a terrible mistake, the killer seeking some other victim instead. Hollinger's head began to ache.

The offensive acceleration of a motorcycle sliced through the night. Some hotshot over on Roosevelt Boulevard, half full of booze and pot, flexing his supercharged maleness. Hollinger longed for a quieter time, a time when people were less rushed and more considerate of each other. Or was such a time just a myth passed on by prior generations in order to make their own lives seem more worthwhile? He put on some clothes and drove over to the Keely house.

He parked in the driveway and looked down at the yacht at its mooring in the canal, then back up at the darkened house. Once again he was impressed by its size and luxurious appointments. Not many houses in Key West compared; and none that he could recall ever endured a double killing. What was it like, to be able to build such a home, to be able to support such an establishment without strain. What was it like to be rich? More questions that would, for him, remain forever unanswered. Some men owned the knack for making money, big money. John Roy Iversen, for one. It came easily to such men and they looked the part. Their clothes drew attention to their wealth, their cars, their women. But that had never been Hollinger's way; just a working stiff trying to get along.

A flash of light brought his head around. He blinked and saw only the shadowed shape of the big house. Had it been his concerned imagination? Did he only wish to see something, hoping for a break that would bring him a solution without the plodding labor usually required? He left the car, leaving the door ajar, and reached for the .38 two-inch that was on his belt. He located the copy of the house key he'd had made and went up to the front portico. Slowly, quietly, he opened the door and stepped inside.

Silence. Not even the night creakings that signaled the complaints of most houses against the long day's usage. The scent of the women who had lived in these spaces drifted into his nostrils and he could almost see again the rows of perfumes and toilet waters in Bettyjane's bedroom. Typically, he'd begun to think of her as a known quantity. Not yet a friend, but someone he was getting to know.

A shuffle of feet drew his attention. He went through the carpeted living room, skirting the heavy glass-topped coffee table, and down the long passageway lined with storage cabinets, toward the bedrooms. Flat against the wall, just outside the doorjamb, he peered into the big room where the two women had died. A small beam of light scanned the bed, the dresser, Bettyjane's vanity. Hollinger pointed the .38, located the light switch on the wall, and went into a firing stance.

"Freeze motherfucker or I'll blow you away!"

A figure in jeans and a sweat shirt stood in front of the huge armoire without moving. "Turn slowly." Hollinger was pleased to see that his hands were steady, his heartbeat regular, that the moment even provided some undefined pleasure; there was still something of the young Dutch Hollinger remaining. "Hands over your head! Jesus H. Christ, it's—you're a girl."

"Woman," she corrected automatically. "Woman."

"Just hold still."

"Stay cool, man. Guns make me nervous."

"What are you doing here?"

Her hands came down and a quick, threatening gesture brought them up again. "Okay, okay. Oh, wow, you scared me half to death. You know that, Hollinger? You're still scaring me."

"You know who I am?" He wasn't surprised. Certain people always knew who the cops were; their self-interest dictated that they know. It occurred to him that she was his first female housebreaker. "Up against the wall."

She obeyed, but displayed annoyance. "Come on, you gotta remember me, man."

He began to frisk her.

"Hey!" she cried. "What are you doing?"

"Hold still, dammit."

"You enjoy that? Is that how you get your kicks?"

"Shut up." He grew flushed, irritated that he had to examine her this way. Even more, he discovered he liked it, appreciated her tall strong body. Her legs were surprisingly muscular, not delicate and soft, the way so many women's were.

"Keep it up," she said. "We just might get to like each other."

He pulled her hands behind her back.

"Hey! What's the idea?"

He cuffed her and stepped back. "Turn around."

"Dammit, Hollinger, turn me loose."

He flashed his shield and identified himself formally, and read her her rights.

"Goddamn," she said angrily. "I am no criminal."

To Hollinger, she looked like a high school cheerleader, fifteen years later. All the fuzziness gone, face and form sharply delineated, no more a child and looking good for the change. Her features were strong, her eyes wide and slightly turned up at the corners, a pale green. Her skin was freckled and her thick almost orange hair flared away from her head in wild wings. She was no longer afraid, at least not much, and growing fiercer by the second. "Take these goddamned cuffs off me."

"Breaking and entering," he recited. "Violating the scene of a crime. I ought to be able to come up with two or three more charges before I take you to the station house."

"Station house! Are you insane? I'm Russell. I work for the *County Journal*. You remember me, Hollinger. Don't you." She ended plaintively. She turned her left breast in his direction. She clearly wore no bra and her bosom seemed no worse for the omission. "In my pocket, my I.D."

He lifted the card case out and the back of his fingers

brushed against her nipple. Long ago he had concluded there existed some mysterious linkage between fear and passion, between passion and anger. The extreme emotions certainly grew out of the same dark source.

The I.D. indicated her name was Annie Russell and she worked as a reporter for the *County Journal*. It also said she was five feet nine inches tall, weighed 125 pounds and was thirty-five years old. She looked five pounds heavier and five years younger, Hollinger decided.

"Okay, you're a reporter. You still committed a crime."

"I'm on a story."

"A criminal, caught in the act."

She cocked her head in disbelief. "Aw, come on, take off the cuffs. I promise not to assault you." Her grin was off center and a thing of beauty. Hollinger warned himself to watch her like a hawk. He removed the cuffs.

"Would you really have shot me?" she said, massaging her wrists.

He put the .38 away. "I still might."

She assessed him. "They say you're an okay guy."

"For a cop."

Again that grin. "For a cop. You shot many people?"

"Is this an interview, or just passing small talk?"

"You haven't answered the question."

"I'm giving you a break. You can go now."

She seemed surprised. "I haven't finished my work."

"Murder was committed here. Any work has to be done, it's mine."

"Mine, too. Just let me follow you around. I won't say a word, won't touch a thing."

He jerked his head once, as if in assent, and she clapped her hands, made a futile pass at her hair. "You see, you're not so tough, after all."

He examined the room once again. Everything was as he remembered it; he drew a blank.

"Was it robbery, Hollinger?"

"Nothing was taken that we know about."

He walked around the house, switching lights on and off, hoping to come across some small sign that would open things up for him. She trailed after him.

"Is it true about the grass, Dutch?"

He went out the side entrance to the pool.

"Call me Sergeant Hollinger."

"The word is out. First-class Colombian, I'm told."

"Everybody on this sandbar burns a little pot."

"Maybe the lady was a dealer?"

"And maybe not."

"Look at this layout! The money had to come from somewhere. Admit it, Dutch, the keys are a haven for dopers. Grass, coke, heroin, anybody can make a buy."

He stopped suddenly, swung around. She almost walked up his back. With a brief apologetic movement of her head, she avoided physical contact.

"Enough grass for a joint, maybe two," he said. "She had it in her purse. Not the stash of some big-time dealer."

Back inside, he examined the kitchen. It was shining-clean, as if seldom used. Bettyjane Keely was a woman who took her meals in expensive restaurants, he supposed. With someone else paying the bill.

Who?

"Fingerprints?" Annie Russell said.

"That's being checked."

"There's a husband, you know. Arthur Keely."

"No kidding! You are truly a crack investigative reporter."

She looked sheepish. "Okay, so you knew."

"We're dumb, us cops. But not all the time."

"Is Keely a suspect?"

"Why should he be?"

"Let me tell you my theory. I believe she had a lover. Her kind would have to, you see. Keely found out and did a job on her."

"What's the boy friend's name?"

"How would I know?"

"Let me know when you find out."

"It's a good theory, Dutch."

"I saw Alan Ladd solve a murder based on that plot once."

"You got a better idea?"

"We're leaving," he said. "Put the lights out."

Back on the sloping lawn, Dutch went down to the edge of the canal. "Some boat," he murmured.

"What's wrong with it?" Annie Russell wanted to know.

"The boat? Nothing, so far's I know."

"My theory."

"Oh, it's okay. I just like to keep a few balls in the air at one time. Try this one: the killer was after Olvera, not Keely."

"The maid? Why, that's beautiful, Dutch! But why? Where's the motive?"

"Haven't got one yet. But I'm working on it." He strode to where he had left his car.

"You are one terrific crime fighter!" she cried, hurrying to catch up.

He climbed behind the wheel and switched on the ignition. The motor turned over crankily, then caught. He was relieved; he had little faith in the internal combustion engine.

"Hey," she said, "give us a lift?"

"How'd you get here?"

"On foot. But it was much earlier then—"

"Go back the same way."

"Cops!" she shouted, shaking her fist at the disappearing car. Her resentment receded rapidly and she grew pleased with the way the evening had worked out. What the hell, he might've shot her full of holes.

She went back to the tiny house which was behind a much larger house, where she lived. Years ago, when the early Cuban cigar makers had come to Key West, they built houses for themselves, one in back of another. Perhaps it made them feel more secure, friendlier and safer, to know they were surrounded by their own kind. Now many of those houses were occupied by marginal people like Annie Russell, people whose income was meager or nothing at all, people who could not afford to pay much rent. Advancing along the narrow alley that led to her house, Annie reminded herself that it was time to again hit Bucky Maddox up for a raise. She was very much underpaid, exploited, doing the work of four good people and being paid much less than she was worth.

But her mind skipped back to the story she wanted to write. It was all in her head and she was excited by the prospect. She enjoyed crime stories, felt the Keely-Olvera murders were her natural meat. She had long ago convinced herself that she understood the mental set of men who committed violent crimes; their unarticulated war with society was part of her battle, too. She figured it would take all night to get the story right, but that was good, that was when she was at her best. Working on something exciting and rewarding.

But Tom-tom was there. Stretched out naked on her mattress sucking a joint, one leg waving in time to the Stones on the stereo. After so long, it still troubled her to see him this way, flaunting his body, using it as a weapon against her. With or without clothes, there was something basically indecent about Tom-tom.

She went to the fridge and poured herself some milk. "You're not supposed to be here."

"I been thinking about you all night. Where you been?"

"Get your clothes on and get out."

"Anticipation puts an edge on everything."

"You can't just come strolling in here whenever you like."

"I've got a key, remember."

"I want it back."

"Never happen. I dig you too much, babe."

"I've got work to do."

"Come on. Who were you with? Did he do you good?"

"It's not like that with everybody, Tom-tom."

"Come over here."

"I told you, I have to work."

"Come and get it."

"No, dammit. That's all over with. There's nothing left for you and me. Now get out or I'll call the cops."

He thought that was funny and said so. "Put yourself down here."

Always orders. Always she was thrust into a subservient position. For how long would it go on? Tom-tom had not been the first . . . "Go away."

He went over to her and took her hair in his hand, led her back to the mattress. "It's up to you. Nice or not nice?"

"Don't hurt me, Tom-tom."

"Say please."

"Please . . ."

"That's better. You see how sweet I can be when you treat me right. Just do as you're told, when you're told . . ."

7

While he slept he dreamed of the big fish that got away. And he woke sweating and quivering with fear. That was the way it always was: the ones you didn't land came back to torment you. The fish, the jungle beasts, the beautiful and unattainable women. The books you could never write as well as you wanted to write them.

He wanted so very much to win. At everything. Life was an ongoing battle joined in various arenas. Winning made everything better: the women you loved, the food you ate, the wine you drank. Winning made up for all the defeats you suffered as a child. Lying now in the inexact flow of a night-light—he had never been able to sleep in the dark—he conceded grudgingly that Freud was right: no one ever truly grew up.

His mother, so lovely and desirable, so steely strong under that gentle, Southern-belle exterior, had dressed him in girl's clothing until he was eight years old, had arranged his hair in long, glistening curls, had imposed checks on all his impulses for roughness and hard play. She blamed it all on his asthma.

"You must be careful, Lawrence. You must not go too far, Lawrence. You must not hurt yourself, Lawrence. You are not strong."

He blamed the asthma on his mother. And so many other things.

He showered and shaved, ridding himself of the stench of Paco's boat. He drank some beer from a can and puffed a Cuban cigar, brought in on a shrimper and supplied to him at a price by a bartender pal. Then he dialed her number.

She answered tentatively, as if expecting his call, fearful, and yet unable not to respond. His voice that rumbled out of that deep chest of his. He was convinced that a man's lowest tones were a powerful stimulant to most women.

"Is Graham back?"

"No," she whispered, as if afraid he'd overhear. "He had to stay in Miami an extra day."

"And the maid?"

"Her day off."

"I'll be right over."

"I'm terribly tired. I thought I'd take a bath and go to bed."

"I'm on my way."

"Oh, please, Lawrence. What if Hilda heard you talking to me this way?"

"Hilda is in Miami, also. Maybe she and your husband are lovers." That made him laugh. "I'd love to see that, those two cold fish trying to work up a sweat."

"You talk the way you write, Lawrence."

She was stalling, and both of them knew it.

"I write the way I live. There is no other way."

"Why don't we have lunch one day next week, Lawrence?"

"Here I come, pretty lady."

"Lawrence, you must understand. I try to be a good wife to Graham, faithful. I believe in the sanctity of the marital bed, in the vows I took, in monogamy."

"Ten minutes."

"I'll be in my bath. You won't be able to get in."

"I'll join you in the tub."

"Oh, awful man. Give me half an hour."

"Exactly thirty minutes, and counting."

"Just long enough for a cup of coffee, before you must go. I mean what I say, Lawrence." But he'd hung up the phone by then.

When he arrived, she was wearing tight black satin slacks and a flowing white silk shirt. Her cheeks were flushed and her eyes were bright.

And why not?

When she was still in high school, Lawrence Grant was already a giant of the literary world. Everyone knew about him. A man larger than life, wild and adventurous, a wicked and dangerous man.

As a sophomore, she'd read *High Country, Low*, still vividly recalled the scene between Hannah and Greg in the snow above Lake Tahoe. They had been on the run, desperate to escape the posse, the danger manifest. But when they had found the trapper's cabin they turned to each other in love and inexhaustible passion.

That scene had fired her budding sexual imagination and Louise had reread it many times until she could not keep her hands away from her own body. Later there'd been guilt, even tears, and regret over something precious lost. Though that had not kept her from repeating the experience, always after reading Lawrence Grant.

Here he was. Huge, imposing, more than a little frightening. He towered over her, blocking out the rest of the world, and kissed her wetly on the mouth. "You look superb."

"One cup of coffee," she warned, going toward the kitchen.

He followed. "Hot and black." His mahogany skin glamed with a thin coat of perspiration and the Teddy Roosevelt grin widened and held. "Ran almost all the way. Didn't want any eagle-eyed gossips spotting the Grant car and enhancing my rep at the expense of yours, pretty lady." He patted her tight round bottom.

"I'll get you something cool to drink."

"Heat up the inside, cool off the outside. Keep it hot."

She filled two cups with coffee. He came up behind her, hands on her waist, sniffing the scent of her, pressing himself close so that she could not ignore his already hardening desire.

"Good, the way you feel."

"Lawrence, please." She pulled away and offered him a cup, went into the living room. She placed herself primly in a straight-backed chair and he sprawled on the deep sofa, thick legs spread, the solid round belly heaving. She could hear the hoarse rasping of his breathing.

"How is Hilda?" she said politely.

He swore. "How in hell do I know how she is? The lady is a sharp pain in the keester, if you really want to know." His ferocity alarmed her and at the same time triggered her emotions. He gave off a primitive maleness that she had never before encountered, raw, blunt, everything magnified out of proportion, dramatized, and therefore exciting.

"You mustn't talk about your wife that way."

"Admit it: Graham is a pain in the ass."

"Graham is a fine, upstanding man. He gives me everything I want."

"Shit on that. Your husband is a stiff-necked pissant. He suffers from emotional constipation. I'll lay odds when he comes he doesn't make a sound."

Louise was caught between a sob and a laugh. "You mustn't."

He put his cup aside and heaved himself upright. "Tell me what's wrong with your husband and I'll tell you what's wrong with my wife." The grin seemed fixed in place, his cheeks glowing crimson, heaving and blowing as he trundled across the room. "Hilda wants to be a writer, but she's all head and no heart. Good writing is from the gut, good anything. All that's worth a damn comes from here." He clutched his crotch as if in offering. "Right here is where creativity festers. It stirs around until it comes to a boil and, writing or screwing, you shoot it out in extended spasms. Only the great writers, like the great lovers, know the secret of it all. You don't teach people to write. Or fuck." He scowled. "Ah, Hilda's okay, but who wants to talk about wives and husbands?"

She wasn't aware of the exact moment she stood up. She hadn't heard her chair topple over. She made a mild effort to retreat, to avoid his hands. He was too quick. He stroked her breasts and his powerful fingers gave her pain and pleasure until she was able to tolerate no more of it. She jerked away and he came after her. His foot hooked the Oriental rug and he went down heavily. For a moment she was afraid he had hurt himself but he struggled up, breathing harder, his eyes small and fiery, and he waggled one large finger at her in warning.

"So it's the chase you want! Well, all right. I love the hunt, and the kill." He lunged, the great body tilted at an impossible angle.

She managed to avoid his great rush and he ended up against the far wall, hands bracing himself. He came clumsily around, head lowered, charged again.

This time there was no escape. The thick fingers of

one hand hooked the waist of her black pants and she tripped and fell. Even before she hit the floor he was on her, pounding against her buttocks, squeezing her breasts, grunting, moaning, saying how good it was to be on top of a real woman.

Seeking a more strategic hold, he shifted, and she took advantage of the momentary respite to roll free. She sought haven under the dining table at the far end of the room. On all fours, hawking, sucking air, he followed.

There was no way out. He pulled her down, and found her mouth, his tongue forcing itself between her lips. She set her teeth against the intrusion until all resolve drained away and she opened herself to him.

He shifted to one side, plucking roughly at her nipples. The buttons on her shirt resisted him and he tore them away. She cried out and her anger provided a surge of strength she hadn't known she possessed. She broke away and climbed to her feet.

"Look at what you've done!"

Her bare breasts incited him even more and he came up grunting, tugging roughly at her slacks.

"You'll rip them!"

"I can almost taste you . . ."

"Let me do it," she said in resignation.

There was no way to take them off gracefully. She worked them down over her feet, removing one leg at a time, then she folded them neatly, draped them over the back of a chair.

Grant had his own troubles. He tripped and almost fell trying to get his trousers off. He succeeded only while sitting on the floor. He worked his shirt off, and then yanked his undershorts down to his knees. Hobbled by Jockey, he stumbled in her direction.

She began to laugh.

His eyes were beady and red. "Don't . . ."

"It's all so funny."

"Is this funny?" He held himself out to her, a semi-turgid offering.

She was disappointed. She had anticipated some great and special prize from the Great Man, an immense ridgepole quivering with glistening passion. His penis seemed not unlike Graham's, or the organs of those few young men she had dallied with years ago.

How sad; a man was merely a man, Pulitzer Prize or not.

She understood that it was not just the man she wanted; there was the Writer, the world-renowned Personality, the Man of the Year, the Hunter, the Fisherman, the War Hero, the Great Lover. Larger than a single life could be, he was a Legend, a Myth, an impossible promise. She eyed that pathetic pink penis in his fat fingers and blew him an encouraging kiss.

He made it all the way across to where she sat, pleading, "Make it hard." He swallowed a harty belch that tasted of beer and hot sausage.

She touched him; he shifted and fell back.

"Do it."

"What?"

"You know."

"I am not very experienced."

"I will teach you."

She examined that wizened wiener sympathetically and delivered a quick, sisterly kiss to its tip.

"Ah," he said. "Ah, ah."

She took it to mean that he approved. But did she? There was little comparison to make. Five years of marriage, and there was only Graham. And he insisted on making love in the dark; once a week whether he needed it or not. All the old jokes were coming back. For a long time she had been wondering what it would be like with another man. A young, strong slender man. Someone like Sam Dickey, for example. Someone always hard and hot and able to do it all day and all night until she was rubbed raw and ready to call it quits.

"Do it," he commanded from on high.

She did it, not well but with mounting enthusiasm for a new skill being learned.

He grunted, twitched, groaned and eventually became firm. He squeezed her hard. He pulled her hair. He issued explicit instructions. He forced her backward onto the couch. They rolled, they bounced, they wiggled against each other. Sweat poured off him and gathered in the hollows of her body making it slippery going. They went to the floor and tried something different.

He licked and sucked and chewed and spit as if desperate for sustenance. Curiosity kept her passion in check;

on-the-job training continued. She matched him lick for suck. She humped and bumped and writhed in simulated agony and desire, urged him to perform more and greater degradations on her flesh.

He obliged. He explored the terrain with the fevered intensity of a Smithsonian explorer in a new land. He spread, he poked, he pinched, inexorably pressing forward, going everywhere, getting nowhere. He suffered spiritual and physical heartburn.

His fingers dug into the flesh of her small buttocks. She yipped in pain and he made a valiant effort to pull her apart. Her effort to put an end to this insidious invasion was futile and his huge forefinger, the one that tapped out fully fifty percent of his literary output, made an excruciating entry.

She yelled.

Thus encouraged, he went faster, breathing in the sweat-sex-scent between her thighs. Sucking air, keeping all parts in motion, he listened to the rush of blood inside his skull. His heart flopped wildly. His legs quivered and his belly vibrated.

She shrieked.

"Great . . ." he mumbled.

"Oh . . ."

"Yeah."

"Nobody ever . . ."

"Great . . . fuck . . . you . . ."

She wondered: would they get to that.

He swore to give her the screw of her life, to elevate her to heavenly heights, to lay one on she'd always remember. He shifted into high gear.

There was, she discovered, a certain pleasure in this rough play. She paid closer attention. She intended to miss nothing.

"Good?" he hushed.

"I'd rather fuck you than read you."

What kind of sneaky literary putdown was that? There was no time to figure it out. His brain whirled and dipped into a warm, hot cloud and he found it increasingly difficult to breathe.

She curled her fingers into his hair and pushed, locking her thighs around his cheeks, making sure he wouldn't get away. He sounded like an old horse running his last race, snorting, wheezing, determined to keep going for as long as he could.

She encouraged him. "That's good, that's nice, right there."

He tried to find the place without success.

"There, too. Do that."

What had he done?

"Better," she moaned. "Better, better."

They shifted. They switched. They went at it, front to back, and the other way around. She stood, he kneeled. She kneeled, he stood. She crouched over him. He sat and she made that work to her advantage.

"I'd like to say some good words about adultery," she announced.

Weariness inhibited his response. Growing depressed, as strength departed his body. He wanted desperately not to disappoint her. Or himself. What if he were unable to consummate this marvelous moment? The possibility of failure triggered a new burst of energy and he went at her with renewed determination.

Not for long. All those extra pounds hanging off his bones, all that booze and good food, all the years he had lived made him aware of how weak and ineffectual he had become. Too many encounters with life, with death, too many battles, too many wars. Victory and defeat alike took their toll.

Longing for comfort, he crawled between her legs, anxious for that young body to be under him, to give what he craved and to take from him as well. He belched and tasted a sour rottenness that defied identification. It wouldn't do to be sick, to puke all over the pretty lady. He blamed it all on that damned big fish. The marlin had extended Grant to the breaking point. What glorious combat! But you paid the price and he was worn to the bone. Which didn't mean he wasn't man enough to close the day out with one last exemplary fuck . . .

"Put the goddamn thing in, for crying out loud!"

That startled her. Even Graham, with his penchant for issuing orders, never spoke to her in that tone of voice. Never demanded that she do *everything* for him.

She reached for him. She tugged, pulled, adjusted her aim. She shifted. She lifted. She turned and widened the avenue of approach. Until he was approximately where

he wanted to be. He bellowed and inched ahead, tested
the terrain, and rammed it all the way home. She yelled
in pain and the old fear that she would be gravely damaged.

She protested.

"Love it!" he gasped. "Love it . . ."

His vigor was overflowing. Listen to her shriek and
shout! Nothing like a screwing by Larry Grant. The Old
Bull still had a few good blasts left. Belt her, baby! Throw
it down! Zing her and zap her!

She gritted her teeth and held on.

Grant bumped her. He buffeted her. He rode her. He
reared back and slammed her down, pounded her heavily
into the carpet, soft clouds of dust rising up. He sneezed
and he coughed, he gasped for air. His heart flipped, it
flopped, it burned. His limbs were drained, growing useless, numb. Desperate to end it soon, he went faster,
harder. He belched some more, muttered, farted, and
began to run down.

She felt better and better. Concentric circles of
warmth. A softening of everything internal, flesh turning
to jelly, bones to liquid, all wet and hot and soft flow.
The active urgency of that great mound of hairy flesh
above her caused Louise to answer back with brief little
bursts of physical activity. She tried this out, experimented
with that, a thrust here, a flex there. When he made no
complaint, she went on.

"Ah," she said.

"Ahah," he responded.

"So . . . much . . . man."

"Oooh . . ."

"Fuck." She said it again, trying it for size and
sound. Never before had she uttered it in the presence
of another human person, though to herself any number
of times. She sought his reaction; he didn't seem to mind.
"Fuckfuck. Fuckfuck."

His strength went fast. The burning in his chest sharp-
ened and was transformed into a deep stabbing pain. Pain
was nothing, he told himself, remembering other pains out
of his distant past. Pain was what life was all about. And
working through the pain, struggling to overcome defeats,
that was what living was all about. He slipped and

slurped around, but his arms failed to support him as before.

"Larry," she said, almost apologetically. She didn't want to disturb his concentration. "I wonder if you could shift your weight a little?"

He had no breath to waste so gave no answer. He was determined to persevere, to ride the storm out to victory. There was, he noticed with dismay, a certain flaccidity to his penis, and in silent compensation he made an effort to go into overdrive. The old familiar signals alerted him to *la petite mort*, as they used to call it in the faraway Paris days and nights. "Coming," he thought he said, but no word was uttered. "Protect yourself!" was the old war cry, that he could give no voice to this time.

He groaned.

She yipped.

He fought for breath.

She rotated her ass.

He was afraid.

She saw the light at the end of the tunnel.

He began to slip away.

She wrapped her legs around him.

"Something's happening," she declared tentatively. "I think, I'm sure, I'm coming, coming, coming."

He moaned in response to the monstrous squeeze that gripped his chest, groaned as it shot up into his jaw, infected his molars and blasted its way into his eyeballs. He opened his mouth and only garbled sound came forth. He fell forward and lay still while she wiggled around in search of the last bit of pleasure the event could provide.

"Boy, do I feel good!" she said.

He didn't answer. He couldn't. He was, as he had once written, dead in the saddle.

PART
II

8

At approximately the same instant that life fled Lawrence Grant's body, Charles Dickey returned to his house with his son. "That was fun for me, Sam, being together again after so long."

"Chez Emile," Sam said. "I must remember that. The food was excellent."

His father went to the bar. All through dinner they had discussed the quality of the cuisine, the bouquet of the wine, pleasantly arguing the merits of New Orleans restaurants versus those in New York City. Was there such a thing, Charles had said lightly at one point, as *good* Conch cooking? No more than there was good Southern food. Except Chinese, Sam had said, causing them both to laugh.

Sam talked of his dining adventures in Europe. In Paris, of course, in Germany and in Rome. And in Corsica, where he had first met Lawrence Grant. They discussed Lawrence Grant at length—the man, the writer, the public figure—and decided it was impossible to break down the triad into separate, measurable portions. They consigned Grant's literary exploits to posterity for a more accurate assessment. Though both agreed that the man was immensely appealing and revolting in the same degree and at the same time. Grant was a monumental personality stuffed to overflowing with contradictions and human desires.

"Some cognac?" Charles offered.

"I don't think so." Sam found himself speaking flatly, formally, as if placed in a lesser position, defensive, trying mightily not to make any mistakes. He could not remember when he had last felt comfortable with Charles.

He looked around and was surprised at the casual appearance of his father's house, the easy disarray: books scattered about, magazines, a pair of tennis shoes tossed against the wall, this morning's breakfast dishes still on the kitchen counter. His mother would not have tolerated it: the Fifth Avenue apartment in which Sam was raised was neat to a fault, spotless, a place for everything, everything in its place.

"Have you ever regretted what you did?" he said, the words out before he could smother them.

Charles showed his surprise, and then a small, sweet smile. "I missed you a lot, Sam. You were a lively child, full of fun, a pleasure to watch."

"To watch? But not to be with?"

"Perhaps I was not the best of fathers. You're sure about the cognac?"

Sam shook his head.

"What about grass?"

"Don't tell me you use the stuff?"

"Now and then. Anything you want, Key West can supply it."

"Smuggler's paradise."

Charles laughed. "Ever since those early pirates. Geography is destiny. Anybody wants to bring in something illegal or immoral or fattening, the keys are a natural. Coves, bays, inlets, canals. There are swamps, beaches, secluded spots where nobody ever goes. And boats by the thousands, coming and going. No way to keep track."

"I might just go into business."

"Don't bother. The competition is fierce, and rough. Too rough, I hear."

"Sounds pretty decadent to me, Charles."

Charles grinned. "Dear, dear, how conservative and judgmental today's young people are."

Sam watched his father arrange himself in a comfortable chair, kick off his loafers. Changes had taken place, subtle and difficult to define. The controls were still in evidence, the slightly aloof sophistication, almost a haughtiness. Yet softened in some way. Charles had always been a handsome man, tall and slender, slightly removed from whatever was happening. Perhaps that was the doctor in him, the necessity to keep from becoming emotionally involved, to salvage one's sanity in the face of repeated onslaughts. Medicine confronted physical and human disaster every minute, blood and guts on the line always. All doctors fought to keep their distance.

Looking at Charles now, Sam saw himself as he would one day become. The same slender but well-formed physique, the same full head of hair (Charles wore his shorter and more artistically trimmed, the gray beginning to come through), the same cool eyes and smooth, pale cheeks. They might have been brothers, Sam thought, correcting himself quickly; he disliked Charles too much for him to be a brother.

"I should get going," Sam said.

"I thought you'd stay here. For tonight, at least."

Sam noted the qualification. Charles no more anxious to have him on the premises than he was to stay. Father and son, two of a kind; save the one from the other.

"I'll check in at some motel, make it easier all around."

"Not for me." Charles seemed to mean it.

Sam had learned to suspect sincerity; it was an effective mask for the hypocrisy he'd experienced so often.

"What I'd like to do is find a small apartment. I thought I'd hang around for a while. This article on Grant."

"Stay here tonight. Tomorrow I'll help you find a suitable place. I know some people . . ."

"You know Grant?"

"Everybody knows Grant on Key West."

"I expect so. On Corsica, it was the same way."

"Surrounded by young girls?"

"Dozens of them." Sam laughed. "If you're around long enough, you get his leftovers."

"Is that what you're after, his leftovers?"

Once Sam would have responded with anger; but he heard no hostility in the remark. "I don't know what I want, Charles."

Charles concentrated on Grant. "The man's had a weight problem for years."

"You're his doctor?"

"In a way. He pays no attention to my advice. He's obsessed with his image. The Big Bear, hairy, huge, horrendous appetite for all of life."

"He can sit around drinking for hours, telling war stories, picking up young girls, drinking, boasting."

"That's Larry. It's very difficult for Hilda."

"She's a lovely woman, but slightly intimidating."

"When I first saw her I thought I'd never seen a more beautiful woman. She was an actress, you know. On Broadway. Grant had a play on and she was in it and they became lovers. He was married to that long-distance swimmer in those days—"

"Cynthia Stillwell," Sam said.

"You've done your homework."

"Research and rewriting."

"That sounds like Grant."

"Stole it from him."

Charles grinned and sipped some cognac. "First night they came to Key West, Grant picked up a girl in a bar and went off with her . . ."

"And Hilda?"

"He left her waiting in the bar."

"And she waited?"

"She loved Grant. Still does, I think."

"Why? What's he got?"

"Ask Hilda, if you dare."

Sam thought about it. "I may have to, to do the article well."

"Good luck. She's been hurt and a damaged woman can be a hard case."

"Remarkable, isn't it," Sam said. "Everybody talks about Grant. Constantly. It was that way in Corsica and in Rome, when I was there. He leaves his mark everywhere, on everyone."

"Great men are like that."

"If only some of them were more attractive."

The phone rang and Charles answered and when he put it down again his face was long with wonder and sudden weariness. He spoke quietly. "It's Grant, Sam. He's dead."

Monte Perrin had spent five years as a professional football player, not good enough to be a regular but mean and aggressive enough to serve on the special teams. Until a series of knee operations took away his speed and made him useless to the hard-eyed men who coach in the National Football League.

Using his poker winnings, Monte opened a shop in Key West selling scuba equipment and offering diving instruction to tourists. The shop allowed Monte to live without economic strain and to spend a great deal of time in the sun.

Monte wore his suntan like a badge of honor over a jolly round face and a body beginning to go to flab. He had sparkling teeth and steady blue eyes and yellow hair that he wore in a Prince Valiant. He drove his van through the streets of Key West carefully, lest he damage its clean, recently painted sides. Eyes on the road, he said, "I never liked the man much."

"Speak no ill of the dead," Charles, in the seat alongside, said.

Perched behind the driver on a corrugated box, Sam offered, "I was fishing with him this morning. He brought in a marlin. Louise Welles was along and—"

"Died in her house?" Monte said, with obvious satisfaction.

"Keep quiet, Monte," Charles said.

"In her hairy old box, I imagine."

Charles frowned. "Try to keep your prejudices in check, Monte."

Sam could almost see it. Louise Welles, so perfectly formed, so pale and lovely. How could she permit the big writer to impose his gross body on her? The vision was grotesque and painful.

"Where's Graham?" Monte said.

"In Miami. on business."

"That's Grant for you. Always flexing his balls, when it's safe. Never pick up the soap in the shower when guys like Grant are around, I tell you."

"Shut up, Monte."

Sam filed it away, not sure what Monte intended. Later he would sort it all out, use it as it fit into his story. Who knows, the article might even be expanded to book length.

"Why'd you suck me into this?" Monte asked in complaint. "He was no pal of mine."

Charles answered patiently. "Because you're the only jock I know with muscle enough to get the job done."

Monte pulled the van into the driveway alongside Graham Welles's house and parked in back. "We're here." He glanced over at Charles. "It's against the law, you know."

Charles climbed out without speaking and they followed. Charles knocked and that brought Louise to the door. They paraded past her and she greeted each man by name, planting a light kiss on Charles's cheek.

"I don't know what I would do without you, Charles . . ."

She wore black slacks and a shirt to match. A delicate gold chain circled her throat. Her lips were pink and perfect and her eyes carefully lined. Sam decided she was the most beautiful woman he'd ever seen, and envied Lawrence Grant his time with her.

She looked at Sam. She blinked and tears welled up in her eyes. "Only this morning, Sam, he was so very much alive."

Sam nodded, not able to think of anything suitable to say.

"We were talking about his last big fish," Louise said, her voice catching.

For a suspended moment, Sam believed her. But the smirk on Monte Perrin's face snatched him back to the real world.

"Leave us alone for a few minutes, Louise," Charles suggested.

Louise lowered her eyes and moved her head in the direction of the living room. "He's in there."

The three men entered the other room. Grant, face turned to the sky, lay naked and dead.

Monte sniffed. "There it is, the last big fish," he said in a poor imitation of Louise Welles.

"Jocks are insensitive clods," Charles said to Sam. "The man was courting disaster. Everything was wrong. Clogged arteries, high blood pressure, high cholesterol, enlarged heart. He smoked too much, drank too much and tried to act like a man thirty years younger."

Sam remembered his first meeting with Grant upon

his arrival in Key West. Had that only been three days before? "He was swimming laps in his pool every day. Said he did about a hundred laps a day."

"Straining an already strained cardiovascular system," Charles put in.

"The poor fool hasn't written a decent book in years," Monte said. "Ugly, isn't he? Never trust a hairy man, I always say."

"What do we do now?" Sam asked.

"They burn books," Monte said hopefully, "what about authors?"

"Not funny," Charles said. "Let's get him into the van and into his own bed, if possible."

"Oh, that will make Hilda happy!"

"Well, what about Hilda?" asked Sam. "Isn't anybody going to tell her?"

"You do it, Sammy," Monte said. "And tell Hilda he went out giving Louise her jollies."

Charles broke in. "Enough of this. Hilda's away. We can't let her know what happened. If we put an end to this conversation we might just pull it off before she gets back. Sam, find Louise and borrow an old sheet."

When the body was safely behind the closed doors of the van, Charles went back into the house. Louise was waiting for him.

"Say nothing about this to anybody, Louise."

"What about them?"

"Monte and Sam? I'll keep Monte in line and Sam will talk only about that fishing trip. He'll say that Larry ate too much, drank too much, exerted himself too much. Paco will confirm everything and, as Grant's doctor, I'll testify to his physical condition. The man was a heart attack waiting to happen and happen it did. Keep your emotions in proportion to your public relationship with Grant and all will be well, my dear."

"I don't know what I'd do without you, Charles."

"Find somebody else, I imagine."

When the van drew away, she locked up and made herself a cup of tea. She carried it upstairs and drew a hot bath, lowered herself into it. The tea, and the steaming water, soothed her inside and out, and the tension began to drain away. What an exciting day it had been. Full of surprises, unexpected rewards and sensations.

She forced herself to think about what had passed, what Grant had done to her, and she to Grant. Everything was vivid in her mind and provided considerable residual satisfaction. She liked what had transpired, was more than willing to do it again. Next time, however, with a man in better physical condition, a man who weighed less, and was much younger.

She felt proud. After all, she had just fucked one of the world's most famous men to death. Not one of her friends had ever done so much.

9

Another Mugging. An elderly couple this time, during their usual evening stroll. Two young white men had knocked them down, snatched the woman's purse and the man's wallet, punched them a few times and departed in haste. The old people were dazed, bleeding and frightened. But not hurt enough to be hospitalized.

Hollinger took the call. The husband was numb, and unwilling to discuss what had happened, as if guilty over his failure to defend himself and his wife. The woman was enraged.

"Where were you when we needed you?" she shouted. "Cops are never around."

"Can you identify the men who assaulted you?"

"Weren't men, were boys. Couple of runny-nose boys. Not more'n fifteen, I'd say."

"Fifteen."

"Are you deaf, young man?"

As if in response, the radio in Hollinger's car began to crackle. He excused himself, listened, then went back. The woman displayed her disapproval.

"How much did they get?"

"Everything we had."

"How much was that?"

"Ten, eleven dollars. May not seem like much to you. But for us, for folks on retirement benefits, it's a lot. Anyway, why can't you make the streets safe for decent people?"

Hollinger put his notebook away. "I'll send a car for you tomorrow morning. Will you go through our mug books? With any luck—"

"Won't do any good

"You never can tell."

"Won't," she insisted. Her husband shook his head as if in agreement. "They were hardened criminals, but young. Won't have a record, not the way judges treat 'em nowadays. Damn permissiveness everywhere. Nobody's safe anywhere. Not a living soul."

"But you'll look through our files?"

"Won't do any good."

Hollinger was anxious to be on his way. He said if they remembered anything else to give him a call, then drove over to Eliza Street, a little more than a block from Bayview Park.

By the time he arrived, four prowl cars were on the scene, flashers spinning, plus an emergency van. The street was crowded with onlookers and kids were running around, as if it were a fiesta. Beer was being drunk and food eaten and a number of peoople were laughing.

Hollinger, pushing his way through the crowd, failed to see the humor. The house was faded yellow, paint cracked and peeling in a number of places. The porch sagged at the far corner where the piling had slipped to an unsafe angle and the railing was broken in a couple of different spots. Some of the steps leading up to the porch had rotted and one showed a large hole. It was the house of people who had stopped caring. Or never had. The house of people who lived with trouble, were used to it, expected to find it every day. And were seldom disappointed.

This time the trouble was very bad, Hollinger told himself. Real and immediate, concocted of equal parts of fear and pain and possible bloodshed. He looked around. On the porches of the houses on either side, neighbors watched solemnly, attentive to the building disaster. The trouble in the yellow house might have been their trouble and if they were able to feel no sympathy for their neighbors, neither did they take joy in what was happening.

A uniformed officer named Grabner took up a position at Hollinger's shoulder. "So?"

"Crazy guy has got his wife inside. Says he's gonna kill her."

"Is he serious?"

"He's got a knife."

"A knife?"

"Big bread knife."

"He's serious. What set him off?"

"Seems like he and his old lady split up, only he didn't like it."

"She kicked him out."

"Yeah. And he showed up tonight to patch things up."

"They argued . . . ?"

"She was with another dude."

"Ah. Where is he?"

"Made it out the back fast. Without a stitch on his back. The wife wasn't so lucky."

"What's the family name?"

"Cruz. Angel Cruz. The wife's is Rosalinda."

"Nice name."

"Wait'll you see her. Built for action. Can't blame Cruz for being pissed off. She's not wearing a thing, either, Dutch."

"Why don't you move some of these people in the street back? We can use some working space."

"Sure, Dutch. Whatever you say." Grabner made no move to go.

A tall woman with orange hair picked her way through the onlookers, smiling as she came.

"Cruz keeps yelling that Rosalinda's a whore and a bum and he's going to cut her heart out," Grabner added cheerfully.

"Hi, Dutch," the woman said. "Remember me?"

Hollinger allowed himself no change of expression.

She sobered quickly. "Annie Russell, of the *County Journal*. Looks like a good story here."

"I thought I told you to move the crowd," Hollinger said to the uniformed man.

"Sure, Dutch. Just about to."

"Do it now."

"Sure, Dutch. Okay, lady," he said to Annie Russell. "Back where you came from."

"Press!" she cried as if brandishing a weapon.

"Move along, lady."

"Don't touch me! Police brutality."

Hollinger tried not to laugh.

"What about the First Amendment?" he said.

"Right on."

"Arrest her, Grabner, if she resists."

"On what charge?"

Grabner looked inquiringly at the detective. "Resisting an officer in the performance of his duty. Obstructing justice. Littering. What the hell do I care? Just get her out of here, and all the rest of them."

Before any of them could act, Angel Cruz and Rosalinda appeared on the front porch of the yellow house. Cruz had one arm wrapped around her throat and held a rather large knife to his wife's naked breast. Cruz rolled his eyes and cried out in Spanish. Rosalinda moaned and prayed.

"What I tell you?" Grabner muttered. "Looka those boobs!"

Annie turned away. "Men."

Hollinger spoke to Grabner. "I want men in back of the house."

"There's two back there, with rifles."

"Christ! No shooting, you understand. Nobody shoots, unless I give the order. Put one man to either side of the porch, out of sight along the sides of the house. Young men, able to move. And nobody does a thing without my say-so. You got that?"

"Sure, Dutch. Any way you want it." He went to see to it.

Annie shifted closer, spoke in an intimate voice. "What's your plan, Dutch?"

"Keep out of my way. Don't complicate my life." He strolled without urgency across the street.

Cruz saw him coming and swore in Spanish. "Stay away!" he shouted. "You come up here, I'll slice her open like a pig."

Hollinger stopped, spread his hands. "Hey, Angel, it's okay to talk a little bit, ain't it?"

"Got nothing to say. Gonna cut this cunt once and for all, you understand me!"

"Sure. Only I'm a cop, Angel, it's my job to be here. Got to do things according to the book." He withdrew his pistol and placed it on the ground, and spread his hands. "You see, Angel, I don't mean you any harm."

"No tricks. I don't trust cops."

Hollinger made himself smile. "Don't blame me. Who would trust a cop? What the hell, Angel, you got your opinion, I got mine, right?"

Cruz said nothing, his feral eyes fixed on Hollinger. The detective walked forward.

"Far enough, cop."

Hollinger stopped. He was close enough to see the point of the knife pressing into Rosalinda's right breast. Her mouth was slack, her eyes wide with terror. Grabner was right about her boobs.

"*Amigo*," Hollinger said. "What do you want to do this thing for?"

"I ain't your friend. This cunt, she was banging the butcher's kid. Eighteen-year-old kid, she's giving it to him. She gives it to everybody, this cunt. So I'm gonna give her something."

"You think I blame you? I don't blame you. Give her a shot in the head, Angel."

"Not enough."

"Maybe you're right. Break her nose for her. Punch her out. Make her know what a real man can do."

"Nobody puts horns on me. The bitch deserves to be snuffed."

"Okay. But what does that get you, Angel? Behind bars forever, maybe. You want to live, don't you? Plenty more where she came from. Just put out your line, Angel, you catch plenty of fish that way."

"Stay back!" Cruz shouted.

Hollinger planted his feet. "Why don't we talk about it, you and me alone. Over a *cerveza*, eh? You got a favorite place, *amigo*?"

"You must think I'm dumb."

Hollinger took a long step forward.

Cruz raised the knife as if to strike. Rosalinda screamed. The crowd moaned and Hollinger yelled, "Don't do it, Angel!"

Cruz grinned triumphantly.

At each corner of the yellow house, the young uniformed cops had worked into position. Hollinger gestured and one cop showed himself. Cruz swore and swung around to face this new threat.

"She gets it, cop!"

Hollinger flicked a finger and the second man came out into the open. Cruz eyed one, then the other, retreated against the wall of the house. Hollinger set the two officers in motion with small authoritative gestures. One by one they climbed over the railing onto the porch.

"Get back!" Cruz screamed, lifting the knife.

There was a split second when he lost sight of Hollinger and in that isolated fragment of time Dutch launched himself across the remaining space that separated them. Cruz came around, but too late. Hollinger got a grip on his knife arm. They struggled until the other two cops joined the fray and together they bore Cruz down, fighting and cursing but helpless. Hollinger came up with the knife and blood flowing from a cut in his right palm. He wrapped a handkerchief around his hand. "Book him," he said to Grabner. "And get some clothes on Rosalinda before some wise guy takes a crack at her."

He was almost back to his car when Annie Russell caught up. "You were great, Dutch. I underestimated you."

He stared at her, then got in the car.

"How about a ride, Dutch? Give me a chance to interview you. Make a great story."

He started the motor and shifted into gear. The hand was beginning to ache and the old familiar aftershocks were setting in. He wanted very much to be alone until it passed.

"I will say this for you, Dutch, you're a good cop, on one level, anyway."

He suppressed an angry retort and drove away. As much as he hated to admit it, he was going to need a doctor's attention.

10

They left Miami after an early breakfast and were able to make it past the road construction and off Key Largo before the traffic built up. Figueroa drove with a sustained resolve, a man singular in purpose, reliable, strong, with a pragmatic intelligence. His hands were extraordinarily large for his size and his wrists were thick and veined. Black eyes peered out from behind wide cheekbones and his jaw was honed down to an aggressive angle. When he was younger, Figueroa had been an athlete, a fine shortstop on one of the professional teams in Cuba, and a quick, aggressive basketball guard. He played no more games; each day he did one hundred sit-ups and one hundred push-ups, and in the evening worked on karate for two hours. The result was a lean, hard body, pared down almost to the bone. It was not an attractive body, all sinews and veins and sharp edges. But it was responsive, able to function under the most demanding and dangerous circumstances without failing what was required of it.

Crossing Islamorada, Welles said in Spanish, "I have always loved best this part of the world."

"Yes," Figueroa replied absently, as if continuing an old conversation.

"I will always be a patriot, a true American, but for me Cuba holds a special place in memory."

"To go back is everything."

"The day will come."

"Next time, I will not leave. Victory or death." For Figueroa, it was an emotional outpouring.

"The last time there was betrayal."

Figueroa hissed.

"Caution is necessary. Speak only to those who must know."

"No longer do I trust anyone."

"You do not mean Hector?"

"Hector? He is one I would trust with my life. Only a few others, my people."

Welles kept his voice flat. Figueroa lacked a sense of humor, would perceive the slightest hint of mockery as an insult. He was not a man who took insults lightly. "I am not a Cuban."

Figueroa considered that for a while. "More than many, you are one of us. Still, it was an American who failed us when we landed at the Bay of Pigs. Your president."

"Even presidents lose their nerve. Kennedy was not alone. Nixon kept insisting he was a great enemy of the communists. Yet he brought to the world that heinous corruption, détente."

"And now the peanut farmer. You trust him?"

"No more than you do. This business about resuming relations with Fidel, very bad."

"An abomination."

"Sanity must be restored."

"I am with you, Commander. Hector is with you. There are others, when we need them."

"The important step is to cause a major alteration in American foreign policy. To return right-thinking men to office. To bring clarity of thought and vision back to Washington."

"We will kill Fidel at last."

"Will that change the thinking of those who make policy at the State Department? Will that bring Cuba to freedom? Or will it only make the walls higher, make our enemies more recalcitrant? No, to kill Fidel is to treat the rash instead of the disease. I have a plan, a war to fight, not merely a single battle. We have powerful friends, men in high places, men eternally faithful to the principles by which they and we live. Nothing will change them. Or us."

"Or us." They rode in silence before Figueroa spoke again. "This affair with Paco Valentín, I do not like it."

"We need him."

"Hector does not like it, either. Why do we need him?

He has changed, this Valentín. He is no longer one of us."

"Once he was among the best, the very best."

"But no more."

"Perhaps, perhaps not. At the Bay of Pigs, he took many boatloads of our people ashore. And when it became bad for them, Paco went back. More times than anybody, he went back to bring out the wounded."

"Some say he left certain people behind who were alive when he was there."

"He left behind those who were dying in favor of those who could live and thus fight again. He is more than a courageous man, he is a smart man. He seldom makes mistakes. Those who speak against what he did at that time are fools, or jealous of him. They do not understand. Do they tell you that when Paco's boat was shot out from under him he swam to shore and fought with a rifle against machine guns, protecting the wounded until help came? No, they neglect to mention such petty details. Paco is a man like few others and he performed very well that time."

Figueroa set his jaw. "Why do we need him this time?"

"Because Paco does what he does better than any man I know. Hector will understand."

"If he changes again, I will kill him. Perhaps I will kill him anyway."

"He is not one who is killed easily."

"If he should kill me, Hector will kill him for me. Hector is impossible to kill."

"There is a cold, dead place in Hector. Yes, he kills very well."

"In all of us who have been betrayed, there is a cold, dead place."

"I understand."

"Shall we triumph eventually, *señor?*" There was a note of pleading in Figueroa's voice, a sound so unusual that it brought Welles around to face the other man.

"With all of me, my friend, I believe that we shall win. You must believe it, too."

"I believe," the Cuban said slowly. "Or I could not go on."

The sun was still low in the sky when the Air Sunshine DC-3 glided in over the salt pond and put down at Key West International Airport. In the old days, when their marriage was young and still sweet, Grant would come out to fetch her in that old white Buick convertible he had loved so much. But much had transpired since, very little of it good, and they came and went their separate ways often now, neither of them taking much notice of the other. She passed under the welcoming sign that claimed Key West as the only Frost Free City in the United States and went through the terminal building and got in a cab.

It was all so sad, she mused as they circled Roosevelt Boulevard and she watched night close in over the water. Life seemed to be a series of High Expectations and Inevitable Disappointments. Failure was the ultimate disappointment. Failure was the dark side of the moon, the ugly sister in the looking glass. Failure was the pain and the agony. Failure was a marriage that didn't work.

The house on Caroline Street was dark when she arrived. Dark and cold to the eye and repellent for the first time. It was difficult to allow herself to recall how much she loved this house, how much she had come to enjoy life on Key West, how rewarding it had once been to be the wife of Lawrence Grant. All that, of course, had been long ago, before she and Grant settled into their rough groove, giving each other bad times, withholding affection and love, engaging in their hurtful games and extracting petty revenges for slights real and imagined.

Inside, she switched on lights and opened shutters to the cooling night air. "Anybody home!" she called once, getting no answer; she expected none. It was the maid's day off and she would be out hustling that hot *latina* fanny of hers, getting it filled up unto exhaustion, as Grant liked to say. Well, why not? What was a good solid bottom for if not to toss it around under some panting stud? Hilda thrust such images out of her mind. Where was Grant? Downtown pulling on a scotch and water, regaling tourists with exaggerated stories of his manly exploits, making it with some teenage chippie? Or, wonder of wonders, was he up in his studio over the pool house, putting one word down after another, as he liked to say?

Christ, she raged silently. I even think like that hairy bastard now.

She set the Norelco coffee maker working and followed the side gallery around to the back of the house. Let Grant know she had returned.

Halfway along the path that wound between oleander trees, Hilda paused to look at the pool. The pool was Grants, his idea to have it put in, his area of recreation, exercise and, whenever possible, entertainment. If there was to be a lasting memory of her marriage to Lawrence Grant it would be the sight of him leaping off the diving board into that pool, arms and legs askew, giving voice to some Neanderthal screech, splashing water for yards around. A sight to remember, devoid of all artistic merit.

An intrusive shadow jarred her consciousness. It was where it shouldn't be, a formless lump, still, and not attractive, but not threatening, either. She went closer, trying to make out what it was. She felt no trepidation, no dangerous emanations, only a mild curiosity.

She was only a few feet away when she recognized Grant. He lay face down, naked and gray in the moonlight, bulging at his waist, hairy and gross. She remarked to herself on the dimensions of his buttocks; what a small ass for such a tub of lard.

"Larry," she said, as if to wake him.

When he failed to respond, she knelt and discovered that he wasn't breathing. She touched his cheek; it was cool.

She stood up and swore. "Son of a bitch," she said aloud. He was dead, as dead as any of God's creatures could be. Cold and growing stiff.

"Mean as you were," she said, "never thought you'd go before me. Figured you'd hang on forever and torment me. Well, thank you, Lawrence Grant."

Then she began to weep. Almost silently, hands cupping her cheeks, gazing at her husband's body. "Damn you," she said softly. "Damn you for dying on me. Damn you for not being kinder and gentler with me, for turning me into a vicious bitch. Oh, damn, Larry, why couldn't you love me as much as I loved you. God, how I loved you, man! And always will, always. If you could only have needed me a little bit more, for a little longer time."

She stepped back and wiped her eyes. "What am I

going to do without you, dammit? How to live without you? You and me, we were opposite ends of the same stick. What good is a stick with only one end?"

She stayed with the body for a while until she began to shiver. She walked toward the house. There was so much to take care of, the strands of a life to be pulled together. She was good at that sort of thing; Grant had been the best of teachers. She knew exactly what to do, he had instructed her very well.

On the veranda, she looked back briefly, spoke aloud. "I never meant to be a bitch, not to you. Not to anyone." Then she went inside.

In the morning, she went to the bank. Two containers were brought out of the vault to a private cubicle and she was left alone. She opened the boxes and found them empty. No novels, no stories, nothing. No cash squirreled away. No rare coins. No gold, jewelry, or other precious objects. The foul bastard had shafted her again.

She went back to the house and checked to make sure Grant was still at poolside. She wished he were still alive so that she might kill him, extract her revenge. But even that pleasure had been denied her.

"I'm going to get even, Grant," she told the stiffening corpse. "You won't get away with this."

Izzy Ben-Ezra stood on Mallory Dock, back to the Chamber of Commerce. Out in the Northwest Channel, he watched a porpoise and her offspring sounding. Overhead, some gulls floated gracefully. A power boat ground noisily past on its way into the Gulf of Mexico. All part of the local scene, superficially interesting, but of no great import to Ben-Ezra since it was irrelevant to his reason for being in Key West. Ben-Ezra was a man who had been schooled to keep his eye on the ball.

Ben-Ezra was doing what all good cops knew how to do. He was waiting. And soon his patience was rewarded. A man appeared from the parking lot, circling like a wary hyena. Long mud-colored hair with eyes to match, a bent body that might be stronger than it seemed, pasty skin, a man who lived on the balls of his feet, always ready to flee. He wore a loose-fitting Levi's shirt and Ben-Ezra guessed there was a weapon of some kind tucked away beneath the faded blue fabric. This was a man who needed all the help he could get merely to stay even.

Ben-Ezra brushed at his thinning gray hair. "You Harry?"

"You Ben-Ezra?"

Ben-Ezra handed over his I.D. "Satisfied?"

"I believe in being careful. Who'd you say gave you my name?"

"I didn't say. A friend who said you might be able to help me out."

"How's that, help you out? Let's walk. Makes me nervous, standing around."

"Buy you a cup of coffee?"

"Just a walk. Help how?"

"What I told you on the phone, information."

"About what?" They strolled up past the Conch Train depot, loading tourists for the sightseeing ride around the island. "Looka the squares . . ."

"What's it going to be, Harry, bullshit or good talk?"

"Jesus, you always so impatient?"

Ben-Ezra gave no answer and they continued walking. Up Duval Street, past the shops still closed, past couples arm in arm, past some middle-aged tourists. A prowl car rolled slowly along, the driver lost in uniformed reverie.

"Cops," Harry snarled.

"I'm a cop," Ben-Ezra answered.

"You are? Private, you told me."

"Used to be public, but that's a long time ago."

"What have you got on the lady?"

"What was that name again?"

Ben-Ezra drove his elbow into Harry's side, the soft flesh under his rib cage giving way. He grunted and pulled back.

"Whatja have to do that for?"

"Don't fuck me around, Harry. I'm on a job. Time is money. You want to play games, find another playmate."

"I don't like rough stuff is all. How much is in it for me?"

They went past Sloppy Joe's, where a few lonely

drinkers were getting an early start. "Let's put the lady aside, give me something meaningful."

"Like what?"

"Like something a cop would like to know."

"You're asking too much of me."

"The money's good, Harry, I promise you. Tell me about the shipment."

"Shipment! What shipment?"

"Around here there's always a shipment. The word is out, I need some particulars."

"Yeah, well, maybe there is a shipment."

"Soon?"

"Pretty soon."

"Big?"

"Pretty big."

"How big is that?"

"A few tons."

"Tons. How many tons?"

"Twenty-five. Maybe thirty."

"Grass?"

"First-class Colombian."

"How's it coming?"

"By boat. Four of them is what I hear. I think we ought to discuss money at this point."

Ben-Ezra shrugged. "A hundred bucks."

Harry let out a cry of protest. "That ain't money. Not for what I'm selling. I'm splitting."

"Keep yelling, Harry. Turns the tourists on. Local color and all that."

Harry whispered urgently. "I'm talking about a thousand, man. One thousand dollars."

"Shit."

"I am not selling crap. I have very sound information here. Security, shipping dates, arrival time. Everything to make you happy, man."

"We'll split the difference—two hundred."

"Two— You think I'm dumb? I'm not dumb, man. I know what I got. And I know who the lady is. Her husband is a big man, lots of bread. He's paying, it don't come out of your pocket."

"Five bills, and that's it."

"Five and five."

"I don't know."

"How can you not know? What I've got here is good dope, straight arrow. You got to have something to trade, you think I don't know. So here it is. Five hundred now, five hundred more closing night."

"Harry." Ben-Ezra took the other man's thin arm in his hand and squeezed hard. "Don't get smart with me."

"Let go. You're hurting my arm."

Ben-Ezra released him. "Okay. Your terms, five and five. We meet an hour before it goes down. Say in Sloppy Joe's, okay?"

"Okay. But I play no part in the action, whatever it is. I stay far away."

"The way you want it, Harry. Now tell me about the shipment . . ."

Harry grinned. "First the dough."

Ben-Ezra paid and Harry began to talk.

11

Off Duval Street, not far from the Pirate Museum, was the Banyan Social and Drinking Society (BSDS). A bar, pure and simple, constructed for drinking and socializing. Food was served in discreet amounts: burgers and French fries, cold shrimp salad with a mustard sauce, fish-ka-bob.

BSDS was at the far end of a short alley, partially blocked by an immense banyan tree, after which the club had been named. Inside, dark and cool, few serious drinkers at the bar at this early-evening hour, a few serious socializers already in the pits, as the space that had once been a dance floor was known.

As usual, Hollinger sat at the small square table in

the far corner of the room, working on his second beer and struggling to sort out his feelings.

Opposite him a woman with long auburn hair that fell almost to her waist. Her features were full and womanly and in the dimness her eyes seemed to recede under a graceful well-formed brow. People had begun commenting on her dramatic beauty when she was twelve years old, had done so repeatedly in the years since, and she was no longer self-conscious about her appearance. She examined Hollinger with a warm, almost maternal expression on her full mouth.

"Can't I talk you out of going?" he said.

She touched his big-knuckled hand.

"You don't want to do that, Dutch."

"If I don't then why am I saying I want you to stay? I want you to stay, Betsy."

"You don't need me."

"The hell I don't."

"I've got to do this."

"You're not sure?" He felt compelled to dissuade her; and at the same time was glad she was leaving. Relief; they had been together too long, she was getting too close.

He took her hand in his. "I'd like it if you'd stay."

She smiled sadly. "I don't think so."

"People are always running out on people. My father ran out on my mother . . ."

"And on you?"

"I would never do that to a kid."

"No, not you, Dutch. You never would."

"Not that I blamed him. My mother was a tramp."

She flinched and withdrew her hand. "Don't tell me about it."

"There were always men around. One-night stands mostly. I can't remember them all. And afterward, she'd cry and tell me how much she loved me, how sad she was, how lonely . . ."

"It must have been very difficult for her."

"She should have tried harder."

"She disappointed you, all right. But she was a human being, she had needs, fears—"

"She died when I was ten years old—"

"And you've never completely trusted a woman since?"

"Why should I? I trusted Laura."

"Your wife."

"Laura walked out on me. She told me she'd had enough. Not enough, no, not enough. That was just the point of it, she wasn't getting enough. Enough of me. I didn't have it to give—enough. I was locked up inside myself, my feelings. As if it were a sin to reveal what I felt, what was most important to me. I loved that woman, I truly loved her, and wanted to go on with her. But I never could tell her so. Not in a way that mattered to her. Not in a way that would make her stay, or let me stay. So damned locked up."

"You tried, you must've tried?"

"I used to believe that I did, really tried. But now I don't know. Maybe not enough. Seems to me it's always been like that where other people are concerned—I just never did what was required, never gave enough. It's not women I don't trust—it's emotions, my emotions. Ah. What I never learned, to let others inside. I never learned to cry. Did you know that about me? I've never shed a tear, at least not in public. You didn't know that, did you?"

"Ah, Dutch, you will, Dutch. You'll see, you'll cry."

"Jesus, this is ridiculous, you know that? A really ridiculous conversation."

"Ah, Dutch." She believed she understood him, in some ways better than he understood himself. "You're an onion," she had told him more than once. "Layer over layer over layer. Where does the real Dutch Hollinger live?"

"Doesn't make any sense to me, your taking off like this."

"Dutch, you are a lovely man. But you hold on to fragments of yourself as if you think somebody is going to steal them. I don't blame you, it's how you've lived, the way you learned. The time for me to go has come."

"First Bill Vail, now you. This sandbar is losing its appeal."

She smiled briefly. "I'm saying good-bye to everyone I know. Bill just went."

"I wonder why. He seemed to have his life all together, tight, shaped up."

"Who knows? Rumors abound, Dutch." She shrugged.

He scowled. "People like to talk about cops, paint us all with a tarbrush."

"Not you, Dutch. There are no rumors about you. Everybody knows you're straight."

The subject made him uneasy. He had always been clean, a good cop, taking pride in his honesty and in the job he did. People weren't concerned with that; they found pleasure in ripping up policemen, making it seem as if all of them were crooks. He wanted to believe better of his colleagues.

"I've used up my Key West time," Betsy was saying. "It was good for a while, a place to get the divorce out of my system, to mark some time. I'm done marking and I want to get out and start living again."

"No insult intended," he said, "none taken."

"We had a once-in-a-while thing, Dutch. Nice, but not for the long run. Two years, Dutch, and I'm on my way."

"Where will you go?"

"Vegas for starters. Maybe the West Coast. As long as it's warm and friendly . . ."

He visualized her in a bikini, a dramatic and startling sight. On any beach in the world, Betsy would make friends easily.

"I'll miss you," he said, wondering if he should invite her back for one last visit to his bed.

"For a day or so. Until you hook up with someone else."

"Never happen."

Neither of them believed that.

"Take care of yourself, Dutch, hear."

"You, too."

"I'll drop you a card, whenever I land somewhere."

"I'd like that. Who knows, when I get some time off maybe I can pay you a visit."

"Yeah." Her mouth twisted up and her eyes avoided his. "We'll have a ball . . ."

He ran.

At about three-quarters speed. Taking a remembered youthful joy in the thrust and pull of his leg muscles.

Aware of the steady pounding of his heart. Sucking air deep into his lungs. He told himself that each jarring stride sweated away a dollop of that extra flesh padding his middle.

Jogging was not for Hollinger. Jogging was for men who wanted to hold back. To inhibit their bodies, do things under restraint, never going all out. It offended him to live by half measures, and yet . . . And yet.

He cleared such ideas from his mind and ran on. Always maintaining a reserve of speed, of power, creating endurance. Intermittently he opened up, testing his body to the far reaches of his ability. Going as fast as he could.

Wind sprints. Absurd for a man in his middle years to fake himself out with the jargon of a young athlete. Still, he had always been concerned with his body, keeping in trim, knowing that at any moment he might be called upon to react with strength, quickness, called upon to test his staying power. All his adult life Hollinger had dealt with the possibility of unexpected violence and danger, death always imminent. That he had survived this long was testimonial to body and mind, to his ability to take only intelligent, professional risks.

Whatever happened, he asked himself, stepping up the pace, to the Dutch Hollinger who took risks?

He ran every day. On mornings such as this, with a thinning mist drifting over the ocean, with gulls squawking, with only an occasional motorist going too fast. Or late at night. But never during the daylight hours when he might be seen. He did not want to be known as someone who went out of his way to maintain his physical condition, or who ran for enjoyment. He preferred a reputation as a man who coddled himself, faintly lazy, without ambition, concern or ego. Just an old cop muddling along.

At the high school, he cut onto Bertha Street and then Roosevelt Boulevard toward the airport, as if on his way to catch a plane. But he wasn't going anywhere. Beyond the Key West-by-the-Sea Condominium he spotted the other runner coming on, still some distance away.

Gradually the figure came into focus and was oddly familiar, which disturbed him slightly. An old crimson sweat shirt and floppy sweat pants. At least no trim and tailored jog suit. At once he knew the runner was a woman, her movements slightly out of sync, arms and legs not quite in harmony. And under the crimson sweat suit, breasts leaping freely about. Wasn't it uncomfortable to run without a brassiere? Then he recognized the orange hair, wild under the slow breaking dawn, and was able to put a name to the intruder in his space.

She waved, came to a stop. Panting and brushing idly at her hair, watching him approach. For a moment he was tempted to keep going, not to acknowledge her presence, to keep at a suitable distance. Instead he brought himself down to a walk. His breathing was regular and his heartbeat slowed almost at once. He still was, it pleased him to know, in pretty fair shape.

"I didn't know you ran," she began.

"You don't know anything about me," It came out harsh and almost angry.

Her brows went up. "Hey, Sergeant, don't you remember me? Annie Russell. Are you always this hostile in the morning?"

"Hostile! I'm never hostile, not to anybody. Just trying to get some exercise, is all. See you around." He began to run.

She caught up and gave him a big sidelong grin. He cranked up a couple of notches and was surprised to see she maintained the pace without effort.

"You were great," she said presently.

"What?"

"The other day. A regular hero."

"Cut it out."

"Can we be friends again?"

"When were we friends?"

"Let's start now."

He gave it some thought.

She laughed, running easily. "I never borrow money, I have no communicable diseases and my manners at the dinner table are impeccable. What've you got to lose, Dutch?"

He thought about that, also.

They went to the Fisherman's Cafe and had breakfast. She ate like a longshoreman; he had hot Cuban bread and coffee.

"You don't eat enough," she told him.

"This Cuban coffee keeps me strong and mean." He meant it as a joke.

She made a face. "You've got a lot of courage."

"Goes with the job."

"I almost forgot that you're a cop."

He examined her. A good face, all the parts in harmony, the eyes steady and unafraid, lively and glinting with good humor. But always the edge, the barbed comment, as if she were testing him, trying him out. "You have a negative fix on cops. Why?"

"I guess I react badly to anybody who can wield coercive power over people."

"Sure, that's me. I go around pounding innocent citizens along the side of the head."

"You carry a gun, don't you?"

"The way a reporter carries a pencil. Tool of the trade."

"Hardly the same thing."

"In the right hands, a pencil can do a lot of damage."

"Come off it."

"What would you do—eliminate all cops?"

"It's not practical, is it?"

"Why not? That way all those pure young kids who get their kicks heaving rocks through windows can do their thing without interruption. And the rebels who set fires and rob and mug people can give free rein to all their heart's desires. And the killers can kill without having their wrists slapped by nasty cops and judges and jailers. I get it, lady."

"That's not what I said."

"That's what you meant."

"You really are quick to defend the faith."

"Just a dumb cop being overly defensive."

"Not so dumb, I think. Maybe you're right. Maybe cops do get a lot of unnecessary flack from people like me."

"Maybe?"

"I'd like to ask you a question."

"Ask away."

"Meaning you might not answer? Fair enough. What about Rosalinda Cruz?"

For a moment or two he drew a blank on the name.

"Oh, the woman whose husband failed to appreciate her extramarital activities. What about her?"

"You know what I mean?"

He was puzzled. "I know we saved her life. I think Cruz meant to carve her up. You know those excitable Cubans—they don't believe in divorce so they have to come up with alternative routes in order to terminate an unsatisfactory relationship."

"Figures," she said. "You're on his side."

"Thanks to us dumb cops, Rosalinda is still alive and walking around."

She shifted closer. "Haven't you heard?"

"Heard what?"

"There's talk in the streets about what happened to Rosalinda Cruz afterward."

"Meaning what?"

"Meaning she was raped. By cops. Four cops gangbanged her."

He finished his coffee and lit a cigaret. "I don't believe it."

"That comes as no surprise. The word is they held her prisoner for five hours and took turns, a couple guarding her while the others were out defending law and order."

He put his hands flat on the table, pushed himself erect. All at once he felt clumsy and weary, aging fast. "If it's true . . ."

"What will you do?"

Standing there, gazing down into those shining green eyes, he felt vulnerable and exposed, as if she knew all the secret details of his existence, could see all his flaws.

"I'm sure you had nothing to do with it," she said.

He stepped away from the table, face clenched with rage and terror. "What do you think we are? Cops are not perfect human beings, dammit. Just guys doing a job. We're not all the same. We're ordinary, we're weak and afraid and we're strong and courageous, and some of us are just not good enough—"

"People have a right to expect their policemen to be better."

"They have no right. They—maybe they do. Most of us do the job. Most of us are honest. We try. We do try. We really try."

She watched him go through the door, head down and shoulders hunched protectively. She said softly, "I know that, Dutch . . ."

Acting Assistant Chief of Police Wilbur Frederic Huntoon was a jolly-looking man with pink cheeks and small bright eyes that darted endlessly about. A casual passerby might see him in the role of a cheerful Santa Claus, soft and pliant and pleasant to all. Hollinger knew better. Huntoon was, under the plump softness, a tough guy, his heart at least as hard as his biceps.

Huntoon was also a self-created equivocator. By training and conviction, he avoided commitment. Dodged a straight answer. Camouflaged his beliefs, his hopes, his ambitions, his needs, behind the dappled wall of ambiguity. He boasted of being a straight shooter, a man direct, simple, unafraid; in a pinch, his best was a definite maybe.

He ushered Hollinger into his new office with a magnificent sweep of a carefully manicured hand, directing him to an uncomfortable chair, already working on a scheme to rid himself of the detective, who had entered with a scowl and a complaint.

Huntoon listened; the first rule of his existence. Pick the other guy's brains, locate the flaws in his argument, the weaknesses in his attack. He allowed Hollinger to run down, then put on his most placating expression.

"Now, Dutch, you don't want to believe everything you hear."

"The original source is a good one."

"Anyone I know?" It was a throwaway line.

Hollinger let it go. "Seems like I'm the only one didn't know what went down."

"Dutch." Huntoon used his smooth rich voice the way a masseur used his hands; to soothe. "You're a good cop, you know rumors spread. People dissemble, Dutch. They lie. They distort for pleasure and profit. Believe half of what you see and less of what you're told. Who put this burr up your ass?"

"I checked it out. Mrs. Cruz, she's been thrown up on the rocks. Beaten and bruised and ready to go under. She began to whimper when she saw me, thought I was there to get some myself."

"I hear she's one fine-looking piece of ass. Always had a fondness for *latina* nooky, smelling of spices and a little unclean. Dutch, face it, some ladies like to fuck cops."

"Four uniformed guys raped her."

"That's a strong word, Dutch. Maybe they pressed their case a little, gave her reasons to put out. Lots of women need a little coaxing, you know that."

"They forced her, Wilbur."

"Not much, the way it came to me. It didn't take much forcing."

"They held her down and took turns."

"Like they say, you can't thread a moving needle."

"They kept her against her will and raped her, sodomized her. Those are crimes, Wilbur."

"Four of our people?"

"That's right."

"She provide their names?"

"Of course not. But she says she can provide positive I.D.'s on every one of them."

"You would like me to charge some of our own people? Imagine what that would do to morale on the force, Dutch."

"We're supposed to fight crime."

"And we do an outstanding job of it. But this—we would need names, witnesses, hard evidence. Otherwise we would simply be taking her word and ruining the lives of four innocent and highly skilled police officers. Dutch, I can't—"

"We know who was there. Let's line 'em up, let her pick them out."

"Her word against that of four good cops. That won't get us anywhere, will it, Dutch?"

Hollinger felt the force leaking out of him. He was making no progress, no impact on his superior. "Wilbur, this isn't right."

"Dutch, face facts. Has the lady lodged a complaint? Officially, that is?"

"She's terrified of coming down to the station, Wilbur. I offered to bring her myself, offered her my protection, promised nothing would happen. She's too scared of cops now."

"No charges, no crime, Dutch. Good rule of thumb, wouldn't you say?"

"We're supposed to be cops—"

"Look at it this way: Rosalinda's husband tried to kill her, and now he's out on bail. She hasn't charged him yet, and I'm betting she won't. I'll give odds she takes him back in, Dutch. What kind of a woman is she? What kind of a witness would she make? Dutch, I understand your feelings. You hear about a supposed criminal act and you spring into action. That's terrific, an intuitive cop at work. Protect the innocent, punish the guilty. Rumors aren't charges and charges don't mean a man is guilty. And when there's a reasonable doubt, Dutch, we always, always have to come down on the side of the accused. Especially if it's a fellow officer. I know you don't want to make waves, Dutch, not you."

Hollinger went back to his desk and tried to convince himself that he'd not just been rolled, whipped, and made to like it. While the mugger celebrated, safe, richer, and honored. He stared up at the sign on the wall—

NOTHING IS BETTER THAN IT SHOULD BE

An hour later, Arthur Keely walked into City Hall through the Angela Street entrance and introduced himself to the first cop he saw. The name meant nothing to the officer and Keely had to explain.

"My wife was murdered the other day, and her maid. Bettyjane Keely was her name—my wife, that is."

It came to the cop that this was the high point of an otherwise drab and unpromising career. He grabbed Keely by the arm and shouted: "You're wanted!"

His voice carried up the stairwell to the Detective Division and brought John Roy Iversen to the scene. He sent the uniformed man on his way and placed Keely under arrest. It was, he congratulated himself, going to be a very good day.

The booking procedure completed, he went back upstairs and boasted to Hollinger of the arrest. "We got one of the bad guys, for sure."

Hollinger, replaying his interview with Acting Assistant Chief Huntoon, was slow to focus.

"Which one?"

"Arthur Keely. That dirty killer is going up for a long visit."

"You sure he did it?"

"Hell, yes. He had motive—jealousy. His wife had a boy friend, at least one, and Arthur knew it. Knocking off an unfaithful wife, Arthur isn't the first to go that route."

"Has he confessed?"

"He will. Trust in the majesty and righteousness of the law, Dutch. I am going to put that wife-killer up against the wall and—pow! Pow!"

Hollinger exhaled. "I wish I was that sure. About anything. The longer I'm on the job the less convinced I am I know what's going on."

"Don't let it throw you, old pal. I can handle Keely."

The phone rang and Hollinger picked up. A loud and potentially violent fight between a husband and wife was in progress. The neighbors were fearful for the wife's safety. Hollinger rushed to cover it, afraid of what might happen if he arrived too late. But by the time he arrived on the scene, husband and wife had reentered a blissful condition. Love and harmony prevailed, flavored by amusement at a cop's protective concern. Hollinger drove slowly back to City Hall longing for retirement, still some twenty-three months and eighteen days away. He wasn't sure he could wait.

12

"Shame!"

Bucky Maddox, owner, publisher and editor in chief of the *County Journal*, was a lean, doleful man. He was seldom still, constantly seeking a comfortable space in which to deposit his knobby, angular frame. Nothing seemed to help. Sitting or standing, he was nearly always in motion, going no place. Now he slumped in an old oak swivel chair, skinny legs propped on the desk that separated him from Annie Russell, squinting as if at a stranger.

"I am very upset," he said.

"What about me?"

"I am disappointed."

"A girl has to eat."

"We are journalists," he pronounced with dignity and despair.

"The paper is making money."

"Integrity used to count for something. This younger generation, so materialistic."

"I'm thirty-five years old," she complained. Guilt filled the cavities of her soul; what right had she to ask more of this dear, kind man? He had done so much for her.

"After all I've done for you," he said.

What? Exactly what had he done? The job was hers by reason of experience, talent, and aggressive reporting. She was a good writer and an excellent investigator. She was worth more money. She *was*.

"And don't think I don't appreciate it," was her answer.

He swung his legs to the floor, crossed and uncrossed them, clasped his bony fingers behind his head. He discovered the ceiling and put his feet back up on the desk. "You were a raw rookie when you came to me."

"With seven years of big-city reporting experience."

"You begged for a job."

"You dragooned me into service after my series on Athletes in Action. They made it into a book."

"Your mother bought a copy, nobody else."

"Bucky the bastard." She smiled when she said it.

"I deserve that. I've been a father to you, a coach, a nursemaid. You know it, Annie, you can always turn to me for help, no matter your problems."

"I need more money."

"Shame," he said again.

"Why do I have the feeling I'm not getting anywhere?" He caused her to feel girlish; no, childish. He was mentor and surrogate father, guardian of her professional and personal well-being. He cherished her as no other ever had. He paid slave wages—especially to women.

"I allow you free rein over assignment. Do what you want."

"Ever hear of equal pay for equal work?"

"Oh, that hurts."

"Even Woodward and Bernstein have to eat."

"Stick with me, I'll make you famous."

"They're famous. They're rich. I'm hungry."

"We are a counterculture newspaper. We are for the people, against the entrenched and the wealthy, the powerful. How you coming on the Keely-Olvera story?"

"The husband turned himself in."

"Nah, that's too easy."

"The police charged him."

"I have an itch."

Bucky Maddox's itches were famous. He expected his reporters and editors to scratch him on demand and at length. The itch was reliable, frequently turning up a good story.

"What are you suggesting, Bucky?"

"That Keely. A beautiful chick. There's more here than meets the eye. A lover? Scout around, see what you can find."

"Scout where? I almost got myself shot in the Keely house. That was your idea."

"Got you next to Sergeant Hollinger."

"I don't think he's very fond of me."

"He's crazy about you."

She sat up straighter. "How do you know?"

"What man can resist, you're a beauty, Annie."

"Let's get back to money, Bucky."

He was on his feet, a fatherly arm draped across her shoulders, guiding her to the door. "Be creative. Imaginative. Daring. Exploit your contacts. Press on until you break through. You've done it before, you'll do it again."

"That sounds like an old song."

"Trust me."

"The money, Bucky."

"Next time we'll talk seriously." He eased her out and quickly closed the door.

"I want my raise!" she wailed, telling herself that she loved the job more than money. Loved it above all else. And wanted very much to believe it.

Graham Welles went directly to his bedroom and un-locked his overnight case, returning every article to its place. Neatness was a necessity in Graham's world. Neat-ness represented order and an ordered world was above all things desirable. To achieve order meant men organized and purposeful had to assume and utilize power. Only then could ordinary mortals live tranquil and secure lives.

Neatness was more than an appearance in Graham's philosophical scheme. Neatness could eliminate altogether, or keep at a minimum, many unsightly reminders of man's evolutionary limitations. For Graham was very much aware of human shortcomings and failures. He existed in concert with a faint disappointment in people and the eter-nal hope that men like himself could change the world for the better.

Graham removed Jake Persky's gift from his bag and undid the wrappings. He placed the Heisler on his dresser and examined it carefully. It had the look of harnessed power. It possessed a crankshaft and headlight, and oper-ating gear distribution, and the tempered cast of authen-ticity. Persky was a gracious and thoughtful man.

Satisfied, Graham went into the kitchen, where his wife was sitting over a cup of tea. She had prepared a cup for him, and a selection of petits fours. He patted her on top of the head, and sipped some tea.

"Ah," he said, "it's good to be home."

She raised her face to his. Her eyes were rimmed with crimson and her cheeks were puffy.

"I missed you," he said, as a matter of course.

She sniffed. "Don't you know?"

"I beg your pardon?"

"Haven't you heard?"

"My dear, let me remind you, I've been away. The better part of three days and two nights, or have you forgotten? Heard what, Louise?"

"About Lawrence Grant, of course."

His curiosity faded rapidly. Grant held little interest for him. The writer was a boor, a bore, a dedicated vul-garian. Further, he was a braggart who exaggerated his exploits and courage as much as he did his location in the literary firmament. Though Grant was an experienced and skilled fisherman, Graham thought little of him even in that role. Grant managed to transform even so impersonal an act as catching a fish into an emotional vendetta. He gave the soulless fish too lofty a role in the simple exercise, as if the creature were equally free in its choices.

For Graham, a chartered day trip was hardly a suitable caldron in which to measure one's manliness.

He spoke crisply. "What about Lawrence Grant?"

"He's dead."

Graham mulled it over. As if considering Grant's demise to be an act over which he might have authority, recall, as if it could in some way not yet clear be useful to him.

Louise felt a twinge of fear. Did Graham suspect her role in all this? Of course not. She had been circumspect, and they had only been together one time. *That* one time. How much she longed to be able to tell Graham about it, to relate in detail what had taken place prior to Grant's death, how she had acted and felt. That, of course, would be foolish, self-defeating. There was still a long life to lead and Graham Welles would necessarily play a large role in it.

"Everybody's talking about it," she added.

He said nothing and she felt compelled to go on.

"The way I've heard it, Hilda had to go up to Miami. Did you run into her up there? When she returned, she found Lawrence's body alongside the pool. They say he'd been swimming before it happened, though nobody could know for sure, could they? Poor dear, undoubtedly overexerted himself. He was no longer a young man and all that excess weight. We are what we eat, after all.

"I never did understand Lawrence's fascination with water, swimming that way, fishing, boats. You men. What strange and exotic beings you are. They say he wasn't wearing a stitch. Absolutely nothing, not even bathing trunks. His heart must have simply surrendered to all the demands he made of it, poor man."

"Have you spoken to Hilda?"

"I couldn't bring myself to call."

"We'll pay our condolences in person. Hilda is to be sympathized with. She is a woman of education, background, style and verve. Marriage to Grant must have been an ordeal. Too bad," he added. "Grant was a passable bridge player. We'll have to look around for another couple for the Tuesday game . . ."

Benny Skaggs slumped down behind the wheel of his Mustang and stared steadily at the old red Beetle across the parking lot to one side of the Holiday Inn. He could see their heads huddled together, and he figured they were going at it hot and heavy. Hand jobs, he told himself wisely. A VW provided very little room for easy loving. When one of the heads disappeared, Skaggs amended his opinion: the girl gave head.

Tom-tom came out of the Holiday Inn and put himself into the seat next to Skaggs. "That's better."

"Nothing like a good piss to quiet a man's nerves."

"What's going down?"

Skaggs laughed softly. "She is."

Tom-tom wasn't interested. "That a fact?"

Skaggs glanced over at the younger man. "You dig head, Tom-tom?"

"Is that an offer, Benny?"

"Very funny, man."

Tom-tom looked at the Beetle. "What's she like?" he said, passing the time.

"Beats me. Never laid eyes on the chick. Just as well, her being Iversen's kid."

"Wouldn't he love that? If he knew, wouldn't Mister Four just love knowing that?"

Skaggs shuddered. "You going to be the one to tell him?"

"Shit."

They sat in silence for a while.

"The man wants the operation expanded," Skaggs said at last.

"What's that gonna mean to me?"

"Just more of the same. We need new talent. Think you can handle it?"

Tom-tom spoke as if by rote. "Fuck night and day, twenty-four hours a day, whomsoever it is, black or white, this hole or that. Never been turned down yet."

"Yeah," Skaggs said. He straightened up. "Lookee there—headwork's done."

"They sure do a lot of kissing."

"Young love, pal."

"I'm tempted to put my butt in that VW and let that little old gal work on my joint for a bit, show her what real action is."

"John Roy would sure look kindly on that, Tom-tom."

"It's moving time," Tom-tom said.

Sure enough, the man had climbed out of the VW and he bent to say a few last words to the girl in the car. They kissed and she drove away. He went over to where a Honda was parked and drove onto Roosevelt Boulevard past the Naval Hospital past the Key Wester. Skaggs followed at a discreet distance. Past Smathers Beach, he gunned the Mustang until it was parallel to the Honda. He turned the wheel quickly and in an effort to avoid contact the Honda went off the road.

Skaggs braked, backed, and parked. He and Tom-tom strolled unhurriedly over to where Marc Davidson was sitting on the ground, rubbing his left knee. He glanced up as they came closer.

"Hey, what the hell's wrong with you guys! You coulda killed me."

"Ah," Skaggs said, "you ain't hardly shook up at all. A very sturdy boy."

"Let's find out how sturdy he is," Tom-tom put in, and kicked Davidson in the back.

A muffled scream lodged in Davidson's throat and he fell over. Tom-tom kicked him again, this time in the kidneys. And again in the ribs.

"That enough?" Tom-tom said.

"Please, don't," Davidson gasped. "Why are you doing this?"

"A leetle bit more," Skaggs said, assessing the damage. "I don't see even a single drop of red."

"Didn't know it's blood you want."

Tom-tom lashed out with his right leg, the toe of his boot landing flush on the boy's nose. Davidson screamed and blood began to flow.

"Right good work," Skaggs said. He hunkered down alongside Marc Davidson. "Boy, you sure are a mess. I would say your nose is busted up pretty good. Maybe a couple of ribs, too. And wouldn't surprise me if you pissed red for the next week or so."

"Why—?"

"Here's how it is," Skaggs said patiently. "You are gonno climb on that motor scooter of yours presently and you are gonna head north, boy. Out of Key West. Far away."

"Why—?"

" 'Cause I'm telling you so is why."

"I don't—"

"Christ Almighty God, boy, don't be dumber than you have to be. You're going is all. With no questions, no farewell visits, no phone calls to your loved one."

Davidson struggled into a sitting position. "You can't do this. There are laws."

Skaggs gestured and Tom-tom kicked out again. Davidson went over on his face. For a long time he lay there moaning. Skaggs hunkered down again.

"Boy, you got to get out of here. Leave—before you get yourself killed. You can see that, can't you?"

Marc managed to nod.

"That's better. You're hurt but you ain't dead, and that's a very big advantage. Give you a minute or two to get your strength back and then you're on your way."

"Where—"

"Anywhere you like, boy. So long as it's outside the state of Florida. I was you, I'd head west. California, maybe. They say it's real nice out there, land of fruits and nuts, they say. You'll git along fine."

Skaggs and Tom-tom helped Davidson to his feet, held him until he could stand unaided, watched him climb onto the Honda. After a slight hesitation, the engine roared into life.

Skaggs grinned. "I was worried it might not work. You go on up old Route Number One, boy, and don't ever think about turning back. And just to be sure you don't commit some awful mistake, me and my friend here are gonna keep you company until you are clear out of Monroe County. Be good, hear? Have a good life. It's the only one you're gonna get."

Sam Dickey found Hilda Grant on her knees on the floor of her dead husband's studio, surrounded by papers, by boxes of papers, by books and letters. She was disheveled, lovely, and protectively fierce. He was reminded of how intimidated he had been upon meeting her on Corsica —her beauty, her hard intelligence, and the fact of her being Lawrence Grant's wife. All had combined to make her seem remote and extraordinary, out of reach of a mere mortal such as Sam Dickey. The apprehension he had felt then returned now and he stood watching her, unable to say anything, sorry he had disturbed her.

She looked up at last. "Jesus, what a mess. Find a place for yourself, sit down. Try the chair behind the desk."

Grant's work chair. Sam could not bring himself to use it. He lowered himself to the floor. "I'm sorry," he said.

"About what?" She recognized the expression on the boyish face; surprise, shock, even hurt. There had been so many like Sam Dickey, hero-worshipers all, come to pay homage to the Great Man, to learn from him, to bask in his literary light. For this one, there would be only the afterglow. She managed a slight, encouraging smile. "I'm the one who is sorry, Mr. Dickey. You were one of my husband's fans."

More than that, he almost said. An admirer, a student, a disciple, perhaps. He answered hesitantly, "He was a great writer."

"There are those who think so." She rocked back on her heels and surveyed the young man opposite. He appeared to be in need of support, protection; he was very young and vulnerable, and quite attractive to behold. "But he's dead now and his legends will harden into immutable truths and his lies will become profound observations. He created his own monument, the memories by which he intended the world to recall him. He was his own most imaginative creation."

"I wanted to pay my respects, see what I could do. I did admire Lawrence. He was the greatest man I've ever known, the greatest writer."

"An opinion many hold."

"He possessed total control over his materials. Everything I know about writing I learned from studying Lawrence Grant, from reading him—"

"Oh, yes, you write, too. Everybody writes, anybody who can speak the goddamn language." She laughed, a tight dry rasping sound without humor or warmth. "He used to say that, over and over. And here I am repeating it, as if the words were my own. The lousy sonofabitch intends to keep a grip on me from the grave . . ."

Sam didn't know what to say. He felt uncomfortable, and rose preparatory to leaving.

"Sit down," she commanded.

He obeyed.

She waved a hand. "Look at this junk. Thousands of words . . ."

"He told me about a new novel he was working on."

"What novel? There is no novel. Just these disconnected ramblings of an old man gone to seed. Unreadable, unpublishable, unsalable."

"I'm not sure I follow you."

"Try harder, Mr. Dickey. Grant was getting soft in the head. This is a journal, bits and pieces about this and that, this person and that person, here and there, Ramblings, digressions, diversions. Excuses for a writer not to work. Macho boasts about women he screwed, women who came before he knew me, and since. He gives names. Names and places. Grant was very big on making it in unusual places. Broom closets, men's rooms, in a hotel lobby behind a potted palm, other romantic spots. Many of the women he mentions were married, the wives of his friends and of his enemies. In most cases, his friends were his enemies. And the young girls. Fourteen-year-olds. A rapacious billy goat. How can I help you, Mr. Dickey?"

"I thought I might help you."

She assessed him coolly. "What do you have in mind?"

He grew flustered. "Anything. The arrangements . . ."

"Ah, the arrangements. So many people can't wait to get dear Larry into the ground. Of course, here in Key West most corpses are interred aboveground. You didn't know that, Mr. Dickey? It has to do with the water table. It's quite high, you know. Not a spot on the whole damned island more than sixteen feet above sea level. You didn't know that, either, did you, Mr. Dickey? Mr. Dickey, has it come through to you that you are not very knowledgeable about a great many inconsequential subjects? There, there, don't pout, dear boy. I'm in a hateful mood. That's what happens when I discover that my husband has screwed half the women in the world and left me practically destitute."

"I'm—sorry."

"Not as sorry as I am. As for the arrangements, Emerson is taking care of them. That's Emerson Gerard,

eminent publisher, editor and *bon vivant*. Emerson was
Grant's editor and he takes a certain satisfaction in making sure his authors get properly planted when they die,
lest they rise up again and go over to Random House or
Scribners. I must be very nice to Emerson. Who knows,
he might just resissue all of Grant's works and I, as the
bereaved widow, might even profit a bit from such a venture."

"I'm sure that will please you."

She examined him with no change of expression.
How incredibly tender and hairless he was. So unlike
Grant. "You are perceptive," she gave him.

"Thank you."

"And sensitive."

"Most writers—"

She cut him off. "Yes, of course."

"I was going to do a long interview."

"*Rock-'n'-Roll Magazine?*"

"*Rock-the-World Weekly.*"

"Of course."

"My editor called me. He wants a piece about Lar-
ry's last days. I was on that last fishing trip with him and
Mrs. Welles. I'm thinking of titling it 'The Last Big
Catch.' What do you think of it?"

"Louise Welles?"

"A very nice woman."

"Very nice," she said thinly. "Perhaps I should have a
stuffed billfish carved on the mausoleum. Grant had such a
close tie to the denizens of the deep, as the critics like to
say. Will you be coming to the funeral, Mr. Dickey? It
should be a jolly outing, full of fun, sentiment, and literary
bullshit. All of Grant's pals will be there. I deed exclusive
rights to the funeral story over to you. That should please
you."

"Well, yes."

"What a time we'll have! The first annual Lawrence
Grant Memorial Book Fair. Every literary hustler in the
Western world will be on hand. Do come, talk to them all,
quotes will abound, witty sayings, literary profundities.
Take pictures, make sketches, expand your article into a
book and advance your career—"

He cleared his throat.

"Of course you wouldn't do that, would you, Mr.

Dickey? No self-respecting person would, would he? Would *she*? Now, if you'll excuse me, the widow is confronted by a monumental task. How to squeeze a buck or two out of this literary residue. It's either that or go back to shaking my fanny at casting agents, and at my age . . . well. See you at the funeral, love . . ."

Sam ran for the street, sucking air and trying to slow his pulse. Hilda Grant was like no other woman he had ever known.

"Tomorrow I can't."

"Some kind of a gringo fiesta?"

"I'm going to a funeral."

"Not family, I hope."

"Not family, but I must go."

"Of course," Figueroa said.

He and Paco Valentín stood in the wheelhoue. Figueroa stroked the polished teak instrument panel.

"Maybe you better charter another boat," Paco said. "Plenty of good captains in the bight."

"I like your boat."

"She's okay."

"Go a long way, will she?"

"Takes me as far as I want to go."

Figueroa nodded agreeably. "Fast?"

Paco resented having to qualify *La Florida*, and himself. But it happened frequently, once-in-a-while fishermen pretending to an expertise they would never possess. "Twenty-five, maybe twenty-six knots," he answered.

"Looks like a lot of boat."

"Plenty of comfort. Three staterooms, private showers, a generator for the air conditioning. Every safety device—radar, CB, VHF, depth finder, automatic pilot, hot water, refrigerator."

"I bet you can stay out for a long time on her?"

Valentín looked across the stern to the dock, to where cars were parked. "How long you intend to stay out?"

Figueroa raised his thick brows. "Long enough to make a good catch is all. Just want to have some good fun."

"Yeah. Well, like I told you, tomorrow I can't. Maybe you better try somebody else."

"I like you. I could phone my friend and tell him it's off for tomorrow but okay for the day after? Is that okay with you?"

"You come all the way down here from Miami to do some fishing. I don't get it. There's plenty of fishing out of Miami."

Figueroa laughed. *"Ay, hombre!* I got to tell you. Both of us got wives. Both of us need a little time out on our own, some recreation, eh, Captain?"

"Well, if you don't want to wait—"

"No, no. You, you're Cuban, so am I, and my friend. We'll all be *simpático,* no?"

"Okay. It's a hundred and twenty dollars for a half-day, two hundred a full day. Up to you."

"Let's make it a full day."

"Just the two of you?"

"That okay?"

"Whatever you say. You'll want food, beer? That's extra."

"I leave it up to you, Captain."

"I'll tell Tody. He takes care of it."

Figueroa, who had started to leave, turned back. "Who is this Tody?"

"My mate. He's good with the engines, good when events begin to happen rapidly."

"Sounds okay. Tell Tody to stock up with good things."

"Day after tomorrow. We'll go out into the Gulf Stream . . ."

"Whatever you say, Captain."

"About four in the morning all right with you?"

"Anything you say, Captain. My friend and me, we'll be here."

Paco watched him drive away, unable to dispel his unease. He reassured himself; the man had said it: they were both Cubans, they would be *simpático,* no?

Maybe.

Charles Dickey came out of his bedroom ready for the day. He wore a linen jacket and tasseled loafers and a striped tie. His shirt was blue, his trousers gray, and he had the look of a man who dotted his *i*'s and crossed only on the green. Correct, precise and intelligent. A physician to inspire confidence.

"Good morning, Ellen."

Ellen switched off the vacuum and straightened up, gave him a quicksilver smile. She almost curtsied. "Good morning, Doctor. Gosh, you look terrific."

"Thank you." He thought her a little too thin, her breasts mere suggestions under a cotton Indian shirt, the nipples in faint outline. From time to time, he'd been made aware of her bottom, round and clenched tightly, as if in opposition to any possible violation. Tight sphincters spoke eloquently to Charles Dickey.

"Can I get you some coffee, Doctor?"

He allowed her to serve him, remained standing as he sipped the hot brew. "You surprise me, Ellen."

"I do?"

"Every time I see you. That such a young and pretty girl should be cleaning my house. It isn't exactly right."

"It's what I do."

"I'm a little old-fashioned, with a body of traditional definitions as to what it means to be a woman."

"Oh, I'm a woman."

"And I'm a male chauvinist?"

"I don't know about that."

He smiled graciously. "I'm glad you're here. I enjoy knowing you're around."

"I enjoy being here. It's a nice house."
he sipped the hot brew. "You surprise me, Ellen."

"I'm good at it. It's fun to take care of nice things. You think it's wrong?"

"No."

"My father does."

"Perhaps your father's the male chauvinist."

"He thinks I'm too good for this kind of work. But there's not much else I can do."

"You'll learn. There's plenty of time."

She nodded. "I brought my bikini. Okay if I use the pool later on?"

"As much as you want."

"Okay if I smoke?"

"Bad for your health, you know."

"Not cigarets!"

He laughed. "As long as you don't get me busted."

After he was gone, she took his cup and refilled it with hot coffee and sat down on the deep soft couch, feet up on the marble coffee table. She drew a burned-down joint out of her purse and lit up, sucking deeply. A few good hits and then she'd give Marc a call. Maybe he'd come over and they could swim together. And afterward make love. Marc was the nicest boy she'd ever known. Not the prettiest, not the best in bed, but loving and so sweet . . .

Big Pine Key; about thirty miles up the Overseas Highway from Key West, comfortably sandwiched between Little Torch and No Name Keys. Take a left off Route 1 and go past Doctor's Arm, up island to a point roughly opposite Mayo Key, this side of where the paved road ends. A track twists down toward the water, ending on a hard flat looking out at Spanish Channel. Here the shoreline is uneven, dented by small coves. It was such a one that Izzy Ben-Ezra and Harry gazed down at from a low grassy hillock.

"Nice," Ben-Ezra commented.

"Perfect spot. They come down the channel, cruise into the cove and drop anchor behind that little tit of a peninsula. Off-load onto some light trucks and split. Done and over with."

"You're sure this is the spot?"

Harry showed his agitation. "Listen, man, I know my business. I followed the Quint dame to where she hooked up with Juan Manuel—"

"You know this dude?"

"He's been around for a while. Juan Manuel Meléndez Gonzáles. Isn't that a fancy handle?"

"Mex?"

"Colombian, I hear."

"Figures. And you think he deals?"

"Hell, yes, he deals. I know that."

"How?"

Harry was startled by the question. "Look, Mr. Ben-Ezra, I am no Johnny-come-lately to this field. You got to me through professionals and you have to respect my professional credentials."

"Now, Harry, don't get hot."

"I am no amateur. I research. I check. I nose around. I follow people."

"You're doing real good work, Harry. Sometimes I run off at the mouth a little."

Harry sniffed.

"What about this Colombian, Harry?"

"About him? Nothing about him. He's a dealer, a big dealer, I hear. Used to work out of New York and before that Denver. He's been around."

"A real wise guy."

"He walks heavy, is the word. Always loaded. And they say he is for hire."

"A professional *pistolero*?"

Harry shrugged.

"Be careful, Harry."

"Don't worry, I don't take any chances. Juan Manuel ain't laid an eye on me yet, and he ain't likely to."

"Yeah. There's one more thing. When's the operation going down?"

"I don't know."

Ben-Ezra gripped his arm hard. "What do you mean, you don't know? Without the timing, I've got zip."

Harry shook himself free. "I'll get it."

"You better."

"Don't come down on me, man. I'm doing my number in your behalf while you sit cool and contented drinking beer and looking at the box. I am overworked, understaffed, underpaid."

"So that's it." Ben-Ezra flashed a roll of bills. "A man does a good job he deserves a bonus. Here's two hundred, Harry, walking money. There'll be extra, once it's in the bag."

Harry's face lit up. "Pleasure doing business with you, Mr. Ben-Ezra."

The Tibbs house was third in line, off the street. Thirty years before it had belonged to Mateo Fuentes, a cigar maker. Mateo had moved into the house because his brother, Felipe, lived in the house directly ahead. And his oldest brother, Jesús, occupied the house on the street. All three brothers had later shifted operations north to Tampa, where the cigar industry had taken hold, working conditions were better, and a good future was to be had. For a number of years, the houses stood empty or were rented on a short-term basis. Until a retired art director from Chicago bought the street house; a black short-order cook moved into the second house; and Marvin Tibbs purchased the third house.

Tibbs was a thin man of no particular distinction. He smoked cheap cigars and drank a great deal of iced tea and liked to suck on rock candy. He lived alone and spent much of his time on his narrow porch, rocking slowly, remembering more exciting times, more rewarding times. That was how Hollinger found him, rocking and drinking tea.

Tibbs waited for the detective to come up on the porch before he spoke. "Afternoon, Mr. Hollinger."

The detective placed himself in a second rocker and got it started. The floor under him squeaked. "How you been, Marvin?"

"No complaints. Like some iced tea, Mr. Hollinger? Sure is hot enough, dries out the throat. Wouldn't be surprised we get a big blow."

"Little rain is possible."

" 'Bout due for another hurricane."

"Maybe hit Cuba, but not here. Surely not this time of year."

Tibbs weighed that opinion, matched it against his own, but didn't argue.

"Marvin, I'm here to talk about Arthur Keely's wife."

"This tea," Tibbs said carefully, "comes already mixed. Just add water. Sugar, lemon and everything, all mashed up ready to go. What a world."

"Bettyjane Keely. Somebody blew her away the other night, Marvin."

"Oh, yes. Too bad about that."

"You were acquainted with her, Marvin?"

"Lived up on Sunshine Lane, didn't she? Rich bitch. Too rich for my pocketbook."

Hollinger stopped rocking. "You ever been in Nevada, Marvin?"

"Might have passed through one time, though."

"Reno, Marvin?"

"One time Reno was big in the divorce business, very big."

"Rumor is you jumped bail in Reno—"

"Me?"

"Say it was for holding stolen goods."

"Must be another Marvin Tibbs."

"I could make a call, get a rap sheet, a picture, prints."

Tibbs stopped rocking; Hollinger started up again. "Gee, good thing you reminded me. Almost forgot about all that, so long ago. You don't want to cause me any trouble, not a nice man like you, Mr. Hollinger."

"Talk to me about Bettyjane Keely, Marvin. She come into the Pirate's Den much?"

"All I do is tend bar. Nothing else."

"I got it."

"Now I remember about Mrs. Keely. Good-looking woman."

"Why would she go to that crummy dive?"

Tibbs seemed mildly offended. "Why? Same reason the rest of them come—looking for a little extra action is why."

"She find any?"

"*¿Quién sabe?*"

"I want some names."

Tibbs gazed off into the distance. Reno had been nice until the trouble. He wondered how Hollinger had learned about Reno. Cops were persistent people, and therefore immensely troublesome. "I'm not much good with names."

Hollinger stopped rocking; Tibbs began again. "Think on it. They say somebody made a switch in Reno involving some very hard-nosed characters. Payment wasn't made when it was supposed to be made. Suppose I did make that call—"

Nothing but trouble. "Never had you figured as a mean man, Mr. Hollinger. A little on the melancholy side, I thought. A person who walked up and down the street, seen it all, knows little can be done to improve on the quality of life. But not mean."

"Keely," Hollinger said.

"Ken Davis."

"That rings a bell."

"Very big with the ladies. Works out of the Slim & Gym."

"Keely and David were getting it on?"

"There were signs."

"More than once?"

"Three, four times that I know about. My professional opinion is they were extremely cozy."

"Anybody else?"

"For her, no."

"For Davis?"

"Davis works dames for whatever he can get. Mostly marrieds."

"Blackmail?"

"Nothing surprises any more."

Hollinger brought out a pad and a pencil, handed it over to Tibbs. "Make a list, Marvin. Other married ladies . . ."

"I hate putting anything on paper, makes me mighty squeamish."

"Write, Marvin."

"About Reno, Mr. Hollinger?"

"Reno?"

"The phone call?"

"Who would I call in Reno, Marvin?"

Tibbs started writing. And Hollinger rocked.

Iversen made himself at home in room 202. He hung his jacket neatly in the closet, draped his tie over the back of a chair, placed his polished black shoes side by side under the bed. He switched on the television set, keeping the sound low, and found himself in the middle of a Humphrey Bogart movie. He was very fond of Bogart, a man of singular style if lacking somewhat in sophistication as an actor.

He poured some scotch into a glass and when it was gone repeated the process. After his third drink, during a station break, he phoned Benny Skaggs.

"I'm ready, Benny," he said, eyes fixed on the screen.

"I'm sending a very nice girl, Mr. Iversen. Very attractive. Her name is Gloria."

"A smart girl, Benny?"

"I prepped her myself, Mr. Iversen."

"The last one was truculent, petty, rebellious. All characteristics I do not choose to tolerate."

"You'll like Gloria."

"We'll see."

"She should be there in about ten minutes."

Iversen replaced the phone and finished his drink and had another. He lit a cigaret. Bogart was kissing Bacall; they seemed to belong together. That was vital, he told himself. That a man and woman match, fit like parts in a puzzle. Physically and otherwise. Most women fell short of that ideal, most disappointed, and continued to disappoint. A knock drew his eyes to the door.

"One moment," he said. He put the drink and the cigaret aside and took off his clothes. He placed his pistol on the bureau, clearly in view. Naked he went to the door and opened it.

She smiled warmly in greeting and moved past him into the room, She was tall, big in the bust and the bottom, but conservatively dressed and wearing very little makeup. Iversen approved of that. She turned.

"Benny told me a great deal about you, John Roy. But he barely scratched the surface."

He locked the door. "Would you like a drink?"

"That would be nice."

He gestured. "Help yourself." She moved gracefully to the bottle. Benny was right; he liked Gloria. She had a certain low-grade flair.

She toasted him and drank, looked him over. "My, my. A man of capabilities. Seems to me Gloria is going to have a lovely evening."

"Get undressed."

She moved to obey; slowly, provocatively, putting each garment neatly aside. Finished, she straightened up and confronted him. "Like what you see, John Roy?"

"What did Skaggs say to you?"

She took a step or two in his direction, watching him watch her. "Only that you were a man of refined tastes."

"What else?"

"He mentioned that you were a man of exceptional influence and power, a good man to know."

"I want to see all of you."

She pirouetted. She turned and bent and peered back at him from between her spread legs, head, hair and breasts hanging. She blew him a kiss as he came up behind her.

"Oh, lover," she cooed. "If there's going to be any rough work can it be on my pumpies. It's where I like it best."

He punched her with all his strength and she went flat to the floor. Before she could move, he was on her, mauling her roughly, prodding and pinching, striking out at her flesh. He yanked her long hair and she rolled onto her back, mouth agape, eyes shining in pain and pleasure. He kneeled over her and filled her up until she began to choke. Abruptly he fell back on the floor and began to sob, to beg her forgiveness, to plead with her to punish him for being bad.

And she did.

"Who did you say you were?"

Arthur Keely filled the doorway of the house on Sunshine Lane. He was tall, lean, sleekly handsome. He looked like a movie star, not a man who had killed his wife. Like a man women would find irresistible, challenging, perhaps, and vaguely threatening. The sort a woman could never be sure of, and so desire all the more.

But he was too pretty to suit Annie Russell. Too close to perfection, as if he'd designed and constructed himself, adorned face and body to enhance his physical gifts. Annie stood still while he looked her over. Top to bottom, side to side. She wished she'd worn a bra, wished she were bundled up protectively from sight. But she didn't own a bra and it was much too hot to wear a sweater.

"Annie Russell, Mr. Keely. I'm a reporter for the *County Journal*."

He made a face. "That counterculture rag."

"We pride ourselves on being on the side of the underdog. My editor is convinced the police are trying to railroad you."

"Well, that's in your favor."

"I'd like to hear your side of the story."

"My lawyer says I'm to keep my mouth shut and maintain a low profile."

"Lawyers are not men who take risks."

"I enjoy taking risks." His eyes held on her bosom. "Big risks."

Oh, subtle man, she thought. She gave him a big, encouraging smile. "Won't you spare me a few minutes?"

"Come inside." She went past him, careful to avoid all contact. She supposed he was checking out her fanny now. She swung around and he lifted his eyes. "Nice, everything about you is nice. How about a swim in the pool?"

"I don't have a suit."

"We'll skinnydip."

"Ask me some other time."

"Business before pleasure? Okay. In here." The living room looked larger in the daylight, complete with cathedral ceiling, ancient beams and expensive furniture. "Sit down. Can I offer you a drink?"

"Nothing, thanks. You have quite a place here."

"How about a snort? Coke? Or a joint?"

"Not when I'm working. I heard you were out on bail."

"Big-time Miami lawyer on a retainer. He might as well earn his way. Anyway, I'm innocent. They can't prove otherwise."

"Proving is one thing. Knowing is something else."

"Meaning what?"

"Only that innocent men go to the slammer sometimes and guilty ones go free."

"Maybe letting you in was a mistake. You believe I killed Bettyjane?"

"That's just it—I'm trying to find out what the real story is. The truth."

"Well, I didn't do it." A puffy sullenness took over the too-pretty face. "Why would I kill her?"

All his attractiveness had dissolved quickly and what was left was a kind of petulance and cunning. Annie wished she were somewhere else. "Another woman?" she asked.

He leaned her way. "If I wanted—you, for example. Would I have any trouble? I mean, I am not the sort of man who has difficulty with women. They like me and don't give me a hard time." He smiled.

"Why would anyone kill Bettyjane?"

His eyes grew hard and hooded. "That's for me to know and you to find out."

"Then you have information? Something you haven't told the police?"

"When the right time comes I'll talk."

"You're saying you're innocent?"

"Innocent, yes. Innocent until proven guilty, that's the way it is in this country."

"One theory is that it was a burglar. He panicked and killed your wife and Livia."

"Could be."

"But you don't think so? What do you think?"

"I told you, when the time comes—"

"The police take the position that you are the only one with a motive."

"Motive? What motive?"

"Your wife wanted a separation."

"Who told you that? Jesus, the things people say. Where'd you hear that?"

"Isn't it true?"

"I've said enough."

"You did move out?"

"I come and go as I wish. It's my house."

"Leaving Bettyjane behind?"

"There were times when she was a royal pain in the ass."

"They haven't found the weapon," she let out.

"They'll never find it." He made it sound as if he were privy to private information.

"What makes you so sure?"

"Call it a hunch."

"Where have you been since the murder? You're going to have to account for that time and why you didn't turn yourself in."

"That's for me to know . . ." Grinning, he allowed his hand to fall on her knee. He squeezed. "There must be something I can do for you, a little present, a new car, maybe, a trip to an island in the Caribbean . . ."

She pushed herself erect. "I'd like to talk to you again."

"Anytime."

"When I've got some more questions."

"Think about my offer."

She knew she would and that troubled her deeply. She wished she were strong enough not to care about the things Arthur Keely had to offer. Strong enough never to consider having them. Or weak enough to accept them without fear or conscience.

13

Jimmy Oreskes, Grant's literary agent for more than twenty years, was the first to arrive; he flew in by special charter the night before. With him were Mailer and Baldwin, and Irwin Shaw, all the way from Klosters for the funeral. Hilda found them beds in the pool house and provided a light supper and a jug of Grant's best scotch whiskey. A second contingent arrived a few hours later: John Huston from Ireland, and Cukor, who'd directed films made from two of Grant's books (the only successful pictures), and Sinatra, Lancaster, Duke Wayne and Maureen O'Hara, a handful of others. They joined the drinkers in the pool house and the decibel count rose sharply and Hilda sent over enough food and liquor for the night.

The New York literary contingent rolled in just after daybreak, headed by Grant's favorite editor, Emerson Gerard. They were tired, hungry and sullen, seeing Grant's passing as an unnecessary reminder of their own mortality. Hilda woke the sleepers and put together a breakfast of eggs, hotcakes, sausages, bacon, Polish ham fried in its own grease, biscuits, fried plantains and coffee. Mailer and Styron mixed a batch of Bloody Marys, which didn't last very long. Some smoked and sipped black coffee and were silent. Others recalled how it had been when all of them were young in Paris, full of ambition and literary dreams. Or on the Greek islands. Or in Africa.

Each of them had a recollection of the Big Bear, as they called Grant, when he and they were full of youth and life. All writers had been suspect in Grant's house, all academics, all intellectuals. Yet all were made welcome. Coarse jokes were told and wild exaggerations and bla-

146

tant lies, but no one saw these as anything but the acting out of an active, creative imagination. In those days, someone said, Grant was happy and laughed loud and long at the more outrageous boasts of his friends and colleagues.

It went on. And for Sam Dickey, who walked in during that extended, gross breakfast, it was a stunning way to launch a day of death and eternal glory. When he could, without attracting attention, he barricaded himself in the downstairs toilet to make notes, to write down some very clever remark by some very famous author, or inscribe a particularly pungent insight by a very drunken actor, or sketch out an obscure but marvelous story about the Big Bear.

It was almost noon when Hilda reappeared, trailed by a trio of women hired for the occasion. "Let these ladies clean up after you slobs," she declared. "Everybody out!" She waved a batch of telegrams in the air. "Henry Miller sends regrets, deepest emotions at this inevitable time, says he'll be seeing Grant soonest."

A round of hoots and derisive hollers went up. Shaw said, "Old Henry'll never go. He'll live as long as those redwoods he has around him."

They settled around the pool, smoking and drinking, launching several literary discussions at once. There was the question of publishers' royalty statements; they all agreed, works of fiction designed to do poor authors out of their rightful profit. The cheapest drunk was a topic that engaged a number of them; high altitudes were recommended and homemade whiskey. All critics were of doubtful lineage, it was decided. And as the morning wore on, it was discovered that more than a few of them had bedded the same women; no one was amused.

"It's over," Bellow said to Terkel.

Terkel nodded sagely. "Chicago will never be the same."

"Anybody want another drink?"

"Boom and you're gone. We're gone. I'm gone. What's it all mean?"

"Read your last novel, you had all the answers."

"Forty is the cutoff date. After that, it's all a fizzle . . ."

"There is no cutoff for a real man."

"Talk is dung. Life is good food, good drink, good ass."

"Your last wife had one, a good ass . . ."

"You bastard, you tried getting some of it often enough."

"Tried . . . ?"

"Is it true Larry went out in a last ride to glory?"

"With his gun going off."

"Yippee eye oh!"

"Way to go, Big Bear!"

"All right, guys!" Hilda yelled from the rear gallery of the big house. "Everybody inside for a last look at the dear departed . . ."

She was the kind of woman cops were always meeting in murder mysteries. Seated stiff and straight behind a small desk, she seemed to overpower it. Long hair bleached almost silver reached to her shoulders, and a large shining mouth set in a perpetual purse, and watery blue eyes vacant of anything remotely like an idea. Her full, fleshy body was encased in a white leotard.

"Hi," she greeted Hollinger. "Something I can do for you?"

He showed his badge. "Tell Ken Davis Sergeant Hollinger would like to talk to him."

"Now?"

"Why not now?"

"He's giving a class."

"Now." Hollinger made his voice hard and his smile terrible.

Impressed, she rose and disappeared down a corridor. Five minutes later she reappeared, deposited herself carefully in her chair.

"They're working on tummies at the moment," she stated. "You know how tummies are. Mr. Davis says he'll be along in about twenty minutes."

Hollinger went down the corridor, the blonde calling ineffectually after him. He opened doors until he came to a large room where an exercise class was in progress. Two walls were completely mirrored and the other two striped red, white and blue. Red-and-blue mats covered the floor and glistening machines were scattered about. There were a jumping horse, parallel bars and weight-lifting apparatus. A dozen women of different shapes, shades and dimensions were doing leg-ups.

Ken Davis, wearing nylon shorts, stepped gingerly among them, dispensing personalized instruction. He was a stocky man, with a hard, muscular body and a face to match.

A chubby woman spotted Hollinger and patted her hair into place. "Man on the scene, sisters," she announced.

A few of them ceased working out and sat up.

"Do not stop!" Davis ordered. "Continue the exercise. Your bodies demand it. Your spirits must not be denied. Lift . . . your . . . legs . . . and . . . hold . . . Spread your legs . . . hold. Bring . . . together . . . hold. Now . . . lower. Slowly, slowly. Breathe and begin again." Davis sidled over to Hollinger, eyes on his students. He spoke out of the corner of his mouth. "You were told to wait outside."

Hollinger summoned up his coldest stare. "How long were you and Bettyjane Keely getting it on, Davis?"

"What? For chrissakes, whataya saying? Keep your voice down, for chrissakes. Anyway, you're wrong. Keely came to work out, that's all. Nothing else."

"If that's the way you want it. Put some clothes on, you're coming down to the station with me."

"You want to ruin me?" Then, to the class: "Take a break, ladies. Be back in five. This way, cop."

A few steps brought them into a sauna. It reeked of sweat and steam. Hollinger sat down on a slatted wooden bench.

"How long?"

"You could be wrong."

"Don't lie, David. Lying makes me nervous."

"How'd you find out?"

"It's my business to find out."

"Ah, it was nothing. I only saw her four or five times."

"You hump all your customers?"

"You the keeper of my morals? B.J. and me, we really were getting it on. We dug each other plenty. A lot in common."

"Like her money?"

"That's a rotten thing to say. I'm all broken up over what happened."

"I noticed. Did she know about you and the other women, Kenny?"

The hard face seemed to melt. "Hey, come off it. I cared for her."

"There were other women."

"She didn't know. You're just taking a blind shot, is that it? Okay, you scored. But B.J. couldn't get enough of what I was putting down."

"She wanted out, didn't she?"

"That's crazy."

"Never kid a kidder, Kenny."

"I had a date with her for that day."

"You went over to Sunshine Lane to work her back into line?"

"No way. She was just some more stuff to me. Look around, man. You think I got the shorts?"

"Do they all have the kind of bread Bettyjane could move your way?"

"A couple of new shirts is all she ever sprang for. She was not very loose with a dollar."

"So you threatened to reveal your relationship to her husband and she laughed at you. She was ready to dump the guy anyway. That got under your skin and you pulled the .22 and waved it around."

"Are you kidding! Guns and me don't get along."

"You argued, and you pumped a couple into her."

"That's crazy!"

"Then the maid showed up so you had no choice—you took her out, too."

"Is this your idea of a joke?"

"Want my professional opinion, Kenny? You are in very serious trouble."

"I didn't kill her."

"Who else had a motive?"

"Her husband. You said it, she dumped him. He was nuts about her, she told me. Couldn't get enough and she treated him like shit. Talk to him, why don't you. Leave me alone."

"Did Keely know about you and B.J.?"

"I didn't tell him. I don't think she did."

"Maybe I will. He's out of the slammer. If he knew about you and his wife, he might do something about it."

"What kind of a cop are you?"

"Got to clean up the streets, Kenny. One way or another."

"That's wild, really wild. You do not have much respect for the law."

Hollinger stood up. "Stay close, Kenny. In case it becomes necessary to continue this discussion. Don't go away without telling me."

"Does this mean I'm a murder suspect?"

"How do you see it, Kenny?"

14

"The coffin was simple, and very expensive. Paid for by Grant's paperback publisher. Made of polished rosewood, it possessed brass handles and a red silk lining. Grant always had a weakness for silk, and for bright colors. His underwear, his shirts, his ties—all silk.

Someone had propped him up so that he was visible to one and all. Not sitting, exactly, but on a gentle incline, as if relaxing in the morning sunlight. But the glow in which he basked was from a low-voltage spotlight meant to illuminate a painting, now removed.

To Sam Dickey, Grant appeared to be bulging out of the rosewood box as if that too limited space could not confine a man of such bulk, stature and literary magnificence.

Across the aisle, Louise Welles. In profile, cool and lovely. Yet with no corporeal substance. A mist shaped by a metaphysical master hand into Everyman's dream of beauty. Expressionless, without care or concern. Or was it simply a pale mask assumed to conceal profound emotion? She seemed vulnerable to Sam, incredibly youthful, and he put the rumors about her and Grant out of his mind. Under mournful black, her breasts sloped to a heavy fullness he hadn't noticed before. Next to her, a straight, slender man with a haughty face and a flat, downturned mouth. This would be Graham, Louise's husband.

Up ahead, in the first three rows, the famous and the celebrated, the rich and the talented; writers, actors, artists in one medium or another. Each appeared different, unique, distinctive in every way. Or so Sam chose to believe. He drew word sketches in his mind: Mailer was flushed and grizzled; Malamud tense and forelorn; Updike a proper Princetonian; and on the aisle, Hilda Grant. She radiated hope and beauty in equal amounts, having found, Sam was certain, some inner peace.

Emerson Gerard, the editor, moved to the front and faced the assemblage, careful not to block off Lawrence Grant from view. He gazed mournfully at Hilda, he cast his eyes to Heaven, he cleared his throat and spoke in a whiskey-saturated voice.

"We, all of us here today, were—*are*—friends of the Big Bear. He was our friend and there was none better. He was friend to millions more. Out there. Readers. Lovers of a good tale well told. Folks who grew up and were nurtured on Grant's great gifts. His manliness. His passion for living. His courage, imagination, his way with the language.

"And now it's over, you say. No, I say. This is where it begins. The life of a great artist never ceases, it transcends death. For out there are untold numbers of folks who have yet to discover his work. Onward to greater and greater rewards for mankind. All that has terminated is this mortal life.

"This death. This death is not an end, not for Grant. The Big Bear was always larger than life and in death he takes on the immense stature that is deservedly his.

"Grant knew the tragedy that every life is. He comprehended the twists, the turns, the sudden dead ends that confront us, every one. He recognized that except in ourselves and in our friends there is no salvation. Life for Grant was all loving and caring and giving and taking it as it came.

"He could weep.

"He could roar.

"He could rock the skies with his laughter.

"In defense of freedom and justice and *truth*, he did more than any of us. He knew more.

"He was the best. Of his time, of all times.

"The cream of a generation.

"A man's man.

"He was—a writer."

Emerson Gerard was breathing rapidly. He went over to Hilda and kissed her on the cheek.

After a suitable interlude, Jimmy Oreskes took the stage. True and faithful agent, he talked of Success. Royalties. Foreign rights and movie sales. The Big Bear, he ended, had always been a bankable commodity. He sat down weeping.

Then Mailer, Baldwin, Ginsberg, Stein, Barth, Bellow, Capote, Didion; names right off the *Times* best-seller list. One after another, talking, lamenting, competing, making points.

Hilda sat in her place in the front row, hands folded in her lap, not moving. But not listening. Wishing that Grant had been alive when she had returned home. Wishing she had been able to speak to him one last time. Wishing she had told him more often how much she needed him and loved him. *The dirty bastard* . . .

Arthur Keely came out of the house on Sunshine Lane and received evil vibrations at once. Something told him it was going to be a bad day. Mainly it was the policeman, a burly man with a weathered face and huge grown hands.

"Good morning, Officer." Keely gave it all the friendliness and cheerfulness he could muster. He smiled, and opened the door of the white Jag XKE that sat in the driveway. The policeman pointed at the rear end of the car.

"There's something wrong, sir."

"Wrong?"

"Obviously wrong."

"What's wrong, Officer?" Keely shut the door carefully and joined the officer. Together they looked at the gleaming white rear of the Jag. Keely loved that car, all seventeen thousand dollars' worth of it. He even loved the windshield wipers that were chronically inoperative. He loved the many creaks and squeaks. He loved the windows that fogged up so often and the defroster that refused to work. Driving the Jag made him feel good, important, better than other men. "I don't see anything wrong, Officer."

The uniformed man took on a glum expression. He reached for a summons blank.

Keely felt his apprehension rise. "What?"

"The license."

"What? What's wrong with the license?"

"The light, the license light."

"What about it?"

"Doesn't work."

"Doesn't work? How can you tell? The car's not running, the lights aren't on."

The officer crouched down and Keely did likewise.

"How do you know?"

The cop smiled grimly. "See for yourself, the light's busted."

True. The small lamp had been broken, the thin glass shattered and scattered. It dotted the asphalt driveway in tiny glittering shards. Keely stood up. "Someone did that."

"Your license, please."

"Deliberately."

"You want to report a crime?"

"I'll have it replaced."

"May I see your license, please."

Keely fished it out. "This is ridiculous."

"Take it out, please."

"What?"

"Out of the card case, please."

Keely obliged.

"This is your car?"

Keely dug out his registration.

"Arthur Keely?"

"You're holding the license and registration in your hand. Yes, I'm Arthur Keely."

"No need to get testy, sir."

"Of course, you're just doing your duty."

"Correct, sir."

"Why aren't you catching criminals?"

"Driving when your lights don't work, that's a violation."

"I wasn't driving."

"You were *going* to drive."

"I admit it."

"I'll have to give you a citation."

"Hand it over, I'm in a hurry."

"Where are you going, Mr. Keely?"

"Why should that concern you, Officer?"

"Answer the question."

"Why?"

"Because you are an accused felon out on bail. Wouldn't want you going off somewhere inaccessible, would we, Mr. Keely?" Gloating suffused the officer's face. He handed Keely the citation.

Keely accepted it. It was going to be a bad day. The first of many, he was convinced.

It was late in the afternoon when the cortege departed Caroline Street at a stately tempo, going south on Duval as far as Truman Avenue, the high school drum corps stepping solemnly out in front. Drums draped in black gave off a muffled, respectful beat.

All commercial activity ceased along the line of march in final tribute to the dead man, an old Key West custom. Stores were closed until the procession passed and people stood in the street watching silently. A local celebrity was departing. But those who came out would have done so for a stranger as well. Besides, trade was slow, it was not too hot, and most of them had nothing better to do.

Off White Street left to Petronia, left again to the City Cemetery, where most of the deceased lay aboveground, under concrete or marble vaults, or in mausoleums. The land for the cemetery, which was purchased by the city in 1847, lay to the northeast of Passover and Windsor Lane, in the heart of a residential district.

The earliest graves on the island were on the western beach, between Whitehead's Point and the town, marked by simple stones. Since no clergyman lived on the island then, services were conducted by various citizens who were so inclined.

Later, Tract Fifteen, between the end of Whitehead

Street on South Beach and the Lighthouse Point, was chosen to be a permanent cemetery. The hurricane of 1846 disinterred a number of the dead, at the same time sending many more Key Westers to their graves.

Still later, during some excavations prior to public construction, a substantial number of human skeletons were dug up. They were the remains of slaves brought to Key West aboard two vessels in 1860.

Standing some distance from the stately tomb that had been made ready to receive Lawrence Grant, within sight of the monument to the battleship *Maine*—the sinking of which was the immediate cause of the Spanish-American War—was John Roy Iversen. At about the same time that he heard the distant roll of the high school drummers, he saw Izzy Ben-Ezra come limping along the bleached-stone path between the grave sites.

Iversen, given to quick judgments about men and women alike, made Ben-Ezra out to be crippled inside and out. A man damaged severely by life, a man never as strong or shrewd or courageous as he might have been. He viewed Ben-Ezra as a member of the herd, a being designed to follow his betters, to do as he was told. He wondered what twist in destiny had made the P.I. and Dutch Hollinger friends.

Ben-Ezra, checking the white gravestones and markers, the mausoleums, avoided making eye contact with Iversen until the last moment; as if to do so would in some undefined way obligate him. Until at last there was no way to avoid the detective.

"Lieutenant Iversen, isn't it?"

Iversen, tall and straight, coldly handsome, gazed down at the sinewy man. Without warning, he delivered his most charming smile, full of warmth and friendliness.

"Good to see you again, Izzy." The big strong hand went out, a fraternal clasp, equal-to-equal. "Hardly expected you to show up here. Respects to a departed literary great, is that it?"

Ben-Ezra smiled sheepishly. "Tell you the truth, I never read the man. I was hoping to find Dutch. You think he'll show up, Lieutenant?"

"Never do know about the Dutchman." Iversen gave

a slow, insinuating wink. "The old boy may be copping a little matinee, if my information is correct."

Ben-Ezra laughed shortly, a secretive, manly laugh. The sound of understanding, of worldliness, of membership in the same masculine society. "Dutch never did do without for very long. Women always went for Dutch."

"Anything I can do for you?" Iversen let the words out casually, a friendly offer not to be taken seriously. He lifted his eyes as if listening to the advancing cortege. "Can't be more than a block or two away. Soon it's goodbye Larry Grant."

Ben-Ezra frowned and nodded. "I got to talk to Dutch."

"Well, you know the man as well as anybody. He could be shacked up in any one of a hundred places."

"No way to get in touch?"

"Can't think of any." Iversen smiled. His senses began to thrum in that old trained cop's way, as if something vital were going down, something he should know about, something he was meant to act upon. He gave no sign that he was interested, no sign of being concerned, no sign that he cared whether Izzy Ben-Ezra stayed or went.

Ben-Ezra shifted his weight off his bad leg. He cracked a knuckle or two and cleared his throat. He tried to sort out his thoughts; he looked at his watch. "It's almost five o'clock," he said.

Iversen glanced at his watch. "Ten minutes to go."

Ben-Ezra sighed. "I went to the station house. They told me Dutch would be here, maybe."

"Don't make book on it."

"I know what you mean." Ben-Ezra's concern surfaced, he began to sweat. It took time to assemble the manpower necessary for this job. There were plans to be made, pinpoint timing to be worked out. He looked at his watch again.

"Sorry I can't help you," Iversen said.

Ben-Ezra glanced sidelong at the big blond man. What was it Dutch had said about John Roy Iversen? Experienced cop. Good at what he does. Probably be chief one day. What better recommendation could a man want? Besides, he was getting good vibes from Iversen and a man had to trust his instincts in this business.

He went to his watch again. Five minutes before five. There wasn't a great deal of time left if the job was going to get done right.

"Ironic, isn't it?" Iversen said in a mild voice. "Here we are about to bury a man and old Dutch is most likely getting off his nuts at the very same minute. Life and death, there it is." He grinned engagingly.

Ben-Ezra, enlisted again in the manly club, grinned back. "Dutch say anything to you about why I'm here, Lieutenant?"

"Just to say you're a first-class man, Izzy."

"That Dutch—him and me worked together a number of jobs. Nobody's better."

"Nobody's better than Dutch Hollinger, I agree."

Ben-Ezra felt his way cautiously. "I'm doing a little job for a certain very important party in New York City."

"Good for you." Iversen fought to mask off his curiosity, stood fast against asking questions, against pressing Ben-Ezra too hard. But on this island, in this place, there was nothing too insignificant to know, nothing too remote to have widespread effects. Information was Iversen's first line of defense, more since Bill Vail's departure than before.

Ben-Ezra felt impelled to make his move. "The thing is, I'm onto something pretty big."

"Too bad Dutch isn't available."

"No chance of his showing up soon?"

Iversen spoke confidentially. "I've known the man to disappear for forty-eight hours at a time. There are certain unnamed ladies in town who claim he is a veritable animal when his sap is running."

Ben-Ezra acknowledged his friend's prowess with a small, sickly smile. He couldn't wait much longer. "The job I'm on—my client's wife is on Key West, playing around."

"They'll do it every time."

"He wants her back."

"Sure he does, though sometimes you wonder why."

"Yeah. Dutch and me, one hand washes the other, y' see."

"You don't have to tell me a thing."

"The idea is, I grab the wife under certain confused circumstances so that she gets the notion I'm doing her a favor, maybe even saving her life or keeping her from a stretch in the joint. I let her know that I'm her husband's man and she's grateful to him for a while."

"Until she breaks out again."

"Something like that. Dutch was going to help."

Iversen seemed bored by the conversation.

"Dutch helps," Ben-Ezra said, "and I give him something."

"That's the way to play the game."

Ben-Ezra weighed the situation. The important thing was to get Janet Quint back to her husband and his chance to do that was coming up. He had to act now, make the necessary arrangements, otherwise it would all be wasted. No telling when he would get a second chance. He made up his mind.

"I was going to give it to Dutch," he shrugged. "Maybe you'd be interested?"

"I don't think so. Never step on anybody's toes."

"No, no, Dutch isn't like that. He'd understand. It's all a matter of timing, you see. The job is going down tonight."

Iversen shook his head. "Are you sure you want to hand this over? I mean, it is Dutch's baby by rights—"

"I can't wait. I'm meeting my snitch at eight o'clock to get the exact timing on the landing. You can see why I'm uptight—"

"You make it sound like a big job."

"It is, twenty-five tons of prime Colombian grass."

Iversen looked surprised. "Coming into Key West?" His mind was racing; he'd lucked out and this dumbass P.I. was right, there was much to take care of before the shipment came ashore.

"Big Pine Key," Ben-Ezra offered. "Three boatloads."

Iversen set himself against a rising anger. How had an outsider stumbled onto the information about the shipment? There had to be a local source—who? He kept himself from grabbing the other man, shaking the information out of him.

The funeral had turned into Frances Street, would soon enter the cemetery. "You trust your snitch, Izzy?"

Ben-Ezra puffed himself up. "I'm not a virgin, Lieutenant. A long time on the job, I've been there before. What I've got is solid stuff, I know."

"Sure, no harm meant."

"You want in, Lieutenant?" Ben-Ezra felt put upon, his credentials in question, his professional competence under hostile scrutiny. It made him value John Roy Iversen even more. "If you don't—"

"If the bust goes down real good, Izzy, I'd want Dutch to share the credit."

Ben-Ezra let his breath out. "That's square of you, Lieutenant."

"How do we work it, Izzy? This is your show."

"Okay," Ben-Ezra said, as the cortege rolled into the cemetery. He would have to remain through the burial and he was a man who had always hated funerals.

15

Paco Valentín and Tody Ellis stood apart from the crowd. As the mourners dispersed, Paco made the sign of the cross and asked God to bless the dead man. Tody added solemnly, "Right on, Lord."

"You ever read his books, Tody?"

"Not lately. The man had lost his edge, you follow my meaning. Getting flabby."

"A pretty good fisherman."

"Better than most," Tody said.

Paco made the sign of the cross again and they left the cemetery. "All-day charter tomorrow, Tody. Two fishermen."

"You want me to load up with food and drinks?"

"The works. Charge it to me."

"You want me to gas up *La Florida?*"

"I'll take care of it. See you later, Tody."

"Later . . ."

Louise said, "This is my husband, Graham Welles. Graham, this is Sam Dickey."

The two men shook hands.

"Your father is a very fine physician," Graham said. "Key West profits by his presence."

"You're very kind to say so."

"Sam was with poor Larry and me."

"You knew Grant well, did you?"

"Not very well. We met in Corsica, a few years ago. He said to come and see him when I was in Key West. I took him at his word. Actually, I was going to interview him for *Rock-the-World Weekly*."

"Another writer?"

"Just getting under way, Mr. Welles. You were a friend of Grant's?"

"We played bridge with some regularity. Competitors, mostly. Friends? Not really."

"I wonder if you might give me some time, to talk about Grant. Different points of view, you see."

"There isn't much I could tell you."

"But, Graham, you knew Larry or such a long time. The way you've analyzed his writings, and his bridge game . . ."

"I think not."

"I'd appreciate any help you can give, Mr. Welles."

"Why doesn't Sam come back to the house with us, Graham? We'll have something to eat and talk about poor Larry. We owe him that much, don't we?" She smiled sweetly, wondering how it would be in bed with Sam Dickey. So young and slender, and gracefully constructed.

"If you wish, my dear. Unless Mr. Dickey has some other plans."

"I can't think of anything I'd rather do."

"How nice!"

Iversen made the call from a public phone. "I've got a job for you," he said.

"I'm tied up right now."

"Meet me in twenty minutes."

"Same place?"

"Yes."

"Shall I bring my little toy?"

"Bring it. I want you to trail a guy, locate a talkative friend of his."

"You got it, my friend."

"Twenty minutes . . ."

Annie Russell, in faded jeans and huaraches, was alone in front of the mausoleum when Hollinger arrived. She displayed little animation when he appeared.

"You an admirer?" he said.

"I used to read him in college. But then he got hung up on the macho game and that put me off."

"This is for old times?"

"Something like that. Solved any good crimes lately, Sergeant?"

"Three muggings in one week, a regular crime wave."

"Kojak could sweep up the bad guys before the second commercial break."

"Kojak wouldn't waste his time on the garbage I get to deal with. All my life I wanted to be a hotshot and look at me—spending time with pitiful old men and women who are afraid of the dark."

"To them you're a hero."

"What about to me?"

"Don't you like yourself?"

"Let's talk about crime."

"Okay, isn't it a crime to move a corpse from one place to another, on the sly?"

"Who would do a thing like that?"

"The way I hear it, somebody moved Grant around, brought him from someplace else back to his swimming pool."

"That's a nice story."

"You don't care?"

"He's dead, isn't he? Nobody's claiming foul play."

"You know why they shifted him around?"

"Even cops get to hear some rumors. But I don't pay attention to rumors."

She inspected him closely. "In my opinion, you are a goddamn moralist."

"No need to insult me, lady."

She made a futile pass at her wild orange hair, gave

him a wide engaging grin, holding it. "Come on, lay back and let it happen. You know you like me."

He filled his lungs with hot thick air and thought about retirement in New England, amid seasonal changes and winter snow. He was tired of a sunbaked life where everything always looked the same.

"Nobody likes a smartass reporter," he said.

The grin seemed to widen. "All right if I call you Dutch, Dutch?"

"My given name is Wolfgang so I guess Dutch is okay."

She began to laugh and hooked her arm in his. She led him out of the cemetery and her breast against his elbow was soft and warm and extremely troublesome. "How about a bite of food, Wolfgang?"

"Dutch," he corrected mildly.

"Anything you say . . ."

They found a table at the rear of a luncheonette on Duval that sold porno books, girlie magazines and tuna fish sandwiches wrapped in plastic. They sipped thin, hot coffee out of paper cups and Hollinger took a good look at Annie Russell.

"Like what you see?" she said at last.

"Be nice," he admonished.

"I don't always know how. It's a hard life."

"It's a big club."

"The truth is, you make me nervous."

"Cops have that effect on people."

"Not because you're a cop."

"What then?"

"I'm not sure."

"Let me know when you find out."

"I'll do that." She sipped some coffee and waited. When he didn't say anything, she decided he had much better controls than she did. "I had a talk with Arthur Keely," she said, trying to make it casual.

"You think you can get me to let you in on police business for just a cup of coffee?"

"What is your price?"

"For you I'm going to work up a special rate."

"Come on, Dutch, give a little. It can't hurt. We both have our jobs to do."

"It is the consensus of my fellow members of the force that Keely did his wife in, with malice aforethought."

"Shit."

"You have a rich and colorful vocabulary."

"Why? What motive?"

"She tossed him out on his butt, how's that for starters?"

"Not good enough. Keely is a ladies' man. He's pretty, he's aggressive, and he's oversexed."

"You found all of that out? I'm impressed."

"Flush out that dirty mind. Nothing happened. But the picture is very clear."

"Even lechers commit murders."

"Not him."

"What makes you so sure?"

"Woman's intuition. Okay, I'm liberated and I should know better. Call it a hunch."

He sat back in his chair. "Keely had a motive, a good one. His wife had a lover."

She was surprised. "How do you know?"

"Even backwater cops like me sometimes get lucky. Or maybe I had a hunch. Anyway, there was a guy and Keely knew about him."

"What's his name?"

"The lover? Uh-uh. You do your job, I'll do mine."

"Cops," she said with exaggerated scorn.

He made a theatrical gesture. "Hath not a cop eyes? Hath not a cop hands, organs, dimensions, senses, affections, passions? If you prick us, do we not bleed? If you tickle us, do we not laugh? If you poison us, do we not die? And if you wrong us, shall we not revenge?"

Her eyes went round and she pursed her mouth. "You are full of surprises, Dutch."

"Would you believe it, some cops are almost literate."

"Okay, so there's a lover. Does that mean Keely shot Bettyjane?"

"Not necessarily."

"Maybe there were other men."

"My sources indicate Bettyjane was an extremely busy lady."

"There you are! I just don't figure Keely as a shooter. He's weak—"

"Weak men often kill."

"—and cowardly, I think—"

"Killers come in all sizes, shapes and dispositions. Keep that in mind and you'll go wrong less often."

"Okay, what does it take to be a murderer?"

"Opportunity and anger. A weapon helps."

"Are you saying Keely killed his wife on impulse?"

"Maybe. And then had to do the maid to keep her from talking."

"Where's the gun?"

"In the Gulf, maybe. If it were mine, that's where I'd've put it. That's what the wise guys generally do, one killing per gun. Makes it hard to connect people that way."

"If you're right, how can you prove Keely is guilty?"

"Basic police work. We'll build a case against the guy."

"I still think you're wrong."

"I have often been wrong."

"Will you keep me in touch with what's going down, Dutch? I can do a good story on this, maybe a series, and if I do—"

"What then? You make yourself a reputation, move onto some big-city paper. Maybe go on television. Another Barbara Walters. You can do it, Annie. You've got the looks, the drive, and you're plenty smart."

She cocked her head. "You do like me, don't you?"

He placed his hands on the table and elevated himself to a standing position. "I haven't come to a definitive conclusion," he said. "I got to go now, there's police work to do. Thanks for the coffee." He started to leave.

"I like you," she said.

That brought him around. "I admit it, you are a terrific-looking woman. But I'm not sure I trust you . . ."

"That," she said after his retreating back, "is not such a bad place to start."

"More coffee?"

Her voice was serrated, made harsh by too much whiskey drunk and a simmering resentment that would not let go of her. It was midnight and she had made a pot of coffee and her cup stood still full and untouched. She chain-smoked and kept her eyes on Jimmy Oreskes, refilling his cup from time to time. She watched him read, fixed on the slightest change of expression on his triangular face, taking heart from the merest hint of a smile, plunging into despair if he scowled or seemed bored. She had limped into the long dark tunnel of uncertainty and feared she would never come out the other side.

Oreskes put the manuscript aside. "I've had enough."

"It's that bad?" Her weak hopes plummeted.

"I meant the coffee." He tapped the pile of papers with one delicate finger. "This is a—problem."

"It's awful, isn't it?"

"You've read it."

"Every goddamn word. Is it as terrible as I think it is?"

"You tell me."

"I think it's unpublishable. I think, even if it were published, it's libelous. If you believe Grant, he screwed every women he ever met. He names them, describes their bodies, what they do and rates them. My God! The lawsuits would go on into the next century . . ."

Oreskes laughed softly and leaned back. "I agree. Unless you'd like to take a crack at rewriting it. Putting it into decent shape. Eliminate the names, or change them. I had no idea Larry had regressed so much, that he could ever write so badly."

"I'm no writer."

He shrugged.

She slumped in place. "The bastard's left me destitute."

"There must be some money. This house, savings, something."

"The house is heavily mortgaged. He spent every penny he ever made. All those other wives, those children; Grant had a great sense of family loyalty, present company excluded. I don't know what to do."

"What about the theater, Hilda? You could pick up where you left off."

She closed her eyes as if in pain, letting the words out one after another. "Grant took the central years of my life. He stole my looks and terminated my career."

"You're still a beautiful woman, Hilda."

"I was an ingenue. Cute, girlish. Pert, as they say. The poor man's June Allyson, except I didn't sing or dance. I'm coming fast up to forty, Jimmy, and there are no parts for a matronly ingenue. There's no going back."

"If Larry had lived, he would have fixed the manuscript—"

"Grant's dead, and I can't write. Not well enough to do what's required here. The hairy ape finished me off for good . . ."

"There's another way."

"What's that?"

"Bring in another writer."

"A ghost?"

"Exactly. Someone with a feel for the way Larry wrote, who understands his attitudes and life-style. Someone who can put these disconnected notes into readable order, in workmanlike prose."

She began to hope again. "Do you have someone in mind?"

"No. But there are thousands of writers. I'm sure I could find someone in New York."

"And everybody in the publishing business would hear about it in fifteen minutes. Mitgang would do a feature story in the *Times*—'Ghost Rewrites Grant's Tomb.'"

Oreskes laughed; Hilda didn't.

"There must be some way," he said.

"There must be," agreed Hilda, without optimism. She felt old suddenly, and without strength, life seeping away, her future dissolving into a white formless blur. "There must be . . ."

But she knew better.

16

Tody Ellis almost floated down the street, his mind going back to the woman he had just left. What a prize she was! Velvety black and smooth, soft and warm and wet when she should be. That body wiggled and squirmed as if to take him all in, to put him where he belonged; going home, mama. What sweet loving.

Her name was Marie and he'd known her for almost two months and never got his fill of her. Even now, minutes after that busy, busy night, his crotch filled up at the thought of her. Maybe he should have stayed on; she'd asked him to, promised finer action if he did. Swore she knew tricks concealed from less passionate females. He believed her. Not new tricks, but old ones made to seem like new. Oh, *lovely*.

Damn, yes, he was going back. This very night. A day out on *La Florida* and then return to the sources of his power and his joy. Whooeee!

He was almost to Second Street, less than a block from where he lived, when the two men jumped him. Slammed him into a wall and began punching him out. He never had a chance to fight back. Or see their faces. Nor did they speak a word. Bleeding profusely, he went down, brain shrinking and closing out the pain and the fear. So this was the way it was to die. Beat up for the bread in his pockets; a poor night's work. He was carrying less than five dollars. Just before he lost consciousness, he remembered Marie and when everything went black he was feeling mighty good.

The two men stood over Tody. One of them drew back his foot. The other stopped him.

"No, Hector," Figueroa said. "It is enough."

"We must be sure he will not be on the boat in the morning."

"Look at him. He will not be there. There is no need to kill him."

"Perhaps you are right. He will not be on the boat."

"Come on, we have other work to do."

17

She said on the phone, "I want to see you, Sam."

"Now?"

"Don't be silly. It's the middle of the night, although that might be nice."

"I'd like that."

"You flatter an old lady."

"You're not old, you'll never be old."

"Tell me that another time. Some of them are still here. The agent, the editor, a couple of drunken novelists. Come tomorrow."

"In the morning?"

"Impatient boy. In the evening. I'll cook for you, something special."

"Yes."

"Tomorrow, then."

"I can hardly wait."

She hung up slowly.

18

In the spotless, polished work kitchen, Louise Welles put together a polite and proper lunch for herself and her husband. Neat little triangles of crustless wheat bread arranged on either side of layers of thin-sliced Virginia ham, imported Swiss cheese and mayonnaise. On each gleaming white china plate, tiny sweet gherkins and potato chips. Tall blue glasses were filled to the rim with English tea and crushed ice.

They dined in the Florida room looking out on a tiny Japanese garden which Graham had designed and built himself: rocks picked clean of dirt and unsightly growth, bonsai trees, gravel paths. Louise enjoyed the garden, tried occasionally to imagine it populated by a community of undersize Japanese, all in colorful kimonos, the men carrying long swords. People said the Japanese took baths together, men, women and children. What would it be like to bathe with strangers, handsome young strangers with bodies tense and smooth?

"Excellent lunch," Graham said. He was in an expansive, almost effusive mood. He'd been working in the railroad room all morning and had completed construction of the new turntable. Just before lunch he'd given the system a trial run with extraordinary results: everything worked perfectly. Switches, signals, rolling stock, the turntable. There was something real and important about railroading, transporting a man back to a simpler, purer time when values were clear and men knew who they were and what was expected of them. Railroading was a solid link with America's past; Graham meant to maintain that link, make it stronger. He checked his chronograph.

Louise made an automatic response. "Do you have an appointment, dear?" She was remembering that day on Paco Valentín's boat, with Grant. With Sam Dickey. The way Grant had hovered over her, imposed himself until the rest of the world was closed out and she knew he alone could provide what she wanted and needed.

"Just habit," Graham said.

She acknowledged his response without hearing what he had said. She put herself back in the living room, on the couch, on the floor, with Grant plucking at her clothes, with Grant on top of her. Inside of her.

"Hilda phoned me about that young man, Sam Dickey. He's doing that story about Larry and she asked would I speak to him."

Louise choked and coughed and wondered if Graham

could possibly suspect her. "He seemed like a pleasant young man." She nibbled her sandwich.

"Hilda mentioned the possibility of young Dickey interviewing you as well."

"I hardly knew poor Larry."

"He was fond of you, I've heard him say so." He finished off one triangle and sipped some tea. "That fishing trip, did Grant conduct himself correctly?"

Fear caused her to grow cold, caused her spine to depress. "What do you mean?"

"Grant was a vulgarian, without taste, manners or background."

"He was perfectly proper."

"Act like a lady and you're treated like a lady. Superb tea, my dear." He looked at his watch again.

"You do have an appointment."

"Not at all. Some acquaintances are embarked on a certain piece of work. I simply wonder how they are coming along. I regret the passing of a single human soul, but Grant did rub me wrong."

She could almost feel Grant rubbing against her. The hairy body rough and grating. She tried to imagine Graham treating her with the same animal abandon, but the image refused to come into focus. Graham was so proper and polite, no matter the occasion.

With sudden horror, she realized that she wanted to tell Graham about her encounter with Larry Grant. Of the way in which the big writer had rooted around inside her like the brute that he was. She longed to let Graham know how much she had enjoyed the experience, enjoyed everything Grant had done, everything she had done. Above all, one thing made her proud: of all the women Grant had known and had sex with, only she had been able to fuck him right into his grave.

Fucking Grant had been good.

Fucking him to death was even better.

What a wild idea! How disturbing that she could think that way. So satisfying . . .

She longed desperately to share the experience with somebody. Somebody trustworthy and reliable, somebody honorable and understanding. But who? She could think of no one worthy of her confidence.

She watched Graham work delicately on his second

triangle. What a washed-out prig he was. An ineffectual, shadowy reproduction of a man. Grant had been real, even with the coarseness; or because of it. He had touched her as no other man ever had. And then been taken away; God's punishment for her transgression.

She sighed. Somewhere there must be another man. Not the same, of course. Someone passionate and gentler, a man concerned with her welfare, her needs, a man to support and delight her in a hundred different ways. Someone very unlike her husband.

Graham provided the framework within which she might exist. But none of the substance of a good life. He was cool, distant, and without deep emotion. She needed more.

What Graham could not offer, other men would. At least she hoped they would. Why not? She was young, beautiful, and her figure was still good. And, thanks to Grant, her old fears and inhibitions had been unloosed. She wanted to repeat everything she had done with him with other men. Many men. More than one man at a time.

"More gherkins, dear?"

"I've had quite enough, thank you."

A new idea sifted up from the underground. Was there any reason why Graham could not be seduced into supplying some small, extra pleasure now and again? Could he not be maneuvered into letting his staid and proper ways fall aside, if only temporarily, manipulated into stepping down from his position of Perfect Grace? Somewhere within him must lie dormant all the passions that other men owned. She would commit herself to stirring them back to life.

But first, make a meaningful contact. Break through the protective outer covering.

"Do you ever think about the navy, dear?"

"The navy?"

"Do you ever miss the life?"

"The navy was my life. Of course I think about it. Of course I miss it."

"Of course," she agreed sweetly.

He drank some tea.

"Why not go back?"

"Go back?"

"To the navy."

"I am retired, Louise."

"I'm sure they would be pleased to have you."

He stared at her. Could she possibly be as dense and unperceptive as she seemed? Not that it mattered. She looked right, she acted right; the perfect wife for a retired naval commander.

"I do manage to keep busy."

"I've been meaning to ask you, what are you working at these days?"

"Just dabbling."

"When I met you you were in the State Department."

"I'm no longer with State, either."

"You're much too young to be inactive."

He wondered how she would react if she knew the truth. "I have my interests."

"Model railroading?"

"Other matters."

"I'd love to hear about them, Graham."

He was tempted to boast a bit, the slightest bit. "I am still active, Louise. Accept that."

"Doing what, Graham?"

"Some . . . government work."

"I don't understand."

"There is always work for a man of dedication and intelligence. Necessary work. Much official business goes on in the shadows, you might say."

"I see. But what do you do, Graham?"

He decided to provide her with a dollop more of information, enough to satisfy and terminate her curiosity. After all, she was his wife. "I never was actually with State, you see."

"Not State?"

"No."

"I don't understand."

"The State Department designation was merely a cover."

"A cover?"

"For the Company."

"What company?"

"The Agency."

"Which agency?"

"Central Intelligence."

"Central— You mean CIA!"

"You'll keep it to yourself, of course."

"Graham, are you telling me you were a spy?"

"An intelligence officer."

"How marvelous! You must miss it, all the excitement, the intrigue, the *danger* . . . Oh, I have it! You must write your memoirs, now that you've retired. Everyone's doing it. That fellow Agee and Snepp and—"

"I'm not one of them."

"Of course you aren't. Still—"

"Retired is not exactly the word to describe my situation. You might say I've kept one hand in the pot."

She began to breathe faster and her eyes went round. "What do you mean? Tell me about the pot."

"I don't think so."

"Oh, *please*. You can't stop now, you can't."

He went ahead reluctantly. "Let's say that I have maintained a certain lasting attachment to Cuba."

She considered his words. "Can you describe the attachment for me, Graham?" She felt herself being drawn into a complex and mysterious plot, one complete with secrets, threats and exotic strangers. It had begun to sound like an old movie with Sidney Greenstreet and Peter Lorre.

"Some of us will never permit Cuba to slide into the enemy camp."

She was under the impression it had already done that and her confusion grew, only to be tempered by the hot flush of her spreading excitement.

"What are you up to, Graham?"

"Steps have been taken."

"How delicious!"

Barely able to contain herself, she bounced in place like some agitated child anticipating a special prize. "What steps?" she sputtered.

He shook his head and attended to the last triangle, chewing thoroughly. He put a spotless, starched napkin to his lips.

"Don't stop!" she cried. "Not in the middle of the story."

"This is not a story."

"All the better!" She squirmed, thighs damp against each other. So much excitement; first Grant and now this. "What steps?"

Her reaction alarmed him and he sought to calm her, to bring her back under control. "Some men are on their way to Cuba—"

"Now?"

He glanced at his watch; then nodded.

"This moment? Why? Why are they going?"

"I've said too much already."

She went around the table, stood at his side, clutching his shoulder. "Oh, Graham, it sounds so—wonderful. Please don't stop now."

"It was a mistake to tell you any of it."

"You can trust me."

"In this work, it is best to trust no one."

She sank to her knees, hands working on his thigh. "I'm your wife."

"Stand up, Louise."

Compared to Grant's massive, muscular legs, Graham was undernourished, feeble. She placed her face between his legs.

He rose quickly and she fell at his feet, holding fast. "A wife does not act in such a fashion, Louise. Not my wife."

"Make love to me, Graham."

"It's the middle of the day."

"Now. Here."

"Now! Here?"

"On the floor."

"My God! What's happened to you, Louise? Get a grip on yourself."

She got a grip on him. He freed himself with a controlled, disdainful display of strength. "I have to go now, attend to certain matters. When I come back, I expect you to be yourself again, Louise. In control. A decent woman acting decently."

"Oh, shit," she muttered, and beat the floor with her fists.

"Louise, you disappoint me," he said before he left.

19

Hollinger pushed himself to the limit. His sneakered feet hit the pavement of North Roosevelt Boulevard hard and his thighs grew heavy, his lungs ached. He went on, making himself run through the pain. His vision blurred and there was an echo in his ears and the parts of his body seemed to take on a life independent of each other. For a long, terrifying interval, it felt as if he'd lost all control, that he would run on forever, or until he dropped, no longer able to command his body and make it obey. He slowed his pace and fought for breath.

Why punish himself this way? A year short of half a century and he was acting like a high school jock on the make. What was he trying to prove?

He bought himself down to an old man's trot. He became aware of the jiggling flab around his waist and cursed the years that had made him middle-aged and softer, weaker, more afraid.

Fear was not something to dwell on. Fear was what crippled a man, other men, not him. Yet he had lived with fear always, a fear that sometimes reduced him to a quivering wreck, a shell of himself, a fear that made him ashamed and afraid that he would not be able to toe the mark the next time out. Yet he always had. No man had confronted danger and death more directly, or with more courage and control. When the shooting began, he was always there. All guts. He would not think about fear. Or about death. He forced his mind to consider other subjects.

Annie Russell. Was she too running around this crowded island? Would he suddenly come upon her as he had the last time? He searched ahead and saw only an empty roadway. Running was still fun at her age, still a challenge to be met and overcome. She could run for the good of her body and the enrichment of her soul. To hell with her soul, she had one super body.

The sort of body a man might never get enough of. A body lush and inviting. And demanding, he added. Not a body for an overweight fifty-year-old to dream about. Such a woman could give the lie to every fragile defense on which a man constructed his life. To consider Annie Russell seriously was menopausal madness. Allow her to get too close and she would bring down the entire house of cards in one painful disaster. Annie Russell was a threat to spirit and flesh that must be avoided at all costs. He had lived too much for her, too differently; he was too deeply enmeshed in being a cop, in keeping his secrets tucked away in darkness, in maintaining himself, in keeping his distance. He was too old for her.

Lately age had dominated his thinking. Maybe it was the muggings and his inability to collar the muggers. Four times they had struck. Two white boys, beating up on old, helpless people, taking money, a watch, a ring, and fleeing. Being young was a trial, getting old was a punishment.

All the attacks had occurred within a radius of six blocks. Hollinger had put cops into the area in unmarked cars but they had turned up nothing. Bad feelings took hold of him when he could not do his job, when he could not protect those who needed it most. He wished the two young muggers would try him on for size. He ran faster; wind sprints.

At Garrison Bight, he stopped and watched the day charters working out of their berths, heading to sea. No matter how many times he saw them, he felt a certain anticipation, as if they were embarked on a trip charged with excitement and unknown sensual treasures. He spotted *La Florida* and made out Paco Valentín in the cockpit, but no one else. Where was Tody? Where were Paco's clients? In the main cabin keeping warm, perhaps.

La Florida sailed along with almost no wake. Gone from where it had been without a trace. Life was like that, his life; he'd sailed along leaving no marker, unnoticed by anyone else. The pain of past failures persisted and though the degree of hurt was diminished with time, it was still sharp. And the disappointment. Nothing was as he'd dreamed it would be. None of his plans had worked out. Once Hollinger had seen himself as a hero: brave, resolute, pure. Instead he'd become bent and flawed, a slightly rotten piece of goods, never quite measuring up. He had transformed himself into that most awful creature, an ordinary man. Regret and sorrow were his constant companions, human frailty his eternal burden.

La Florida had left the Bight, was out of sight. Why had Tody Ellis not been at the stern rigging lines, preparing bait, setting the outriggers? Why no fishermen in the fighting chairs? Perhaps Paco was not on a charter. He might be going out for a cargo of illegals, to be run into the Upper Keys. Or a load of dope. A mother ship might be waiting at a rendezvous point off-loading to smaller craft for transport to shore. It was an easy day's work, with only a minimal chance of being caught. Not the Coast Guard, not the sheriff's office, none of the enforcement agencies had men or money or boats enough to stem the tide of the smugglers. Even if they wanted to.

All energy spent, Hollinger walked all the way home, carrying his failures with him; as a man, as a cop, as a genuine, gold-plated all-American folk hero.

The poker game was over and Harry was a big winner. First time in a long time. Mostly he lost. At cards, at craps, at whatever he tried. But now he was a winner and it felt great. More than a thousand dollars stuffed into the pockets of his jacket.

Harry hurried along Margaret Street, toward Fleming, his pocket stuffed with Ben-Ezra's money. And later, when the job was done, there would be more. He was anxious to get to Albert's house, to boast of his good fortune. Albert was Harry's friend, his lover, his roommate. Albert would be proud of his exploits this night.

All the lights were off in Albert's house, which was strange. Albert didn't like to sleep in the dark. But dawn was breaking and Harry was able to make his way into the bedroom. The bed looked slept in, but Albert wasn't there. Harry was annoyed and for a brief moment felt a stab of jealousy. Then he scolded himself: Albert was not like that. He was steady, reliable, faithful. Harry took off his jacket and went into the bathroom.

Albert was in the bathtub. Albert was dead, his throat

cut, bathing in his own blood. Harry opened his mouth to scream but no sound came out as the man with the knife came up behind him, flung one arm around his throat, and thrust the knife into Harry's back. The pain was excruciating and accompanied by an old, nighttime terror. Harry struggled, but without strength or purpose. The man with the knife stabbed him again, and allowed Harry to fall to the floor. Looking up, Harry saw the man step into view, leaning, and watched the knife slice forward to cut his throat.

When Iversen came out of his bedroom, Ellen was waiting. "What have you done to Marc?" she said.

Her suitcase was on the floor next to her and she was dressed for travel. "Marc? That boy you were dating? I haven't seen him."

"He's disappeared."

"I'm sorry."

"It isn't like him to go without telling me. He loves me."

He exhaled. "Men don't always say what they mean. They speak about love when what they want—"

"What did you do to him?" Her voice rose, shrill, in anguish.

"Nothing. I did nothing to him."

She picked up the suitcase. "Good-bye, Daddy."

"What are you doing?"

"I'm leaving. For good."

He took the suitcase out of her hand. "I won't let you do this."

"I'm going anyway."

"I had nothing to do with Marc."

Her head swung loosely from side to side. "You want to run my life. I can't let you. I won't let you."

"Because I don't want my daughter cleaning other people's homes?"

"Because it's impossible for me to live the way I want to live with you around."

"I'll find you, wherever you go."

"This time I'll be harder to find. Who knows, maybe this time you won't find me. Or if you do, then next time I'll be more cunning. I'll get away one day."

"I can't discuss this now. I've got a big job going on.

Wait for me. In the morning we'll talk it over. Then, whatever you decide will be all right with me."

She stared at him until he avoided her gaze.

"Will you wait?"

She shrugged.

"Please," he said, before he left.

She lit a roach and perched on a high stool next to the kitchen counter and tried to force her head to work efficiently. Eventually an idea began to form. A superwonderful idea, an idea that sent her soaring much higher than the best grass would ever do.

Iversen was alone in the Detective Division. He sat at his desk and drank hot black coffee and chewed listlessly on a glazed doughnut. The phone rang. He picked it up and said his name.

"One down," the familiar accented voice said.

"Dammit, you're not supposed to call me here. Which one?"

"The snitch."

"And the other?"

"He's in his room at the motel."

"You told me it would all be over by now. Get him."

"I can't go busting in there. The guy's loaded. He's an ex-cop, he knows his way around. What am I supposed to do?"

"You're the expert."

"Get him out of there."

"I don't want to be involved."

"Get him out and your secret goes with him."

"How long will it take you to get into position?"

"I'm ready when you are."

"Okay. I'll call."

"Just get him out."

"Okay."

The phone rang. Ben-Ezra picked it up and said, Hello."

"Izzy, it's Iversen."

"Everything set?"

"It's all up in the air."

Ben-Ezra felt sweat break out on his palms. "What's wrong?"

"Harry Waterman, he's bought it."

"Dead?"

"Someone cut him good, and his roommate."

Ben-Ezra wanted to run, to hide, to remove himself abruptly and forever from the closing danger. He felt he should say something meaningful, make known his objections, his fears. He hadn't mentioned Harry Waterman by name to Iversen, or to anybody else. Maybe he wasn't the man he used to be, but he was too good a cop to spill a snitch's name around. He kept his voice steady.

"Where is he?"

"I'm at the station house, I'll take you."

"Give me five minutes."

Ben-Ezra hung up and went into the bathroom, swallowed a Valium, then put on his jacket. He pushed the short-barreled .38 on a .32 frame under his belt and buttoned up. Then hurried outside.

He made it past the swimming pool and into the motel parking lot when the first slug ripped into his throat, hurling him backward. Rolling reflexively, he tried to reach his gun, cursing himself for a fool, for being too trusting, too impetuous, for never correcting his character flaws. The second slug smashed in the back of his head before he could get his gun out and he died in the street alone. Just the way he'd always feared it would happen. Just the way he'd always known it would happen.

Going out without Tody made Paco feel bad. In the many months that Tody had been his mate, the slender black man had proved himself reliable, a hard worker, a man of his word. His failure to put in an appearance worried Paco; it was unlike Tody.

Paco had thought about canceling the charter. But that was a bad thing to do. Word got around that a captain was not dependable, that he altered schedules, failed to fulfill commitments. It was bad for business.

And his clients were on board on time, ready to go. Tody had filled the cold locker with beer and soft drinks, and there were plenty of sandwiches and fruit, chocolate bars, and coffee.

"Can't you handle the boat yourself, Captain?" Figueroa had pressed him.

"It is safer with two men."

"No reason to anticipate problems, is there?"

"No reason at all." Tody had undoubtedly overslept. Or had a little too much to drink the night before. Such things were not unheard of. "No," he repeated. "We will go out."

Once out of the Bight, Paco put the diesels up to three-quarter speed. A glance over his shoulder showed Figueroa and his companion in the fighting chairs, talking quietly, looking back at where they had been. Figueroa glanced up and smiled, then returned to his conversation. His friend kept staring across the bow. At once Paco felt uneasy and it occurred to him that he had not seen the man's face, that no introduction had been made, no name given. Was it simply an omission, or personal rudeness, or did Figueroa's friend have something to hide? He shrugged such thoughts away and pointed *La Florida* toward the Yucatán, to a location where the fishing was almost always good, always easy. He would give them their money's worth.

Figueroa came up behind him, saying his name. An enigmatic smile curled his sensual mouth. *"Ay, capitán,* we seem to be heading west . . ."

"You have a good eye, *señor*. South, southwest would be closer. Into the Gulf of Mexico."

"My friend and me, we'd rather go south."

"Where I am taking you, the fish run in schools and—"

"South." The smile had altered slightly and made Figueroa resemble a snake.

"I don't sail south," Paco said.

"You got a superstition, *amigo*?"

"South is where Cuba is. I keep my distance."

"This time, make the distance smaller. Take us to Cuba."

Paco turned in time to see the second fisherman leave his place and come forward. He was of medium build with a feline grace, his narrow head riding lightly on a strong, long neck. As he came into the light, Paco recognized him.

"Buenos días, Hector."

"¿Cómo stá, Paco?" His face was bony, the cheeks depressed and pocked, his eyes black and icy and set back deep in his skull. He did not offer his hand, nor smile,

but his voice when he spoke again, in English this time, was not unpleasant, though untouched by personal warmth. "You lookin' good, Paco."

"Not so young any more."

"You always had a little gray in your hair. I'm glad to see you, Paco."

"Hector, it does not please me to have you on my boat. I am finished with your kind of work."

"Take us to Cuba, Paco."

"I don't make that run any more, Hector."

"One more time, Paco. Like the anglos say, for old times' sake."

"You want to fish, I'm for hire. Anything else, *nada, amigo.*"

"I got to talk to a guy back home, Paco. It is very important."

"Find another boat. I'll put you back on Key West. Ask around, plenty of captains will make the run if the pay is right."

"I want you."

"Sorry."

Figueroa grinned. "Somebody cut off his manhood, Hector. Somebody cut out his heart."

"Tell your friend to watch his mouth, Hector."

"I spoke very well of you to Figueroa, Paco. He is disappointed. But I am confident you will change your mind."

"I do not go to Cuba."

"A special favor."

"No favors, Hector. I told you a long time ago I was finished. What's done is done. I am a fisherman now, a captain of this boat. That is all. All."

"I will make him change his mind," Figueroa said, and produced a pistol.

Hector laughed shortly. But there was no humor in it and his eyes remained flat and watchful. "Hey, Paco, peace, eh? It's your mother—she is dying."

"Do not lie about my mother."

"I have got word. She is sick and she is dying. I will take you to her."

"And what else?"

"And you will get to see your baby brother."

Paco filled his lungs with air. "And if I say no?"

"There is always the gun."

Figueroa grinned. "You take us to Cuba, no? You will visit your mother and brother. We will take care of our business. We will all leave together."

"And if there is trouble?"

"You were never afraid of trouble," Hector said.

"If there is trouble?"

"All the arrangements have been made. There will be no trouble. Old friends traveling home together. It will be peaceful and good for us all."

"And afterward?"

"Afterward? After it will be over. We will each go our separate ways, Paco."

Paco stared at the smaller man.

Hector finally smiled a small smile, a slight movement of his lips, no teeth showing. "You can trust me, Paco."

Not for one minute, Paco thought, as he swung *La Florida* onto a course for Cuba. Not for one second.

PART
III

20

"He was a friend."

Hollinger turned away from the sheet-draped body on the table and fixed his attention on the far, flat wall of the dead room in the basement of the hospital.

"I'm sorry," Iversen said.

"We ought to have a morgue," Hollinger said absently.

"The town won't put up the money."

"The killings, they're coming in pairs now. We ought to have a morgue."

"Who was this guy, Dutch?"

"A friend, a P.I. on a job. Nothing important. Nobody important."

"Why would somebody knock him off?"

"And Waterman, a small-timer. A snitch."

"Snitches don't figure to last long, not anywhere."

"What about Izzy? A stranger in the neighborhood. No enemies, just chasing a runaway wife. It doesn't figure."

"You figure there's a connection, Dutch? Did Ben-Ezra say anything?"

"Izzy used to be a pretty good guy, John Roy."

"Maybe he pushed too hard and somebody got his back up."

"Maybe. Maybe he talked too much, I don't know. He used to talk too much. He was older, slowing down. Just enough left to chase runaway wives."

"Any idea who he was after?"

"Janet Quint." The name almost fell out of Hollinger's mouth. Instead he shook his head.

"Doesn't matter much, does it?" A second name surfaced: Juan Manuel Meléndez Gonzáles. What was it Izzy had said? ". . . he leaves a bloody trail wherever he goes."

"Is there a connection?" Iversen said again.

"Between Waterman and Izzy? They bought it separately, you said. What connection could there be?"

"The bodies are piling up. Gives the place a bad name, Dutch. I'll cover these two, give it my best shot"

"If you don't mind, Izzy was a good friend. We had some good times together. I'd like to take it myself."

"No sweat, pal. There's enough to go around. You need a hand, say the word."

"I'll do that, John Roy."

Dr. Charles Dickey brought a fresh drink from behind the bar to Monte Perrin, and sat next to the ex-football player on the couch. Perrin tasted the drink and indicated his approval.

"All your drinks are perfect, Charles."

"I try."

They sat silently and stiffly for a moment, neither looking at the other. Then Perrin took the other's man's hand in his own.

"Don't," Charles said.

"I've always wanted to. I care for you, Charles."

"I'm not like you, Monte."

"You care for me. You told me you did the last time."

"It was a mistake. One mistake, one lapse. Not a way of life."

Perrin raised Charles's hand to his lips, kissed each knuckle tenderly. "I'm not some raunchy hit-and-miss faggot, Charles. I do truly care for you."

Charles shuddered.

"We can be happy together," Monte said.

Charles went to the bar and freshened his drink. "You better go now, Monte."

"It's not new to you, Charles."

Charles turned as Monte approached, made a small gesture that stopped the other man. "It's not new," he agreed. "It cost me my marriage—"

"Ah, it isn't fair, the way life penalizes people like us. Just for loving."

"No, it isn't fair."

Monte embraced him and very tenderly, very warmly, they kissed. And went arm in arm into the big bedroom.

Ellen Iversen located the Smith & Wesson Police Special in the top drawer of the built-ins in her father's bedroom closet. It felt ponderous in her hand, ominous, and at the same time oddly reassuring. Out of the box of ammunition, she lifted a single bullet, walked back into the kitchen. There, in the hard light of day, she inserted the cartridge, snapped the cylinder into place and spun it around. Spun it again.

Sitting on the floor, back against the wall, she placed a transparent plastic bag over her head. It was oppressively warm inside the plastic bag. She put an inch of the gun barrel into her mouth. The cool taste of metal was unpleasant. She worked the hammer back, counting the clicks, placed her thumb on the trigger.

When it went off, how much pain would there be? Would it hold at a tolerable level or rise to a pitch beyond her ability to deal with it? In answer, she giggled around the muzzle of the pistol. A momentary flash was all that was possible. Then, blackness. Oblivion. An acceptable end to all questions and all answers. No more problems.

Unless.

Unless there was something after death. Some improved form of existence. Perhaps she would find greater, more lasting joys on the other side. A solid string of kicks. A meaningful, lasting high.

She considered her father. How would her suicide affect him? Would it affect him at all? And, if so, for how long? He was not a man to linger over such minor dislocations as a human death. Even that of his only daughter. He existed without regrets or doubts or spiritual anguish. John Roy was a pragmatic man who dealt with things as they were.

She decided that her death would be a triumph for her father. He would be rid of her at last. Free of her

problems and the embarrassment she so often caused
him. He would confront her violent departure with a firm
expression, courage, his chin held high. All man, John
Roy.

She understood that she wanted to live on. Wanted
to find a better and different way to go. She was optimis-
tic about the future and there was so much pleasure and
satisfaction still to be had.

But she wanted to punish her father. Hurt him in
the same way that he had hurt her. Had hurt her mother.

As if seeping up under pressure, the bare bones of
an idea surfaced and began to take shape. Until it turned
itself into a well-formed drama, fully fleshed, a beautiful
thing to see. A work of art, if only she were able to
execute it in all its marvelous ramifications.

She put the pistol back where it belonged and left
her father's house. He would not find her this time, not
until she was ready to be found.

Sam Dickey was taking an early swim. As he cut
through the pool's blue water, he imagined Lawrence
Grant doing his morning laps. What a great splashing of
water. What a great spitting and coughing. All those
rough exhalations and noisy thrashings as if by sound and
physical strength Grant meant to subdue and enslave the
water. Grant versus the pool; and Grant had won the
battle in his mind, as he won all battles in his mind. But
Sam understood that day that Grant had lost the war, as
he lost all wars.

Now, swimming in that same pool, Sam wondered
if Grant knew that his wars all ended in defeat. Or if
he cared. Like the writer or not, appreciate his gifts as an
artist and a man or not, you had to give him this: Grant
never quit being what he wanted to be—the Big Bear.

Sam swam with the rhythmic kick of a trained swimmer, which he was. He swam without effort, riding high
in the water, staying abreast of Hilda Grant. Like her
late husband, she worked much too hard for the results
achieved, dissipating strength and energy above the surface. He might have corrected some of her bad habits,
but he was there to collect rather than dispense information.

"Had enough?" she said after a dozen laps. She was breathing hard.

"Whatever you say."

They dried themselves with beach towels and settled onto Brown Jordan lounges under the warming morning sun. There was iced tea in tall glasses and plenty of cigarets for Hilda. She closed her eyes and smoked.

"Key West has its pleasures," she said after a long silent wait.

"I never cared for the life here."

"Neither did I, at first. But Grant taught me. Now, like him, I feel a part of its history, almost a Conch. Funny, isn't it, people naming themselves after a seashell."

Sam laughed. "They make a chowder out of the conch. They grind up the animal, pulverize it, tenderize it —it's tough as hell—and spice it pretty good, give it a short cook and you've got a damned tasty soup."

She sat up and he looked her over. She was remarkably lean, free from blemish or bulge. Despite a delicate frame, she was wide at the shoulder and round at the hip. Sam had known women twenty years younger who lacked her fine physique.

"There are times you talk like Grant. He cared about the way things were made, or how they tasted and smelled or looked. He wrote that way."

"Teacher to us all."

"He used to deny it, but you're right, he was a teacher. It was there in his sentences and paragraphs. Reading Grant thoroughly was better than four years at an Ivy League college. He knew it, too."

"One good word after another . . ."

"Yes, that's his." She took time to look at him. "There's fuzz on your cheeks, you're too damned thin, you've still got a lot of growing to do."

"I'm twenty-five, I've got the time."

"What have you done with your twenty-five years? Grant said men are made by their experiences. Victories and defeats are good for nothing, except to shape men. Writers have to be men first. Men writers make books."

Words from an Outcast. He really wrote that book right."

"You think you can write as well as he can?" She

watched Sam narrowly. They were sitting facing each other, knees only inches apart.

He looked into her eyes and saw a glint of mockery in them. As if she were able to penetrate his mind, knew his desires, and was laughing at the temerity of them. "I'm a good writer," he said defensively. "But I'm not Lawrence Grant."

"But you'd like to be." He shrugged; she smiled. "You've read all of Grant?"

"Every word. Many, many times. They gave a course in college—only Grant. We dissected every book, every story, every sentence. I can quote you—"

"Can you understand what made him tick?"

"I think so."

"Be certain, always be certain. Can you capture the style of the man, the way his mind worked, his libido, his fears? Can you empathize with his appetites and his rages, the way he perceived the world?"

"Yes."

"Not much conviction there."

"Yes."

"That's better. It sounds better. Can you put words on paper the way he did? Choose the images he would have chosen? The words he would have chosen? Link them up so they read like Grant wrote them? Can you do all of that?"

"I don't understand."

She stood alarmingly close to him, his eyes on a level with the girlish rise of her belly. He had to struggle to keep from taking hold of her, from burying his face in her, from putting himself where Grant had been so many times.

"Grant said you fell short. He said you were talk, back then on Corsica, in Casa Pablo where we all drank chilled rosé wine and ate cheese, and everybody boasted of the great things that lay ahead. Grant saw right through you."

He stood up and backed away in order to let the space between them cushion the rising emotions. "If he said those things, he was wrong."

"Grant was wrong about many things, never about the character of men. Never about writers. You had it in you to become a fair journalist, he told me. Nothing

more. A seeing-eye reproducing bones and dust and thinking that it mattered. Grant said you were small-time. He
had you pegged."

"Bitch," he bit off.

Without a word, she left him, moving without haste
toward the house. At the foot of the gallery, she turned:
"Grant left me with pages filled with words. A journal of
gossip and innuendo and libel. A manuscript worthless to
me. What I want is someone to put it all together, make a
book out of it, a book by Lawrence Grant—" She
was on the gallery almost shouting.

He shouted back. "I'm not a goddamn ghost. I write
my own stuff."

"Grant had you pegged. All shit and no poetry, he
used to say." She took hold of her crotch. "I need a
man with balls and talent and shrewdness. A man willing to take risks . . . Grant had it all. You've got none
of it."

"I can do anything Grant could do, all of it."

She laughed scornfully, legs planted solidly apart,
arms flung out. "You can have it all. The work, the
money, the fame, and me. If you've got guts enough to
come after it . . ."

He started forward.

"No. Not yet. Bring me something you've written.
I'll decide if you can handle this assignment. If you
can—"

"I'm not ready to be read."

"I'll judge."

"What if I say no?"

"Then get out and don't come back."

He hesitated. "I have a hundred pages of a novel.
Rough but solid. I could show them to you—"

"If I approve, you'll read Grant's journal. If you honestly believe you can handle it, we'll work together.
Closely. As closely as literary collaborators can get. Night
and day. As closely as lovers. You'll get everything Grant
ever got, and more. It's what you want, isn't it?"

"Yes," he managed to say. He went forward.

Her upraised hand stopped him. "Bring me your
manuscript. So I can read it and judge you. Go now, get
it now."

"Goddamn," he said, "I will."

There were two maps on the wall over Hollinger's desk. One of the keys stepping their way out of the Gulf of Mexico east and north to the tip of the Florida mainland. And a large street map of Key West. Two red pushpins marked the Sunshine Lane house where Bettyjane and Livia had been murdered. Now he put a blue pushpin in place to indicate where Harry Waterman had died and a yellow pin at the spot where Ben-Ezra had been shot. He studied the map and substituted a blue pin for the yellow; he was not yet convinced that no connection existed between the two murders.

The two women had been killed with a .22 pistol. Harry had been knifed, weapon not found. But Izzy had been shot also. And from what the medical examiners had dug out of him, Hollinger was sure the weapon had been a .22. He expected the ballistics report to show that the same gun had killed all three people. A .22 was an unusual weapon for a killer to use. It lacked the power and killing force most shooters liked; it was a target pistol, mainly. Or a weapon kept by women for their own protection. Though it had little kick, it was accurate at close range, and was comparatively quiet. In the hand of someone efficient and purposeful, it would certainly do the job, as the trio of deaths indicated. Should the weapon prove to be the same one, what then was the connection between Izzy Ben-Ezra and Bettyjane Keely? Hollinger could forge no connecting chain.

Except . . .

Something eluded him. Some insignificant piece of information that had been overlooked, or pushed aside as irrelevant. By the end of the day he had strained his mind to the breaking point and become short-tempered, irritable. He insulted a secretary in the city manager's office and yelled at two uniforms, both of whom were good and reliable men.

Disgusted with his foul mood, he decided to run the poisons out of his body. He went faster than usual for longer stretches until the tension began to drain away. Exhausted at last, he went home and shaved and showered and donned fresh clothing. He drank a beer and returned to City Hall, made some phone calls. To Ben-Ezra's office in San Diego, to the Minneapolis headquarters of Quint Food Supplies, to the New York apartment of Hillary Quint, where a man with an Italian accent answered.

"Mr. Quint?"

"Who is calling, please?"

Hollinger identified himself.

"Just a moment, please. I am the butler. I will see if Mr. Quint is available."

Almost five minutes ticked away on the wall clock at the far end of the room before Quint came onto the phone. He spoke in the petulant fuzzy tones of one who had spent a lifetime indulging himself, whose every wish was automatically a command.

"Isaac Ben-Ezra is dead, Mr. Quint," Hollinger said for starters.

Quint thought that one over. "Are you sure you have the right party, Mr. Hollinger?"

"Sergeant Hollinger," Hollinger reminded him. "Key West Police Department."

"Why are you calling me, Sergeant?"

Hollinger refused to play that game. "Your wife is a doper, Mr. Quint. She's down here now with an operator named Meléndez Gonzáles. Either talk to me now, Mr. Quint, or talk to the newspapers. Murder is involved, drug dealing and using, maybe kidnapping. There's no way to stay out of it. Izzy is dead, I told you. Shot twice, a professional killing. I figure Meléndez Gonzáles got him. Maybe he found out Izzy was closing in on your wife, Janet, Mr. Quint. Maybe Janet was in on the shooting—"

"Oh, no. No, that can't be."

"The point is, I want Izzy's killer."

The voice out of New York was getting shaky, fainter, as if the current was slackening, the connection worsening. "What can I do to help, Sergeant?"

That was much better. "What can you tell me about Meléndez?"

"Meléndez? Why nothing. I never met the man. He was one of my wife's contacts. I knew the name, of course. She always made sure I knew the names. She's very considerae that way. But we never met. Janet would announce her new friend, announce what he could do for her—in a number of different areas—and then disappear. You understand, Sergeant, she wanted me to know everything she was doing. She took great satisfaction in knowing that I knew, knowing how much it pained me."

"But you didn't stop her?"

"How could I? What would you have done?" Hollinger made no attempt to answer the question. His was no exemplary life to hold forth to lesser men. He had not done so well, not in any way. "She went with the assurance that I wanted her back. She went knowing that I would send someone after her, to bring her back. Someone like Izzy. I'm sorry he's dead, Sergeant. I liked him. Did he have a family? I'll send them my condolences, some money. Do you have an address?"

"Izzy was alone," Hollinger said. As he, too, was alone. Going through the motions, the fine, hard edge of life worn away. The past was a collection of discolored memories that possessed no reality. "All alone," he added. "There's nothing you can do now."

"I'm sorry." Quint's voice grew stronger, a rising self-confidence. "What about my wife?"

"That's your problem, isn't it?"

"Don't hang up, Sergeant," Quint said. There was renewed cheerfulness in his manner, as he maneuvered himself onto secure and familiar terrain. "With Ben-Ezra gone—well, somebody must take his place. I want my wife brought back and I'd be willing to pay for that service. Pay very well. You sound like a man who can be depended upon to be discreet in the execution of your duties. You're on the scene, you have official status, the assignment might be a relief from your daily routine and it will be, I promise you, rewarding. What do you say, Sergeant?"

For a cop, temptation was always around, Hollinger reflected. Just open your hand and close your eyes, take whatever was offered. For him, never the big deals. His conscience would never allow it. But the small transgressions that could be overlooked, eventually forgotten: drunk driving by the offspring of the well-connected, an ounce of grass in the pocket of the high school football star, a well-married lady who took delight in performing for porno films. Small falls from official grace, minor chips in his once flawless armor, insignificant gratuities accepted. A little cash, a new suit of clothes, a bottle of booze at Christmas. Never anything big. Nothing really wrong ... nobody's perfect.

But not this time. Not for Quint. Or his wife. This time what he did he would do for Izzy Ben-Ezra, a friend, a colleague, a dead reminder of what all of them had once been like.

"Sorry, Mr. Quint. I've got a heavy work load right now."

"What about my wife?"

"This is a small island, Mr. Quint. Come down and see. You're bound to bump into your wife one way or another."

"Oh," Quint said, as if the idea startled him. "I could never do that ..."

Iversen sat behind the wheel of the Valiant on Boca Chica Key on the backside of the air base, peering into the dark, smoking a cigaret and waiting. Being a cop taught a man how to wait, how to set himself against the anxiety, against the fear or the worry. He'd arrived on time, expecting to be first. These things never went off as scheduled. So he waited and smoked and tried not to think. Occasionally he glanced up into the rearview mirror.

Forty minutes later, another car pulled up. The lights went out and a man got out, leaving someone behind, marked in place by the glow of a cigaret. Iversen opened the door on the passenger side and the man slid in beside him.

"*Buenas noches, Señor Iversen.*" He was a dark-skinned man with the studied movements of a bullfighter and a face and body to match. He smiled a lot and was overly polite; it was his style, but Iversen could not help being bothered by him.

"You're late."

"These affairs do not run by the clock. The boats did not arrive on time and one of the truck drivers was sick and a replacement had to be found."

"Drunk?"

"I think so."

"Don't use him again."

"I did not intend to, *señor.*"

"It went off well, then?"

"There was no trouble. Just that the change in plans made it all a little clumsy."

"I couldn't take any chances. Ben-Ezra might have told Hollinger about the landing at Big Pine."

"Perhaps. Sugarloaf was good, even better, maybe. We rendezvoused up at the point, there is a *laguna*—"

"A lagoon."

"*Sí*. A small inlet, where a dirt road leads to the larger road. It is sheltered by pine trees and was very quiet, very good for our business."

"And the goods?"

"The transfer to the trucks was made without incident, *señor*. Everyone was paid with proper bonuses and the boats are gone again, the shipments on their way north."

"Good." Iversen looked up at the rearview mirror. In the car behind, he saw the glow of the cigaret as it was sucked on. "Is that the woman?"

"She is trustworthy, *señor*. She depends upon me for many of those things that make her happy. She uses heavily and cannot do without."

"No user is trustworthy." He paused, aware of the volatile nature of the man he was talking to. "Hollinger knows your name, Juan."

"How?"

"I don't know. Maybe the P.I. Maybe some other source, but he knows you are with the Quint woman. Somebody else is bound to come after her."

"I will take care of it when the time comes."

"It would be better to take care of it tonight."

"Kill Hollinger?"

"Kill Janet Quint."

"Ah, *señor*. I have grown very fond of her, I would prefer to keep her aound. In the bedroom . . . she is like no one else I have known. Hollinger, I would kill at once, if you wish. But the woman . . . I am not ready for that yet."

"She'll cause trouble."

"I can take care of trouble."

"Some trouble, none of us can handle it. If it was me, I'd get rid of her."

"No, *señor*. But the cop . . . ?"

"Listen to me, Meléndez. On Key West, kill a house-wife, or a Colombian housemaid, kill a Jew private eye or a sneak of a snitch, nobody cares. We don't need 'em, that's the attitude. But wipe out a Conch cop and you'll bring everybody down on our heads. Dutch, he's one of us, so it's hands off."

"And what if he gets close, *señor*?"

Iversen sighed. "Well, things can change, can't they?"

San Miguel de Allende spread lazily over a rocky incline about a mile from the sea, a farming village of no particular distinction. The land in the vicinity was poor and the villagers often were able to grow only enough to feed themselves. Cash crops were almost unknown and many of the young people had left to join the army or to attend university in Havana or to work on richer lands elsewhere.

Still, few people complained. No one went hungry, and if the Revolution had failed to bring more water to the parched lands of the village, it had erected a new school building on the northeast corner where it could be easily seen by everyone. It was a low structure made of wood with a metal roof, the walls brightly painted. There were a field cleared for soccer and three basketball courts. It was more than Batista had ever done for San Miguel.

It was still dark when Figueroa led Paco Valentín along a narrow path up from the shore to the village. In the east, the dull first glow of daylight, and the hoarse cry of a rooster greeted it. Somewhere a dog barked and it was answered by another and someone shouted in Span-ish for the dog to be quiet and let a workingman sleep, or die. The dogs barked some more.

"It is the same as when I was a boy," Paco whis-pered.

"Little changes in such a place."

"I could have come myself. The path is the same, the houses, everything."

"This way is better, safer."

"Hector said there was no danger."

"There are no soldiers in this area. But there are al-ways those willing to take up a rifle for Fidel. Each village has a political and military cadre. They instruct the people in the correct way to think and to live, Fidels' way, the communists' way."

"These people," Paco murmured. "I know them. Politics doesn't concern them. They are farmers, they fish a little, they raise their children."

"Still, it is better to be careful. There, up ahead, your mother's house."

It stood low on the hillside, thick walls of stone and plaster painted white, the roof of old red tiles. Wooden shutters closed off all but one window and a dim light glowed inside.

"I will wait for you here," Figueroa said at the door.

Paco turned to the wooden door without answering, and went inside. Everything the same. The fireplace in one corner, coals still glowing from last night's fire. On the far wall, the ancient gas stove, a chipped enamel sink, a noisy refrigerator. In the center of the room, a rough-hewn table, the social core of the house, of the family. Here he once sat and argued with his father which were superior, American baseball players or Cuban. Here he sat and laughed at Kiki, his brother, twenty years his junior, born three days after his father died of cancer. The old man had been unable to get satisfactory medical care anywhere on the island. Here he sat and informed his mother that he was going up into the mountains to help make a revolution with the lawyer Castro and the Argentine Guevara, and others. Here, too, he had sat and told her that he could no longer support the things Fidel was doing, that he had to fight against the Revolution which was betraying the Cuban people. It seemed as if all of it had happened in another century to somebody else, like an old movie faintly remembered.

He touched the table lightly, then went into his mother's room. Candles flickered on either side of the bed and the old wooden crucifix still hung on the wall above her head. Her hands were folded and her eyes were closed.

Next to the bed, a figure rose up out of a wooden chair. "You're too late, she's dead."

Reflexively, Paco made the sign of the cross. "Kiki . . ." The brothers embraced and kissed and Paco felt the tears running. He pounded softly on his brother's back. "When . . . ?"

"Just past midnight. There was no pain."

"She was sick . . ."

"And very old, tired, Paco."

The big fisherman turned toward the bed and went down on his knees. He held his face in his hands and prayed for his mother's soul to be received gently. *"Ay, mamacita,"* he ended. "I would have come sooner had I known." He stood up and looked down at her.

"You have used two blankets, Kiki. That is good. Mama was never fond of the cold."

Without answering, Kiki led the way back into the front room. There the men embraced again and examined each other.

"Ay, Paco, you are all white-headed and getting old. I kept remembering you as you were."

"Nobody is as he was. But I am still not so old I cannot handle the baby brother."

They talked of how it used to be when the family was complete and living together. They drank thick hot coffee with lots of sugar and smoked and talked of how their mother had worked to raise Kiki to manhood after Paco had left.

"I could not remain in Cuba," he said.

"I could never leave," Kiki replied.

"There is nothing for you here. Fidel has turned against the people. There is no freedom and there will be no future. He must make an arrangement with the United States or he cannot continue. The Soviets will not continue to pour millions of dollars into this island."

"What the Russians do or the Americans do is not important, Paco. What we do is what matters. Cuba is free of tyranny. There is good health, work for all, no whores in Havana and no Yankee gangsters running the casinos. We are one people, free, and we go on."

"I do not want to argue with you, Kiki."

Figueroa knocked at the door and called out, "We must leave soon, *mi capitán.*"

"Who is that?" Kiki wanted to know.

"A friend. He brought me here. Now he needs me to take him back."

"I do not understand."

"We came on my boat."

"I see. You are not here legally?"

"I came to see my mother."

Kiki stood up. "And you have seen her. Now it would be better if you left."

"Ay, Kiki, I feel more a father to you than a brother. I wish you would come along."

"This is where I belong. I teach in the school. I do good for the people, the nation. We all work for the future. We all belong to the future."

Figueroa knocked again. "Paco, it is past time—"

"If it becomes possible," Paco said, "perhaps I will one day come back to see you . . . legally." They shook hands, embraced, and parted. On his way down the hillside, Paco looked back. Kiki stood in the doorway but gave no indication that he saw Paco when he waved.

Halfway back to Key West, Hector offered his condolences to Paco. "I am sorry we could not get there sooner."

"She was very old. But I would have liked to speak with her once more. You accomplished your mission?"

"Everything to my satisfaction. You did well for me, Paco."

"This one time. There will be no other."

"You have always been a valuable asset to the movement, Paco. More valuable than most. I would hate to lose you forever."

They didn't speak again until they had docked in Garrison Bight, and then only to say good-bye. It was over and for the first time Paco considered how easy it had all been. No hint of trouble. So easy. Too easy . . .

Hollinger held the dead phone in his hand as if expecting some special afterword that would put to rest the pervading uneasiness that had taken hold of him recently. Four murders in the space of a very short time. Four murders in a place where one was sufficient to cause a public and political uproar. Four murders which defied any investigative logic he was able to apply.

What was Quint's role in this? Not Hillary, but Janet? For it was she Izzy had been after. And it was she who

was drug-linked, at least in Izzy's mind. It was she who ran
with Meléndez Gonzáles, a known operator.

There seemed to be no connection. Was it just coincidence that Quint was the object of Ben-Ezra's interest?
Was she just a not-so-innocent bystander, uninvolved
in the killings? Did that mean that Meléndez Gonzáles was
also outside these killings? Was there no relationship between the four murders?

No. No, there had to be.

It made sense. But often what made sense in an investigation made no sense at all. The one abiding logic of
police work was that there was no logic to many crimes.
No apparent logic, he amended. Afterwards, the parts of
the puzzle dropped into place and all the answers stood
out in bold letters for everyone to read and comprehend.
Afterward, it all made sense. He shook the questions and
unsatisfactory answers from his head and wiped his mind
clear. There was only one thing left to do: go over the
same ground again.

He went to see Arthur Keely and discovered him at
the side of his swimming pool with a blond woman of
spectacular proportions. Keely made it clear that the visit
was unwelcome.

"My lawyer advises me that I don't have to say a
damned thing to you cops," he began.

Hollinger made an effort not to look at the blond.
"We both want the same thing, I believe."

Keely rubbed the blond's long brown thigh. She
mewed and smiled at Hollinger.

"What do you think that is, Sergeant?"

"To find the person who killed your wife."

"I'm beginning to think that whoever did it did me a
favor."

"Your lawyer would advise you against making that
kind of remark."

"My lawyer says you don't have a case against me."

The blonde stood up and stretched. Her breasts, barely encased in the bikini top, were cantilevered for hard
usage. Hollinger was impressed. She dived into the pool,
splashing water on the detective's tousers.

Keely laughed. "I've got an alibi."

"It won't stand up."

Keely laughed again. "I was with—a lady." A glance at the blonde in the pool. "A different lady."

"The lady in question denies your presence in her company at any time."

Keely paled. "You can't bluff me."

"She's married, right?" Hollinger made it sound authentic. "Never trust a married woman. She cheats on her husband for sex, she'll cheat on you for her reputation. You put your money on a bummer, Keely."

"Damn. She knows my life's on the line. I begged her, the rotten cunt."

"The conventional wisdom at the station house is that you are going up for killing your wife."

"I didn't do it, dammit. Why won't you leave me alone?"

Hollinger made his voice ugly and uneven. "Ken Davis."

"What about him?"

"You don't deny knowing him?"

"The Slim & Gym guy. Sure, I met him once or twice at parties."

"Davis and your wife . . . ?"

"What are you saying?"

"You want to claim you didn't know about them?"

"Know about them! Listen, you have no right to insinuate . . . she's dead, her reputation—"

"Davis and your wife were making it."

"I don't believe you. I— No, no, it's not true."

"The hell it isn't. She was and you knew she was."

"You bastard."

"You knew about it and you killed her for it."

"No."

"And there were others, other men?"

Keely's finely boned face seemed to melt. "She wouldn't stop. I loved her. I really did. I loved her. But she wouldn't stop. I tried not to notice but she began to tell me about it, about what she was doing, who she was doing it with. Everything they did—"

"Until you couldn't stand it any more?"

"No man could stand it. No man would have taken what I took."

"Until you had to kill her?"

Keely seemed startled by the question. "Of course

not," he replied calmly. "I left, that's all. I walked out. There is no reason to let a woman dump on you forever, now is there, Officer?"

"Motive and opportunity," Hollinger said slowly. "What does your lawyer say to that, Mr. Keely?" Hollinger turned to go.

Keely shouted after him. "Let me alone! All of you people, let me alone!"

21

The lawyer's name was Muir. He had the face and build of a recently retired middleweight. Thickening around the middle, but still light on his feet. Even sitting, he appeared catlike and ready to spring.

Acting Assistant Chief Wilbur Huntoon fiddled with a paper clip at his desk and arranged his features in what he hoped was a suitably grim visage. At his left shoulder, tall and handsome, looking the way every cop wanted to look, Acting Lieutenant John Roy Iversen.

Next to Counselor Muir, Arthur Keely, replete in a five-hundred-dollar custom-made garbardine suit, a blue button-down shirt, and a Paisley tie. He looked terrific and felt it. He was, he was convinced, in good hands.

The scene made Hollinger uneasy. Everybody was somber, serious, except Arthur Keely, who smirked as he savored the approach of a delicious victory.

Huntoon cleared his throat. "Counselor Muir is leveling a serious charge against you, Sergeant Hollinger. Against the department."

Hollinger didn't have to be told what was coming.

"It's your show," Huntoon said to Muir.

Muir set his eyes on Hollinger's face in his best courtroom manner. He was no Key West lawyer, Hollinger knew. Probably down from Miami or flown in from Dallas. He listened for some regionalism in his speech that would give it away. But Muir had carefully honed away every hint of an accent; he could've been a radio announcer.

"The rule of law," Muir said, pronouncing each word clearly, as if reluctant to let it escape. "It remains in force from border to border, from coast to coast."

Hollinger glanced over at Huntoon and saw a threatening vacancy in those rheumy eyes. And Iversen gazed stolidly into space as if any human encounter would prove irreparably destructive. Recognition came: Hollinger alone was the target. Or more accurately, the goat staked out as a lure for the scavengers, put forward to deflect attack from others more vulnerable and more powerful.

Muir pontificated in his best courtroom manner, "Key West or the nation's capital, this is a nation of laws, not men."

The words were familiar to all cops. Lawyers made their legal points in the same way, argued from traditional platforms, attacked with old weaponry over recognizable terrain. The differences, Hollinger, hardly listening, remarked to himself, were primarily stylistic. Assumed rage, feigned friendliness, boyish eagerness; all an act, the lawyer's tools. Legal pieceworkers, paid by the performance. Muir played the sophisticated tough guy, forceful, strong, steady. "Get off my client's back!"

Hollinger said nothing. Tactics were what this was about, not guilt or innocence. Pretrial strategy. Establish cause for a possible reversal in a higher court should the verdict go against Keely. Damage police efforts, slow the investigation, inject a large dose for uncertainty into the legal mechanism.

"Harassment," Muir shot out, and went on for three minutes with no loss of wind. He invoked the Constitution, state and federal, the Bill of Rights, three Supreme Court decisions, including *Miranda,* of course. He went on.

He was good, Hollinger gave him that. Sleek and slick, every shift in emphasis, in wording, in tone, carefully considered and done for a purpose. Muir was better than most. He raked the three officers with a fiery, warning glance that told them he was only getting warmed up.

Huntoon shifted in place. He too had heard it all before but he was susceptible to threats, to intimidation, to political pressure.

"Police investigatory procedures require questioning and—"

Muir waved him quiet. "My client's friends have been awakened from their sleep in the middle of the night. They have been warned that their cooperation is expected and given vague threats of police punishment—"

"My men don't make threats."

"Nor do your men always identify themselves."

"Department regulations state—"

"There are phone calls, direct, vicious, sometimes obscene—"

"If you wish to level charges—"

Muir made a derisive sound. "Charge who? And with what?"

"Well, then—"

"Huntoon, we both know what is going on. I want it to stop."

"Want what to stop, Counselor? My men function within the framework of accepted police procedures. Are you asking me to call off a murder investigation— I am sure Mr. Keely wants the person who killed his wife brought to justice as much as we do."

Muir stood up, looked around. "My client is innocent."

"Until proven guilty."

"Exactly."

"His alibi won't stand up, Counselor. There is provable motive and opportunity aplenty."

"All disputable. With the case you have, we'll never see the inside of a courtroom."

"The investigation is not yet over."

"What you call investigation, I call harassment. Car checks. Speeding citations when he is doing twenty-five. Mailbox vandalized. Interruptions when he is entertaining . . . It must cease."

"My men do not—"

"Your man—Sergeant Hollinger here—intruded on my client in the Gondola Restaurant two nights ago while—"

"He was with a known prostitute."

"If the lady commits a crime, arrest her. Don't pass moral judgment on my client or his companions."

"More than two ounces of marijuana was found in the trunk of his car—"

"Liar!" Keely yelled.

"Shut up, Arthur," Muir said. "Charge him, if you want."

"Not for using, Counselor. For killing his wife and the maid. Oh, we'll get him, all right."

"You'll never see the day, Huntoon. Now get off my client's back."

"If you're not satisfied, maybe you'd like to see the chief, tell him your troubles."

Muir allowed himself a thin grin. "Watson's got the office, Huntoon. You've got the power."

Hollinger agreed in silence. Police Chief Henry C. Watson was a flabby man inside and out, a political hack who avoided direct contact with his men whenever possible. There were those who insisted his only function was to serve as bagman for the city manager, but Hollinger doubted that. Surely Watson served other masters as well. Whatever the case, Hollinger wanted no part of it. He never talked about Watson and when others did he found some reason to excuse himself. He wanted to know nothing about payoffs in high places or low.

Huntoon pushed himself to a standing position. He made a visible effort to suck in his belly, to lift his chin, to stand erect. "You wouldn't want to obstruct a police investigation, would you, Counselor?"

"Shit," Muir said, and led Keely out.

"Feisty little terrier," Huntoon said, when they were alone. "Snaps, spits and growls like he means it but all it adds up to is a fart in the wind. Keely did his wife and the maid, so I say get the bastard. Worry him until he breaks. He's gonna be glad to get it off his chest, you'll see." Huntoon studied each of his men before waving a hand in dismissal. "Oh, Iversen, got a minute?"

The door to his office closed, Huntoon leaned back.

"I am working up a great fondness for this office, this job. But I sure do miss Bill Vail."

"A good all-around man."

"Dependable."

"Yes." Iversen brought a number ten envelope out of his pocket.

"That's important. Had his priorities in order. Got things done right. What do you reckon happened to ole Bill?"

"Hate to say it, but I believe he bought it."

"Dead?"

"Dinner for the sharks."

Huntoon sagged in his chair. "Why? Why would anybody do poor old Bill?"

"Some people say he had enemies."

"Don't we all."

"Course, he could be sunning himself in Costa Rica, or some place like that."

Huntoon liked the idea. "Or playing the ponies in Rio."

"With one of those fantastic-looking señoritas."

"Bill always did good with the ladies."

"I always liked Bill."

"Dependable."

"True enough."

"I depend on you now, John Roy."

"I'm your man, Chief."

Huntoon enjoyed the sound of the title. "You're smart, John Roy."

"Kind of you to say so, Chief." Iversen placed the white envelope on the desk. He squared it in front of Huntoon.

"How'd you happen to get onto that shipment of grass, John Roy? A very fortuitous bust."

"One of my snitches."

"The truckload just came rolling off the Overseas Highway onto Key West, and there you were to put the arm on it. Very nice."

"The driver never said a word."

"Almost as if he expected to be busted?"

"You might say that."

"Could be he wanted to be busted."

"Why would he want that, Chief?"

"I hear big dealers turn over part of a shipment to us

now and again. Just to keep us happy, give the public
something to chew on. They turn over one of their guys
and take care of him, his family. Pay him off big when he
gets out of the slammer. Nobody suffers that way, they
say."

"Could be."

"How big was the load?"

"Eight tons."

"That's nice."

"Just a lucky break."

Huntoon touched the white envelope. "The usual?"

"Yes, sir."

"How do you propose to dispose of all that good
grass, John Roy?"

"Burn it, I guess."

"Oh, my, won't that make all the heads in town
mourn. Isn't there a better way?"

"You got a suggestion, Chief?"

"If somebody were to mix a ton of the stuff with some
hay or weed or whatever else is handy and torch it, I
reckon the gulls would get just as big a high as with a full
load."

"Sounds about right to me."

"Well, it's just a suggestion."

"And a good one, Chief."

Huntoon hefted the white envelope. "There's a rumor
going around that the incoming shipment was about four
times eight tons. Anything to that, John Roy?"

Iversen knew when his bluff had been called. He
cleared his throat. He smiled sheepishly. He spread his
hands. Huntoon's cources were obviously very good and he
was not yet prepared to confront the other man. "Twenty-
five tons."

"An accurate count?"

"On the nose."

"Give the story of the bust out to the press, John
Roy. Make it sound good and take all the credit for yourself. Just make sure what doesn't get burned gets out on
the street in a hurry. Don't draw no interest laying
around."

"Yes, sir."

"And this envelope, John Roy. The usual isn't going to

do any more. The unusual is in order, if you follow my drift."

"I'll take care of it as soon as I get word out of Jacksonville."

"Sounds good." Huntoon dropped the envelope into his desk drawer. He spoke without looking up. "Don't much care what a man does to augment his salary. High prices, inflation, taxes. It gets harder and harder to live well. Run some girls, a few hustles, hijackings, whatever else is going down. But never, never forget one thing, John Roy."

"What's that, Chief?"

"I run you, John Roy."

"Never doubted it for a second, Chief."

"One more thing. Stay on Keely's back. Break the filthy motherfucker. He killed those two pathetic women and I want his ass in a permanent sling. Can't let a man get away with murder."

22

Inside the Time Machine, a blast of heavy sound. Of shifting strobes. Of revolving mirrors. Dancers twitched and jerked as if guided by unseen hands. Waitresses in brief, sequined costumes wore devil's maks and bushy tails. The uninitiated discovered to their horror that the terrified faces staring at them were in fact their own reflected images. In the Time Machine contacts were made, severed, and made again without notice. But no one dared be alone for very long.

Hollinger found a stool at the bar and drank a scotch and water and waited for Casey, the barman, to come over.

When he finally did, Casey looked properly regretful and guilty. "I can't help you, Dutch. Not much coming my way lately."

"I'm looking for a lady, Casey, name of Janet Quint. She's with a guy who's called Juan Meléndez Gonzáles. The word is he deals."

"Never heard of them, man."

"But you might?"

"Never know, Dutch."

"You heard about Harry Waterman?"

"Oh, sure, everybody heard."

"And a P.I. named Ben-Ezra?"

"I heard about him, too."

"Ben-Ezra was a friend of mine, Casey. I want whoever wiped him out."

"I wish I could help."

"Okay. Stay with me, Casey. It's smart to do so."

"Ah, Dutch, you know me."

Hollinger returned to his drink. All his sources were dry. Nobody knew anything, or so it was said. Where was Janet Quint at that very moment? What was she up to? Meléndez, Quint and Ben-Ezra. The linkage was weak but worth looking into. He nursed the scotch until someone drilled a forefinger into his spine and said, "Freeze, copper," in a poor imitation of Cagney. "Got you covered."

He swung around to face Annie Russell. Amid all that sound and movement, the blinding color changes, the furious turbulence, she appeared tranquil and rooted in her own center. Perhaps it was those steady green eyes, or the flamboyant orange hair flaring out wildly as if she hadn't combed it recently. Perhaps it was the confidence that came from being a woman aware of her beauty and her maturity, reveling in her own worth.

"Package it," he said.

"What's that?"

"You look special to me."

"Why, Dutch, how you do go on." She looped her arm in his and gazed into his face. "I didn't know you cared."

He led her to a booth in a far corner where the sound was comparatively muted and the flashing lights less obtrusive. A waitress came along and he asked for another scotch and a glass of white wine on ice for Annie.

They talked about how noisy the Time Machine was, and agreed it was difficult to carry on a conversation. He said rock music was hard on the nervous system. She said tranquillity seemed a remote state for the younger generation. He said she was a member of the younger generation. She told him he was a calendar freak. They laughed and went silent until the drinks arrived.

She lifted her glass. "To Cayo Hueso."

"What?"

"That's what the early Spaniards called Key West. Didn't you know, you a Conch?"

"Bone Key," he translated from the Spanish. "Why Bone Key?"

She laughed briefly. "The Calusa Indians occupied some of the keys, a long time ago. Then another tribe moved in and forced the Calusa out. They fled until ahead lay only mangrove swamps. The Calusa decided to make their stand on the last piece of solid ground, and they were slaughtered. The enemy tribe then pulled out, leaving without burying the dead. When the conquistadors started island hopping—Cuba, the Bahamas, into the Caribbean—on the hunt for gold, adventure and Eternal Youth, they landed on this island. They found all those bleached bones of the dead Indians. Therefore—Cayo Hueso."

"It's a nice story. You believe it?"

"Sure. It makes as much sense as any other slice of history."

"Okay, how did Cayo Hueso become Key West?"

"Ahah! You think you've stumped me. Not so, my fine fellow. The British were responsible. Kay-o Wesso, was what the Spanish said the name was. Our British friends turned that into Key West."

"Linguistic imperialism."

"Say, Dutch, are you putting me on?"

"Do you know how Key West became part of the U.S. of A.?"

"Your turn."

"In the early part of the nineteenth century, an Alabaman named Simonton bought the place from Don Juan Pablo Salas, over drinks in Havana. Simonton intended to use the island as a base for a wrecking business. Turned the island into a rough, tough seafaring town."

"Now I'll tell you one. About how Commodore Porter and his Anti-Piratical West Indian Squadron—"

"Good guys and bad guys. We're still playing that game."

She clamped her mouth shut and attended her glass. He did the same and neither one of them spoke until the glasses were empty. He called for another round.

"Why did you call me?" he said, breaking the impasse.

"You are an attractive man." She waited for his reaction.

"Aside from that," he said, unable to keep himself from feeling self-conscious, aware of his too-wide body and his chipped face etched with crevices and hard bulges. He peered at her from eyes set back in deep shadows and spoke in that strangely serrated whisper. "What are you after?"

"I do like you." She spoke with an alarming frankness as if he were expected to accept her words at face value. He was pressed to remember when last he had done that with a woman. With anyone.

"I could be your father."

She tried that on and put it aside. "No way. An older brother, maybe." Her smile was lush and made him want to smile back.

"I don't play games. Why are you here?"

"Games are okay, if both players know the rules. All right, Dutch, I'm a reporter working on a story. You've become one of my best sources."

"What story?"

"Murder and chicanery. Keely and Olvera, Harry Waterman and Isaac Ben-Ezra. What's the connection?"

"There isn't any, as far as I know."

"Maybe you heard, a couple of corpses were found just off Interstate 95 north of Miami. Two guys who are known to operate in the drug trade. Small-time guys, truck drivers. Each one had a bullet in his head."

"So?"

"So they found substantial amounts of Colombian grass on each of them."

"And you think there's a connection . . . ?"

"Both were shot with a twenty-two-caliber pistol. Just like the Keely woman, just like your pal Ben-Ezra."

"Coincidence."

"You know better, Dutch. I'll bet when the ballistics report comes in it'll show the same gun was used in each case."

"Let's wait and see."

"Whatever you say, Dutch." She moved the ice cube in her glass around with the tip of one finger. "You know what's being said in the streets?"

"You tell me." He was mocking her.

"This is business, Dutch."

"Too bad. There goes our grand passion."

"Everything in its place. The pot bust your pal Iversen made: the way I hear it, it was a couple or three times as big as reported."

"Talk is cheap."

"Twenty-five tons or more, I hear."

"Talk."

"Most of it went north on two trucks."

"The two corpses outside Miami, is that what you mean?"

She nodded, watching him.

"Coincidence," he repeated without conviction. "What about the rest of the shipment?"

"Here in town. Being moved right now."

"How could that be? Iversen made the collar, and it's a good one. Eight tons of grass—"

"The grass is being sold on the street and the rest of it disappeared up north."

"Iversen—"

"How well do you know him?"

His face warned her. "Talk softly, lady. There are some things I will not sit still for."

"How well do you know Iversen?" If she was cowed, she gave no sign.

"He's a good cop. Experienced, smarter than most, hard-working. In a pinch, he's there. Always there."

"Are all cops honest?"

"Are all reporters honest?"

"No, Dutch. Nor are all psychiatrists competent. Nor all priests spiritual. And all doctors are not— Dammit, Dutch! You know what I'm saying to you. Keep an open mind. Six people murdered in a matter of days and nothing's being done."

"We're working on it."

"Hah! Burying the true story, most likely."

He stood up. "We don't make the laws. We don't pass judgment. Politicians and judges, they're the ones who do that. But cops have to exist with the daily reality of what life is truly like, and a lot of the time at the risk of our lives."

"I know. I saw what you did to save the Cruz woman. But that gun on your hip. So much power, the ultimate means of coercion."

"If I use the gun, there's a reason."

"Not every cop can say that. Cops can be cruel, brutal, cowardly, corrupt—"

"You don't know anything about it. You remember only the occasional case of police brutality or venality or incompetence or cowardice. Day after day there's courage and dedication by cops. That doesn't register with you people. Day after day, ordinary guys doing extraordinary jobs, doing damn good work, too. You throw up the crud and forget the danger, the hard work. Goddamn, I don't need this . . ." He was moving away.

She hurried after him. "Hey, Dutch, we're just getting to know each other. Wait for me!"

They strolled out to the end of the White Street Fishing Pier and looked out at the Straits of Florida in the night. Talk shifted from one subject to another without purpose, random exchanges, each moving tentatively ahead, picking their way through a thick social underbrush in which neither was at home.

"I could never be a cop," she said, as if continuing some earlier conversation.

"It's what I do."

"And you like it?"

"Sometimes . . . I hate it. Mostly, it's what I do. Once in a while, it delivers a supreme satisfaction and makes me know exactly what I am."

"A cop."

"Yes."

"And you've always been one?"

"For a while, I was a soldier."

She groaned. "Always with a gun."

"When someone else uses a gun, you better get a guy to go in and take it away. A guy who knows how."

"Well, you were too old to be in Nam."

In the darkness he couldn't see her face; he was glad she couldn't see his. He wished he were ten years younger; five, anyway.

"I was there," he said without emphasis.

"Then you killed women and children—"

"I hope not."

"You aren't sure?"

"I hope not, I said." The hardness crept into his voice and she warned herself not to push him too far.

"I was a cop and when Laura left—"

"Laura?"

"My ex-wife."

"Oh."

"So I re-upped. You're right, I was too old but I'd been in before and they made me a captain so they took me back."

She waited before speaking again. "What did you do in the army?" She wanted to know about him, even about those things she didn't like. He was a strange man, keeping a distance between himself and other people, coating himself in a soft mist, camouflaging his true self behind a painted costume.

For a moment, he wasn't going to answer. But he did with an energy that surprised her, told her that the army had been important in his life and, in some way he didn't quite understand, still was.

"I took a leave of absence from the cops and went back. In the Rangers. I was a good soldier, a professional. There was some training and getting used to things again and after a while they sent me over to Nam. I didn't even know who the enemy was. I didn't hate anyone. Just a soldier, you see, responding to orders. They put me out in the field, working with the Montagnards. The Nuangs. A couple of other tribal groups that had moved down out of China over the centuries. They didn't even speak Vietnamese. Good people, honest, hardworking, and exceptionally courageous. They told me who the enemy was."

"And you believed them?"

He spoke without looking at her, the words issued without expression. "The North Viets would come into the villages at night. They stole the men for their army and the women and children for their work force. They killed when killing was in their political interest. They destroyed families when that seemed in order. The tribespeople hated them and that was how I learned who the enemy was, who to hate. No politics, no ideologies, no theories of dominoes created by lofty thinkers in the Pentagon or the State Department. Just some people treating people I knew badly."

"So you killed them?"

"I fought them."

"You killed them."

His eyes glazed over and the chipped face, set in planes of seamed granite, grew stolid. "There was so much fear, so much courage. It was rotten, arms and legs blown away, a man's balls, his face. It came out of nowhere when you least expected it and when you were set and protected in every way you could think of. It was rotten. A palpitating madness that gripped us all and didn't let go of some of us. Yes, I killed. Dealing death is what soldiers are supposed to do."

"You enjoyed killing!"

The glaze dissolved and his eyes turned moist and soft. A shudder wrenched his big body. "You get caught up in what's happening. The awful sound of the killing, the stink of men who are dead and the cries of those who are dying. You keep fighting because that's why you've come to the damned war. You keep fighting because there isn't any choice. You fight for the friends who have fought and been killed, because you don't want to join them."

"You're obsessed with an early death. You want to kill and you wanted to be killed."

He stared at her for a long time until she was unable to hold his eyes any longer. "You're right."

The response surprised her, startled her, made her a little afraid of him; and drawn to him even more.

"I had become a killer. A gun was a natural part of me. Shooting it was natural. Walking into enemy fire was natural. I didn't care if I was shot, if I died. In a way, I would have welcomed death."

"You frighten me."

"Yes. It frightened me when I understood what was happening."

"Is that when you quit the army?"

He shook his head. "I was wounded and hospitalized

and I went back again and fought again. I left something
of myself in Nam."

She looked him over. "What do you mean?"

His face was screwed up. "Sometimes when I'm
alone, I remember. And I hurt. And I miss what I left
behind. Like those amputees who feel pain in the missing
part."

She wanted to touch him, to comfort him, but didn't
dare. "It's hard for me to understand . . ."

"I did things I didn't like. Many of us did. On both
sides, I believe. I discovered so much of myself that I
loathed, that disgusted me."

The words she spoke came out of their own volition.
"You're different now."

"No, not so very different."

"You couldn't walk into enemy fire now."

There was a mocking note in his voice. "I could and I
would. The changes a man makes in himself are small."

"You couldn't kill any more."

"I'm not so sure."

"I am. I am."

"Well," he answered, looking up at the stars. "The
war is over. But I have to tell you, we could have won it."

"Soldier's talk."

"We should have won it."

"More soldier's talk."

"We fought with our hands tied. With our feet tied.
And that's not right. If you send men out to war, you have
to allow them to try and win. We could have won, if they
had allowed us to."

The intensity with which he spoke startled her, almost
convinced her. But it went against all the accepted wisdom
she had listened to and read, all that she believed.

"It doesn't matter any longer," she said softly, as if to
stroke and gentle him.

"Oh," he said with a diffident smile. "It matters, all
right. But there's nothing to be done about it. Come on, I'll
take you home."

She refused to budge. "I'm not ready yet. Everything
I've heard about Nam, like something out of Kafka."

"Make it the *Inferno*." He recited simply, " '. . . I
came to myself in a dark wood where the straight way
was lost.' A lot of us got lost."

She tried to penetrate the darkness, see through to the core of him. She kissed him lightly on the mouth and he made no move to hold her, or respond in any way.

"Maybe you are too old for me," she said, trying to keep it light.

She lived on the second floor of an old two-story building that had been thoroughly renovated, transformed into small apartments. Hers was reached by a black iron staircase. On the second step up, she faced him, a warm, pleased expression on her face. But it was clear she meant him to go no farther.

"This used to be a cigar factory," she said, with a wave of her hand.

"More history? Always a mistake to spend time with a woman who reads."

"Male chauvinist—"

"You're probably right."

"Since you admit it, I forgive you and I'll tell you the story. Six thousand men used to work in the cigar industry in Key West. It was a three-million-dollar-a-year business and in 1890 they turned out one hundred million Key West cigars. All Cubans, you see."

"Thank you for telling me."

"The big migration from Cuba commenced in 1868. This building was put up a few years later."

"Whatever happened to the cigar industry?"

"You're being snide, but I'll tell you anyway. They were induced to move up to Tampa. Labor trouble, government regulations, that sort of thing."

"No more cigar business."

"You don't smoke them?"

"The smell keeps the ladies away."

She cocked her head. "You telling me something, Dutch?"

He tried to remain calm. "Not me." There was a disturbing directness about her at times that left him edgy and uncertain as to what she might say or do next.

Her voice was almost inaudible. "You're the kind of man I could get high on, I think."

He took a step toward her.

"I don't mean now, of course."

"I better go."

"Everything's so damned complicated."

He took a few steps and looked back. "I enjoyed the history lesson."

"See you around, Dutch."

"The likelihood is strong."

She went inside and found an open bottle of Pouilly-Fuissé in the fridge. She sipped a glass and smoked a joint and contemplated the turns her life had taken. Where was she going? She cursed herself for thinking in square terms, for entertaining square visions. All that mattered was where you were. The past was gone, and there was no future.

Tom-tom was asleep when she came to bed but he woke and reached for her. She resisted briefly; she had never been very good at saying no to a man. They made love with the easy familiarity of those who have done it many times. When it was over, Tom-tom lit a cigaret.

"I was with Helen and Marty for a while this afternoon."

"Don't tell me."

"They asked for you. Both of them."

"No, thanks."

"You loved it, for a while."

"For a while."

"It got you free of the old hangups."

"Don't you know the difference between liberation and perversion?"

"Since when are you a moralist?"

"I've had it with that kind of action, Tom-tom."

"And if I haven't?"

"Do anything you want. We're both free operators. That's how it began with us, how it still is."

"What are you telling me?"

She rolled onto her side, back to him. "I want you to split."

"Because of Helen and Marty?"

"Because of them. Because of you. Because of me, mostly. I want to pack it in."

"And if I say no?"

"Then I'll leave."

"It's your place." He considered the situation. "You found another stud?"

"Not yet I haven't."

He reached between her legs.

She protested.

"Look at you, you can't hold still. I always could turn you on."

"I'm trying to break loose, you fool."

"One for the road?"

She freed herself. "This is not a class reunion. It's over. I want to go to sleep. I've got a big day in front of me and I need the rest. There's a cop I mean to get . . ."

23

Ellen spoke into the phone. "I won't be working for you any more."

"I'm so sorry. You did such good work."

"You have so many lovely things."

"What will do you, Ellen?"

"I'm going into another line of work."

24

"Hey, man, you look awful," Paco Valentín said, keeping it light.

Tody Ellis worked up a weak smile. "You oughta see the other guy."

Paco took Tody's hand. "How'd it happen?"

"I got jumped is all. These two dudes, see. They climbed up one side of me and down the other."

"Muggers?"

"That's it, Paco. They didn't take nothing. Not my money, not my watch, not my gold ring. How do you figure it?"

"A couple of nuts. What do the cops think?"

"Some guy was here, asked a lot of questions. But I ain't got a single answer for him. I didn't see the guys. Never had a chance, the way they moved. They were good, Paco. Boom, boom, they took me out."

"You got an enemy, Tody?"

"I'm a lover, man. No, no enemies."

"You're lucky, they could've killed you."

"A concussion, a few lumps, and a busted nose. Seems to me they didn't want to kill me, just put me out of circulation for a while."

"Why would they do that?" Paco's brain began to turn over and he was unhappy with the answers it threw up.

"*¿Quién sabe, amigo?*"

"Yeah. You get a rest."

"Sorry I missed the charter. Go all right?"

"A couple of turkeys. You didn't miss a thing."

"I'll be back on Friday."

"Take the weekend off."

"I don't want to stick you, Paco."

"Everything's okay. I see you around."

"Later, man."

"Yeah."

She reminded him of his wife. The same extended line of hip and shoulder, that same sinuous action when she moved. Her hair was the same color Bettyjane's had been, but cut short and curly. And her breasts were larger, swelling out of the loose-fitting blouse she wore. Her name was Grace and he'd been calling her Princess all night.

They had dinner at Delmonico's and stayed on to kill two bottles of red wine and do some disco dancing. When they went back to the table, they were hot and laughing and clutching at each other. Two men were sitting in their places.

Keely let go of Grace and wiped sweat from his upper lip. "This is my table—"

John Roy Iversen indicated the two empty chairs. "This won't take a minute."

Iversen showed his badge to Grace. "Sit down, miss. Detective Cadoux and I are investigating the murder of Arthur's wife and her maid. Were you acquainted with Arthur's wife, miss?"

"You've got no right!" Keely sputtered.

"Two young women," Iversen said. "Shot dead. Not a nice way to go, is it, miss?"

Grace wet her lips and worked the gaping front of her shirt closed. "It has nothing to do with me."

"Killing gets to be a habit," Cadoux said. He was a stocky man with spaces between his teeth and a quizzical expression on his face.

"That's right," Iversen said. "Chicks should stay clear of a guy who killed his wife."

"I didn't do it!" Keely hissed.

"Boy, you sure have got terrific boobs, miss," Cadoux said. "Don't you think so, John Roy?"

"You a hooker, miss?" Iversen said conversationally.

Grace paled. "I have a very good job. I—"

Keely set himself as if to strike out. "You dirty bastards—"

"Be nice," Iversen said softly. "Unless you want me to break your back." The all-American boy's face lit up with innocence and zeal. "Murder is one thing. Calling police officers names is an entirely different matter. We are still human beings, Arthur."

"I'm getting out of here," Keely said.

"When I'm through with you."

"You ever done time, miss?" Cadoux said.

"Oh!"

"If she's a hooker, I'll bet she's got a record," Iversen said.

"You got a record?" Cadoux added.

"Please . . ." she whimpered. "I don't want any trouble."

"Of course you don't," Iversen said. "She give head, Arthur? I bet you give good head, miss."

"I've seen her hustling on Duval Street," Cadoux said, straining his memory.

"No," she said. She was crying and trying not to. She wiped her eyes and her blouse fell open again.

Cadoux clapped and softly said, "Hurrah!"

Iversen stood up. "Take care of yourself, miss. A man like Arthur here, he could get you into a real bind, if you grasp my meaning. Now you take care of yourself, Arthur. When the trap is sprung, I want you in good working order, aware of what's going down." The detectives left.

Grace's shoulders were jerking, her breath coming in short takes. "Ah, Princess," Arthur said. "You don't want to pay any attention to those guys." He pressed his thighs together, afraid he was going to wet his pants. He excused himself and went to the men's room and emptied his bladder. Then he called his lawyer. Muir said he would take care of everything in the morning. When Arthur got back to the table, the Princess was gone, which really wasn't very nice since he'd paid in advance for nightlong services.

Jimmy Oreskes tapped the manuscript in his lap. "The boy can write."

"When Grant was his age, he'd already published two novels."

"Okay, he's not the Second Coming. But he can do the job that has to be done. His prose is more like Grant than Grant's was in the last few books."

"Then you believe he can do it?"

"There's still the libel problem. Those names—I'm afraid of it, and so will the publishers be."

"Sam had an idea, Jimmy."

"Tell me?"

"He wants to do the journal as fiction, as a novel. Change the names and dramatize the encounters. All those fistfights Grant claims to have had, the women, the trouble with his publishers, his other wives."

"It might work."

"Sex, violence, conflict, and Lawrence Grant's name on the title page. How can it miss?"

"I think you're right. But it must be kept secret. This fellow— What's his name?"

"Sam Dickey."

"He's got to agree to stay behind the scenes. No

written contract, no checks drawn to his name, nothing that would prove he's done the writing."

"He'll agree."

"You can control him?"

"I think so. If you're with me?"

Oreskes thought it through. "Once I met a young agent with the William Morris Agency. Kept saying he was a radical, a revolutionary. Can you imagine a talent agent who is a revolutionary? All he was, of course, was a salesman, hustling after his ten percent. He got rich on the job and opened up his own agency. He's worth millions and still calls himself a revolutionary. He's full of crap, of course. All he wants is his ten percent. All I want is my ten percent."

"Can we make a lot of money, Jimmy?"

"Posthumous novel from Larry Grant. On this one, I'll grab a cool million for the movie rights. The agent, the wife and the ghost. What an unholy trinity we make. A sure thing, I'd say."

"I need a cushion, Jimmy."

A soft knock drew their attention to the front door. She stood up smiling, looking almost girlish again, and virginal, almost virginal. "That will be Sam. I don't think it serves our purpose for you two to meet."

"Hell, no." He was on his feet, moving toward the rear of the house. "I've got a late flight to catch for Miami. I don't need to meet the writer. Tell you the truth, I've never met a writer I really liked."

Teddy's Smoke and Variety Shop was midway between the Gulf and the Atlantic Ocean on Duval Street. On your left, as you entered, a magazine rack; beyond it paperback books. To the right, a glass counter from behind which were sold cigarets and candy, and such sundries as captured Teddy's fancy. Teddy, a man designed to attract almost no attention in any company, worked the cash register. Having lived his life trying to put his hand in someone else's pocket, Teddy trusted nobody; except when he had to.

He greeted Hollinger gloomily. "Evening, Sergeant."

"Hello, Teddy." Hollinger seemed cheerful and that made Teddy nervous; happy cops always meant trouble. His right eye began to twitch. Hollinger went to a table in the rear corner, unattended until a waitress drifted alongside, eyes cast aside as if she were about to commit a mortal sin.

"Yeah?"

"Coffee," he said. "And some key lime pie."

"I don't know if there is any."

"If there is, I'd like a slice."

"Suit yourself."

The waitress went away and Teddy came over, shuffling in place.

"What's up, Dutch?"

"Sit down, Teddy."

"This is my busy time, Dutch. I got to get back up front."

"Besides me, there's one customer in the place and he's looking, not buying. Sit down, Teddy. I'm here on business."

The waitress brought the pie and coffee.

The coffee was watery and the pie was almost sweet. "It's a local delicacy," Hollinger said.

"What?" Teddy kept checking out his register.

"No one's going to crack it while I'm on the job, Teddy. It's not supposed to be green."

"What?"

"Key lime pie, it's supposed to be yellow. This island is famous for it and you're gulling the tourists with green pie."

"What are you talking about?"

"The juice from key limes is colorless, Teddy. Somebody put a green dye in this pie. I'll bet there's a health regulation against it."

"Listen, Dutch . . ." Teddy's eyes glowed triumphantly. "If the damn limes got no color how come the pie's supposed to be *yellow*?"

"Egg yolks."

Teddy didn't know what to say.

"Yeah? How come you know so much about it?"

"Because I've got a couple of key lime trees in my back yard. I make my own pies now and then." He leaned back in his chair, lit a cigaret. "Why is there suddenly such a good supply of grass on the street, Teddy?"

Teddy turned sullen. "Why ask me?"

"You deal, Teddy."

"Not me, Dutch."

"Call me Sergeant. You deal and I know you deal."

Teddy chewed his lip. "Not much, Sergeant. Just a little here and there, just grass, which is good for people and not addictive."

"And against the law. What do you say to a couple of years in jail, Teddy? Maybe three?"

"Ah, Sergeant."

"There's first-rate Colombian on the market. Where did it come from, Reddy?"

"I don't know exactly. There's talk a shipment came in a couple of nights ago."

"There was a bust a couple of nights ago."

"Yeah, well, same thing, isn't it?"

"Don't stop, Teddy."

"There isn't any more." A desperate ring indicated Teddy didn't possess further information. He was a functionary with limited contacts, limited information.

"The word I got is there have been organizational changes. New dealers working the streets. Who do you buy from now, Teddy?"

"Well, that's privileged information, Sergeant. If I went around blabbing—"

Hollinger stood up. "Let's take a look in that cash register of yours, Teddy."

"Sit down, for chrissakes, sit down. Okay," he went on in a hurried whisper. "Uncle Alan is my man."

"Alan Toomay?"

"Yeah. Or Brother Merle. Sometimes I make a call and one of their kids makes a drop."

"Who gets the money?"

"Uncle Alan. Once a week, regularly."

"Uncle Alan isn't the top dog?"

"I guess not."

"Be sure."

"I'm sure."

"What makes you sure?"

"There was some mention of somebody else . . ."

"Name, Teddy?"

"Mister Four, they said."

"Who is Mister Four?"

"I swear I don't know."

"Anything else you'd like to tell me, Teddy?"

"Nothing else, nothing."

"You did good, Teddy."

"Thank you, Sergeant."

"Call me Dutch."

"The Heisler is a gem. You're very good to me, Jake." Graham Welles handed a small package over to Jacob Persky. They strolled without haste along the row of ticket counters in the Miami Airport, two middle-aged travelers attracting no attention as they wasted time until their flight was called.

Persky hefted the package. "Also a locomotive, Graham?"

"It's the B-40, Jake."

The wispy little man shot up his brows in surprise and pleasure. "The Baldwin for the B & O Southwestern? Where did you find it? I will treaure it always."

"It's a kit, Jake."

"Each hour will reinforce our friendship, Graham. You are a good man, the best."

They walked for a while before retracing their steps. "I spoke with a mutual friend recently—Sergio Fernández."

"He's in Florida?"

"No, in Cuba still. He does good work for us."

"A most valuable man. You went to Cuba?"

"Sergio insisted the intelligence he had collected required a certain amount of discussion. He was right."

"Do not keep me in suspense, Graham."

"As you know, a major military strike against Cuba had been planned. Our forces were well equipped and trained, ready to go. Then the government—the United States government—discovered our plans and cracked down on us. That was the end of the invasion plan. Sergio has supplied me with the names of the people—there were three of them in Miami—who betrayed us."

"They must be attended to."

Graham brought a folded piece of yellow paper out of his pocket, handed it over. "The names are written here."

Persky accepted the paper. "I'll attend to it."

"Sergio believes there was one other traitor. A woman. But he has not been able to identify her. He will keep trying, naturally."

"I understand why you went to Cuba yourself."

"There is more. At this very moment, there is in Havana an American trade commission meeting with their Cuban counterparts. This president of ours is determined to support and recognize Castro's regime, give it legitimacy."

"Once that happens—"

"I agree. And that brings me to Sergio's next bit of information. It seems that there is talk of a secret cultural exchange."

"Painters, professors, they can't hurt us."

"I don't agree, Jake. They—historians, journalists, poets, novelists—they can influence men's minds against us and for Fidel. They must be stopped."

Persky grew thoughtful. "A secret exchange, you said?"

"Yes. It seems they're afraid that we might do something to disrupt their plans. The conference is to take place on a certain plantation that formerly belonged to one of our friends."

"Roselli?"

"Roselli."

"Life is funny."

"Yes. Some of the best-known intellectual and academic personalities in the United States and Cuba will gather there."

"And you intend to disrupt the meeting?"

"We'll launch an attack from the sea and kill the Cubans. Teach Castro a lesson. Teach those in this country who—"

Persky interrupted. "No, no. There is a better way. Think it through, Graham. This is a monumental opportunity and we must not miss it. Listen to me, entertain another idea . . ."

Graham attended the other man's every word. Jacob Persky was, after all, a master craftsman in this line of work.

Ken Davis pranced across the wall of mirrors in his exercise room, secure in his solitude. He turned and posed.

He flexed his biceps. He puffed up his pectorals. He admired his hard round buttocks. He was, he concluded, an absolutely superb specimen of the species. Perfect in every way. Focused intently on his own hard, masculine beauty, he failed to hear the door open.

"Looking good, Kenny," John Roy Iversen said, the all-American face glowing.

Davis commanded his muscles to loosen, recede, rest easy under his taut skin. He turned to face the intruder with what he hoped was a confident, pleasant set to his face. Cops as a class made him edgy; this one made him downright uptight. He perceived too much inconsistency in Iversen and a lack of consistency in an officer of the law was a serious and worrisome defect.

"What a nice surprise, Mr. Iversen."

Iversen put his hands on the high balance beam and hoisted himself up to a sitting position, legs dangling. He produced one of his warmest smiles. "All those muscles, Kenny. You ever play football?"

"No, sir. Not football."

"Baseball, basketball, you run track?"

"None of those, Mr. Iversen. I work with weights, that's all."

"I hear you're good with your fists, Kenny. Anything to that?"

"A man has to take care of himself."

"All those muscles—you'd last about thirty seconds with me, Kenny."

"Whatever you say, Mr. Iversen."

"Or any other real man. You would never be much good in a serious mix-up, Kenny. Your kind never is."

"I don't know what you mean."

"I mean you ripped off a couple of lesbians last week —stereo, TV, Zenith Transoceanic, couple of other quick-sale items."

"No, sir, not me. You got the wrong party."

"You dealt the stuff off to Ollie Whiteside up on Marathon."

"There's been some error, Mr. Iversen. I don't go in for house work. I would never—"

"You did the job without proper consent, Kenny.

You have been told that permission is required for any job. Any job. You failed to get permission."

"The timing—"

"Don't crawl, Kenny. Never crawl."

Davis wet his lips. How good would Iversen be in a fight? Davis was better than the detective realized, meaner, braver, and damned good in close.

Iversen, as if reading his mind, smiled thinly. "Try it, Kenny."

"You got me all wrong, Mr. Iversen."

"I got you right, pal. Penny-ante hustlers can make me look bad when they break the rules. Rules are very important, Kenny. On this island, there is only one fence. Sergeant Jackson is your contact. From now on, deal with him."

"I'll make it up to you. I will—"

"Yes, you will." Iversen pushed himself off the balance beam, landing lightly. He possessed the natural grace of an athlete whose body remembered how things were done. "The Keely house, it's yours tonight."

Davis made a face. "What happens at the Keely house?"

"Mess it up a little. Take a helper along. There are paintings, slice 'em up. Gut the furniture, cut up the rugs, go over the joint so that it doesn't look too good."

"The Keely place, I'd feel funny."

"Conscience, bubba? What the hell, you screwed the man's wife, here's your chance to screw him, too . . ."

"You smell sweet."

In his past experiences with women, odors were currency for conversation. He squeezed her thigh.

"And you're smooth. Clean and without hair."

He massaged her belly as if to quiet her.

"Grant always smelled like something had spoiled. Sometimes it was booze. Or sweat. Sometimes it was other women. It's true, the bastard came to me after rutting around in another cunt. Didn't even have the decency to wash himself off."

"Jesus . . . !"

"He gave me syphilis when we were hunting Kodiak bear in Alaska. Contracted it from that French singer who used to be a hooker in Paris. Don't worry, darling

Sam, I'm clean now. Penicillin works wonders. He screwed himself to death."

"That's just talk, Hilda."

"He was with Louise Welles. The Big Bear had been after her for months. First time he made it she put him into his grave."

"Do you know it for a fact?"

"I believe it. You're stronger than you look with your clothes on. Hard, sinewy, and so incredibly young. Nobody is that young any more."

"I'm not so young."

"What's your record for comes in a night?"

"I never counted."

"Grant said every man counted. He insisted every man was in competition with every other man. It wasn't enough to get your gun off, he'd say, you got to be *numero uno*." She laughed softly.

"I'm not ready to challenge the champion, I'm afraid."

"No complaints so far." She licked his throat. "You taste salty, I like it. Grant had to be best at whatever he did. He swore that he once did it twenty-eight times in twenty-four hours, with seven different women."

"My God!"

"My God!"

"When he was twenty-three. He was an awful liar. Last year or so, he could hardly get it up. Obviously he succeeded admirably with Louise." She bent over him, kissing wetly and sniffing. She licked him. "Ah, see! How nice, how very nice it is."

He watched her with growing curiosity. From this angle, she looked like a young girl. Slim, strong, breasts slumping forward but still firm and round. Did she mean it? Was he truly better for her than Grant? What a coup it would be!

Would Louise think so, too? Hilda was right about Grant and Louise, he knew that. But he intended never to reveal that he had been part of the crew summoned to cart the Big Bear's body to a more sedate locale. As his excitement grew, he thought more about Louise Welles and wondered what it would be like to make love to her.

Later, much later: "You can move in here."

"I don't know."

"We'll be working together, we'll be sleeping together. It makes sense."

"I'll think about it."

"Are you turning me down?"

"It's a fine invitation."

"Let me tempt you some more."

"You"—he took a firm hold on her bottom—"you are a reality, no longer a temptation. How good is your arithmetic?"

"My arithmetic?"

"Keep count. I think I've got a shot at the world's record . . ."

Maribelle was waiting on deck with a terrycloth robe. He put it on and she rubbed his hair dry with a towel.

"Ay, Paco, you are loco, I tell you."

"I could use a beer."

She went to the locker and came back with an open bottle. He took a long pull and led the way into his cabin. He pulled off his trunks.

She laughed. "You don't look so big to me now, Paco."

"Blame the water."

"You are the only fisherman I ever knew who enjoyed the sea enough to swim in it."

"It is good exercise."

"It makes you little."

"When it matters, I am big enough."

"¡Ay, qué creído!" She lay back on a bunk on her elbows watching him. "Braggart. How far did you swim this time?"

"A few miles."

"I cannot swim a hundred meters. What is the most you have gone?"

"Twenty miles, maybe."

"Nobody can swim such a great distance."

"Maybe twenty-five." He stretched out beside her, the robe tied tightly.

"I will tell you something. Swimming has never made me tired, not since I was a boy."

"Then how do you know when to stop, when to turn back?"

"I swim. When it gets boring I swim back to land. But never tired."

"You are some fisherman, Paco."

"I try." He reached for her.

She pushed his hands away. "Why am I here? Why do I wait for you? I have a large bed. A real bathroom. Everything in the kitchen. This boat, it is so tiny."

"Ay Maribelle, you insult me when you insult *La Florida*. She is my lover, my life, and my burden. I owe a lot of money on her. You are here because I could not wait to put my hands on you after my swim, that is why."

"You are too old for me, I think."

"You know a younger man who never gets tired?"

"In the sea, you mean?"

"You want to make love in the sea, I am ready for that. Ay, Maribelle, what a body you have!"

"And yours is thick in the center and your hair looks like iron and there are creases in your face. But I tell you something, Paco, there is nothing about you that I don't like."

"How come you have on so many clothes?"

"That's a very good question." She began to undress. "You like to watch, no?"

"I like everything."

"It is good with you, Paco."

"And with you."

When she was naked, she opened his robe. "Ay! That little thing—where did it go?"

He laughed with pride and pleasure.

She murmured lovingly, "That is a weapon. It is a good thing we are not enemies."

"I would not want you to be my enemy, Maribelle."

"I have never been your enemy, not even when you went over to the other side and I remained behind."

"That was not how it was. I saw how life had become under Fidel and I could no longer tolerate it. Many times I spoke to Fidel about the way things were going. To Che. To Raúl. Nothing helped; they did not hear my meaning."

"The society had to be altered drastically, Paco."

"So you kill your own people? So you put them in jail? You cannot keep from being tainted by such matters.

You cannot call yourself a free country when you do such things. Such a society is not a just one."

"Remember, I left Cuba, too."

"Yes, you left."

"After you, but still I went. I left my homeland."

"You were more deeply involved, in a personal way."

"The business with Fidel was over long before then. That was not my reason for leaving."

"Calm yourself, woman. Such a temper."

"Always it is the same with a man. You believe a woman does what she does because of a man. Cuba was finished with me and I with Cuba, that was how it was."

"You went back and did work against Fidel."

"It was necessary."

"Is it still necessary?"

She sighed and her heavy breasts rose and fell and he enjoyed watching the movement. "There is a Maximum Leader, he still wears army clothes after so long, a pistol on his belt— Yes, it is necessary still."

"Yet you remain in the beauty shop?"

"And you take fat old men fishing."

"But if there was a call, if it was necessary . . . ?"

"Then I would go back. I would work or kill, do whatever I could do. But I am not looking for such an assignment."

"Nor I. So you grow rich in the shop."

"And please you, I hope."

"Sometimes when I am in the Gulf and the gulls are flying around calling and the smell of the water is in my head, I make myself remember what it is like to be with you. The way you look and feel and smell. It is a very unsettling pastime when you must run a boat."

"You are a man of strong passions."

"With you only." He went after another beer, offered her the bottle. She took a pull and gave it back. "There is something going on."

She had learned when to press him and when to wait. This time she waited.

"The last charter, Hector was aboard."

"Hector Todaro!"

"Yes."

"*¡Dios mío!* Why is he here?"

"There was a man with him, Figueroa, from Miami. Does the name mean anything to you?"

She shook her head. "What did Hector want?"

"For me to take him to Cuba."

"You?"

"Yes. They said my mother was dying. She was dead when I arrived. I spoke with my brother, Kiki. I felt as if I were his father."

"And Kiki?"

"He asked me to stay, to become a part of the new Cuba."

"They know nothing of life outside, the young ones."

"Nothing."

"Hector," she said slowly. "He is a bad man."

"When there was fighting, he was good to be with."

"He did not take you so you could say a prayer over your mother?"

"He met a man, they talked. I do not know who."

"It is better not to know."

He swallowed some more beer. "The night before we left, Tody Ellis was beaten by two men. It was a very good job. Enough so that Tody had to remain in the hospital. Not so much as to damage him for long."

"Hector?"

"I think so. They did not want a stranger along."

"Hector was always thorough."

"There is much about all this I do not like. Including how easy it was to get inside Cuban waters, to land, and get out again. They did not require *me*. Anyone could have taken them."

"Then why . . . ?"

"It is not ended yet, I think."

"Perhaps you should speak to somebody."

"The Commander, you mean?"

"This business, it does not sound right. He knows about such matters."

"He is retired. He has a young wife to keep him busy. He does not have anything to do with the old days."

"I do not want you to get hurt, Paco. Or killed."

"I will tell you what I think. I think they are planning something bigger, more important, and it is intended that I become a part of it."

"Talk to Mr. Welles, see what he thinks."

"We will see."

"It can do no harm."

"We will see."

"And don't trust Hector. He kills quickly and with much relish."

"I remember."

"Now finish your beer so that I may discover how much of a man you are. Or has the swimming taken too much of your strength away?"

"Poor woman, do you not listen? Swimming has never made me tired. Not for anything, you see?"

"Ay, I see."

25

Acting Assistant Chief Wilbur Huntoon hovered over the paper platter of Key West pinks and smacked his lips. He dipped one of the jumbo shrimps into a fluted cup of sauce—mustard, mayonnaise, horseradish, spices—and delivered it to his mouth, chewing with great powerful bites. He grinned at the two men on the other side of his desk.

"You got to try some of these before you leave Key West, Counselor. They are the best."

"I am registering a complaint," the lawyer, Muir, said.

"Pink gold some folks call 'em. Can't find better shrimp anywhere. Fisherman named Slavador took to trawling at night back in 1949 and discovered the beds. Shrimping was daytime work before that."

"Very interesting, Chief," Muir said. "But I'm here because my client's house was burgled and vandalized last night in a cruel and inhuman fashion."

"Sorry to hear that, Mr. Keely." Huntoon nodded

sympathetically in Arthur's direction, then attacked another shrimp. "Height of the shrimping season, we get as many as five hundred boats prowling our waters. Down from Mobile, Texas, New Orleans, name it. There's plenty for all. Most of it gets processed right here, then shipped out by refrigerated truck. Big business, yes sirree. Sure you won't try one?"

"Fourteen oil paintings were slashed and very effectively destroyed," Muir said.

"Worth millions," Keely added.

Huntoon clucked while he ate. "Mean suckers nowadays. Not like in years past. Then, a man came to rob, he did a job and left. Didn't even carry a weapon. Just a craftsman doing his work. Too bad."

"They took five color television sets."

Huntoon stopped eating. "Now what in the world would anyone want with five TV sets?"

"They took my client's clothing—"

"Even my shaving equipment, my hairbrush."

"Jewelry."

"Rings, chains, bracelets."

"You wear bracelets?" Huntoon said to Keely.

"My wife's."

"Condolences," Huntoon mumbled.

"There is no way to replace those works of art. Not to mention personal mementos, gifts with emotional attachments."

"Insurance?" Huntoon said through a mouthful of shrimp.

"It isn't merely a question of money."

"Burglars get more daring every day."

Muir glowered. "Sounds to me as if you admire them."

"Oh, I wouldn't go that far. Still, in my line of work you develop a certain admiration for professional competence. Can you provide us with a list of the stolen items, Mr. Keely?"

"That may take days—"

"No rush."

Muir said, "My client believes this was no ordinary burglary."

"I agree. A very special job. Carefully planned and executed."

"What I mean is, we believe it was done to cause my client additional personal distress."

"Explain, please."

"My client has been the object of considerable police harassment."

"Now look here, Counselor, unless you care to make specific charges against specific individuals I will not tolerate that kind of talk." Huntoon picked a sliver of shrimp from between his teeth and wiped his mouth with the back of his big red hand. He smiled sheepishly. "Could eat those things all day."

"You've got to put a stop to it."

"As long as it's legal, Counselor."

"The perpetrators must be caught."

"Tell you what I'll do. Put one of my best men on the case—Acting Lieutenant John Roy Iversen. If anybody can get results, Iversen can."

"He's been harassing my client!"

"Not Iversen!"

"It's true. The entire department has been on my back."

"It is the job of the Police Department to investigate, query, inspect, track and ultimately determine the guilt and innocence when a crime has been committed. Police techniques often demand—"

"Assign another man," Muir said.

Huntoon considered the request. "Okay. Sergeant Hollinger. He knows everyone—"

"He's been after me, too."

"What you're saying is that my men may have been a little too zealous in their efforts, I'll speak to them."

"What we want," Muir said, "is for Mr. Keely to be able to leave Key West. His life has become intolerable here. He is followed, annoyed, questioned at delicate moments, not permitted to pursue a normal existence. His friends are pestered and nagged and he has been robbed, threatened over the telephone, and—"

"He stays," Huntoon said.

"Things cannot continue this way, Chief. Let Arthur go up to Miami, that's all. He'll remain there until his presence is required."

"No can do."

"I'll get a court order."

"On a charge of first-degree homicide? You can try, but I know Judge Gunn. You'll get nowhere fast. If it was up to me, Arthur'd be behind bars right this minute."

"I'll go over your head, Huntoon. To the chief. To the city manager."

"I'll have somebody show you where their offices are."

Muir, strutting like a bantam rooster, led Arthur Keely out of the office. When he was alone, Huntoon undid his belt and let his belly expand, emitted a monumental belch. "Jesus," he said, thinking about Iversen. "That sonofabitch is going to spoil everything." He reached for the phone, intending to call the detective on the carpet, but thought better of it. He replaced the phone with a trembling hand and for the first time realized that John Roy scared him half to death.

Duval Street at night was a costume party. Tourists strolled in pairs and groups dipping into souvenir shops and restaurants, checking to see what looked safe. Rock music blared out of bars and here and there some moved in time to the rhythm. Young people in jeans and Mexican shirts hung out doing nothing; killing snakes, as they say. Pretty girls pedaled along on bicycles and an occasional Harley-Davidson polluted the soft night air. A couple of freaks panhandled with elaborate politeness and two pickpockets worked their way along without haste, confident that the tourist trade would always be there.

Uncle Alan, having left his shiny red Ferrari in the parking lot of La Concha, bounced along taking it all in. Duval was his street, home away from home, his place of pleasure and business. Brother Merle materialized out of the Shirt Tale wearing a T-shirt which read:

A KNIGHT TO REMEMBER

They slapped palms and exchanged grins and Merle gave Alan a brown envelope stuffed with money. It disappeared into Alan's jacket. Another envelope appeared and made the return trip.

"Do your number, little brother."

"The business is out there."

"Well, good."

They were about to part when Hollinger crossed the street, circling like a wary dog, stiff-legged and sniffing the air.

"Something going down, boys?"

"Not a thing, Sergeant," Alan said. "Later, Brother Merle."

Merle took two steps when Hollinger grabbed his belt and yanked him backward. Merle squawked and gasped for air.

"Hey, man, that hurt!"

"Stand still, Brother Merle. You, too, Uncle Alan. Until I say otherwise. Let's all move around the corner, and assume the position. Spread those legs, get those arms apart." He frisked Alan, then Merle. "Lookee, lookee. Two fat brown envelopes. What could they contain?" He inspected them. "Money, money, so much money. And this one has a number of little glassine bags, Brother Merle. And, would you believe, there's some white powder in each of them. Aren't these what are known as dime bags, Brother? Dime bags of cocaine? Which sell for ten bucks a snort?"

"I just picked that up off the ground, Dutch. Honest."

"And this bread, Uncle. You pick it up off the ground, too?"

"You have no legal right."

"Shut up." He smiled cheerfully. "I noticed where you parked your car, Alan. Why don't we all stroll over in that direction? I have never frisked a Ferrari up to now."

"Without a warrant, you can't make it stick—"

"I can stick my fist down your throat, Uncle. I can break your head. Maybe kick in your nuts." Again he manufactured that terrible smile. "See how many options are open to a policeman when he allows his imagination free rein?"

"Ah, Dutch, be nice," Alan said.

They arrived at the Ferrari. "What a fine-looking automobile," Hollinger said. "Guess I'll never be able to afford one."

"Take it," Uncle Alan pleaded. "It's yours. A token."

"Is that a bribe, Uncle? I don't take bribes, haven't you heard?" He drove his fist into Alan's midsection and the tall man doubled up, holding himself. "Who is your source, Alan?"

Merle stepped forward. Hollinger lifted his fist and Brother retreated against the Ferrari.

"Somebody's going to give me a name. Which one of you?"

Neither answered. Hollinger hit Merle on the bridge of the nose. The cartilage made a squishy sound and blood began to run. Merle began to sob and held a handkerchief to his nose.

"You broke my nose."

"Police brutality," Alan said.

"Who?" Hollinger said.

"This is a terrible thing you're doing, Dutch," Alan managed to get out. "You must know the answers, you have to."

"Who?"

"We can do business, Dutch. Let's be reasonable, all of us."

"Who?"

"Who do you expect to get?" Merle said weakly.

"The man on the top."

Alan, standing straight now, massaging his solar plexus, shook his head. "If I knew, I wouldn't say. Only the name we hear kicked around."

"Mister Four?"

"If you know, why are you doing this?"

"Who's your contact?"

The two brothers looked at each other. "Tell him," Merle whimpered.

"Tell me."

"Vic Jackson."

Hollinger forced himself to breathe easily. "Sergeant Victor Jackson. One of the uniforms?"

"The same."

"He supplies you?"

"And collects the bread. If there's a hassle, we're supposed to tell him."

"You tell him about this little encounter, Uncle, unless I get there first."

"Ah, Dutch, what are you making waves for? It's all out in the open. You can buy an ounce of grass from

your own people in the prowl cars any night of the week,
except Saturdays. That guy on Saturday nights is straight."

"I'm glad to hear somebody is."

"I thought you were in on it."

"You thought wrong."

"You going to bust us, Dutch?"

"Not if I can't find you."

Uncle Alan looked puzzled. "What do you mean,
Dutch?"

"He means we should split," Merle said.

"I never realized Brother Merle was the smart one
in the family. That's right. Disappear tonight and never
be seen around here again, boys."

"But this is where we live, Dutch."

"No more."

"No more," Merle agreed.

"Uncle?"

"No more, Dutch."

Keely and Muir exchanged concerns and assurances
on Angela Street outside City Hall before going their
separate ways. Keely fell into step a few yards behind a
woman in tight turquoise slacks and studied the muscle
play in her substantial round ass. It was too big for his
taste but it set his imagination on fire; callipygian adventures had lately turned into the ultimate sexual trip for him
and he wondered if this woman, big as she was, would
make herself available. He increased his pace and considered grabbing her butt without preliminary. Would she
shriek in fright? Remain calm and impervious? Would it
turn her on as the idea did him? Thus involved, Keely
remained unaware of the two men who had been follow-
ing him and who now were catching up.

He made up his mind about the woman. He would
strike up a conversation, say something outrageous. Blunt-
ly and obscenely sexual. If she reacted well, he would take
her back to his ruined and filthy house and do it to her on
the floor. Roughly, meanly, showing no mercy, no tender-
ness.

The first of the two men was on his right, bumping
him slightly. "Excuse me," he said automatically.

The man pushed him and Keely protested, his

mind still on the woman ahead. He was falling behind, she was getting away. He couldn't allow that to happen.

The second man yanked Keely by his jacket, spinning him around, hurling him into a narrow walkway between two wooden buildings.

"What's going on?" he said.

The first man slugged him and Keely fell backward against a wall. Then both men were beating him and there was a spreading pain and he tasted blood in his mouth. He went down and felt them kicking him, sharp pains shooting into his hip. He lay still, panting, moaning, while they took his watch, his wallet and a gold chain with hollow links from around his neck. It was his favorite chain, he thought idly, and they might have left him that. Then he lost consciousness.

The Martello towers, East and West, were constructed to protect Key West ocean approaches from Confederate naval vessels. Successful in beating off attacks, the Martello tower was widely used in Europe during the Napoleonic era. Built of brick in a circular pattern, it has a square tower at the center. Should the outer walls be breached, riflemen in the square tower would be able to fire at the invaders through gun slits in the walls. Eight ten- and fifteen-inch Rodman and Columbiad cannons completed the forts' armament.

Neither fort came under attack during the Civil War, and with the end of hostilities their usefulness as strong points was ended also. Today, West Martello houses the Key West Garden Center and its regular and special exhibits are open to the public the year round.

East Martello, situated just outside the airport, contains the Key West Art and Historical Society's Gallery and Museum. Key West's vivid history, from the time of the Calusa Indians to the present, is on permanent exhibition. Locally collected shells are on display, a silver tea set that once belonged to Dr. Samuel Mudd, who set the broken leg of President Abraham Lincoln's assassin, John Wilkes Booth, rails from Flagler's Folly, equipment for cigar making, old bottles found on local beaches, spongehouse tools, replicas of Indian villages, relics from the battleship *Maine* and other historical objects.

Accustomed as he was to the peaceful, unchanging atmosphere of the past, it was with dismay and shock that the curator of East Martello arrived on this particular morning to find the body of a woman lying outside the tower, as if cast out of a car speeding past on Roosevelt Boulevard.

It took him fully five minutes to calm himself enough to phone the police, who confirmed his worst fears: the woman was dead, made so by one bullet in her chest and another in her brain.

In the course of time she would be identified as Janet Quint, but only when her husband consented to visit Key West and confirm Detective Sergeant Hollinger's suspicions.

Hollinger also took it upon himself to have the slugs that killed Janet Quint dug out of her body and sent up to the FBI laboratory in Miami. He was convinced, from the look of them, that they, like the bullets that killed Bettyjane Keely, Livia Olvera and Izzy Ben-Ezra, all came from the same weapon. A .22-caliber pistol.

The FBI technician in Miami agreed, and suggested that in each instance a silencer had been used. Hollinger became increasingly distressed; life was becoming too complicated, troublesome, veering off in directions he had not planned to go.

26

Ellen began drinking at Sloppy Joe's and after a couple moved on to Captain Tony's, where a stout, pink-cheeked tourist bought her one and offered a hundred dollars if she would spend the night with him. She thanked him for the drinks, kissed him on the lobe of his right ear and went over to Rusty's Nail, a discotheque. The Stones were wailing over hidden speakers and people jerked and shuffled and rubbed against each other as if they were alone.

At the bar, Ellen watched the dancers, a vacant expression on her delicate face. After a while she studied her reflection in the mirror behind the bar, thinking about the pink-cheeked tourist and his offer. Wouldn't that blow John Roy's mind, his daughter hustling? It was a well-worn fantasy and she tired to imagine what weird and different feelings it would unloose in her should she go in that direction.

Up at the bar, a tight-assed dude in French jeans was dealing drugs, goods for cash, all in the open. The dealer held his spot and the buyers kept coming. Ellen weighed the pros and cons of making a buy, decided against it. Liquor was a sometime thing with her—not always good, not always productive—but easing her now into an easy, delicious state of suspended reality. She ordered another.

A figure intruded on her private space and the uninvited presence annoyed her, irritated the tranquil sense of apartness she had drifted into. She shifted a couple of stools down the bar. He followed, as she intuited he would. Came on with the smug arrogance of a man who usually got what he wanted.

"Never saw you here before," he confided.

"That's your big news?"

He was attractive, but sinister. His hostile features were craggy, their unevenness enhancing his beauty. His eyes glittered as if coated with layers of plastic and his teeth shone in a challenging snarl. His hair, a red-and-yellow mix, fell almost to his shoulders.

His expression held. "A smart mouth," he drawled. "That's shit in a chick."

She tried to stare him down and gave it up as a bad job, putting her back to him. He made a sound that no one would describe as laughter and said, "Come back, little lady."

She lifted her glass. Before she could drink, his immense hand closed over hers and he drew her around, his face close and mean. She remembered a caution she had read in Kipling a long time ago. Never look into the eyes of the cobra, for the fear will be so great that there can be no escape.

"You a boozer?" he murmured.

She waited until he released her hand. "I'm drinking."

"I'll buy you another."

"No."

He examined her openly. "Good-looking, good mouth. Wide mouths are in. Terrific body, too."

"Next stop—Miss America."

He squinted her way. "You a user?"

"What kind of a question is that?"

"Grass, maybe. Not hard stuff. You don't have the look."

"One for your side."

"I'll score some good grass and we can go somewhere and smoke."

"The cat in the fancy jeans?"

"I own him."

"Own? You can't own people."

He flashed his teeth. "Consider a short-term rental, in that case."

"I'm not so sure about you."

That seemed to please him. "Come on, you, me and the grass. We'll have a party."

"Where is this party going to be?"

"My place. Just moved in, very sharp. You'll like it."

"I don't even know your name."

"Tom-tom."

That made her laugh. "Like in jungle drums? Boom-boom-boom."

"What do you say?"

"I say this for you, you sure are persistent."

"That's my business."

"What business is that?"

"Later. What's your handle?"

She told him and he said it a few times as if trying to taste it. He stood up and spread his hands, for the first time backing off, giving her room. "Come with me?"

"I'm still not sure about you," she said. But she was, sure that he was exactly what she'd been looking for, fantasizing about. Here was a man with answers, a man who would put those formless dreams into a tight, supportive structure.

"Come on," he said, reaching for her hand. "I'll take you where you want to go."

Could he read her mind? "And where's that?"

"Follow the yellow brick road." His grin was engaging, seductive, malevolent. "If you get antsy, you can always split."

"Promise?"

"Sure. We smoke a little. Dance a little . . ."

"And?" She accepted his hand.

"And whatever else happens to come up."

"Don't talk dirty." She slid off the stool.

"Give me one good reason."

She was stuck for an answer.

"Oh, my God!"

"You really turn on."

"Oh, my God, yes."

"When did you start?"

"Don't get personal."

"When?"

She wanted him to know. "Less than a year ago."

"Some chicks start getting it on when they're ten, eleven years old. You must be retarded."

"Thanks."

"How many times? Different guys, I mean."

"Three. But not many times with the first two."

"A lot with number three?"

"Not as much as I wanted."

"Where is he now?"

A vision of John Roy faded into view and she shivered. "What difference does it make?"

"Right on. All that counts is what comes down now. You dig what you got?"

"Put it in jars. Advertise on TV."

"Hey, that's okay. Sell it like toothpaste."

"Keeps a girl from getting nervous."

"There's no chick I can't turn on." He tried not to think about Annie Russell; something special about that one. And strange. Imagine, putting him out in the streets. Weird lady. "No chick ever split on me."

"If you say so."

"Look at this."

"I've already made eye contact at close range."

"Look, dammit!"

"If it makes you happy."

"Big, right?"

"Wow!"

"And in first-class working order."

"You can have my endorsement."

"You're okay— What's your name again?"

She told him, feeling nothing, almost glad he hadn't remembered. Sex with a complete stranger. And no shame, no guilts, nothing but pure body pleasure.

"Ellen," he said. "You are in for a long, happy night. The best ever."

"Nobody's stopping you, Tom-tom."

"And in the morning, I'm gonna lay a little proposition on you."

"Oh. Am I going to like it?" Her heart began to pound faster.

"All fun and games, and piles of bread."

"You haven't said anything bad yet."

"Stay with me, baby, you can't go wrong."

"Maybe you ought to tell me what you've got in mind."

"Later. First I am going to wind you up until you beg me to put you out of your misery. How's this for openers?"

She gave no answer.

He lifted his head. "What's wrong?"

"Nobody ever did that before."

"You're kidding."

"Just a little nibble, a little kiss, that's all."

"Tom-tom provides a full-course dinner."

"Oh!"

"All right?"

"Oh, yes, all right."

"There?"

"Just there . . . and there, too. *There.*"

He laughed as he went, reveling in his craftsmanship. "I," he announced to her palpitating thighs, "am going to play you like a fiddle."

"Music . . . has . . . always . . . turned . . . me . . . on."

"What if I don't like it?"

"You'll love it."

"You're so damned sure."

He took her chin in his hand and squeezed. "Be nice."

"I never even thought about it."

He shoved some eggs and toast into his mouth. They were in the coffee shop of the Motel-by-the-Sea and he was on his second breakfast. She had never seen a man eat so rapidly or so much.

"You're a liar."

She made a move as if to leave.

"Sit down," he commanded. She obeyed. "All chicks think about being hookers. What the hell, they give it away, half the time to guys they don't know. Why not get paid for it? You thought about it."

She had, of course. Had seen it as a way out of her dilemma, an escape, a weapon of revenge. But could she actually do it? Sex had always been something friendly and personal. You did it with someone you liked and if you loved that person, all the better.

"I never made it with a stranger."

"You made it with me an hour after we met."

"I guess so."

"Sure, don't make a big deal out of it. The johns introduce themselves, they pay good, they want a little fun. The money is good and you do what you do for free anyway. Just wait for my calls. I set it up, every trick. No hassles, no sweat, no hard work."

She wet her mouth. "What about the cops?"

"It's taken care of."

"Who else is involved?"

He eyed her warily. "What's that supposed to mean?"

"You report to somebody? I get the feeling you're just a front man."

For a long moment, she thought he was going to hit her. Then he leaned back in his chair and wiped egg off his mouth. "Smart chick. I got a boss, if that's what you mean. He handles everything, the fixes. You just do as you're told. What I tell you."

"And if I don't like it?"

"You love to ball, don't you? You'll like it. Whataya say?"

She hardly hesitated at all. "Okay," she said in a small voice.

He grinned. "Okay. Tonight's the night. There's a dude down from Detroit, a businessman. Auto executive for GM. Lots of bread to spread around. He's out fishing all day and at night he wants to lay around and enjoy himself some more. Okay?"

"What about you and me?" she said, not sure why she bothered to ask. Whatever his response, she knew the truth, perceived the future.

"You and me, babe? We're a team, you don't have to worry."

"I don't like to be hurt."

"So we keep you away from johns who are a little too weird. Okay?"

"I guess so."

"You want to be sure, for starters."

She nodded. "I'm sure."

27

Sam Dickey exulted on the way back to his father's house. A sense of impending triumph enveloped him, made him airy and alive, drenched in well-being. It was all within reach now, all the dreams, the rewards, the happy times, everything he had ever wanted and never dared to believe he could achieve. Soon it would all be his.

He envisioned Hilda Grant. How good it had been to bury himself inside of her, to embrace that still-firm, writhing body. To listen to her passionate moaning, and the words she had spoken against his ear. The most exciting woman he had ever known. What a great sense of his own manhood she had evoked in him. Even now he could taste her flesh and smell the thick womanly odors she gave off.

She reeked of Grant. Reeked of that great fat-laden body, reeked of booze sweated out in bed at night and of semen spent on her belly. He had rubbed his face in every crease and crevice, wherever the Big Bear had put himself. They spoke of it, of his taking Grant's place in her bed, in *her*. Nothing was left out.

She told him bitterly how Grant was and was not. Itemizing his shortcomings as a man, a husband, a lover. She said Sam was better in every way. Every way. The look of him. The feel of him. The way his flesh jerked in response to her caresses.

She drained him.

And went after a little extra.

And found it.

And vowed to do it all over again. And later they talked about the work.

The *work*.

Going down the street, reconstructing all the sensual moments, rolling it around his memory banks, he gave a silent cry: *"Up yours, Lawrence Grant!"* Up yours, all who had scoffed, mocked, disparaged his ambitions. Take that, all who had delivered slights, stigmatized him as a Dreamer rather than a Doer.

"I fuck Hilda Grant!" he almost shouted, and giggled at what the neighbors would think. *"Whatever Grant can do I can do better . . ."*

Was it so? Had Hilda been telling the truth? Had he been the man in bed Grant professed to be and was, only in print?

Why lie? There was nothing to gain.

He would do much more than fuck Grant's wife. He would write Grant's book. Better than anything the dead man could do himself. Could he pull it off? Why not . . . He was young and vigorous, bursting with zeal for the written word. For the perfect sentence. The paragraph. Why not him?

Hadn't he read everything worth reading? All the great ones—James, Dickens, the Russians, Jane Austen, Conrad; the poets, the playwrights. Studied literature:

B.A., Dartmouth; M.A., Northwestern; Ph.D., Yale. English lit, American lit, sixteenth-century Spanish poetry, all the Elizabethans. He knew literature. He knew how to make the ordinary great. He knew and he could do it. He would do it.

What an incredible opportunity.

But Grant would get the credit.

Still, Hilda would know. And the editor, Emerson Gerard. And Jimmy Oreskes, the agent. The publisher would know. Every one of them would be surprised and amazed, delighted to offer him a chance to develop his latent gifts. Soon enough he would become rich, famous, lionized in the literary salons of London, Paris, Brooklyn Heights.

He made a decision. No TV talk shows. Let Mailer and Vidal do their turns as stand-up comics. Let them dance and grin and wear funny intellectual hats for the unwashed; not Sam Dickey. No personal publicity of any kind. No interviews for the Sunday *Times* Book Review. Screw that crap. Sam Dickey and Pynchon, two of a kind. Here is the novel, sir. Publish if you will and allow me to do what I do best: compose, create, write my books.

He increased his pace, kept in enthusiastic motion by the brilliant future that loomed so large. The stained-gray light of dawn lit the horizon by the time he reached his father's house. In the front room, a single lamp burned, a paternal consideration to light his way to bed.

In the kitchen, he gulped cold orange juice from a container that tasted faintly of wax. His thirst quenched, he made his way to the john and emptied his bladder. He took off his clothes and, carrying them, headed for the small room at the back of the house that had been assigned to him.

The door to Charles's bedroom was ajar and Sam looked in. Angelically peaceful in sleep, Sam Dickey's father and Monte Perrin, hands clasped in sated possession.

Still clutching his clothes, Sam fled to the street, where, naked and shivering, he emptied his guts until all that remained was tormenting spasms that threw up nothing.

Arthur Keely went back to his car and discovered that all four tires had been slashed. The car sagged on its rims like a crippled animal, pitiful, helpless, its fate in other hands.

Keely touched the car, as if to comfort it. And seemed to make up his mind. He walked the nine blocks to Aida's bodega and asked for Perez. Aida suggested he try the Emperador, a small Cuban restaurant not far from the Turtle Kraals. Perez was at the bar, a young man with frightened black eyes and a smile that arrived a little later than was natural.

"Can we go somewhere and talk?" Keely said.

"This is a good place to talk," Perez replied.

"I want to do business."

"Ah, business. Why didn't you say so?"

They went to Perez's house, which was littered and dirty and smelled of stale tobacco and beer. There were cards and chips scattered on a round table and a dozen cats watched the two men without moving.

Perez went to a closet and brought out a green duffel bag. "What're you looking for?"

"I don't know exactly."

"That's okay, my friend. I got all kinds of good goods." He began to unload the duffel on the card table. "Don't be embarrassed. People, they don't know much about guns, which is why I am here. It's a service business, you know what I am saying to you? Goods and services, right. That's what America's all about. Tell me how you got in mind to use it? Gonna knock some dude off or what?"

"Oh, no. No, nothing like that. Self-defense, that's all."

"Protection." Obvious approval from Perez. He rubbed his hands together. "In a world so fucked up as this world is you cannot let other people push you all around, ain't that right. Otherwise, can you call yourself a man? You cannot. You are an okay guy, Mr. Keely. Put your eyes on this weapon. This here is a very pleasant piece manufactured by the Colt Firearms Company. It shoots six rounds on a trigger that is not too resistant but not too quick to give up the bullet, if you follow my explanation. This is not what I would call a risky gun. A thirty-two-caliber, but with a much higher impact. Look down the barrel, man, and Pow! What you see is what you shoot. Give it a feel. What I tell you? That's some gun. You like her?"

"I guess so."

"Sure. And I'm asking only one hundred and fifty only. Self-defense. Self-defense is a full-time proposition. You walk the streets, you drive your car, that little lady is your full-time companion. You ask her, she puts out just fine. But what about when you are home, Mr. Keely? When you are in your God-given house, protected by the Constitution and state law against intruders, burglars, murders and rapists. What about then? A man's home is his castle. Got to keep the moat filled with crocodiles and the drawbridge up, ain't that a fact, Mr. Keely? Let me show you a real crocodile."

Out of the green duffel came a twelve-gauge shotgun. "Over and under, Mr. Keely. Boom-boom, blast the dirty mothers away. Quick-loading, too. Break her open just like so, flip out the spent shells and slip in a couple more. At twenty feet you get a spread of shot big enough to wipe a couple of wise guys out."

"How much for both?"

"Mr. Keely, it's a pleasure to do business with you. So for you, a special bargain . . ."

Hollinger sat in his car and waited. Waiting was so much a part of police work, yet he had never been comfortable waiting. All that time for fear to grow and take hold, to make a man question himself, become uncertain about his courage and his ability to do what had to be done. Waiting gave you that rare opportunity to think about yourself, what you were doing with your life, the worth of your commitments, the mistakes you had made, your unfulfilled dreams.

What shit, he thought and closed his mind off. To his right, El Salvador Methodist Church. At this late hour the church doors would be locked and all the parishioners watching Johnny Carson on the tube, having a final *cerveza* before hitting the sack, watching the lizards on the wall catch insects. The island would be overrun were it not for the lizards, he told himself.

A car pulled up behind and stopped. A man got out and walked up to Hollinger's car, got in.

"Hey, bubba, what's so hot it can't wait until a respectable hour? My lady gives me fits when I split in the middle of things, you take my meaning."

"A policeman's work is never done, Victor."

"Ain't it the truth. The creeps are out in force these days. Break-ins by the dozen, trouble in the streets, car thefts . . ."

"And those killings."

"I could use a dozen more uniforms on my watch."

"And all that dope coming down."

Victor Jackson nodded sagely. He was a tall man with a broad, flat face. His features were large, his head massive and devoid of all hair, the results of a childhood disease.

"Don't seem like the citizens are willing to get up the bread for a truly effective police force, Dutch. They ask too much of their cops."

"They ask us to do the job."

"But don't let us free to do it. Rules, regulations, the Supreme Court. No my chile, it ain't easy being a lawman."

Hollinger grunted softly and shifted around to face Jackson. "How do you manage the extra money, Victor?"

Jackson's expression froze. "Meaning what, Dutch?"

"Don't fuck me around, Victor. The bread coming down from outside interests. Safe-deposit boxes, overseas accounts, or the old mattress? I could learn a trick or two from you, Victor."

Jackson's face folded into a relieved grin. "Never can tell about a man. I always figured you were outside of things, Dutch. Too straight to bend, as they say. I use the Bahamas myself. Reliable and easy to get to. Some of the boys bury in their back yards or something. Not me, I want money doing a job for me. How do you handle it, Dutch?"

"Money's always been a problem for me, Victor. Holding on to it, I mean."

"Know what you mean, my pal."

"Victor, you supply the Toomay boys, and I reckon a number of other people. Care to fill me in?"

Tension flowed back into Jackson's flat face. "Supply, Dutch? I don't know what you mean."

"The hell you don't, Victor. We're talking about dope. Answer the question."

Jackson's face grew hard but he failed to meet Hollinger's hard stare. "Maybe you better talk to somebody else, Dutch."

"Sure, Victor, give me a name."

Jackson looked away.

"Mister Four, maybe?" Hollinger persisted. "Another year or two and you ought to be able to hang it up, Victor. Isn't that right. How much do you handle every month? A half-dozen kilos of coke sounds right to me. Maybe more. But Mister Four, he's the smart guy. Doles it out so as not to flood the market. Keeps the prices up and the excess gets shipped up north. Is that the way it works, Victor?"

"I think you're making a mistake, Dutch. You better talk to the man yourself."

"I may have to do that, Victor. First chance I get."

28

Annie Russell perched on the bed, back against the wall, in a cone of light from the small lamp hanging on its own cord from the ceiling. Across her knees, a slab of one-inch plywood and sitting on that the old Hermes 2000 she had purchased secondhand a dozen years before. Or was it longer? Time went so quickly and girlhood, her young womanhood, had disappeared with only faint markers to lead her back along the trail.

Not that it had been so bad. Many good interludes. Many good adventures. Seldom time enough in one place or with one person to be bored. Being bored was a load she did not choose to carry, had fled whenever it raised its bland and ugly head.

Journalism had saved her from boredom. Journalism and the ability to adapt, to make changes; always quick on her feet. "Keep moving," the old vaudeville adage went, "they may start throwing things." How ironic to spend half a life avoiding the dull and the mundane, only to discover that there was less and less in the world that excited her.

Journalism had indeed saved her. It had given life to her sense of history—though she knew very little history, in fact. But she had learned that the past was inexorably connected to the present, gave shape to the future. Everything she had ever heard, or learned, or experienced, was relevant to her work as a reporter. Newspapering dealt with the present and that was the only imperative to which she could freely respond.

With Tom-tom departed, the apartment seemed peculiarly hers again, a place to hide in and be safe. Tom-tom had been a bully, physically and in his head. He enjoyed humiliating people, hurting them whenever possible. But when you stood up to him, Tom-tom backed away, a man on a deliberate journey from nowhere to oblivion.

She read what she had written and tore the page out of the Hermes and inserted another, began again. She was doing a feature story about the American Man's love affair with his own masculinity. "Macho Loves Macho," she intended to call it. It was geared to such violent articles of manliness as war and fighting and football.

Why? Why this overweening concern with men's activities? Why the rough-and-tumble life? Why jocktime? Killing time. Why police work?

Dutch Hollinger was a man.

She should have been born a man. The genes had been disordered, displaced, her parents dismayed. They wanted a boy, found a girl inadequate and insufferable. Broke her father's psychological back when he discovered she'd begun screwing at age fifteen. Broke her mother's pride when she became pregnant at seventeen. Broke her own heart when she submitted herself to an abortionist.

Dutch was a tough nut.

How ironic to long for manhood when she had given so much of herself to women's causes. She was all for Sisterhood, yet she lived in a peculiar and singular manner few women could understand. She clung desperately to that singularity.

Write about Dutch . . .

Hollinger fascinated her. Soldier, cop, weary station-house philosopher.

Would he talk to her? Really open up?

She was professionaly anemic. She yearned to make her mark. To do important work. Build a reputation. Turn her journalism into a high art. She had to follow her star and there were times when the star seemed to have fallen irretrievably into a black hole. She dialed the station house.

"Sergeant Hollinger speaking. May I help you?"

Preoccupied, words slurred from having been spoken so many times. The voice of a man expecting nothing and with not much to give. Not the kind of man a vibrant, driving female wanted. Or desired. Oh, no.

"You overwhelm a girl, Dutch."

"Who is this?"

"Annie Russell."

"Oh."

"Oh," she mimicked. "God, you make me feel wanted."

"I'm on a job."

"You're always on a job."

There was an unnatural silence. "Seems that way. What can I do for you?"

She made her tone crisp and efficient. "I'd like to discuss something with you."

"I'm on my way out."

"I can be there in a few minutes."

"It's a job, I told you."

"Let me come along."

"Impossible—"

"Will you wait till I get there? Please."

"You've got five minutes."

He was at his desk when she arrived. He sat with his feet up, hands clasped behind his head, staring intently at the map on the wall. "Look at that, will you?" He spoke with more heat than she had ever heard from him before.

She checked the map. "So?"

"Here, here and here. All those colored pins. Within

a six-block area. You can walk it through in fifteen minutes and no sweat."

"I don't know what you're talking about, Dutch."

He was on his feet, moving toward the door. "You can wait if you want."

"I thought we were going to talk," she wailed, but he was gone.

Fifteen minutes later, an old man limped into the room, weight balanced precariously on a wooden cane. "Got a cop named Hollinger around here, lady?"

"Out."

"Out where?" The old man's voice was shrill and charged with annoyance, as if he'd been betrayed. "Lookit the joint, not a copper in sight."

She grinned, the green eyes glinting.

"Dutch! What kind of a game is this?"

"Damn! It won't work."

"What are you up to?"

"Some punks have been ripping off old people." He indicated the map again. "I thought I'd give 'em a shot at me."

"It might work, if I come along."

"The hell you say."

"I could make myself look old, too."

"Forget it."

"I need to talk to you."

"Not when I'm working."

"Come on, Dutch, be a pal. An old couple out for their nightly constitutional. Make it all seem very legit. Want to see my rheumatic shuffle?"

He looked forward to a long lonely evening. Some company would make the time pass more quickly. "Okay, let's see what wardrobe I can supply." He left, and returned minutes later with some women's clothing. "Try these for size."

She began to undo the buttons of her blouse.

"Not here!" he cried in alarm. "The ladies' room."

Delighted with his reaction, she went out laughing.

They proceeded along Truman Avenue, down Watson and across United, in a deliberate geriatric shuffle, as if the sidewalks underfoot were the enemy. Once around without attracting any apparent attention.

"We're getting nowhere," Annie complained.

"Slow down. You walk like an old hooker trying to remember how it's done."

She gave him a look of disdain. "That limp is phony. Nobody's going to go for it."

"Listen, this is cop's work. Split anytime you're ready."

"No way. There's a story in this. Maybe dull, but a story anyway."

"When they hit us, you back off. It could get rough."

"If they hit us. And don't worry about me. I know my way around with tough guys."

"I'll bet you do."

"What is that supposed to mean?"

"Keep your voice down."

"I'm not sure you're a nice guy, Dutch."

"I'm on the job, remember?"

"So am I, remember?"

"Too bad you didn't bring a photographer along."

"Oh, there's a Nikon in my purse."

"Always prepared."

"For ever-y-thing."

"Jesus," he muttered disconsolately.

They moved on. Ahead of them, three teenage boys, jiving their way down the street. Tension rippled the skin along Hollinger's spine.

"Stay loose," he cautioned.

"Don't worry about me."

"You keep saying that."

"Well, I mean it."

"Don't look at them. Just keep shuffling."

"Okay, dad."

The teenagers broke ranks. Two of them drifted over to Hollinger's side, the other nearer to Annie. Hollinger stiffened, curled his fingers into fists. The teenagers went past without word or incident, comparing the relative merits of a Big Mac and a Whopper.

"Myself," Annie said with relief, "I go for Big Mac."

"Kids," he answered sullenly. He shouldn't have brought her along.

"They're all animals, right?"

"You're putting words in my mouth."

"Is that a fact!"

"The trouble is you look too damned young."

"The hell I do. I look the part, dammit. Old, decrepit and run-down. I wish I were twenty years younger."

"You're supposed to be playing a part."

"No, I don't wish it. I like it where I am exactly. Mother of God, what a miserable teenager I was. Dutch, old people don't want to be old. It just happens."

"So I noticed."

"You're becoming a crab in your old age."

"Walk, don't talk."

Ten yards later, she said, "What's hot on the Keely killings?"

"Arthur's hot, guilt does that to a man."

"You're so sure of that?"

"I'm not sure about anything, not any more."

"Hey, you're beginning to sound like a real human being, Dutch, instead of a badge who walks in the night."

"Funny lady. Maybe you should be the cop."

She giggled. "Maybe. I love it, I really do."

"Go home, get married, have babies."

"Are you proposing?"

"I'm a three-time loser. I have withdrawn from the marketplace."

"Three wives! Dutch, you fascinate me. You and marriage are not a natural team."

"I've noticed that."

"Well, console yourself, it takes two to tango, as the saying goes."

"I blame myself for my problems."

"A man who believes in individual responsibility. That's unique in our time, Dutch."

"Well, good," he said, "we agree on something." She would never understand how he felt, how he viewed the world. He had been brought up in an age where a man took blame for his errors, the flaws in his character, the various ways he fouled up his own life. A man also took silent credit for the good things he did, knowing that ultimately only he was responsible for his own fate.

She came out of a different time, lived in a different society. Young people today, blame your father if you can't hold a job. Or blame the system, your teachers, blame

God or your ex-wife. Blame men or the economy. Never yourself. Especially not yourself.

Christ, he thought. He had transformed himself into an old-fashioned moralist, a dinosaur, out of place, out of step. He was trapped in some ethical glacier, unable to break free.

"I don't know why," she was saying, "but I really like you."

"Wait till you're asked."

"Tough guy."

No, he wanted to say, setting his teeth against any revelation. Not me, I'm not tough. That was the Old Man. Helmut Walter Hollinger, gut swollen with too much beer drunk, and a heart turned to stone against those who loved him most, needed him most.

Were they so different, father and son? Two stubborn Dutchmen carved out of the same chunk of clay. Men locked into emotional place, willing to sacrifice anything, anyone, rather than admit their own vulnerability.

There was a difference. Dutch's father had not been a strong man. Oh, all the outer accoutrements were present—the great, powerful body, the willingness to strike out, the intimidating temper, the great voice used as a weapon. But no real strength. In the face of human trouble, in the face of someone else's torment and need, Helmut always withdrew, retreated, ran like hell for the hills. Until one day he kept going, and never came back. Never called. Never wrote. Never again made his existence known to wife or son.

Ten years old and no father, Dutch remembered. How much that had hurt. And frightened him. And made him wonder what he had done wrong to deserve such punishment. It was not until much later that the chilling anger set in, the hard knot of fury that made him want to destroy his father, to kill him, to make him suffer.

"You know what I think, Dutch?"

He brought himself back to the present, stared at her as if seeing her for the first time. "You're going to tell me."

"I think we might just get it on."

"Forget it."

"We might even fall in love."

"I've been there."

"Did it hurt so much?"

She had a way of summoning up ancient images, unsettling memories, the bitter past. Hurt? Hell, yes, it hurt. A deep, rampaging hurt that left unhealed wounds in its wake. Sometimes the anguish sliced into him with enough force and cruelty to make him want to cry. But crying was something Dutch Hollinger never did. Except . . .

"Who knows, we might move in together."

"Get married? You and me?"

"Who said anything about getting married? Marriage isn't necessary. Two people can just live together, love each other—"

"Screw," he said harshly.

"Sure. Have sex. Make love. Get it on. We could even have babies."

Babies cry.

Cry over that sweet little boy. That happy, active creature that had been Hollinger's son. His only son, only child, his baby.

They called him Willy, after Laura's father. A bright-eyed boy with freckles across his nose as if painted into place. Cuddly and trying so hard to be older than he was, trying to be brave when he hurt himself, trying not to be a baby any more. He had been just four years old when the virus hit him. A few sneezes, a runny nose; nothing to be concerned about. And eighteen hours later, that precious child was gone, dead, killed by an unidentified virus that no one could explain or fight or pray away.

Hollinger had cried often in the weeks after that. And now, thinking of Willy, he felt his eyes moist over and he blinked them clear. He avoided looking at the woman at his side; in some strange way she managed to get inside of him, activate all the carefully concealed and delicate circuits, raise up specters out of his past. He made himself a promise: watch her carefully.

"You'd make some kid a terrific father," she told him. "Strong, warm, loving, with lots of smart things to tell him."

"Keep quiet and keep walking."

"You've stopped limping."

She was right. He put the limp back into his act. On their fourth trip around, she grew impatient.

"This isn't working, Dutch."

"Time is on our side."

"I'm getting tired."

"A runner like you?"

"There is a psychological difference between running and walking."

"I didn't notice."

"What have you noticed, Dutch?" She craved a personal response from him, some verbal intimacy, a hint of interest. And she was ashamed that she felt compelled to tempt him this way.

He said flatly, "I've noticed that cleanliness is next door to godliness and honesty is an Allstate policy."

She suppressed a laugh. "I am not sure where you are at, Sergeant."

"Just an old cop plugging along."

"Cops," she drawled.

"Don't generalize."

"Color them blue and hang a gun on their hips."

"All the same, right?"

"Right."

"Wrong."

"That's a cop's point of view."

"Bingo! All my life I've listened to it, cops are the same. Cops are crooks. Cops are freeloaders."

"Say it ain't so, Dutch . . ."

"Depends. The person, the city you're working, the degree of crookedness in that city. Training, education, the mentality of the chief, the morality of the politicians, not to mention the citizens in their purity."

"You've thought about it."

"A lot, lady."

"Limp, Dutch."

He did. "Cops exist pretty close to the basic rhythms of life. A good cop is steeped in the job, a good cop thinks about the day-to-day problems, a good cop gets stirred up over the ethical questions."

"I was right, you are a moralist."

"Every cop is. Honesty, courage, guilt; plumbers needn't trouble themselves with such cosmic concerns. Or carpenters. Most jobs, you can turn away from such unsettling subjects."

"But not a cop," she returned softly.

"Not a cop."

"Dutch, about making babies . . . ?"

"Hold on to my arm, keep still, and try to look like you're on your last legs."

"Everyone says I've got terrific legs."

"Keep 'em moving."

"Cops," she drawled.

They were back on Watson for the fifth time, closing in on Virginia, when two men materialized from out of the shadows, separating, making their approach from different angles.

Annie squeezed Hollinger's big bicep. "Oh, here it comes!"

He shoved her aside. "Hold it right there."

"Don't move, mister!" one of them shouted.

Hollinger saw a flash of blue in the soft glow of the corner street lamp. He swore softly.

"Take it easy, men." He reached for his badge.

"Freeze!" the second man yelled, reaching for his pistol. "We're cops."

"It's a damned convention," Annie said. "So are we! At least, he is."

"What's that!"

Service revolvers and badge made it out in a dead heat. The larger of the two uniforms edged closer, squinting suspiciously. "Hey, Seymour, he is a cop."

"You're sure, Charley?"

"Sure he's sure, asshole," Hollinger snarled. "Put those damn guns away or I'll get you flopped over to collecting garbage."

"Well, I'll be damned," Charley said, holstering his pistol. "It's Sergeant Hollinger."

"Hi, Dutch," Seymour said.

"Batman and Robin," Hollinger snarled. "Look at those poor-ass Conchs, without brains enough to get in out of the rain."

"Fearless crime fighters," Annie said. "I could do a story about them."

"You'll set police work back a century."

Seymour was grinning as he came closer. "Gee whiz, Dutch, that's a fantastic makeup job. You undercover or something?"

"No, I'm just trying to find out what it feels like to be a hundred and two years old. Can you believe these guys?"

"We got a complaint," Charley explained.

"I got a complaint," Hollinger said menacingly.

"Aw, Dutch." Seymour eyed Annie speculatively. "You gonna introduce us to the lady?"

Hollinger straightened up and rubbed his back. "Not a night for catching muggers, I reckon."

"Win some, lose some," Seymour said.

"Please, Dutch," Annie said, "can we leave the scene of the crime?"

Hollinger offered her his arm and off they went into the night, a sprightly old couple out for a bit of a stroll. "Cops," he muttered, when they were out of earshot.

"You can stop limping now," she said.

"I'll take you home."

"What a rotten idea."

"Okay. I'll buy you something to eat."

"I'm not hungry."

"Want a drink?"

"Is that the best you can do?"

"Give me a minute, I'll come up with something."

"I'm not encouarged."

"What do you want?"

"I think we ought to get it on."

"What?"

"It's where we're headed, isn't it?"

"You are weird."

"You do like women, don't you?"

"You're not exactly shy."

"Does shy turn you on?"

"You're a unique case, I'll tell you that."

"Okay, go ahead."

"What are you talking about?"

"You believe in the man's inalienable right to initiate the action, don't you? Go ahead. Initiate."

"Now you wait justagoddamn minute!"

"Misplaced anger will get you nowhere, Dutch."

"Don't lay that on me."

"Okay, then."

"What?"

"Do it."

"Oh, yes. Well, sure. Why don't we go over to my place for a nightcap?"

"We haven't known each other very long. Do you think it's proper?"

"What?"

"Can I—you know, trust you?"

"What?"

"After all, a lady has to consider her reputation."

"What the hell kind of a game are you running? First you—"

"Yes."

"What's that?"

"I said, 'Yes.' "

"Oh. Well, then . . ."

"Shall we go?"

"Yes."

On Hollinger's old couch, positioned obliquely so as not to confront each other, carefully arranged to make no physical contact, avoiding eye contact, Annie and Dutch sipped Dubonnet over ice. They produced considerable small talk, thus establishing a secure emotional separation, masking off vulnerabilities, tucking fears away behind rhetorical barriers.

Nevertheless, Hollinger rode a rising tide of resentment. He was too old, too charged with street smarts, too worldly-wise, to have permitted himself to be sucked into this stressful engagement. He plotted retreat, withdrawal a cunning getaway, increasingly desperate to be safely and comfortably alone. He itched for solitude but was unable to scratch. He shifted around. Anxious. Antsy. "Damn," he complained, wishing he'd kept quiet.

"What?" She inspected him with languid interest, as if comforted by his unease.

"We're not making any sense."

She put her glass aside. "Must we be sensible?"

One brief look, and his eyes swerved away.

She spoke intimately. "Are we going to get it on, Dutch?"

He folded his hands in his lap like an obedient schoolboy, and faced to the front. "You have a truly romantic nature."

She presented a cheerful visage, pleased with herself and with him. "Too honest for you, huh?"

"Let it all hang out, you mean. Save it."

"Okay if I smoke?"

He shrugged.

"Not a cigaret."

"A joint?"

She brought a thin brown cigaret out of her pocket, displayed it.

"Suit yourself."

She lit up, sucked hard. "You angry with me, Dutch? You have no cause to be."

"Don't be silly."

She offered him the joint. "Maybe I shouldn't have come here."

"I asked you, didn't I?"

"I think I pushed you into asking. I think the timing may not be right."

He glared at the smoldering weed. "A cop, and you smoke grass in my place."

"Please, Mr. Policeman, don't arrest me."

That made him smile. "No easy busts for me."

"Is that it, Dutch? Am I too easy for you? Have I usurped some of your precious male prerogatives?"

A quick flush of anger washed away, replaced by an unaccustomed gentleness. "It's not that way at all, Annie. Would you believe it—I'm scared."

Her eyes grew large and moist. She kissed him lightly on the mouth and when he failed to react, she leaned away. "You are a special man, Dutch. I haven't known many like you, maybe none. It's reassuring that you're scared, that you're not sure of yourself. Or of me. I like it, Dutch, that you're an honest-to-God human being and not one of those sex machines."

Annie; so charged with sexuality, so open and free. She must have known many men who were sex machines, and loved them for being so. He wiped the thought from his mind, the dirty pictures; and loathed himself for thinking that way.

"I honestly believe we are going to be okay with each other," she told him.

"I'm not so sure."

Her grin angled upward. "Nobody's a hundred percent sure."

"Women keep quitting on a man, he begins to wonder about himself."

She kissed him again, a little less casually, a little more insistent. Her hand rested on his chest, fingers drumming softly in reflex. She extended the joint.

"Go on, take a hit."

"Doesn't do much for me."

"You've tried it?"

"A couple of times."

"You are full of surprises." She dropped the joint into an ashtray and her arms circled his neck. "Come on, Dutch, give a girl a hug."

He wasn't convinced he wanted to go on with this, wasn't certain he was capable of meeting the demands Annie, in her essence, made of him. Obligations to other people, people close to you, were so difficult to fulfill; his past was a crooked trail of disappointments. It was easier being a good cop than a good man: keep your distance, avoid involvements with victims and bad guys alike. A secret part of him was wearier than he dared to admit; he was ready to retire, from all of it.

They kissed again; he stroked her solid, pliable body, tracing soft curves to where they gracefully dissolved. Admit it, Dutch; the lady is perfect; nothing wrong anyplace.

"I'm sorry," he said, fear taking hold in his chest, and at the same time ashamed.

"What are you talking about?"

"Nothing is going down."

"Ah, Dutch. Don't make waves. Just let it happen and it will. We like each other, we really like each other. I can tell, Dutch."

"Love conquers all, is that it?"

"You're a cynic."

"It goes with the job."

"In case you haven't noticed, this is your free time." She stroked his cheek, his neck, his chest. "You are the most man I've ever known."

"Sooner or later, a man gets broken—"

"A little bent, that's all. It's only natural. Here, let me—"

He lifted her hand away.

"Ah, don't put limitations on me. I feel so much, Dutch . . . affection. I like you, you know what I'm saying to you? I like you." She kissed him for a very long time.

"I suppose lots of women have told you what a first-rate kisser you are."

"Best on the block . . ."

"I mean it . . ."

She nibbled at his lip, licked the corners of his mouth, pushed her tongue against his teeth until they parted to admit her. Without warning his arms closed around her with such force that she began to worry about her rib cage. His grip loosened and one hand found its way to her breast. She clung to him, enjoying the sensations unloosed in her body, waiting for the tensions in him to ease. When he reached under her shirt, when his great fingers touched her bare breast, she shivered and her nipple grew hard and erect and she pressed up to meet pressure with pressure.

"So good, good . . ."

For him, too; as if for the first time. Her breast; she *fit*. The full, firm weight, the diffused warmth, the silky skin. Small, furry sounds in her throat and the extraordinary look of her roused him further.

Her hand was on his thigh, then his belly, exploring, digging in, going on. Fear gave way to desire and she went between his great strong legs and for an extended moment she expected a rough refusal, anger. But it wasn't like that.

"You are a new kind of woman for me."

"I think we talk too much."

The talking fell off soon after and the kissing increased, kissing of such an intensity and variety that Hollinger made a mental note to catalog this remarkable experience. Annie used her body, her limbs, her hands, her lips with immense skill and a refined delicacy that delivered a series of tiny shocks to Hollinger's nervous system. Skittering bursts of pleasure suffused his middle and caused his muscles to harden and grow stiff.

"Ahh, look at you."

She bent over him, crooning wordlessly and planting soft, moist kisses wherever her mouth came to rest. She worked his clothes away and filled herself with him, lost in the act of joy given and received.

"Annie, you are so good for me. So very good . . ."

In time, they became naked and moved without effort to his bed, where they came up against each other in easy harmony. There was no thinking now, only the feeling as each ministered to the other's flesh, turning, twisting, adjusting until she reached to guide him.

Abruptly she was filled as never before. A profound emotional gratification for so long longed for. His insistent bulk, his great size and strength, vaguely frightening and more exciting for being so; and the pulsating hardness, the startling dimensions, the heat radiating up into her belly. Her need intensified and drove her body into wilder searches for relief. She rolled and rose and fell back, panting in a deeper desperation.

He pressed down. In her. Struggling to cross distant borders, to penetrate secret niches, to invest them with his strength, his gift for life. Pounding powerfully as she, without words, urged him on. No concern now, no fear. Only a vague awareness of himself as a corporeal being; he was elevated to planes of delight always denied him in the past.

There was a swift gathering. A focus. A frozen instant when all of him drew down to one place, one clearly defined dot of existence. Muscle and joints, sinews, nerves, the flow of his blood, all waited. At last he plunged and she took all of him and locked arms and legs around him lest he fall away from that ecstatic peak and damage them both.

Much later, he reached back to the way it had been with awe and gratitude.

"So . . . nice," he said.

"Better than nice."

"A nice way to end the day."

"A nice way to begin . . . something."

A faint alarm went off in his mind; that was something to think about.

The house was empty.

Iversen knew it was empty, that Ellen had gone. For good. An empty house gave off an oppressive aura, as if touched by a communicable disease. Treatment was in order, some specialist brought in to bring it back to good health, to put things in working order once more.

Iversen felt Ellen's hatred as a palapable object lying against his skin, making him uneasy, and he longed to scratch it away.

He stripped off his clothes. Shirt, underwear, socks, into the hamper. Shoes put back in place, lined squarely up with the twenty or so other pairs he owned. Slacks and jacket placed across a chair, ready for the cleaners. Iversen never wore an item more than once without having it sanitized.

He took a shower. He wet himself down thoroughly. Letting the spray play at length into his armpits, into his crotch, spreading his buttocks to its hot sting. He soaped his body and rinsed. Next his hair, using a delicate baby shampoo that promised cleanliness without harm to even a single follicle. He dried himself with an oversize bath towel, patting not rubbing.

He shaved. A slow, careful process. And applied a medicated lotion that stung his cheeks and left them glowing, smooth and healthy. He examined his body in the mirror. A slight thickening at the waist betrayed the advancing years; otherwise, he was hard, flat, without unsightly hair.

Using cuticle scissors, and a small hand mirror, he trimmed his pubic hair, brushed away the excess. He walked naked into his bedroom and neatly folded the comforter back, exposing the cool white sheet. From the rosewood chest on the far wall, he brought forth the panties and bra. Both were delicately constructed, a pale pink color edged in black, and they belonged to her. He arranged them suitably in place on the double bed, lay down alongside.

He stared at the ceiling until the whiteness began to blur and his brain emptied of all thoughts and he lapsed into a state of tranquillity seldom available to him. For a long time, arms extended along his sides, palms up, fingers curled, he lay without moving.

Until a faint vision shattered the white void. A woman appeared, drifted closer until he was able to recognize his wife, Clarice, her face closed and sullen. At once she was naked, that lean, perfect body displaying itself in a tormenting dance. Thrusting herself forward, so that he was forced to watch her small pyramidal breasts as they shimmered in the soft light, and spreading her thighs and directing his vision between them.

A soft animal sound came out of him and he cupped himself with his hand, as much for security as for passion.

But his hand could not encase the thick, growing member that suddenly was central to his being. His fingers fluttered in counterpoint to the Clarice who was in his head.

She made coarse gestures, executing broad, obscene movements. Using her hands on herself. Floating backward whenever he reached for her. Mocking him, questioning his manhood, daring him to follow. His fingers bent around himself, stroking in tempo to Clarice's erotic choreography. He cried out for her to come to him, to give him what only she could give, to help him. Taunting laughter, and she went faster.

Faster.

Restraint was futile. For he had slipped into the throes of a desire so great and so overwhelming that he could no longer withstand its demands. He rolled onto his side and pulled the pink-and-black panties to himself as the spasms began ...

And at that moment Clarice no longer danced in his head. Another had taken her place. The body the same, the face so alike, but sweet and youthful, unspoiled.

"Ellen," he muttered, his body jerking into severe muscular contraction, a spastic creature out of control, crying out in despair and fulfillment, wanting it to go on and loathing his weakness. "Ellen," he said again, just before he fell into the dark oblivion of sleep. "Ellen ..."

29

Arthur Keely placed himself very gingerly on the polished slate floor of the entry hall of the ruined house, his back to the wall. It was the only space that had not been violated by the vandals. Except the bathrooms, of course. But the bathrooms were all shining marble and tile, much too impersonal for him at this time.

His eyes were fixed on the front door. At any moment they would come crashing in on his life once again. They would nag and pester him, they would beat and rob and threaten him. They would hassle him forever, embarrass and shame him in front of his friends. All for their pleasure and his pain.

No more. His mind was made up. He picked the shotgun off his lap and pointed it at the door. Pow! Pow! Let them come, if they dared.

He drew the .32-caliber pistol from his belt and hefted it, twirled the cylinder, aimed it, finally put it on the floor between his legs, within easy reach. He turned his attention back to the shotgun. He had never owned such a weapon before, had never fired a shotgun. The barrels were smooth, giving off a dark dull glow, much longer than he had supposed they would be. He raised the muzzle and inhaled the faint thick scent of gun oil. He touched the tip of his tongue to the cold metal and was surprised to discover an adhesive quality, as if the shotgun insisted on his close and continued attention.

He inserted both barrels into his mouth and peered down their length. How far away the trigger assembly. He raised his knees and rested the fine wooden stock on them, leveling the weapon. He located the trigger with his thumb. Pow! Pow!

Always at him, the bastards, allowing him no respite. Making him feel as if he were the cause of all the world's troubles. Making him feel bad. "Well, fuck you, boy," he said around the shotgun and pulled down on the trigger. And in that blinding, deafening, anguished moment, as his brains were splattered against the immaculate and expensive wall that Bettyjane had herself designed and loved so much, he realized that he had made a mistake.

The worst mistake of his life.

PART
IV

30

"No way."

Bucky Maddox squirmed around in his old oak chair as if trying to screw himself into permanent possession. He heaved his long legs onto the desk, crossed them at the ankles and promptly uncrossed them. He made his doleful face longer, the look expressing pain far worse than he actually felt.

"Don't oppose me, Annie. I know what's best for you."

"I'm a big girl now."

"You're a journalistic child."

"Oh, Christ, Bucky, I'm thirty-five years old—"

"I thought you were thirty-six."

"You have a nasty streak. Thirty-*five* and a reporter for a dozen years. I'm overworked, underpaid and, like most women, without any real power. I want to follow through on the Keely case."

"He's dead, it's over."

"He killed himself, but I don't believe he killed his wife."

"Forget it, kiddo. Go with Grant."

She made a face. "I never could stand that overblown ego with a typewriter."

"There's a story there."

"Give it to Henry Gerber."

"Uh-uh. You."

"Gerber loved Grant, all that muscles-and-balls crap."

279

"Think about it. A major literary figure takes the count under less than clear circumstances. All those rumors about buying it in the hay—"

"Who cares?"

"People care. Sex, mystery, art; all the ingredients for increased circulation."

Bucky, you talk the radical line but you've got the heart and soul of a contemporary William Randolph Hearst. Circulation and profit."

"Don't knock it. It pays your salary and keeps the paper going. Now about Grant—womanizer, boozer, self-aggrandizing writer of shifting literary values, macho extraordinary . . . what a hell of a story you are going to do. Make that a series."

"Speaking of salary, let's discuss my raise."

It was as if she hadn't spoken. "I want you to interview everyone who knew Grant. Check deep into that rumor about humping himself into the grave. If we can put a name to the chick involved—"

"Why me, Bucky? I'm happy on the police beat. I'm happy doing sports. And what about Keely?"

"Forget it, I said. Dig up everything on Grant you can find."

"Bucky, you do not hear what I'm saying to you. I want a raise."

"Advertising is down. The word is Graham Welles's wife, Louise, was on a fishing charter with Grant the day before he bought it—"

"The day before he was *found*," she corrected.

"Ah, see how sharp you are! I knew you were a winner. Go all the way, Annie. I have an itch about this story.

"Contact Grant's publisher. His agent. Editors. Friends, relatives, ex-wives and ex-lovers. I'll make a deal for syndication. Maybe there will be a book in it. You'll be famous."

"I don't want to be famous," she wailed. "I want to be rich."

He guided her to the door and sent her on her way, speaking intimately. "I was sure you were thirty-six . . ."

"The case is closed," Acting Assistant Chief Wilbur Huntoon intoned with official sonority.

He reminded Hollinger of a mortician, slamming

shut the lid of a coffin on the dearly departed, the harsh and final act of life. "Keely didn't do it."

"The man is dead," John Roy Iversen reminded them.

Hollinger struggled against the increasing rage he felt. "Dead or alive, he deserves justice."

Iversen thought that was funny. "Nobody gets justice, Dutch. The lucky ones get away with it. That's life."

Huntoon thought that was funny. "What kind of a way is that for a cop to talk? I ought to call in your badge." He moved his eyes over to Hollinger, again serious, solemn. "The man killed himself, Dutch. What more do you want?"

"Suicide is not an admission of guilt."

"Why else did he do it?"

"He was being harassed, by all of us. The whole damned force was on his back until the poor sucker broke and couldn't see any other way out."

"Life is cruel," Huntoon said piously. "Life is hard. A real man doesn't take the easy way out."

"Once I believed that. Now I'm not so sure."

"You're soft, Dutch," Iversen said.

Huntoon shuffled papers in dismissal. "Out, both of you. Call somebody, make a report, investigate something. Stop wasting my time. The Keely case is finished. Move on to something else . . ."

Out in the lobby, they each took a long drink from the water fountain near the dispatcher's window and followed that with a trip to the men's room. Hollinger was dismayed to see that his stream was diffused, colorless. Alongside, Iversen pissed an authoritative flood into the urinal, all manly yellow liquid.

"Keely," Iversen said, zipping. "That's over, a *fait accompli*. Nobody put the gun into his mouth."

"We gave a helping hand."

"Screw that. The gutless mother knocked off his wife and the *latina* maid. He got what he deserved."

"There are two small areas of disagreement, Mister Four," Hollinger said, not looking at the other man.

"What are they, Dutch?" Iversen's manner was withdrawn, but tense.

"I don't believe Keely was the killer, that's one. Second, nobody deserves to have his brains blown out."

"Take a walk with me, Dutch."

"You heard Huntoon, get to work."

"This is business."

They circled around to Duval. "Dutch, that jacket you're wearing," Iversen said finally. "Must be two, three years old."

"Four."

"Still driving that beat-up Chevy?"

"Still. But not far."

"You got no class, Dutch."

"Agreed. No class, no style, no future."

"All three are within reach."

"Just drop into a tourist shop and order up. A couple of pounds of class, please. And fifty cents' worth of future."

"Money buys everything."

"And everyone?"

"Everyone. Everyone."

"I would rather not believe that."

"Vic Jackson talked to me last night."

"Good old Victor."

"Said you and he had been jawing on and off."

"One time only."

"Said you'd been talking to the Toomays?"

"They had to leave town."

"Those were my people, Dutch. The Toomays were okay out in the street. Medium tough, medium smart. Victor is very tough, but not very smart. Few of the people around here are big in the brains department. But they have to do. I have to make do. *Those are my people, Dutch.*"

"So you said, John Roy."

"You're the only one I've ever been worried about, Dutch. You're real tough, you're real smart. There was no way you wouldn't get onto things, sooner or later."

"Later, it seems. Tell me, John Roy, whatever happened to Bill Vail?"

"Seems to have just up and disappeared, Dutch."

"Did you feed him to the sharks? Or just dump him into some mangrove swamp? How'd you handle Bill Vail?"

"You give me too much credit."

"You stepped into his shoes quick enough."

"Let's talk about the present, Dutch, about you and

me, and a number of other people. Some very important, very powerful, very short-tempered people."

"You giving them up, John Roy?"

Iversen curled his mouth in a thin, grim smile. His eyes crinkled properly, making him handsomer than ever, the kind of man you'd like your daughter to marry. "You planning some kind of a move, Dutch?"

"Be poor strategy to talk."

"Don't do anything dumb, Dutch. You have never been dumb."

"I do believe you are threatening me."

"Be careful. This is no penny-ante operation."

"I get the picture."

"This is my special deal, Dutch. Mine and the others'. It's better than ever since I took over, bigger, more profitable. Nothing can be permitted to go wrong. Nobody is allowed to interfere. Nobody. Dutch, in this town, everything is connected, everyone is connected. Join up. Save yourself a lot of grief."

"Good advice, I suppose. But I'm a cop."

"So am I. See things my way, the way most of us do. Most everybody has something going down, a little vigorish."

"Except me."

"Except you, Dutch. Honesty is not necessarily the best policy."

"I'm beginning to get the picture."

Iversen stopped and faced the other man, hands spread almost in supplication. "Oh, man, you want in, you are in. You want a piece, you've got a piece. Something significant. Middle management, with all the benefits, a staff of your own. Your people, your operation. Answer to me, only to me. It's safe, it's rewarding, it's what's happening, Dutch."

"The American way of life."

"That's one way to put it. What do you say?"

"We're cops."

"You keep saying that."

"Somewhere along the line, we must do what we're sworn to do."

"And what is that?"

"Catch the bad guys."

"Meaning me?"

"You said it, pal."

Iversen let his hands fall and walked on, Dutch at his side. "Why are you so damned stubborn?"

"Why did you blow Izzy away?"

"Who?"

"You don't even remember his name. Izzy Ben-Ezra, the private investigator. He was a friend."

"You can't prove that."

"He was a friend, an old friend. Killing him upset me a lot. Seems to me I have to do something about that."

"I was wrong about you, Dutch. You are a fool. Take care of yourself."

"And the same to you, John Roy . . ."

Ellen knocked and the door opened as if he had been standing at the knob waiting. The man was portly and pleased with himself. He held a glass in one hand.

"Welcome to the party."

"I'm Ellen."

"I'm Marvin."

She stepped into the room and looked around. "Looks like I'm the party."

"You bet." He leered and teetered.

"You're nice, too."

She swung around to face him, arranging a wide, provocative smile on her face. Her feet were solidly planted in the deep shag carpet of the motel room and she wondered why she wasn't afraid. Not even nervous. She felt only slight numbness.

"You," Marvin said, "are something. Benny was right —you're terrific."

"You're not going to believe this, Marvin, but I never even met Benny."

The information left him vaguely alarmed. "Ellen, right? Benny said your name would be Ellen."

"He set it up. I just never met him, that's all."

"Well, as long as it's all okay."

"I wouldn't want to go that far."

"How far will you go, Ellen?"

"Name your game, Marvin. What you get is what you pay for."

He lowered himself to the floor, drinking deeply from the glass. "Get undressed."

She made it last. Folding each item neatly, placing it carefully. Letting him see her from every angle. Naked, she turned his way.

He put the glass aside. "Come on. Come on over here. Just keep walking right to me. Closer, closer. Ah, baby . . . baby . . ."

She felt nothing. Nothing but his warm breath on her skin, his lips, his wet tongue. No physical response, not even a twinge of desire. Which was as it should be, the way she wanted it to be. She waited an appropriate moment or two and moaned, and moaned again. Then commenced the deliberate rotation of her hips. She matched her movements to his, exactly as Tom-tom had instructed her. Going into her act, holding back on nothing.

And in return she received—nothing.

On the morning Tody Ellis returned to work aboard *La Florida*, Hollinger invited Paco Valentín for a coffee. On White Street, between a bodega and an Italian delicatessen, was a narrow store that served sandwiches, orange crush and coffee. They sipped heavily sweetened Cuban coffee and Paco smoked a Cuban cigar smuggled in by a shrimper. They made small talk for a few minutes, until Hollinger broke it off.

"There's a hell of a lot of rough stuff going on, Paco. Maybe you heard."

"I know about Tody."

"That snitch, Harry Waterman, bought it. And a private investigator I knew. The Keely woman and her maid, Livia Olvera. You know her, Paco?"

"All this talk about killing. I'm a lover, Dutch. Let's talk about loving."

Hollinger had known the fisherman for a few years, but they'd never gotten really close. Paco was not an easy man to know. From an occasional poker game, Hollinger recognized him as a shrewd, perceptive man with a tough, controlled intelligence. Other players were flashier, but none won with more consistency. He was always around after all the others had quit. Or been forced out.

"In New York," Hollinger said, "nobody'd lift an

eyebrow. But a tight little island like Key West—lots of ripples and raised eyebrows."

"You'll work it all out, Dutch. You're that kind of a guy."

"Yeah. Let's talk about drugs, Paco."

"Never use them myself."

"How about running some?"

"What kind of a question is that?"

"A man gets desperate, he asks desperate questions. Talk straight to me, Paco."

"What's it matter how I answer—yes, no, maybe? Some of the time. You know me."

"Sure, I know you. I hear the shrimpers, some of them. Go out for weeks, some of them, meet a mother ship, and bring the load in whenever they return."

"I'm no shrimper, Dutch."

"But you hear things."

"Not so many things."

Hollinger decided to try a different approach. "I don't believe Arthur Keely did his wife that way."

"They say he did."

"The man was not a killer."

"He killed himself."

"That's a point."

"If not the husband, who?"

"I got a theory, Paco. I'll try it out on you."

The cigar had gone out. Paco struck a match and puffed hard.

Hollinger said, "I make it out that the shooter was after Olvera."

"Why the maid?"

"You never answered my question. Did you know her, Paco?"

"She's a Cuban?"

"Colombian."

"I'd've remembered a Colombian. Not many of them around. I don't know, maybe I met her once. Or twice."

"Did she use, Paco?"

"How'd I know? Maybe. Most young people use these days."

"Maybe she was a dealer."

"I don't think so. You're asking the wrong guy."

"I know you, Paco. You hear things."

"Not so much. Maybe somebody once said something, I can't remember for sure."

"Said what?"

"Like she carried this or that, here or there."

"She was involved in drugs?"

"Some seemed to think so."

"Any talk that she was involved in Iversen's operations?"

Paco's expression hardly altered, yet change took place. A shift of angles, a hardening of lines, the black eyes flattening out. He put his big brown hands on the table and pushed himself to his feet. "Thanks for the coffee, Dutch. I got work to do."

"If I go after this thing, Paco, I wouldn't want any of my friends to get hurt."

"*Amigo*, you do what you got to do. I'm all right with the law."

Hollinger stood up, eyes level with Paco's. "What I would like is a name. Somebody who did business with Olvera. Would you know such a name?"

"Maybe. You ever hear of a cat named Tom-tom?"

"Just Tom-tom?"

"That's all there is."

"I'll look him up."

31

Annie Russell stood on the front gallery of the big house on Caroline Street and spoke to Hilda Grant through the closed screen door.

"There will be no discussion of my husband," Hilda said, her manner icy and aloof.

"He was a great man—"

"There is no point in any further exchange."

"He was so much a part of Key West. I had hoped to talk to—"

"You may talk to whom you please. Grant knew many people, few of them knew him. Really knew him. I will not cooperate in some ghoulish journalistic endeavor to exploit a man's death."

"Mrs. Grant—"

Hilda withdrew and in that split instant before the door slammed shut, Annie imagined Sam Dickey came floating into her field of vision. She marked it down to a hallucination of mind and eye; what would he be doing in Grant's house at such a time? And stark naked?

Annie called Louise Welles. "A few moments of your time, Mrs. Welles."

"I was barely acquainted with the man."

"Bits and pieces, that is how such a story will be put together."

"My husband and I played bridge with Mr. Grant. But bridge doesn't encourage conversation or intimacy."

"Do you think Mr. Welles will give me some time?"

"You might call him one evening."

"He and Grant went fishing together?"

"Why don't you ask my husband?"

"There are certain rumors floating around, Mrs. Welles . . ."

"Rumors?"

"About you. About you and Grant."

"What do you mean? What a vicious thing to. say! Larry and I were friends, that's all—"

"You said you hardly knew him."

"Yes, that's true."

"Can't we talk, Mrs. Welles? I don't want to misrepresent your position in my story."

"There is nothing to misrepresent, Miss Russell. Nothing to talk about. Good-bye."

Annie began to believe Bucky Maddox was right; there was a story here.

"You knew Grant pretty well, I guess?"

Paco shrugged. "He went out with me lots of times."

"He was a good fisherman, I suppose?"

"Not as good as he wanted people to believe, but good

enough. Some of his stories, well, things don't happen the way he wrote they did."

She felt herself relaxing. Valentín seemed willing to talk to her, if without special enthusiasm. It was a change that she appreciated.

"They say he was a great swimmer?"

Paco looked over the stern of *La Florida*, across Key West, in the direction of Cuba, and asked himself what reason he had for living on. He had maneuvered himself into a routinized existence, with no profound purpose, allowing the days to flow one into the other, no one different from the others. He had sought tranquillity and quiet when he came to Key West, and had discovered exactly what he wanted. It made a man wonder.

"Grant worked too hard at everything," he said. "As big and strong as he was, he misused his strength. If he ever learned to relax, he'd have been a fine fisherman and a superior swimmer. He fought the water instead of using it. Let the water hold you, I used to tell him, keep the kick strong but regular, without strain. Save your arms and breathe right. He never learned."

"I didn't know fishermen were ever swimmers."

"When I was a boy, back in Cuba, a boat was sunk from under me and my father. We swam back to shore."

"How far was it?"

"Eight, maybe ten miles."

"How old were you?"

"Eleven."

"At age eleven you swam ten miles?"

"It was the best swim I ever made, in a way. I did not know I could go that far. But my father kept talking to me, saying if I would become a man I had to act like a man at that time. Once in a while, I rested and he supported me. But not for long, or both of us would have drowned. He said it was up to me to take care of myself, no matter where I was. So I made the swim."

"I'm impressed."

"My father was a very good man."

She made a note, not so much to remember what he was saying as to clear her mind. She was supposed to be interviewing him, but she felt that he was guiding the conversation where he chose, manipulating her, telling her nothing of consequence. She filled her lungs with air and looked up into his black shining eyes.

"You took Grant and Louise Welles fishing a few days ago?"

"You have talked to others before me?"

She had a flash of inspiration. "Sam Dickey was along, wasn't he?"

"Dr. Charles's son—yes, he was there."

She decided to take a direct route. "Did you know that Grant and Mrs. Welles were having an affair?"

He ran his strong brown fingers through the wiry iron-gray hair. "I know nothing of such matters."

"What about Sam and Hilda Grant?" It all squared off, if true; or was she merely playing bedroom guessing games?

"What about them?"

From his tone, she gathered the interview had come to an abrupt end.

"How may I help you, Miss Russell?"

"May I come and see you, Dr. Dickey?"

"If you call my office, the nurse will make an appointment—"

"I thought we could talk about Lawrence Grant. I'm doing a series of articles."

"Oh, I see. It would be a waste of time, I'm afraid. There's nothing I can add to the public record."

She decided to plunge right in. "Is it true that he died while making love, Doctor?"

"What a romantic idea!"

"It does happen."

"To many men, according to statistics. But Grant was found lying at the edge of his pool, by his wife. Heart attack. All supported by his physical condition and—"

"Rumor has it he and Louise Welles—"

"Don't believe everything you hear."

"Your son, Sam, and Louise were on a fishing charter with Grant—"

"I would suggest you pursue this, if you must, with Mrs. Welles. As for Sam—"

"I believe I know where to find him."

"Which is more than I can say."

Graham Welles answered the phone.

"This is Annie Russell, Mr. Welles. I spoke to your wife."

"So I understand. Good-bye, Miss Russell."

Click.

Annie sat at the bar in Old Louie's Free Lunch, which of course had no free lunch, and sipped a dark beer. It went with the place, aged woods and a molded tin ceiling; the only light coming in from the double windows to the street. Two men drank at a far table; otherwise, the place was empty.

Old Louie resembled his bar. Darkened by time, unfashionable, and slow to change. He was a small tight-bodied man with the face of an ex-pug, which he was.

"You bet I was his friend. Real pals, both of us."

"What was he really like?"

"Everybody asks that—a swell guy is what. One of the best, none better."

"All that hunting and fishing stuff, fighting, war. Some people say he was a cruel man."

"Ah, come on. Not the Big Bear."

"Would you call him gentle?"

"Yeah, and kind, you understand what I'm saying to you? Treated people like they were gonna break, y' know."

"He liked women?"

"Boy, did he? And they were nuts about him. Guy was hung like an elephant, excuse my language, lady. But you get my meaning?"

"There's talk he died making love."

The pug's face closed up. "I didn't hear nothing like that."

"What if I mentioned a certain lady's name?"

"I don't wanna hear it. Say, who are you, anyway? Why all the questions?"

"I'm a newspaper reporter. I'm doing a story on Grant."

"Yeah. Well I got a terrible memory. Too many right hands to the head in the old days. I got work to do, lady."

The call to New York went through finally and Jimmy Oreskes' secretary came on, asked Annie to hold. Presently the agent greeted her like an old friend. They had never met.

"God, how I love Key West," he said. "God, how I loved that man. How may I help you, Miss Russell?"

"I'm doing a series about Lawrence Grant."

"And you think there may be a book in it? I represent the estate, the widow, I imagine that might be considered conflict of interest. Why don't you try another agent? There are dozens of good ones."

"I want to interview you—"

"Agents don't know anything."

"You knew Grant."

"I know contracts, deals, percentages."

"There's a rumor about how Grant died—"

"We all die the same way—alone."

"It's a conspiracy," Bucky Maddox lamented.

"Nobody's going to talk."

"Get tricky."

"I've already gotten nasty."

"Get nastier."

"I'm beginning not to like myself."

"Did Bernstein and Woodward give up?"

"Get them on the story."

"I got you."

"I don't like it, Bucky."

"You're getting paid, do your job."

"Speaking of pay, what about my raise?"

"You disappoint me, Annie."

"Bucky, I used to trust you."

"The reporter-editor relationship is sacred, Annie. Never forget that."

On her way out, she swore.

It took half the afternoon and into the early evening to track Hollinger down on the telephone. "Are you trying to avoid me?"

"Annie, you have a suspicious nature."

"I must talk to you."

"Meet me at my house."

She laughed. "That's better. Did you hear, Graham Welles is having a huge party next weekend?"

"I'm invited."

"Does that mean I get to go along?"

"I intended to invite you."

"How nice! You mean it?"

"Of course."

"Well—"

"Why?" he said.

"Why what?"

"Why are you still talking?"

She shut up. She hung up. She rushed right over and when she got there he was ready.

32

Old Timer's Day & Night. Done up to resemble a Western dance hall, complete with reclining nude over the bar, mirrors on the walls, and a staircase leading to private rooms. The barmen wore green sleeve garters and the waitresses were dressed like cancan girls. The bouncers were easily identified by the hard gray derbies on their heads. The owner was called Wild Bill and he carried a two-shot silver derringer in an ankle holster and a switchblade in his side pocket.

Beer was the big seller in Old Timer's, at two dollars and fifty cents a mug. Tourists mingled here with young locals, and comfortably padded ladies from Topeka or San Antonio or Cleveland frequently disappeared with one of the younger men, all of whom wore tight jeans and shirts unbuttoned to the solar plexus.

Sam Dickey was at the bar when Annie Russell appeared. He raged silently at the crowds of people push-

ing in on him, at the intrusive sound of them, at Annie
for being late. And he tried not to see his father lying in
bed with Monte Perrin, tried not to know what his father
was, fought hard to quell the fear that he was in every way
his father's son.

"Sorry I'm late," Annie began, taking the stool alongside him.

"It makes no difference."

She groaned to herself. He was already drunk and
loaded with self-pity. She considered splitting, then decided his condition might work to her advantage.

"You and Grant were pretty close, I understand."

He glared her way. "That sonofabitch."

"In that case, I understand you and Grant couldn't
get along?"

"I never gave him the chance."

"How'd you manage that?"

"The trick is to stay arm's length away from all
egomaniacs. That's what he was, you know."

"But that didn't have much effect on you?"

"He scared me shitless."

"Why is that?"

"The man was a potential danger to everyone. Hostile, violent, a repressed homosexual, if you want my
opinion."

"I thought he was very big with the ladies."

"Talk is cheap. I know better."

"How?"

"What do you mean?"

"How do you know better?" She kept seeing him
flitting across her line of vision through Hilda Grant's
screen door, naked and furtive. It had not been her imagination at play. "Is that what Hilda claims?"

"Hilda's got nothing to do with it."

"You and she, you're together."

"What kind of a crack is that? The lady's in mourn-
ing and—"

"I saw you there."

He examined her closely, a wily expression fading onto his smooth face. "You are trying to provoke me."

"I saw you. In Grant's house."

"Why should I tell you anything?"

"I saw you there, I'm going to write it up."

He gripped her arm hard. "Don't do that."

She shook herself loose. "Then give me something else. I'm not interested in Hilda's bedroom activities, I am interested in Grant's."

He gazed off into space. "There is nothing else."

A light of recognition broke inside her head. Sam was taking Grant's place in more than one area. She spoke in a matter-of-fact way. "You're doing some work for Hilda?"

"Forget it."

"What kind of work?"

"You get nothing from me."

She sensed his essential flabbiness, his need to speak of whatever he was into. His desire to boast, to let her into his private and apparently important activities.

"What kind of work?" she said again. The light flashed again, brighter this time. "Some sort of writing?"

"I've got nothing to say."

"He still scares you, is that it?"

"Shit."

"You won't pull it off, Sam."

He cocked his head curiously.

"You won't take his place, not seriously. You're not half the man he was, not half the writer."

"Go to hell."

She stood up. "Talking to you is a waste of time."

"Wait a minute." She watched him carefully. "Grant had one final go at it. But the man couldn't cut it."

"I don't understand." She sat back down. A man like Grant was a barnacle, clinging to life even when gone. Rumors, hyperbole, lies, legends—true or false, all rooted in the Big Bear's reality. Put it all together and you came up with the real Lawrence Grant, a truth larger and more vivid than any of his fictions.

"Grant was writing something when he died."

She took a chance. "When Louise screwed him to death, you mean?"

"No secrets on this little island. Rumors are facts, facts are lies, lies are the stuff of all our lives. I thought he was going to get it on with her on *La Florida* that day. He was all over her and after a while she turned on to it, she liked it. He was a letch, he devoured younger women."

"And Hilda knew all about the other women?"

"Never underrate that lady. She is someone special. Smart, tough and a survivor."

"Tell me about the novel."

"There is no novel."

"You said Grant was writing something."

"Not a novel, a memoir, an autobiography, a journal. A piece of literary bullshit."

"You've read it?"

"I am *studying* it, lady."

"A journal'"

"Bits and snatches of stuff. The old man had lost it all, become a parody of himself. All those sentences saying nothing. Gossip, brags, all crap."

"He would have rewritten, fixed it up—"

"No way. He had nothing left, in bed or at the typewriter. Needs a fresh eye, a strong hand, a growing talent."

"All of which you are going to supply?"

"Am supplying."

"How is it coming?"

He tried to remain casual. "When it's done, it's going to be a superior piece of work."

"Grant's work?"

He shrugged and swallowed some beer. He looked her over. "Grant at his best couldn't do it better."

"His journal, your work?"

"His final novel. I'm doing it as a novel. Supplying story, characterization, narrative, virtually everything. The old bull's last shot."

"Nice work if you can pull it off." She came off the stool. "You should get together with Louise Welles. Certainly she can supply some interesting anecdotal information, insight, just the thing an aspiring genius can use."

"Hey, what's that supposed to mean!" He reached for her, one hand coming to rest on her bottom. "Nice," he leered. "Big enough but not too big."

She disengaged. "I can see why Hilda has employed you. But save it for the widow . . ." Then she was gone.

He went back to his beer. A slender man with brooding eyes and brass-colored hair took her place. "Your wife isn't coming back, is she?"

"Not my wife."

"Bet you're not even married. You don't strike me as
the sort. Can't stand women, you see. Not to touch them
or be near them. The way they smell some of the time . . .
My name is Roberts."

"Sam is mine."

"Buy you a drink, Sam?"

"I buy my own." Sam kept thinking about Charles
and Monte. Roberts reminded him of his father, though
they looked nothing alike. "Fuck off, mac."

"Oh, say, there's no need to be vicious. We both
know what we are, what you are."

Sam struggled to clear his mind. Next to him, Roberts seemed to sway forward, a mocking turn to his sensual mouth. "I find you irresistibly attractive, Sam." His
hand came to rest on Sam's thigh.

Sam hit him between the eyes, sending him to the
floor. Both hands swinging, Sam went after him. Blood
began to run and somebody screamed.

A pair of bouncers in derbies and brocaded vests
dragged Sam to a room under the stairs. Seconds later,
Wild Bill led Roberts in.

"Fairies cutting up. Jesus. What am I supposed to do
with you girls?"

Sam went for Wild Bill and one of the bouncers
jerked him away, immobilizing him in a chair.

"Call the police!" Roberts shrilled.

"No need for the law," Wild Bill said.

"I want this animal put behind bars," Roberts said.
"I insist on it."

"Well," Wild Bill drawled. "Maybe that's the best
way after all . . ."

Hollinger floated in thick dark space, at some middle
level, going nowhere, and all of it was good. He resisted
all efforts to drag him free of that treasured haven. A
flashing light became blindingly bright, penetrating to the
core of him. Then a clanging commenced and jarred him
upward toward a nagging resentment. He clung to that
now precarious perch, he kicked and struck out, thrashed,
and finally woke up.

He reached for the phone, and mumbled his name.

Annie, at the far side of the double bed, complained
and rolled, burrowing against him for psychic comfort.

She was, he acknowledged sleepily, the wiggliest woman he'd ever known. And wonderful to be with.

"Who is this?" he said.

"Hilda Grant, Dutch. I woke you, I'm sorry."

"What time is it?"

"Dutch, it's Sam Dickey, Charles's boy. He's in jail."

He sat up and located his cigarets in the dark. "What he do?" He struck a match.

"Smoking gives cancer," Annie muttered.

Hilda answered. "Nothing much, Dutch. A bar fight, is all."

"Where—?"

"Old Timer's Day & Night . . ."

"That sump hole. Who was the arresting officer?"

"I don't know."

"Doesn't matter. I'll talk to Wild Bill, he'll drop the charges."

"That's just it, Dutch, Bill isn't pressing charges. It's the guy Sam hit. A homosexual."

"Jesus, Hilda. Nobody hits gays these days. It's politically unsound. Civil rights."

"Well, Sam did. Seems the guy made a pass."

"Sam was drunk, I suppose?"

"Stinking, from what I hear. Dutch, can you straighten this out for the boy?"

"Sure, in the morning. Let him sleep it off for the rest of the night."

"I appreciate it, Dutch. Sorry if I woke you."

"One thing, Hilda, why you? Why isn't Charles the one to call?"

"Sam found out about Charles, and I guess that set him off. He's a nice boy, Dutch."

"But a boy." Having said it, he wished he hadn't.

"No lectures, Dutch."

"You've got it. I'll take care of things in the morning. Good night, Hilda." He lay back down and embraced Annie, filling his hands with her lush, heavy breasts. "I hate skinny women."

"Nobody ever called me skinny before."

"Exactly my point."

"You know what I think? I think you aim to take advantage of a woman half asleep."

"What gave you that idea?"

"You're a sex maniac, Dutch."

"Everybody should have one."

She came around and faced him. "I think you are one beautiful man, mister. How nice of Hilda to call. Why was she calling?" she ended suspiciously.

He told her.

"I was with him earlier in Old Timer's. He was boozing pretty good and more than a little hostile. I think he made a half-ass pass at me."

"You're not sure?"

"I'm sure."

"Did you accept or reject?"

"Reject."

"That's what did it, your rejection. The poor guy went berserk, beat up some faggot. Be careful with your turndowns, lady."

"Nobody likes a wise cop. You interested in why I was with him?" She didn't wait for his reply, outlined the story she was working on. "You believe Grant died on top of Louise Welles?" she concluded.

"Everybody in Key West is cautious. Small place, too small to contain many secrets for long. But talk isn't proof, rumor isn't evidence. In this town, everybody knows everything that's going on. But nobody does anything about it."

"Except you."

"I'm a cop."

"Everybody's got to be something, I guess." She reached for him. "My God, Dutch, you are a constant surprise to me, and a source of inspiration. Am I to take that as an indecent suggestion on your part?"

"A firm declaration of intent."

"Firm is right."

"Don't talk any more."

Jack Roberts owned a sandwich shop on Front Street. Sandwiches, soup of the day and a green salad, key lime pie and seven-layer cake. Coffee and tea. That was the extent of the menu. Good, simple food served at a reasonable price, quick service. Roberts prepared all the food himself every morning and worked the sandwich board at lunchtime while two waitresses worked the tables.

Hollinger entered the place, showing his badge. Roberts, his lip swollen and one eye squeezed shut, glared at him. "Dammit, Dutch, I know who you are."

"Just to let you know this is a semiofficial visit."

"Semi? That boy is going to do time if I have anything to say about it."

"He really worked you over, Jack."

"For no reason at all. Coffee?"

"No, thanks. Why not forget the whole thing, Jack?"

"I won't do it."

"You'll have to testify. You made a pass at the boy. Unnatural suggestions. You'll look bad and no jury will convict, I'm giving you my best professional advice."

"He's insane. Look at my face, my face. All I did was display a certain amount of friendly interest."

"A couple of days, you'll be as good as new. Let the kid off the hook."

"Why should I?"

"He's Charles's son."

"Charles Dickey?"

"The same."

"Ironic, isn't it?"

"Apparently the boy recently learned about his father. It came as a shock."

"Pardon me if I'm short on sympathy. Being gay is no crime, no perversion, no moral stigma."

"A choice not an echo, you mean?"

"Give it a try, Dutch."

"I've got my own problems. Say the word, Jack, and Sam goes free."

"He's guilty."

"Aren't we all?"

"Save the philosophy. I hurt, I want him to hurt. I want justice."

"Justice? I'll see that you get your share." He waved an arm. "Nice business you've got here. Too bad about the Health Department . . ."

"What about them?"

"I've got a feeling an inspector will be scratching around Front Street before long. Maybe this afternoon. This inspector, he's a bad egg, tough guy. No compromise.

Lacks all humanity. Keep him out of your hair, Jack. If you can."

"I've got nothing to hide."

"Everybody has, Jack."

"Like what?"

"Like roaches—"

"Roaches! There are no—"

"A dirty storeroom, a freezer that doesn't work properly, hair in the hamburger and—"

"Goddamn, that's not right."

"Justice, Jack. You want justice, you'll get it."

"And that kid is free to beat up on some other poor gay."

"I'll talk to him. Why not come down to the station house, drop the charges, clear the air. Do it right, Jack, so there's no mistake."

"Jesus! You know what I think?"

"What's that, Jack?"

"It's a rotten world."

"So it seems, a great deal of the time."

Charles peered at his son through the bars of the cell. "What started it?"

Sam made himself confront his father. "The dirty cocksucker wanted to get it on with me."

Charles winced. "Can't we talk, Sam? There's so much I'd like to explain."

"Okay, you do that, explain. Mother found you in the sack with a guy and now I've had the same pleasure. There's nothing to explain."

"Your mother and I never did very well together. Sam, I tried to be a good husband, but I failed. I meant to be a good father—apparently I failed in that, too. Can't we establish a new relationship? We're both adults. I'm not a criminal. I'm a man and—"

Sam whirled away, facing the wall. "Get out."

Charles did so. He had lived for so long with his failures that one more hardly added to the burden.

That afternoon, the Muggers of United Street, as they'd come to be known, were captured. It was their own fault; they committed a terrible error in judgment. In broad daylight, they jumped two middle-aged ladies on their way home.

The ladies were both lesbians who had, out of fear and general antipathy toward the male segment of the population, become well schooled in karate, judo, plus a working knowledge of many foul and dirty tricks. The two ladies took the Muggers of United Street out with dispatch. Breaking the arm of one, and knocking him senseless; severely bruising the testes of the other, and cracking his jaw in two places.

Two hours later the Muggers were released in the custody of their parents, both being under age. Hollinger entered their names, addresses and method of operation into a file and marked it Active.

"Police work," he told Annie that evening, "is a dandy pastime. One glorious triumph after another."

Maribelle eased herself out of the bunk, careful not to disturb the sleeping man. A slow trickle of sperm went down the inside of her thigh. To carry a man's juice around inside you, on your skin, for an entire day was something special. Paco Valentín was a special man, manly, one it would be easy to love and live with.

She let herself out of the cabin and went out onto the pier where her car was parked and drove out along Roosevelt Boulevard to where a line of houseboats were moored in Cow Key Channel. She entered the red-and-blue houseboat at the end of the line.

The man waiting inside greeted her affably, indicated a chair and offered her a drink. She sat down and watched him as if he were about to strike.

"It has been a long time," he said.

"I did not know that you were here, Felix."

"I am not here. I'm in New York City, living in one of the apartments belonging to our delegation. I seldom leave the city, or the apartment, except to attend to business at the United Nations."

"Why did you want to see me?"

"You were always direct, more so than most of our women. I have always had a great deal of respect for you."

"Why?" she repeated.

"There is work to be done."

"I am through with your work."

"People in our profession, we are never truly free of the work. By temperament, we require it."

"And if I refuse?"

"Of course you will not refuse. You and I both know you will not refuse. There are too many connections. Too many loose ends, in this country and in Cuba."

"No me jodas . . ."

He grinned thinly. "I do not screw around, you know me better than that."

"Bastard."

"All in the cause of the Revolution."

"Qué se joda. La Revolución . . ."

Still grinning, Felix sat back and talked in a soothing, confident voice.

33

"Find another way." Huntoon kept his eyes cast down. More and more, it became impossible for him to confront John Roy Iversen. More and more he questioned his own strength and courage. Their relationship was disintegrating and his own position in the daily order of events grew shaky and diminished. "There has to be another way."

"I didn't want it this way. But there's no longer a choice. Unless you can suggest something?"

Iversen was taunting him, Huntoon was convinced of it. Mocking his weakness, his inability to act with dispatch and equal ruthlessness. Well, he wasn't Iversen, never would be. He didn't want to be like the other man. His resentment turned into anger. "There's been too much of that since—"

"Since Bill Vail left us? Since I took over his spot?"

"I didn't say that."

"If there are complaints take them upstairs. Discover the sentiment at the top."

"It's simply a matter of judgment."

"The man in the field has to exercise judgment on the spot. Mistakes are inevitable. There are always risks."

"Maybe we should talk to the chief."

"Suit yourself. But he doesn't care about nuts-and-bolts work. Just keep the envelopes coming, end of each week. The man's got a good thing going."

Huntoon squeezed his eyes shut. He opened them. "I like Dutch."

"I like Dutch. So what?"

"He's a good cop."

"If he weren't, he'd be with us. And no threat."

"What if something goes wrong?"

"He's a good cop, but no superman."

"Twenty-eight years on the force, I never used my gun."

"Twenty-eight years, and all of it behind a desk."

"Watch your mouth, Iversen."

Iversen answered with no change of emphasis. "Would you like an apology?"

"I think I would. Yes, I would. Apologize, Iversen."

"Go to hell."

Huntoon blanched. "Remember who's in charge here."

"Is there any doubt?"

Huntoon looked away. "As long as you remember, that's all."

"Then it's agreed?"

"If it has to be done."

"It does."

"You feel it's absolutely necessary?"

"A matter of survival, in my opinion."

"Survival. Yes, survival. Well, in that case, all right."

"I'll take care of it."

"Don't tell me the details. I don't want to know details."

"I said I'd take care of it."

"Fine, fine."

"You can arrange an inspector's funeral. All the trappings. A little ceremonial excitement. Ought to perk up the tourist business in town . . ."

"Louise and I are having a few people over, Paco," Graham Welles said over the telephone. "We'd like it if you came."

"I am not good at parties, Graham."

"It would give us a chance to talk."

"Graham, there is nothing for us to discuss."

"I think there is. Come early, Paco. The food will be excellent, the liquor good, the company fair. Do you like model railroading, Paco? I have a first-rate layout I'd like to show you. Yes, by all means, come early."

Even as Paco refused the invitation, he knew that he would attend the party. Graham Welles had always been a difficult man to oppose.

Hollinger spent the early part of the evening in the station house. The files, at best incomplete and poorly organized, failed to throw up anyone named Tom-tom. A call to the FBI office in Miami had drawn a blank. He'd put in an armed services check and come up empty again. Drug Enforcement could tell him nothing.

His snitches told him this: Tom-tom had been in Key West for more than a year. He dealt drugs on a small scale, had great success with women, was handy with his fists and possessed of an evil temper. Nobody liked Tom-tom. Nobody trusted him. Nobody knew where he was.

Hollinger gave it up finally and bought a bottle of Pouilly-Fuissé and went over to Annie's. She had prepared a shrimp casserole, delicately flavored, and a green salad. He ate more than he should, drank more than he should. Afterward, they shared a couple of joints and listened to a Beethoven sonata and made love leisurely and well, falling asleep in each other's arms. A heavy knocking at the door woke them both.

"Expecting somebody?" he said, after a while.

"Must be some kids, playing games."

"At this hour?" A male voice called Annie's name. "He seems to know you," he said.

"Not any more."

"Sounds like he's going to kick in the door."

"He'll go away."

"If it were my door, I'd want him to stop banging."

She sighed and got out of bed, got into a short robe, went into the living room. "I'm coming," she called.

Hollinger put on his pants and cinched up his belt, slipped his holster onto his belt at the small of his back. He went after her.

"Go away," she was hissing at the still-locked door.

"Open up or I'll break it down."

"No," she said.

"I think you ought to let him in," Hollinger said.

She faced him, a frightened look in her eyes. "He's out of the past, Dutch. He has no right—"

"Open up and settle things, before he wakes the neighborhood."

"Damn," she said. "Damn all of you . . ." She unlocked the door and opened it.

He came charging in as if anticipating resistance, a big man with long hair, his hands balled up into lumpy fists. If he noticed Hollinger, he gave no sign. He went directly to Annie and slapped her hard; she fell to the floor.

"Dirty cunt!"

Hollinger helped her up. "Are you all right?"

"Yes, okay. It's all right. Please, Dutch, no trouble."

"No," he said softly. "It's not all right."

"Since when do you get it on with old men, Annie? You always went for hard young cocks, like this one."

Hollinger eased forward, hands spread placatingly. "Please, no trouble . . ."

"I want some, Annie, and I want it now. The old bastard can watch if he wants."

Tom-tom never saw the blow that put him down, a short right hand. He rolled as he fell, coming up in time to take a second punch.

Tom-tom rose, his face showing crimson lumps where he'd been hit. His eyes were moist and drool trickled onto his chin. "Nobody ever—"

"I did. I will again. Be smart, hide. And go."

The man spun around and was gone. Hollinger closed the door and locked it. "You seem to have had a fascinating past . . ."

"Someday I'll tell you all about it."

"Do us both a favor, don't."

He finished dressing himself. "Does your violent friend have a name?"

"Forget it—please."

"I always like to know who I've been slugging. Call it a cop's idiosyncrasy."

She shrugged. "Tommy Thompson. Everybody calls him Tom-tom."

Nightlife was an after-hours club situated on the site of an old cigar-box factory, not far from Jackson Square. Inside the old building everything was softly lit and there were red velvet walls and deep chairs and sofas to sit in. On the main floor, two bars did a thriving business, one to the plinks and plunks of an old-fashioned piano, the other to the driving beat of acid rock. Dancers filled up the space with considerable energy. In the rear, a restaurant consisting of four rooms, each decorated differently and serving a superb continental cuisine.

On the second floor, the gaming rooms. Roulette, craps, blackjack, poker. The players were serious, the smoking urgent, the drinking incidental and sex something to be postponed to a less important time.

On the third floor, Ted Wallingford's private apartment and office. A large man with a heavy jaw and dull eyes guarded the door. A bulge under his left arm announced what he was carrying. But Hollinger had never heard of a shooting at Nightlife and trouble was always kept at a discreet and acceptable minimum. Noses might be occasionally bloodied, even a jaw fractured in the heat of the moment. But at Nightlife no one was ever seriously damaged, except financially.

The large man recognized Hollinger. "Ted's expecting you."

He was passed into the office, a spare room designed for work. Wallingford was a small man with white hair and the quick, feral eyes of a professional gambler. Nothing escaped him. He had been in business for a dozen years, local, state and federal law to the contrary. He was a confidant of the city manager and was married to the mayor's youngest sister. He dined regularly with the chief of police and went scuba diving off the reef with the county sheriff. He was shrewd, judicious and well con-

nected from South Beach to Jacksonville. It was said
that Wallingford and the present governor had been room-
mates in college.

"How can I help you, Dutch?"

"I'm looking for a guy, Ted. He calls himself Tom-
tom."

"I know him. A hustler. Women are his main bag."
Hollinger set himself against the dirty pictures of Annie
that came into his head. "Tom-tom is what I'd call a re-
cruiter."

"A pimp?"

"That's the word."

"In business for himself?"

"Not exactly. Maybe he runs a girl or two on his
own, but he's no entrepreneur."

"Does he work Nightlife ever, Ted?"

Wallingford was mildly offended. "Dutch, I run a
straight operation. Tom-tom comes around now and
then, has a go at the tables. If he pitched a chick in here,
I wouldn't know about it. But if I did—" He broke it off.

"Okay, Ted. Where do I find Tom-tom?"

"*Quién sabe,* my friend? Try Duval Street, wherever
the groupies hang out. That's his way, latch on to some
runaway kid and suck her into trade."

"Who does he supply mostly?"

"I have a bad memory for names, Dutch."

"I *need* a name, Ted."

Wallingford gazed up at the ceiling.

Hollinger cleared his throat. "Max Ferrera?" he said
inquiringly. "No, not Max. He's his own man, no helpers.
Alty Moore? A possibility, eh? Getting warmer. What
about Benny Skaggs? Bull's-eye! I take it there is no sense
in going on?"

"Why waste time?"

Hollinger edged toward the door. "Always good talking to you, Ted."

"Anytime you want to try your luck on the tables,
Dutch, my chips, my tables, you got to be a winner . . ."

"Sounds good, Ted, but I pay my own way. See you
around."

Benny Skaggs lay sleeping between the McGuire sisters when Hollinger arrived at his house. Helen McGuire

was fifteen, Leona was sixteen. The sweet scent of burned pot hung on the air, tinged with the smell of Chablis consumed or still standing in open bottles.

Skaggs answered Hollinger's knock with an angry complaint. "Who the fuck is it, this time of the night?"

"Open up, Benny, it's Dutch Hollinger."

"Oh, shit," Skaggs said, but he opened. He was naked and his face resembled a worn and weary bloodhound, jowls sagging and eyeballs cupped in cushions of soft flesh. His big body blocked the doorway. Hollinger put one hand on the hairy chest and shoved hard. Skaggs stumbled backward. "Hey, you got no right."

The detective walked in sniffing. "Place stinks like a whorehouse, doesn't it? That is your trade, Benny, whoring? Jesus, you're an ugly insect. Put something on, you turn my stomach."

"You got no right to come barging in here. I don't want to talk to you, cop."

Hollinger let him have a medium shot in the belly, slightly harder than intended. The air whooshed out of Skaggs and he doubled up. Hollinger was distressed at his lack of control, at how much anger he was carrying around. Damn Annie Russell. Damn Tom-tom. Damn, damn . . .

"Sorry, Benny." He went to the bedroom door. One of the McGuire sisters stirred, the sheets falling away. "Nice-looking girls, Benny. But they look under age."

"If you haven't got a warrant—"

"Oh, Benny, put on some clothes."

Skaggs located a green-and-purple-striped robe, complete with monk's cowl.

"That's better."

"Why you hassling me, Dutch?"

"Tell me all about Tom-tom."

"Shit."

Hollinger raised his fist. "Tom-tom?"

"I could make a telephone call," Skaggs said.

"And I could run you in for statutory rape, Benny. Those two innocent kids—"

"They said they were twenty years old."

"In these matters, Benny, the victim doesn't even have to press charges. Look at it this way, I have got you by the balls and if I squeeze you holler. About Tom-tom?"

"He's a pal, a man doesn't give up his pals."

"Tom-tom or you."

"What do I get if I do turn him over?"

"I leave and you can go back to your two little friends in there."

"It can't be too serious—"

Hollinger waited.

"All right. He's shacking up with a chick named Russell, a reporter for the—"

"Get your act up to date," Hollinger broke in. He didn't want Annie's name spoken here, wanted to keep her out of mind.

"Look, I don't follow him around."

"He recruits for you."

"I don't know what you're talking about."

"Where's he sleeping these days?"

"I told you."

"Guys like Tom-tom, there's always a backup. I want it."

"Behind the Athena Diner, a little apartment. Just a couple of safe rooms, you know. Is that what you want?"

"It should do. Don't make any phone calls when I leave, Benny."

"Tom-tom doesn't even have a phone in that pisshole."

"Not to anybody."

"You can trust me, Dutch."

Skaggs waited till he heard Hollinger drive off before he made the call. It rang once and he hung up, dialed again. This time he let it ring three times before hanging up. He waited for a full minute and dialed once more. A man answered and Skaggs said, "Dutch was just here. He's on his way to Tom-tom's place right now . . ."

The door to Tom-tom's apartment was ajar. Hollinger took out his pistol and followed it inside. No one was there. The bed was rumpled and still warm. Some clothes were scattered about and a wallet containing nearly three hundred dollars. Hollinger holstered his gun.

Skaggs had alerted Tom-tom and the long-haired man was on the run. Where to? Would he leave Key West, never to return? Possible, but not likely. Tom-tom would show up again, he was sure of it.

He considered paying Benny Skaggs another visit in order to chastise the pimp for breaking the rules. But it was much too late and he was much too tired. He decided the smart thing to do was to go home and get some sleep. Or try to.

As soon as he turned in to his street, Hollinger sensed something wrong. Halfway up the block, under a tall palm, a car he had never seen before, lights out. Instead of stopping, he drove around the block, trying to decide what to do.

There would be two of them at least. Waiting inside, where he'd be trapped, limited in his movements. He parked on the corner and walked swiftly back to his house, circling until he located the slashed screen that told him how they had made entry. He hoisted himself through the window and dropped silently to the bedroom floor. From the front room came the sound of hushed voices. The fools were making it easy for him.

On his belly, into the living room, gun in hand. Using their voices, he picked them out in the darkness. One was seated in the tall black leather chair, amateur. The other sprawled out on the couch. Very slowly, very quietly, Hollinger rose up reaching for the light switch. He filled his lungs with air and moved swiftly.

Bright light flooded the room and the two men came up shouting and shooting.

Hollinger crouched. "Police! Drop your weapons!"

They kept firing. Hollinger snapped off a shot that missed, then spotted Tom-tom running for the nearest window. From behind the black leather chair came a single shot and Tom-tom went sprawling on his face.

Hollinger froze for an instant and in that instant the second man dived out the window, footsteps pounding down the street. By the time Hollinger reached the street, the man was gone. He went back inside. Tom-tom was breathing harshly and there was blood all over his upper back.

"Tom-tom," Hollinger said. "You run with bad folks. Your pal shot you. Who was it?"

"He said you'd be easy."

"Who?"

"Meléndez."

"Where do I find him?" Tom-tom's eyes fluttered shut. "Who ordered me hit, Tom-tom? Give me his name . . ."

But Tom-tom was dead.

34

"That was stupid!"

"Nobody talks to me that way."

"I do, dammit. You're risking too much."

"Okay. I had a few too many, I blew up, that's all."

"The hell it's all. A fag makes a pass and you beat up on him. Dumb, dumbness, that's what it is. The worst that happens to you is a night in jail. But what about me?"

"What the hell do you have to do with it?"

"Everything. I've committed myself to you in every way, Sam. My life, my welfare, depends on you. But you depend on me, too."

"A small mistake."

"Because of your father? A fag makes a pass and you see red because of Charles. That is dumb."

"I've heard enough."

"Sit down."

"You don't own me."

"What do you know about being owned? Grant owned me body and soul for too many years. He used me in a hundred different ways, abused me, ignored me and made me feel rotten about myself. And I'll tell you something—in many ways it was the best of times for me. To be owned by a man like Grant, to be used by him. I wish it had never ended. I wish— I hope at the end, I hope at that moment that he had a damned good time, the bastard . . ."

She struggled to contain her anger, to breathe more regularly. "When I found his body, I promised myself that I was going to reclaim some part of my life. Not the part Grant stole, that's gone. But I am going to get what's left to me, revel in every day, every minute, use my body and mind, enjoy it all. That's Grant's legacy to me and if you think I will stand by while you spoil it for me then you are truly stupid."

Her intensity made him afraid and he yearned to flee. He saw her suddenly as a powerful woman, a living threat, an opponent too strong to defeat and too quick and wily to avoid. "You don't own me," he said again weakly.

"You're repeating yourself. Grant said that when a man repeats himself under stress he's given up his guts. Bore in for the kill, Grant taught me."

"Fuck Grant."

She laughed and touched his cheek. He jumped away as if seared by flame. "Grant's dead and gone forever. There's nothing you can do to him, except his public memory. Make that journal work for me, Sam, for both of us."

"I've fucked Grant's wife, and that's enough."

"No, not for you, Sam. Anyway, I was unfaithful to Grant a dozen times, maybe more. The sonofabitch virtually put me in bed with more than one man. He enjoyed the idea of my doing it with somebody else. He loved it when I came home with the stink of another man on me. He was never more excited than when I told him what I had done with other men." Her eyes were gelid and her voice a sibilant flow. "Look at you, you're so much like him, but you won't admit it. You like the idea, too. All right, I'll let you fuck Grant posthumously. I'll tell you about him, about everyone I was ever with while we're together. But ultimately there's only one place to do it, and that's at the typewriter, if you've got the balls for the job."

"You underestimate me."

"Not a bit. You can pull it off. With your words. With your ideas. Your head, only yours. What do you say?"

He found it difficult to speak. He jerked his head once.

She let one hand come to rest on his chest, circling lightly. "And no more Annie Russell."

"You're jealous!" The idea pleased him.

"I'm smart. She poses a danger. A newspaperwoman. Nobody can be permitted to learn what we're up to. This must be Grant's work publicly, his book, otherwise the entire project will go down the drain."

"I know. I feel as if my brain's being lifted out of my head."

"Use your brain, Sam. And we'll use your body together. In ways you never dreamed of."

He watched as she went to her knees, hands working at his belt.

"You really love it that way, don't you?"

"Better than anything else."

"And Grant loved it?"

"Yes."

"And you did it to him?"

"All he had to do was ask."

"And to those other men?"

"Every one of them. Many times."

"You're no goddamn good. Oh, God! Don't think you own me. Nobody owns me. I go and come as I want. Jesus, that's good. If I want another woman, you're not going to stop me. Anybody. Anybody, anybody . . . Holy Mother of God! What are you doing to me? What are you doing? Oh, God, God, go on, go on, go . . . go . . ."

There was a curious, almost suspended quality about Graham Welles's party. All the parties he had ever given. As if every guest had entered into a tacit contract to do and say nothing to upset the delicate mechanism that Graham had designed to make the evening work. Yet, at Graham's, there was always a puzzling mix of people that provided an innocent onlooker reason to believe a social explosion was imminent, perhaps even desirable.

To a sprinkling of retired admirals and generals, some lesser ranks, a number of businessmen, industrialists, financiers, add writers, published and otherwise, a painter or two, a sculptor, the obligatory poet, shopkeepers, a surprising number of young people, roaming artlessly while attempting to fulfill their economic or predatory aims.

There were straights and gays, the mayor, the city manager, the chief of police, members of the Board of Education and a few men whose incomes were derived in ways no one ever spoke openly about. They were, in short, a cross section of Key West, getting along in silent consent lest they rip each other to shreds. It was agreed, without being mentioned, that social and political peace reigned in Key West as long as no one rocked the boat, as long as no one reached for too much too fast, as long as the power remained in the hands of the powerful.

Gossip was one of Key West's favorite activities, ranking no lower than number three on anybody's list, and gossip at parties where tongues were loosened by alcohol was often bright and witty, and touched by thinly veiled venom. But there were rules. No direct accusations of wrongdoing were allowed. Facts were artfully disguised by exaggeration and laughter. And one never touched on a husband's or wife's infidelities, at least not in front of the spouse. Nor was a thief ever accused to his face of being a thief, or a liar a liar. Dissembling and hypocrisy were considered necessary virtues, the grease that permitted society's gears to mesh smoothly. Key West, it was widely held, was no different in this from the remainder of the nation, except in degree.

Graham's parties were a microcosm of the island. You might meet anyone there. You might talk about anything there, as long as it was done with style and discretion. For along with the invitation was the implicit expectation that everyone would abide by the rules. Graham, everyone understood, believed firmly that good manners alone separated man from the beasts in the jungle. Still, there were always those who fell from grace. The sneaks, the conspirators, the cheats.

Graham's party. Louise was simply an appendage, a prettily contrived decoration on Graham's party cake. She had a role to play and she never forgot her lines. In a long black lace skirt and a pink silk blouse, the collar modestly high, she looked beautiful, youthful and well bred, the perfect mate for Graham Welles. A stranger might have mistaken her for Graham's virgin daughter, but Louise felt otherwise. Her skin tingled with anticipation and excitement pulsed along her limbs, her eyes raking every new man who appeared, as she asked herself if this one would do for her. Louise had made up her mind: she intended to break the rules again. And again. And again.

In the garden, a four-piece band played Latin rhythms. Paco Valentín stood not far away while Maribelle moved sinuously across his line of sight. A Cuba Libre in one hand, a cigar in the other, he watched her warily.

"Paco, dance with me?" she murmured.

He shook his head in admiration. Dressed or naked, Maribelle was a marvel of sexuality, her body a snare, her face a lure, her spirit constantly vibrating with a love for life. No man could resist her, he had long ago decided, and he less than most.

"I am too old to dance," he answered.

Her hips rotated in one fluid circle and she offered her arms to him. He dragged on the cigar. What a beauty she was! Among men, he was surely the most fortunate.

"Perhaps you are too old for other things as well."

He scowled. "You will let me know if I am."

"Oh, yes, I will let you know." She laughed, her head thrown back, and he followed the arch of her throat down to where those exquisite brown breasts swelled up out of the shining red gown she wore. "Oh, yes, I will let you know."

"There are times when I wonder about you, Maribelle."

She pursed her lips and laughed again, softly, invitingly. "Smile, Paco."

"I should not have come. I am not happy in this house."

"We are together, we will be happy together."

"Let's return to *La Florida* now."

"What would we do there, just the two of us?"

"Ah, Maribelle, what a woman you are!"

She kept dancing.

Someone said, "It's not the same Key West any more."

Greg Barney loved parties. He loved to drink, particularly when the booze was free and plentiful. He loved Graham's parties because the free booze was always excellent. Greg, a retired advertising executive, drank quickly, in long swallows that amazed onlookers and worried his wife, Lynn.

"You're drinking too much," she whispered.

"Fuck off," he told her with a smile.

"I won't stand by and watch you—"

"It's a party, enjoy yourself. That's what I intend to do."

"I can't drink the way you do."

"You can't do anything the way I do."

"I won't stand by and—"

He went after a refill.

First woman: "I loved your last play, Mr. Williams."

Second woman: "I loved all your plays, Tennessee."

Playwright: "People do, you know."

Hollinger thanked Louise for inviting him.

"You're always welcome, Dutch, you know that. Graham and I are both very fond of you."

"It's a nice party," he said.

She thanked him and excused herself. He moved off toward the bar when he spotted John Roy Iversen and picked his way through the crowd toward the other man.

"Let's talk, John Roy."

"Here? Now?"

"In this bunch, nobody listens to anybody else. Not in any way that matters. Last night, John Roy, I was set up."

"So I heard. Glad you made it out safely."

"Two guys waitng for me when I got home."

"That's a bad business. But you took them out."

"Tom-tom bought it."

"I know. The other shooter got away?"

"All those fireworks, puts my teeth on edge, John Roy."

"You were always a good man in a pinch, Dutch. Nobody better on the end of a gun."

"I don't like it any more. I don't need it any more. I don't want it any more."

"We're all getting too old for the cowboys-and-Indians

scene. I'm glad you got Tom-tom, instead of the other way around."

"I didn't shoot him."

"Oh! Who did?"

"That leaves only his partner. We're running a check on the slug, maybe make a match."

"Why would Tom-tom's partner take him out?"

"I keep asking myself the same question. They knew I wanted Tom-tom, maybe the partner decided if he couldn't get me the next best thing was to wipe Tom-tom out."

"Logical."

"Maybe it was ordered to hit Tom-tom."

"Ordered? By whom?"

"His boss, whoever that would be."

Iversen's handsome face showed concern. "You're a good cop, Dutch."

"Can you think of a reason why anyone would want to knock me off, John Roy?"

"Cops make enemies."

"The dudes I sent away aren't the kind to do a job like this. No, no enemies, John Roy, outside of the department. Outside of you, John Roy."

"You do make waves, Dutch, and that makes people unhappy."

"I didn't think it would ever get this rough, John Roy. But since it has—well, you know how I am. If it happens again, John Roy, and I make my way through it, I'll be coming after you. I'll kill you, John Roy."

The boy in the flowered shirt smiled sweetly at the lanky former general. "I've always had an inordinate fondness for tall men."

"Faggot," the general answered stiffly.

"Tell me something I don't know."

"Why are you addressing me, sir?"

"I could make you very happy."

The general grew flustered. "What? What? What are you saying to me?"

"I'd love to give you some head, my dear."

Clamping his sphincter down, the general marched away in martial splendor.

Hilda arrived fifteen minutes before Sam Dickey, according to plan. They were to be polite to each other in public, but spend little time together. Hilda meant to keep their relationship out of the public eye. She wanted no idle talk, no scandal, no suggestion of Sam's work in her behalf.

By the time Sam got to the party, Hilda was surrounded by a dozen men and women who offered their condolences, who clucked over her lonely state, who professed unending affection, friendship and assistance. She listened to their words and assessed the odds against any of their promises being fulfilled: small chance.

She spotted Sam talking to Annie Russell and had to restrain the impulse to separate them.

Someone said, "Key West was better in the old days."

"All right to talk to you?" Sam began.
"Last time you didn't do too well."
"Maybe you're a jinx."
"Maybe you attract trouble."
"Touché," he said, with a disarming smile.
"Still working on the Grant piece?"
"I could ask you the same question."
"I manage to keep busy."
"Good for you. Now, if you'll excuse me. I see a cop I know . . ."

Greg Barney, glass in hand, lurched off in search of a bathroom. Too many years, too much booze, had wreaked havoc with his bladder. Once he could drink and play all night and never go to the bathroom. No more. A few drinks and taking a leak became a pressing necessity. As he went, he felt a drop or two squeeze its way into his Jockey shorts and he hoped he would arrive in time.

Graham Welles sat on a high stool at the control panel operating his model railroad. He ran a passenger train with twin engines over a horseshoe turn around the base of a heavily treed mountain. At the same time, a diesel-drawn freight advanced steadily in a wide swing along a meandering river.

"What do you think of the layout?" he said when Paco appeared.

"Very impressive, Commander."

"I have long been fascinated with railroading. Almost every unit is handmade. The bridges, the terrain, the water areas."

Paco watched the freight.

Seeing his interest, Welles said, "Would you like to operate it, Paco?"

"It would make me uncomfortable."

"Playing with toys, you mean?"

"Being responsible for another man's precious things."

"Ah," Graham said, and touched a dial on the control panel. Both trains came to a sudden stop. He smiled at Paco. "Every man should have a hobby."

"Why did you insist that I come here?"

"There are things we have to discuss."

"Such as?"

"Such as Cuba."

"Cuba," Paco echoed. "Always Cuba."

"Until Cuba is free again some of us can think of little else."

"I am finished with all that. Key West is my home. Cuba belongs to the past."

"For a Cuban, there is always Cuba. You are a patriot, Paco."

"I am a charter fisherman, that's all."

"Hector informs me you did well on the trip."

"It was easy, almost as if it had been arranged."

Graham smiled. "It had been. Even in a socialist paradise, men can be bought. I wanted you to see your mother, Paco."

"She was dead when I got there."

"That is regrettable. But you did see your brother."

Paco waited without comment.

Graham stood up. Even in these informal circumstances, he resembled nothing so much as a cadet on parade. His eyes were still, searching, always cold. "Good men are always difficult to find, Paco. Men with experience and the will to see a job through. You are such a man, rare and priceless."

"I am finished with it."

"One more trip, Paco."

"The last one was the last one."

"You have my word."

"There are other boats, other captains."

"There are two aspects to the job ahead. One has to do with your brother."

"What about Kiki?"

"He is one of us."

"I don't believe you."

"Ask him when you see him."

"He spoke well of Cuba, of Castro, of his life there. I do not believe it."

"He is our man there and the time has come to bring him out."

"He is in trouble?"

"He soon will be. Word has come to me that they are onto him. As of this moment, they are still not certain. But they watch him, monitor every move. Either he comes out soon or he is finished."

Paco felt some essential element seep out of his middle, some primary stiffening agent, a fundamental link in his manhood. He was trapped, even as Welles had known he would be. "Two aspects, you said?"

"We have before us an opportunity that no true *cubano* can resist. It is possible to strike a huge blow against Fidel. All this stupid talk about détente, about normal relations between Cuba and the U.S. Once and for all, Paco, we can end it once and for all. This chance is rare and must not be missed. I want you with us, Paco. I need you."

"If I go in, I want your word that Kiki will come out with us. Unharmed."

"You have it."

"I don't trust you, Commander."

"I'm sorry to hear that, Paco."

"I trust no one any more, no one who believes as strongly as you do. To believe so strongly is to make it inevitable that you would lie, cheat, kill, whatever is demanded in order to make your dream come true. No, I do not trust men of ideals any more."

"I will not betray you, Paco."

Paco shrugged. "If you do, it would be wiser to have me killed, for I shall certainly find and kill you."

"Understood. Do we have an agreement?"

"I will be with you on the job, but I am not for you

any more. What you do you do for yourself, not for me, not for Cuba. Not for the people of Cuba. Never come to me again."

The chubby, puffy, gimlet-eyed novelist down from New York signed autographs and agreed with his fans that he might very well be the best living writer in the world.

A pretty youth asked for his autograph.

"Have you a piece of paper?" he said.

"I was thinking of someplace more intimate," the youth said.

The novelist's round pale face glowed. "Such as?"

The boy brought out his penis. "Will this do?"

The writer signed in a flowing script.

"Good evening, Sergeant Hollinger," she said, coming up on his blind side.

He came around as if unable to make up his mind. "Detective Sergeant," he corrected, stalling for time.

She produced her friendliest smile. "If we're going to be all that formal, you must call me Ms." She laughed when she said it.

He yearned to respond easily to the flirtation, but was unable to do so. He was, he accused himself, irrevocably damaged by the longtime stunted condition of his emotions. Having been hurt, disappointed and dislodged from his normal, comfortable groove, he swelled up with self-pity, petulance and a simmering hostility. It occurred to him that some of his wildest and most acclaimed heroics in the army and on the force had come out of a deep, silent rage that anyone would, or could, stand between him and the immediate gratification of his wishes. He wanted to strike out at Annie Russell, to deliver pain; but she was just too damned good-looking to stay mad at for very long. He vowed not to give in too quickly, however.

"What are you doing here?"

She gave an exaggerated shiver, hugged herself. The gesture made him remember what a fine, responsive body she possessed.

"You promised to bring me. But it must have slipped your mind, because a man of your moral strength would never, never go back on a promise."

He studied her closely. "You know about Tom-tom?"

"Yes, It was inevitable."

"I was there."

"I heard."

"He and another guy, they meant to take me out."

"So you got him first?"

"No. His partner shot Tom-tom. Obviously, the deal was to gun me down and then wipe Tom-tom out. Both of us presented somebody with problems."

"Who wants you dead, Dutch?"

"What difference does it make to you?"

"Stop it, Dutch. You're being childish. It was over with Tom-tom even before you and I got it on. I made him get out, told him it was the end."

"He didn't seem to believe you."

"And neither do you . . ." She turned and started away. He reached out and took her arm, gently bringing her back.

"I'm sorry," he said.

"Damn, damn. There was feeling for Tom-tom once, and I can't just cut it off. I knew he was wild, and into some wild things, but he could be very kind, sometimes, even tender. And there were moments when I felt he actually needed me." Her eyes were round and glistening and her mouth worked into a wistful smile. "I warned him, Dutch. He didn't have the character for the rough side of the street. He wasn't as smart as he thought he was, and he wasn't as brave, and he wasn't so hard. But something in him made him keep on going. I warned him, and he laughed, said he could take care of himself." She touched him lightly, hand remaining in place. "Buy me a drink, Dutch?"

"Not here."

Someone said, "In the old days, there was always Havana."

Sam Dickey had been watching Louise Welles for nearly thirty minutes as she drifted from group to group, person to person, being her husband's perfect hostess. Finally, he intercepted her.

"I've been watching you," he began, grasping her upper arm.

"That hurts."

"I want to talk to you."

"Let go, Sam." He released her and she massaged her arm, looking up into his flushed and drooping face. Even drunk, he was incredibly attractive, and being drunk seemed more vulnerable and younger than ever. "You're much stronger than you look."

"Someplace private."

She considered him briefly. "All right, Sam."

The general pissed with authority. A strong yellow stream that made a strong satisfying splash in the pool at the bottom of Graham Welles's guest toilet. The general perceived his urinary effort as the inevitable result of years of sound military training and self-discipline. He liked to do things with dispatch and competence. Get it on, get it done, move on to the next objective.

He was somewhat surprised, therefore, when he heard the door open. He had somehow neglected to lock it and even the least behavioral omission disturbed his sense of order.

He pivoted around, cock in hand, as if to repel the intruder. He had expected it to be that queer in the flowered shirt. Instead it was Greg Barney, drunk as usual, a glass in one hand and fumbling at his fly with the other.

"Taken, Barney," the general growled. "Be done in a second."

"Jesus, General, that tool of yours is just like the rest of you, long and narrow and stiffer than it should be. You always half hard or did I interrupt a little hand job?" Barney giggled. "Look at mine, shriveled up and soft. Kind've cute, don't you think? In action, it occasionally comes through." He finished the rest of his drink and went down on his knees.

"What the hell are you doing, Barney? Get up at once!"

Barney took the general's penis in his hands and held on tightly.

"My God, man! What are you doing? Let go of me, do you hear?"

If Greg Barney heard, he gave no outward sign, committed to his present course of action.

The general hit him on the ear, knocking him against

the tub. He bounced and cried out in pain. The general kicked him in the face and blood began to flow from his nose. Barney began to cry and the general drew back his foot as another figure appeared in the doorway. It was Lynn Barney.

"Don't hurt him, please," she said.

The general stammered indignantly. "Your husband, madam, has performed perversely."

Lynn Barney helped Greg to his feet, pressed a wet towel to his already swelling nose. "If you don't mind, General, would you put that thing of yours away?"

The general pushed and stuffed with all the dignity he could muster. "Your husband, madam, is a . . . a . . ."

"I know," she said cheerfully. "But only when he's drinking. Otherwise he's straight as hell . . ."

"I hear," someone from the mayor's office said, "that the desalinization plant broke down this evening."

"This place will become a desert," two people responded in unison.

"Bullcrap," said someone from the city manager's office. "That could never happen."

"It did once before."

"Safeguards have been taken . . ."

"Would you believe it—they're turning the convent into a condominium?"

"Will they sell to non-Catholics?"

"They're likely to use the confessionals as elevators."

"What will the Pope say?"

"Oh, they'll only sell to young singles . . ."

Someone said, "In the old days, every married man had a *pied-à-terre* in Havana and you could fly over in a few minutes."

"I know about you and Grant," Sam said, when he and Louise were alone.

For a long beat, she couldn't reply. Her senses clouded over, her brain was numb, her tongue refused to function.

"No," she got out. "There was nothing—"

"He screwed you—"

"No—"

"He left a journal, he wrote about you."

"He couldn't have. He died—" She broke it off and abruptly the confusion and fright turned to anger. "You cheap sonofabitch, what are you after? Why are you trying to hurt me?"

He drew her toward him and her struggles were ineffectual. "He wrote about what he wanted to do to you, in detail. I wonder if he had the chance to do all of it? Tell me, what you did to him?"

"Bastard!" She struck, nails curling toward his cheek. He avoided the blow easily.

"That's all the confirmation I need. How was it, fucking a man to death?"

"I'm a happily married lady—"

"Half the island suspects what happened, the other half is sure of it."

She stared at him, mind racing. A surge of pride and defiance flooded all the hollow spaces of her head. She wanted to admit what she had done, boast of it, share the feelings she had had, feelings that remained with her still.

"You are on your way to becoming a local celebrity, Louise. The Conch Train will bring tourists around to show them your house, where Big Bear was humped into eternity. They'll engrave your name onto a bronze plaque, a landmark forever."

"You bastard." It was a struggle to keep from laughing aloud.

"Tell me all about it, Louise, and I'll tell you something equally wicked and delicious."

Temptation plucked at her resolve. "What can you possibly tell me?"

"That I am the ghost of Lawrence Grant, come back to haunt you. Haunt lots of other people."

"You sound a trifle mad to me." She stepped back and was vaguely disappointed when he released her readily.

"Grant left a journal. Names, dates, gossip, exaggerations and distortions, outright lies. I am going to rewrite it all. Change the great man's bullshit into a work of fiction worthy of his reputation. I am making a novel of it,

Louise. Truth as fiction which the world will accept as truth, not fiction."

"You're confusing me."

"I'll put you in the book, Louise. In suitable disguise, of course. What an ending, Big Bear pounding away on that marvelous body of yours, sweating and grunting as death closes in. It'll send the publishing world into shock."

"You mustn't."

"Oh, yes, I must."

"My husband—"

"He'll never know, unless I want him to know."

"You wouldn't tell him?"

"I might, unless you buy me off."

"How?"

"I want what Grant had."

"You are a bastard," she said, without emphasis.

"That day on the boat, how I envied him."

"What if I say no?"

He opened his belt. "You won't."

"Don't do that."

He pulled his trousers down.

"You are crazy. This is my house. Someone might walk in any minute. Graham—"

"Quickly. Don't make me wait any longer."

"You bastard—"

"There, that's good. Oh, much better. You must tell me how it was with Grant. And I'll tell you about Hilda, how she is with me. I'll tell you everything. We'll do everything. Everything . . ."

Someone said, "Parties are just not the same any more on Key West."

"Nothing is," someone else said.

"Or ever was."

"It was," Graham Welles said to Louise, after switching off the night lamp next to their bed, "a perfect party."

"Perfect, Graham."

He adjusted the covers up to his neck. "I've some business to attend to later in the week," he murmured. "Out of town."

"Must you go?"

"Of course I must. Or else I wouldn't. It's only for a day or so."

"I'll miss you," she said with expression. "Where are you going?" she added, not really caring.

On impulse, he told her about Jacob Persky, about Spencer Forester, about Hector and Figueroa and the trip aboard *La Florida* to the Roselli plantation in Cuba, which made Louise remember that fishing trip with Grant, and the time with him on the floor of the living room. She shivered and Graham misunderstood.

"You mustn't worry about me, I can take good care of myself."

"You're my husband, it's my place to worry."

Graham placed a reassuring hand on her thigh and removed it quickly lest she take the gesture for a sexual advance. He was much too preoccupied to make love this night.

"I'll be all right," he said.

"Oh, I know that you will," she said. She lay awake for a long time hoping something would go wrong and her husband would be killed in Cuba.

35

Sam Dickey kept his eyes to the front, fixed on the place alongside the pool where Lawrence Grant had been discovered naked and dead, and so very much alone. Grant had written about the terrors of dying, unattended and unloved. He had feared such a death. Death, as readers around the world knew, was a most enchanting lover for him.

And in that erratic and so often irrational journal, death was on Grant's mind again and again. Out of the Book of Job, he had copied: "If a man die, shall he live again?" And later on: "My days are past," as if he had a premonition of his end. Gradually, seductively, a fresh sympathy for the dead man seeped up into Sam's awareness. An identification with the raw humanity that for so long had been concealed in that huge, powerful body screened out of sight by a personality almost always gruff and too often cruel and malicious.

" 'The king of terrors,' " Sam muttered.

"What?"

"Just thinking out loud," Sam said.

"Concentrate," Hilda instructed him. "There's much work to do and little enough time to do it in. You have it in you to write much better. Those first three chapters, they have to be redone completely."

"Grant was terrified of going out alone."

"Grant afraid!" A mocking lilt came into her voice. "The bastard wasn't afraid of anything alive or dead. He was coated in machismo, drenched in it."

"True and yet not true. For a man like that to die alone—"

Her lip curled back, her voice harsh. "He died on top of that Welles bitch, I told you that. Now stop this. Grant is gone and we're left to do his work. Go back to the typewriter, go back to work."

"You don't own me."

"Keep on repeating it, Sam, and maybe it will come true. But until his book is done to my satisfaction, you do belong to me. Part of Grant's meager legacy. You're an extension of that damned old Smith-Corona of his, so stop moaning and do the job."

His eyes flickered across her face. All that beauty suddenly seemed tamped down, without vigor or emotion. A hard-edged piece of clay, well molded but lacking any life. "I have been thinking about my father—"

"What the hell has he got to do with this?"

"Ultimately we are all alone, aren't we? Grant, Charles, you, me."

"You have me, Sam."

The sound of her voice startled her. It was flat, chilling, remote. What had life done to her? What manner of woman had she become? She fought back the urge to go to Sam, to embrace and comfort him, to reassure him. He was her lover because she needed a man in her bed.

He was her employee because she needed a writer. The needs existed, but she looked upon them as weaknesses, flaws in her character. Grant had said it: "Show the bastards the tough side of you. Fight and win. Never let them know you're the way they are—frightened and uncertain."

"I want to talk to my father," Sam said, standing, moving away from the poolside.

"I give you everything a man needs," she called after him. "Everything. Thanks to me you'll become rich, successful, in command of your talent. Trust me, Sam, and one day I'll make you famous."

"I won't be back for dinner . . ."

She was on her feet now. "What? Listen, Sam. There's so much to do. We must talk, work it all out. I planned—" She stared at his long back, the high, broad shoulders. "It's Louise, isn't it?"

He stopped without turning. "I always wanted to be like Grant. To be Grant. At the typewriter, in the bedroom. I'm doing his work, I'm sleeping with his wife. Why not his last lover?"

"You dirty bastard!"

He continued on. Halfway to the front gate, he heard her running, heard her shortened breath as she called to him.

"I'll wait up for you, Sam. Whatever you do is all right. Whoever you do it with. No matter how late it is, Sam, I'll be waiting. Please, come home tonight. Please, Sam . . ."

He went through the gate without answering.

There was so much to think about. Sam went over it all in his head as he looked at the charter boats moored in Garrison Bight. Here was where it had all begun, that fishing trip with Grant and Louise. What great expectations he had that day. Since meeting Grant on Corsica, he had steeped himself in the writer's work, reading, rereading, putting aside any doubts about Grant's standing in the literary firmament. He allowed no questions to interfere with his worship of the great man. Grant was genius on the hoof, a purveyor of word magic, an intellectual gladiator of rough ideas in a world gone mushy and effete.

But the doubts remained, pricked at him like persistent thorns. Once larger than life, Grant had gradually been reduced to manageable proportions. The god had become comprehensible, even likable, thus destroying his godliness. Now Sam perceived him with warts in place, tolerated, pitied, cared for. Lawrence Grant, human being.

Take Grant's place! What an absurd idea. As if any man could replace another. The empty dream of a hollow man. A grisly, obscene joke.

He couldn't laugh.

He looked around and noticed a slightly built black man coming his way. "Afternoon," the man said.

"Afternoon," Sam replied.

"Mr. Sam Dickey, ain't that right?"

Sam nodded, on edge, suspicious, unable to place the stranger.

"I'm Tody Ellis, Captain Valentín's mate."

Of course. "Good to see you again." He offered his hand. "No fishing today?"

"Paco's laying to, waiting."

"For what?"

"For the word to come down. A big charter is on the way. Be set in a few days, Paco says. The thing is, he's furloughed me until it's over. Don't know what is going on. Paco says it's for my own good. Don't know what he means."

"That's curious."

"Ain't it, though? It's Paco's boat and he's paying me for time off, so it can't be bad. A week with my lady and nothing to interfere with the loving time." His laugh was a rising peal. He waved and went on.

Sam watched him go. Tody's words possessed a hidden meaning, something significant that remained elusive, tantalizing, beyond his understanding. Perhaps he should talk to Paco Valentín, put the question directly to him. Instead he walked off in the same direction Tody Ellis had gone, to keep his date with Louise Welles.

They sat in her car at the end of White Street Pier, looking out toward Cuba. Louise dropped her hand onto Sam's thigh, massaging in quickening circles. "I want him to die," she said.

He had been unable to stop thinking about Charles. He had plunged deeply inside his head in an attempt to answer the awful questions that tore at his innards and allowed him no rest. What made a man go against his nature, his entire being? Or had Charles in fact turned nearer to what he truly was? Sam grew afraid of an enigmatic destiny. He was, after all, his father's son.

"Die!" he said, with some alarm.

She giggled. "Mustn't take me seriously. It's simply that I want so much to be alone with you."

He shifted and her hand fell away. "Do you mean your husband?"

She nodded. "He's taking a trip. He could get shot."

"Who would shoot Graham?"

"The Cubans, of course." She directed his hand on her breast. "Ah, Sam, I . . . just . . . love . . . it . . ."

He shifted again in order to put distance between them. "What are you talking about?"

She lifted her skirt; she was naked underneath.

"It's broad daylight," he admonished.

"No one can see. Touch me here, Sam. Please, Oh, God, there must be someplace we can go."

His mouth tightened. "Grant really pressed the right button, didn't he?"

"Yes, dammit, Grant. Ever since Grant I've been crazy. Insatiable. But it's better with you, Sam. The way you look and taste and smell, Sam. The night of the party, I kissed Graham, a long, wet kiss, with the taste of your semen in my mouth."

"I may not be the man for you, Louise."

"Don't say that, Sam. Please, I need you so much."

"Tell me about the Cubans." Concentric circles of fact and fiction dipped and flowed inside his skull, tantalizingly close to forming up a single, revelatory picture. The answer to everything he was, everything he wanted, or could be. "The Cubans?" he said again.

"I promised Graham I wouldn't tell." She was being cute, girlish, coquettish. She was in fact suddenly dull and transparent, not at all to his taste. He began to experience an active dislike.

"What about this trip?"

She lifted her chin, a movement studied and awkward. It made her seem very earnest, intense, an all-American girl standing her ground. "Graham is going to Cuba."

The information confused him further. "What for?"

She spoke matter-of-factly, fast losing interest. "He's a spy, you know. Has been for a long time. CIA, or he was once. Bay of Pigs, and all that. There's a job to do and Graham and the others are going to do it. Something dangerous. Maybe he will be killed," she tacked on hopefully. "Then I'll be free, Sam, and nobody will be able to interfere with us."

"What others?" The circles slowed, ground down to a logical tempo. Facts fell into place, and the nonsensical began to make sense. "When?"

"That's just it, my darling." Her eyes began to glow again and she wet her lips. "Tonight, late tonight, on Paco's boat. Graham and a man named Hector and somebody named Figueroa. Oh, what does it matter? They'll be away for at least forty-eight hours, Graham said. Two whole days. I'll call you as soon as he's gone. I'll be showered and smelling sweet and naked when you arrive. You can do anything to me, anything you can think of. And I'll do to you whatever you want . . ."

Yes, Paco's boat. But without Tody Ellis, who might be in the way. A dangerous mission, for whatever illegal purpose. He felt a stirring, a rising curiosity, a need to know. This was the kind of story he longed for, the kind of work he was meant to do. To pursue life wherever it led, at whatever cost it extracted. Pay your dues, man.

"Start the car," he said.

She pouted: "I'm not ready to leave. I want you to do something for me, to me."

"Take me to my father's house."

She objected, but finally gave in. But Charles was not at home, and his office was closed. Sam phoned Monte Perrin.

"Charles flew over to New Orleans for a medical conference, Sam," Perrin said. "He'll be back day after tomorrow. Any way I can help?"

"Tell him—" Sam clamped his mouth shut. It occurred to him that he had never asked forgiveness of anyone before, had never sincerely apologized to anyone for anything he had done, had never wanted to until now. He said, "I'll call again in a few days . . ."

36

Hollinger drove out to the airport and parked his car. A man waved to him from alongside a Chrysler sedan and he knew it would be John Roy Iversen IV. Iversen opened the door and Hollinger got into the seat next to the driver. Iversen slid behind the wheel and took them out onto Roosevelt Boulevard without speaking. It was Acting Assistant Chief Wilbur Huntoon who broke the silence, from his place in the back seat.

"Dutch, you're making a lot of people very antsy."

Iversen had arranged the meeting, on Huntoon's behalf, he had said; Hollinger had established the seating arrangements. He wasn't going to sit in front of Mister Four in a moving car.

"Seems to me cops are supposed to do that, Chief."

Iversen cursed, but Huntoon cut him off.

"Listen to me, Dutch. This is not going to do any of us any good. You've got to pull back."

Hollinger placed himself so that Iversen was in profile to him and at the same time he could look at Huntoon. "I'm not sure I can."

"Have you considered retirement, Dutch?"

Hollinger grinned in the darkness. "Two long years until pension time."

"Arrangements can be made."

"That pension is very important to me, Chief. I'm not a rich man, you know."

"There, you see, John Roy. I told you Dutch would respond to reason. Money is no problem, Dutch. It should never be a problem among friends."

"Early retirement," Iversen said with no color in his voice. "I suppose a medical could be worked out. There must be something wrong with you, Dutch. At your age, all of us begin to run down."

"As a matter of fact, I'm in very good shape, John Roy. Run four, five miles every day."

"I'm impressed, Dutch," Huntoon said quickly. "What do you say to heart trouble?"

"I've always taken a kind of pride in the condition of my heart, Chief."

"I know what you mean. There's always hypertension. A few words to the doctor and—"

"Forget it," Iversen said in a thin, hard voice.

"A back, then?" Huntoon said with a hint of desperation. "The medics can never be sure about a man's back. In the army they used to say—"

"Forget it," Iversen repeated.

"Consider it, Dutch," Huntoon said wistfully. "Mull it over overnight."

"Dutch doesn't want to be friendly," Iversen said.

"All my life I've been part of arrangements, compromises, overlooking things."

"You've been a good cop, Dutch," Huntoon said hopefully. "There's no cause to put yourself down."

"I've been a bad cop."

"No, no. Be fair to yourself. After all, we're all just human beings. Fallible, weak, hungry for a little bit of the pie, right, Dutch?"

"All these years, I've been hanging around. Oh, sure, there's some rough work, a shooting, send for the Dutchman. I do my job, keeping the peace. But where the big stuff is, the big guys stealing the city blind, cheating, lying, using the badge to commit the worst crimes, I kept a blind eye to it all. Never made waves. Never rocked the boat. Good old Dutch, just waiting for his pension. Marking time."

"You won't be sorry, Dutch," Huntoon said anxiously. "A man is entitled to his fair share. Just like a civilian."

Hollinger felt awkward, a stranger in his own skin, the joints stiff, the parts not working well. "A cop is different. A cop takes an oath. A cop wears a badge. People depend on cops to protect them, their property, to play it straight. Uphold the law."

"That's naive, Dutch. Life isn't that way. This is a jungle and what you get is what you can take."

"Forget it, Wilbur," Iversen said.

Words poured out of Huntoon as if his vocal chords were out of control. He didn't want to believe that he faced a man who chose to be his enemy. "Just say the right words, Dutch. So everybody can relax. Business as usual, right?"

"Iversen tried to take me out."

Iversen concentrated on his driving. They were on Truman Avenue now, rolling past the Catholic church. "Everybody needs a jolt now and then, Dutch."

"You certainly jolted me, John Roy."

"There's your answer, Wilbur," Iversen said.

"Dutch," Huntoon pleaded. "For God's sake, Dutch, use your head!"

"Let me think about it."

Huntoon began to breathe again. "There. I knew you were a person of good sense. Adjust, that's the trick to life. Adjust and get along. I have always considered you a man of excellent judgment and discretion."

"How much time have I got?"

"Twenty-four hours."

"That's long enough."

They drove back to the airport and Dutch went back to his car. When he was gone, Iversen said, "He's not with us."

"He said he'd think about it. He'll make the correct decision, you'll see."

Thirty minutes later, Iversen made a phone call. "Do it," he said. "As soon as possible. And this time do it right."

"Consider it done."

When Hollinger arrived, Annie was seated on the narrow front porch of his house, hugging her knees, looking solemn and frightened.

"What are you doing here?"

"Ah, don't be such a hard rock, Dutch. I was worried about you."

He went inside and she went after him. "You want a beer?"

"Mind if I smoke?"

"Why not?"

He fetched a can of beer from the kitchen and re-turned to the living room to find her curled up on the couch. He sat an arm's length away and examined her, decided she had the kind of face a man never grew tired of looking at. He took a long pull on the can.

"I want to tell you about me and Tom-tom," she said, letting the words out one by one, as if weighing each for truthfulness and impact.

"Forget it. That's none of my business."

"Yes it is. I want it to be. It was over between us."

"You said that already."

"Sometimes a woman gets involved with a guy and she shouldn't. She knows she shouldn't, I mean. It's as if you're off in space, watching it all take place. Chastising yourself for being a fool, for subjecting yourself to punish-ment and pain, wondering when you'll take charge of your life and live right. You know what I'm saying to you, Dutch?"

"There's no reason to talk about it."

"I can't forget anything I've ever done, or been, or felt, or dreamed. That's the goods of my life, Dutch. I don't want to forget. Tom-tom played a role and it's over now. But he was there and in some way I cared for him, wished it could have been better, y' know?"

He nodded once and drank some more beer.

"I'm sorry he's dead, but I don't want him back again. Does that make sense?"

"Lots." He finished the beer and went after another. She waited for him to settle down. "I care for you, Dutch."

"Look. I am into a lot of things you can't really know about . . ."

"Tell me."

"It's not your business."

"If it's yours, I want it to be mine."

"Don't be a child."

"I'm a woman, Dutch."

"Compared to me, you're a child. What I'm into is heavy, the heaviest."

"I can help you."

"No one really can."

"I love you, Dutch." She said it so softly that it was almost inaudible. "I love you a great deal, Dutch."

He looked away and sighed. "They offered to buy me off," he said presently.

She didn't have to ask who "they" were; she knew. The powers that manipulated lives in Key West, that pulled strings, pushed and shoved, damaged people in the flesh and in the spirit. "They" existed everywhere, the powerful and the corrupt, the devious ones, the destroyers of people and lives. The bad guys.

"They'll arrange for an early pension," he told her. "And more. Enough to be comfortable on for the rest of my days."

"You'd be done with the hassle, Dutch."

"Yes," he said, working on the beer can. Then: "But I'm like you, I would never forget."

"And if you don't take the deal?"

He rolled his head to relieve the tension. "They've come after me before, they'll come again."

"Sooner or later they'll get you."

"That's a reasonable assumption."

"I don't want you killed, Dutch."

He laughed mirthlessly. "I'm with you, babe."

"Take the deal."

"I don't think I can do that, Annie."

"You fool," she hissed, with an intensity that captured his attention. "What good are you dead? To me? To anyone? A hero cop. They'll give you a jazzy funeral and play taps over your grave."

"I can't run away."

"Of course you can. We'll run together. I'll love it, running free, out of this muck. In the end, all there is is two people caring for each other, taking care of each other. Nothing else adds up in this spoiled world."

"Maybe so."

"Tell them you'll do whatever they want you to do. Pick up the phone and tell them. Do it now, Dutch. While there's time. Then we'll split and I'll make love to you until you do forget. You will forget. You will."

"That makes a lot of sense."

"Make the call, Dutch."

"That's what I ought to do."

"Do it, Dutch."

37

Graham led his men aboard *La Florida*. Paco recognized Hector and Figueroa, but the others were strangers to him. Four young men in ordinary clothes, looking no different from young men anywhere. But they were different, he knew. These were another breed of the True Believers that infested the times. Fanatics dedicated to freeing a land they had never known, perhaps never set foot on. Emotional killers on the search for a way to legitimize their compulsion to destroy and to kill. In the name of some Singular Truth, they would act out their destructive fantasies.

Welles took his place alongside Paco. "These are very good men," he said.

"For killing, yes."

"There is a time for killing."

"Once I would have agreed. Now I am not so sure. Men kill in order that others may live, they make war for peace, they lie and steal and cheat in order to create a better world. The contradictions trouble me more and more, Commander."

"You are not for Fidel?"

"No. But I am not for you either, Commander."

"So you've made clear." Welles's smile was short and tight. "You have always been a good man, Paco. You still are."

"This time. I take you where you want to go, you do what you have to do and you bring my brother Kiki, out. But do not ask me to fight. I will do no shooting. I will do no killing."

"Take care of the boat, Paco. The rest, my men and I will take care of the rest. Now let's get under way."

"Cast off forward," Paco commanded. Moments later *La Florida* was outward bound, looking to a casual observer like any other charter boat on her way into the Gulf for a fishing trip. In the dim light in the cockpit, Welles's bony face was hard. His eyes were unmoving. "I have faith in your seamanship, Paco. In your courage. Your perception of political realities is limited. What we do on this expedition shall change forever the face of Cuba and the Western Hemisphere. We strike a blow for freedom and justice everywhere."

For the first time, Paco began to feel afraid.

Maribelle sat in her car until *La Florida* departed Garrison Bight. Only then did she return to her house. She poured a cup of coffee out of the Norelco and took it to the phone and dialed. Listening to it ring, she lit a cigaret. A woman answered.

"Let me speak to Felix," Maribelle said.

"*Momentito*."

Felix came on the line. "*Bueno!*"

Maribelle said her name. "They've gone. Paco and Graham. Plus six others."

"They are armed, I suppose?"

"They carried duffel bags."

"They are armed. Very well. From here on it is my responsibility. Your cooperation will not be overlooked."

"Do not call me again, Felix."

An amused note slid into his voice. "Of course I shall call you, Maribelle. Whenever the need arises. You are very good at what you do. The Revolution cannot afford to lose people like you."

"Fuck," she said softly, and hung up.

She went into the bathroom and took off all her clothes. She let water into the tub and climbed in with her coffee and cigaret. She drank the hot liquid and smoked and watched the water rise higher around her body. ¡Ay, *Paco!* How much she would miss him. ¡Ay, qué hombre! One remembered such a man for a very long time. The good of him, the evil. There would be pain and regret, shame and guilt, until it all passed. The worst of life passed. One became used to everything. If one managed to live long enough.

Louise grew itchy. No other word so suited her present state. The persistent creeping of desire under her skin. Raunchy. Horny. Hot. All the words pleased her and stimulated her even more.

She craved Sam's presence. She could taste him in her mouth. Smell the manly odor of his flesh. Remembering how it was with him, she was unable to remain still for long.

She tried to locate him.

She called to his father. Charles said he was anxious to talk to Sam himself. If Louise heard from him first, deliver the message, please.

She poured a rum and Coke and jiggled her crossed leg and tried to work up nerve enough for the next call. Finally she dialed.

"This is Louise, Hilda," she began.

There was an extended, plainly hostile silence.

"Yes, Louise?"

"How are you, Hilda?"

"Widowhood takes some getting used to, my dear." Verbal safeguards against the unexpected intrusion.

"If there's anything I can do . . . ?"

"What do you have in mind?"

"Anything—"

" 'Anything is nothing,' Grant used to say."

Under assault, Louise considered withdrawal. But the itching persisted. "I understand Sam is doing some work for you . . . ?"

Hilda swore to herself. The little prick couldn't keep his mouth shut. Who else had he told? How widespread was the leak? How much damage already done? "A minor assignment," she said with adolescent innocence. "Some research, filing, that sort of thing. Sam is good at details, if nothing else."

Louise chose her words with care. "I'd like to get in touch with him . . ."

"Oh," Hilda said, "do you have some work for him, too?" She regretted the comment immediately. Sam was servicing both of them, and each of them knew it. To mention it, to get involved in discussing that supposedly private act, would be a horrendous mistake that could only hurt her plans for the future. It was absurd to allow

jealousy to interfere. Sam was a passing necessity in her
life and, as long as she got what she wanted, nothing he
did mattered. As for Louise Welles, she mattered not at
all. "Sam's not here," she tacked on, not unkindly.

"Thank you."

Louise hung up, frustrated, still itchy, wondering what
to do with herself. For herself. By herself. In time she
came up with an answer.

38

Hollinger showed himself.

Hiding would only postpone the inevitable. Caution
might complicate his defense. And surrender, he intuitive-
ly knew, was no longer possible. Or acceptable.

So he showed himself, day and night. Attending his
case load. Asking questions about this crime and that one.
Picking up snatches of information from informants,
passing time in a bar here or a coffee shop there, joking
with street hustlers and ignoring anything that would keep
him too long in one place, anything that might dilute his
concentration. Or alter his purpose.

Along Front Street, up Duval, circling back to the
Public Library, down to the docks where the shrimpers
put in. After dark he bounced from club to club, drinking scotch and dropping an easy trail to follow.

By the time Paco Valentín was two hours out to sea,
Hollinger had embarked on his deliberately casual walk
home. For the last thirty minutes, he had been aware of
the intense, sinewy man, an ominous shadow going everywhere Hollinger went.

Off Duval into a poorly lit side street. Even at this
late hour, half a dozen boys lingered in hushed fraternity,
some black, some *latino*, some white. They paid no atten-

tion to the detective. Two blocks along, around a corner, he ducked between two parked cars. The tail stepped up his pace, anxious not to lose his quarry, closing fast.

The man swung into view and saw the empty street in front of him. He swore and broke into a run. Hollinger waited until the last possible moment before showing himself. He came from between the cars swinging a heavy fist. The sinewy man showed quick reflexes, shifting and turning, causing the blow to glance off the side of his narrow skull. He went down to one knee and suddenly a pistol leaped into his hand and he was shooting.

Hollinger dived over the hood of the nearest car, aware that he'd been hit just under his ear, a deep burn that caused him to swear. He landed in the street, and rolled, went charging to one side.

Concealed behind a blue Mustang, he hesitated briefly, then launched himself toward the gunman. The little man reacted at once in a graceful pirouette, leveling his pistol. He got off one wild shot just as Hollinger struck his gun arm. The pistol went flying and down he went. Hollinger struck twice, short heavy blows. It was over.

Hollinger cuffed him, hauled him erect, breathing hard. "I'm a cop, *amigo*. You're under arrest for attempted homicide for starters."

"*Ay, hombre*. I am a poor man with a wife and three sons in Bogotá. I am not a criminal but I am desperate for some money."

Hollinger's neck was beginning to sting. He put a handkerchief to the wound. Blood. He glared at his prisoner.

"Be quiet, man! Look what you've done. You hurt me. It makes me sick, the sight of my own blood . . ."

According to his I.D.—and Hollinger was certain it was a fake—his name was Juan Manuel Meléndez Gonzáles of Bogotá, Colombia. He was a coffee salesman, he said, on holiday in the United States.

"Why the pistol?"

"The stories of criminals in the United States have reached my country. I was afraid."

Hollinger pointed out that Meléndez Gonzáles had been carrying a .22-caliber with attached silencer, hardly a common weapon of self-defense. He suggested that the

pistol might be the same one used to commit a certain
number of homicides in recent weeks.

Meléndez Gonzáles insisted he'd found the gun in an
open trash can. Fingerprints were taken and Hollinger
ordered a check in Washington and in Bogotá. "Test-fire
that twenty-two and match the slug with the ones that
killed the Keely woman."

Word of Hollinger's activities reached Acting Assistant Chief Wilbur Huntoon and he promptly summoned
the detective to his office. "What's all this about?"

"I have a hunch this is the gun used in the Keely
killing, and to take out Izzy Ben-Ezra."

Huntoon grunted, indicated the bandage on Hollinger's
neck. "You going to be okay?"

"He tried to snuff me."

"Ah, why would anyone do that?"

"He's a hit man. Somebody ordered it."

"Who would do a thing like that, Dutch?"

"I thought you might know something . . ."

Huntoon rolled his massive shoulders. "Go home,
Dutch. Get some rest. Can't afford to have any of our
good cops getting shot down. Take a couple of days off."

"I might just do that."

"By the way, Dutch. That little talk we had, you
reached any decision?"

"Still thinking, Chief."

Huntoon shuffled some papers. "I am certain you'll
come up with the correct choice, Dutch."

Hollinger went directly to Annie's place. She was
getting ready to go to work. She fussed over him, put him
to bed, and brought hot tea with lemon and honey. He
tried to make love to her but she broke away, insisting that
she wasn't going to do anything to open his wound.
He claimed never to have felt better.

"Which proves you must be in shock," she answered,
keeping her distance. He sipped the tea and watched her
hopefully and after a while she sat on the edge of the bed
and held his hand.

"Hasn't it broken through to you, Dutch, that you
have a pretty bad job?"

"I like being a cop."

"That's ridiculous! You may *need* to be a cop.

You may *want* to be a cop. But only a masochistic creep obsessed with death could enjoy it."

"That's me, I reckon."

"They're getting too close, Dutch."

"I'm getting close."

"They'll get you yet."

He patted her leg. "Not as long as I've got my good-luck piece."

"I know a beach in Mexico. A village with no TV and no telephones. No crime, Dutch. People fish and butcher a wild pig once in a while. The swimming is good and we can make love and smoke leaf and watch the sunsets. No hassles, Dutch."

"This Meléndez, he was their best shot. He is going to open up to me, Annie. He has to. Otherwise it's maybe twenty years in the slammer. When he talks, I'll have the evidence I need."

She stood up. "Damn you, Dutch. I've finally figured you out, you're a romantic. A knight on a white horse. Gary Copper at high noon. Leo Durocher was right, don't you know? Nice guys do finish last."

"Go to work and let me rest. A few hours' sleep and I'll be better than ever."

"I'll stay with you."

"I'm all right."

"But am I?"

He slept for six hours and when he woke she spoon-fed him a thick minestrone with saltines, and then he slept some more. The next time he woke, it was night and he ate some scrambled eggs and bacon, bread and butter, and plenty of coffee. Despite her objections, he showered and dressed and went down to the station house.

The uniformed man on guard asked how he was and Hollinger said all right. "What about your prisoner?"

"An angel, Dutch. Not a peep out of him for hours."

"I want to talk to him."

"Sure, Dutch, go right in."

Juan Manuel Meléndez Gonzáles was hanging from a steam pipe on the ceiling of his cell by his belt. His eyes were popped open and his mouth was agape as he twisted slowly in the still air.

"Suicide," Wilbur Huntoon announced solemnly. Chief of Police Henry C. Watson, behind his neat, shining desk, nodded wisely. "There can be no doubt."

The city manager said he agreed with the finding.

The mayor cleared his throat and concurred, his very word.

Acting Lieutenant John Roy Iversen, from his place against the far wall, turned his eyes to Hollinger. The handsome face wore a slightly quizzical expression, the clear intelligent eyes glinted in amusement, the finely etched brows lifted imperceptibly in question. In challenge.

Hollinger felt like a fool. "It was murder," he said.

"Why do you keep saying that?" Chief Watson asked sadly.

Huntoon growled. "We have no evidence of foul play."

Hollinger, as if alone, spoke to a point in space. "Many crimes are being committed around here. We have no proof, no legal evidence, no arrests are made. Meléndez Gonzáles didn't hang himself."

"What makes you so sure?" the city manager, a slight man with the myopic intensity of a certified public accountant, wanted to know.

"Yes?" the mayor put in. "We all respect your professional abilities, Dutch. But why turn a simple suicide into a murder that will undoubtedly prove to be unsolvable?"

"Meléndez Gonzáles was a professional hit man. They don't kill themselves."

"Idle talk," Huntoon said.

"A good cop trusts his hunches," Iversen said, his enjoyment clear. He was relaxed and very much in charge. Rank had little meaning here; the chain of command had been shredded, going off in strange and alarming directions.

"He'd been given a contract on me. He expected to be protected by his employers. He expected to be turned loose eventually."

"Then why did he kill himself?" Chief Watson put in.

"He didn't," Iversen said, cool authority in his stance. "That's Dutch's point, right, pal?"

"Meléndez was a dealer," Hollinger said.

"Drugs?" the city manager said uneasily. His eyes skittered around the room, pausing nowhere.

"A direct line from Colombia to here. Important shipments of top-grade grass and coke."

"Cocaine!" The mayor seemed surprised. "I didn't know—" He broke off and examined his shoe tops.

"Proof?" Huntoon demanded.

"Let's go back to the Keely-Olvera shootings." Hollinger warned himself to end it, to stop the charade. No matter what was said in this room, it would change nothing. These men, for reasons best known to themselves, were not interested in his theories, in the tangled web of fact and intuition, of rumor and evidence, which he had compiled. But he had been a cop too long to break it off, not to try and convince his superiors that he was on the right track. And as he talked, he was aware that Mister Four, against the far wall, was silently mocking his effort. "We began thinking it was a burglary, or a paid job bought by Bettyjane's estranged husband, or even a disgruntled lover after her. That was a dead end. The killer came to Sunshine Lane after Livia Olvera. She was a mule in the pipeline out of Colombia, carrying cocaine. As far as I've been able to find out, she made at least a dozen trips in the last fourteen months. Under three different passports, three different identities. It took a lot of time on the phone to check that out, but it was there."

The chief of police said, sensibly, "Okay, she ran a little coke—lots do."

"She ran a great deal of coke, a couple of kilos every trip. She was after more money, threatened to blow the lid on the entire operation—"

"You can prove that, Dutch?" the mayor asked nervously.

"Yes, proof?" Huntoon said, shifting around to face Iversen. "That's conjecture, Dutch, and both of us know it. A nice, neat line of thought, but all in your head."

"There's talk in the streets and—"

"Not enough to go on trial with," the city manager said. He was standing straighter now, thin lips curled back over long, yellow horseteeth.

"The slugs will match. The weapon will prove out and we—"

Chief of Police Watson leaned forward, a narrow look of triumph lighting up his face. "One small problem, Sergeant. The gun you speak of, it's been stolen."

Hollinger's perceptions slowed and he saw everything through a thick, distorting jelly. He felt aged, crippled, drained, at once furious and unable to care. He struggled against the impulse to give up, to weep, to turn and run. "Stolen?" He heard his voice as if from a great muffling distance.

"Out of the property room," Iversen explained.

"Incredible," Huntoon said, calmly. No longer interested in the proceedings.

"Almost impossible to believe."

"There'll be an investigation of course," Watson said.

"The police property room robbed," the mayor said in awe. "We'll be the laughingstock."

"The bullet . . . ?" Hollinger knew better. Disaster had come down all around and there was no way to avoid its terrible results.

"It was with the pistol, tagged and ready to go up to the FBI in Miami. Too bad."

"That doesn't leave us much in the way of physical evidence. Sorry, Dutch, all the work you've done."

Chief Watson stood up. "Well, that's it," he declared with executive dispatch.

"I suppose so," Huntoon said.

"Not much choice," the mayor added.

"Case closed."

39

Louise woke in a strange place and was immediately aware that her body ached and throbbed. She forced herself to sit up and discovered she was surrounded by sleeping bodies. Three naked men, sprawled out limply. Every-where the lingering smell of burned marijuana and cigarets and the offending odor of stale whiskey.

She came off the bed and found bruises on her thighs and one breast was tender. She began to remember; the burly man with the thick mustache she had picked up in Chico's Disco. He reminded her of Grant. The burly man brought her to a party, gave her something to drink and something to smoke, then took her to bed.

A bed already peopled by two men making love to each other. None of it seemed to matter at the time and when the burly one was through with her, she hardly noticed when the others took their turns with her. Vaguely she remembered the fight—or was it a fight?—blows were exchanged and she had been beaten and when the beating was done they were at her again, each of them, more times than she could remember.

Walking now was a painful process. She picked her way into the next room where there were more naked bodies asleep. She tried not to think about what she had done, or had done to her. She searched for her clothing.

A tiny blond girl also naked, appeared, a container of orange juice in hand. She took a long drink and silently offered it to Louise. Aware of a pervasive thirst, Louise drank.

"I'm Marcia," the blond said, offering her hand.

Louise said her name, eyes hunting for her things, She spotted her shirt and moved toward it. Pain shot through her groin and she winced and groaned.

Marcia put on a sympathetic face. "Those guys hurt you, honey? Sometimes things get a little rough."

"I guess so. I don't remember too much."

"It'll all come back."

Louise took another step and stopped, gritted her teeth.

Marcia reached out and placed her hand lightly over Louise's pubic area. "Poor baby," she murmured.

Louise froze in place, unable to move, unable to speak.

"Men don't know what it means to be tender, lov-ing . . ." She leaned over; her kiss was a cool alien caress. Louise felt herself stiffen, yet offered no resistance. And gradually, reluctantly almost, the tension seeped out of her and the great muscles of her thighs gave way and spread and she felt herself being led, maneuvered, directed. No longer aware of the pain, she floated, warm and sentient, until nothing that had been mattered. Not Graham, nor Grant, nor Sam Dickey. At last she had come home.

"Hello, Hilda!"

The agent's voice over the long-distance wire was faint and crackling with electricity.

"Jimmy, can you hear me?" Her mind was made up; things could not go on as they were. She could accept Louise Welles as a rival, even as the third point in a sexual triad. She could not accept carelessness, failure to perform the work, a lack of professional concern. Sam had displayed all of those shortcomings. Despite every effort she made to inspire him, to firm up his commitment to the book. It was as if Sam were determined to fail, and in so doing drag her down with him. No way she'd permit that.

"I hear you very well, Hilda. How's the novel coming?"

"That's why I called. Sam can't cut it, Jimmy."

"Sorry to hear that. What's the next step?"

"I'd do it myself, Jimmy, but I am not a writer. I can direct, edit, support a writer, but not do the work myself."

The crackling on the line increased and she grew irritable, afraid they'd been cut off. "Jimmy! Are you still there?"

"I was thinking. Do you know Stewart Browne? Done a couple of novels. Published, but with no commercial success. A good man, a good brain, a growing talent. Stewart could do this job."

"Will he do it?"

"I can talk to him." He hesitated. "He's young, Hilda. Strong-willed, but very much the pro. He reminds me a great deal of Grant, the way he talks and acts, the way he writes. Yes, he'd be perfect."

"Do it today, Jimmy. My funds are running low. I must make some money."

"I'll get back to you. Maybe we can get an advance

on this project, a sizable advance. I think Stewart will work cheap—"

"Call me as soon as it's settled."

"Trust me, Hilda."

The hell with that, she thought afterward. Grant had warned her: "Never trust a man who does his job only for money. Agents, stockbrokers, bankers; dollars are their only reason for being." Grant was right, of course, as he'd been right about so many things. What would she do without him? He had been like a great bullying security blanket under which she'd been shielded, if not entirely safe. She poured herself a substantial drink. "Fair weather or foul," Grant used to say, "booze is a man's best friend." She raised her glass in a silent toast to her late husband, a man so often right. Right, right, right; except where time mattered most.

40

Iversen opened the door and arranged a smile of welcome on his handsome face.

"I wasn't expecting anybody, Dutch. Come on in." He preceded the other man into the living room. "I'm having a beer, how about you?"

Hollinger shook himself as if trying to shake off a terrible burden. He brought his police .38 out of his belt and aimed it at Iversen.

"Is this some kind of a joke, Dutch?"

"Sit down."

Iversen sat. The smooth-featured face grew mottled and lost its usual self-assurance. The keen blue eyes were cloudy.

"Don't make any mistakes, Dutch."

"You have a bad habit, John Roy. You keep trying

to waste me. It's getting so I keep looking over my shoulder. Jittery, you know. I'm getting jittery, John Roy."

"That's over, Dutch."

Hollinger cocked the pistol, one notch.

Iversen paled and talked rapidly. "There's no need any more. You can see that. It's over. Even if you wanted to go on, the case is closed. You're not a threat any more."

Hollinger eased the hammer back another notch.

"For chrissakes, Dutch!"

Hollinger jammed the muzzle of the pistol between Iversen's eyes. The beer can fell to the floor.

"Izzy Ben-Ezra was a good guy, John Roy. He saved my life. We lived separate lives, but he was there when I needed him. He was a friend and he was doing a job. You had him blown away—"

"No!"

"The hell you say! And the Olvera woman and Bettyjane. And all of us played a part in Arthur's death. Harry Waterman, a smarmy little creep, but a human being. You had him knocked off."

"You dont understand, Dutch."

"And maybe Bill Vail, so you could take over the whole rotten business."

"That's all it ever was, Dutch, business."

"You're a cop."

"Man, don't you know? Practically everybody's got his hand in the till. I'm just stage-managing it all."

"A cop is supposed to uphold the law, not break it."

Iversen pulled back as far as he could go, the words coming out in a snarl. "Who the hell are you to preach! You're going to blow me away. What for? Where's your proof? Who made you judge and jury, executioner? What makes you such a special moral case?"

Hollinger's internal resolve wavered. A failure of nerve, of concentration, of *belief*. Pull the trigger and he was no different from Iversen, or the others. Perhaps worse, for he pretended to be a good cop. In that suspended fraction of time he realized that he wanted, *wanted*, to kill John Roy Iversen. Wanted to destroy everything the other man was and stood for.

"What good will it do?"

Who had spoken? Hollinger couldn't be sure. A loud

echo ricocheted off the sides of his skull and his eyes began to water and ache. Take Iversen out and then what?
A substitute was waiting in the shadows for the opportunity. Blue corruption extended up and down the line,
from side to side, in uniform and out. It reached, he was
convinced, into the highest levels of life on Key West.

He took a quick step backward and eased the hammer back into place. Iversen, pale, his cheeks moist,
slumped in place.

At the door, Hollinger said: "Don't tip the scales,
John Roy. I'm a man who changes his mind."

"You'll never be sorry, Dutch."

Hollinger knew better than that.

41

Halfway to Cuba, cruising under a high crescent
moon, Hector and Figueroa hauled Sam Dickey out of
the dry locker where he'd been hiding. They dragged him
topside and beat and kicked him until Graham Welles
stopped them.

"Did you know about this?" Graham said to Paco.

"He was a stowaway."

"How did you find out about this trip?" Graham said
to Sam. The battered youth opened his mouth as if to
answer, then reminded himself who was asking the question. If he admitted Louise had been his source, Graham
would want more information and Sam was not sure he
could resist their method of questioning.

"It really doesn't matter," Graham said, straightening
up.

"What are we going to do with him?" Paco said.

Graham gestured to Hector. "Put him over the
side . . ."

PART
V

42

The sea was up and *La Florida* pitched and rolled, bringing Graham out of the cabin. His eyes swept the deck, coming to rest on Sam Dickey huddled in the corner of the wheelhouse. Watching him, Welles said, "Are we in for a blow, Paco?"

"The radio says it'll pass, just a squall. You want me to turn back?"

Welles lifted his eyes. Nothing showed. "No, no. We mustn't disappoint our intrepid reporter friend here. Oh, we'll continue on to the rendezvous." He went back below.

"You're really going to take them to Cuba," Sam said. One eye had begun to swell and his nose was crimson, crusted with blood. His back hurt when he moved and whenever he shifted around pain shot out of his left knee.

"That's right."

"But why"

Paco grimaced. "Because Welles and me go back a long time together. Because he asked me in a nice way. Because he and those boys in there have every kind of gun you can think of. Now it's my turn—why are you here?"

Sam struggled to his feet. Every part of his body ached. "I'm a reporter after a story."

"Somebody put you onto this trip. Before this is over, Welles is going to ask you who."

357

"I won't tell him."

"Of course you will. The beating you took—just a little whipping to teach you a lesson. Welles knows plenty of tricks to make men talk."

"I'm tougher than I look, Paco."

"You are a fool. Have you forgotten how close you were to being dead a little while ago?"

"You saved my life, I appreciate it."

"I postponed your death, *amigo,* that's all."

"Postponed?"

"What do you think? Do you think Welles will bring you back to Key West so you can do a story about this operation? Listen, he will kill you first."

"Can't you stop him?"

"You wanted a story! Men are going to die soon, many of them. Pray for them, for all of us."

"I'm an atheist," Sam said, trying no to sound afraid.

"Ah," Paco said. "Maybe you better convert, *amigo . . .*"

They were within one hour of Cuba. The sea grew calm and through patches in the cloud cover they glimpsed an occasional star. They proceed without running lights, the diesels set to give off a minimum of sound. Paco cautioned his passengers to speak softly and posted some of them as lookouts.

"What happens if we run into a Cuban warship?" Sam wanted to know.

Hector laughed thinly. "Boom-boom."

"Oh, no," Figueroa said. "Fidel will have a marching band waiting. There will be a parade before they shoot us."

"They will give us a trial," one of the other men put in. "Fidel enjoys theatricals. He will make much propaganda."

"True. A large trial with all of my family looking on. They will try not to cry and at the same time they will publicly condemn me as a traitor."

"Imperialist running dog," Hector said without humor.

"*Aieee!* If only it were so."

They all laughed at that and the joking continued until Welles said it was time to check the weapons. After that, there was only the ominous clink of tempered steel upon steel.

"I think it is appropriate now," Paco said to Welles, "that you tell me our destination."

Welles brought out a map, spread it open. He pointed. "Here is where we are going."

"The Isle of Pines!"

"No, Cuba itself. Here, where the land is like a horn, there is a small cove, safe, protected, and invisible from the sea." He gave a pleased smile. "They call it the Bay of Redemption, a fitting name, no? We are the redeemers this morning. We will go ashore at this point, in the rubber boats."

As if to underscore Welles's words, two black rubber life rafts were broken out and inflated, set up astern.

"Am I to remain aboard *La Florida*?" Paco said.

Welles gave a small laugh. "Ah, Paco, could I be certain you and the boat would be where I left you when we return?"

"Commander, have you lost your faith in your fellow man?"

"What about me?" Sam Dickey said.

Welles eyed him coldly. "You will come, also." Welles checked the compass. "It is time," he said. "Turn west, Paco."

"So you are also a navigator," Paco said. He swung the wheel until they were headed into the Yucatán Channel. "The patrols here are frequent . . ."

Welles glanced at his watch. "We are making the passage between patrols."

"You have considered everything," Paco said dryly. "Can you tell me how it is to be done?"

Welles glanced briefly at Sam. "Why not? Nothing can stop me now. The old Roselli plantation, you remember it, Paco?"

"I have heard of it."

"Fidel uses the place, his leadership. It serves as a luxury hideaway for the top command of the army and the political infrastructure."

"Fidel will be there?" Sam said.

Welles gave no sign he'd heard.

"Last fall, a select group of Cuban scholars and poets and writers attended a meeting under the auspices of Yale

University. For security reasons, they met not in New Haven but at a certain rural location in New York state. There, in the lap of capitalist luxury, they patted each other's backs and egos, convinced that their words would change reality.

"Old friends from the academic and intellectual communities met and wept and commiserated with the lot of the other. The Cubans very cleverly sent along a non-Communist economist, the appearance of plurality in a Communist dictatorship. A very strategic move which undoubtedly had a telling influence on those most gullible of men, university professors.

"Now Fidel has reciprocated. Two dozen American academics and artists have been invited to attend a similar meeting in Cuba."

"The Roselli plantation?" Paco said softly.

"Fidel will make a speech calling for peace, understanding and open international relationships."

Sam Dickey understood that he was privy to an important news story, an eyewitness. Even better, a participant. He forgot about the pain, about the danger.

"You're going to assassinate Castro?" he blurted out.

Welles glanced over, as if surprised to find him still present. But it was Paco who spoke.

"Killing Castro is too obvious, Sam."

Welles waved an arm in the direction of his men, just beginning to come out of the cabin. They wore army fatigues. "Cuban army uniforms," Welles said. "The weapons they carry are Cuban, too—Russian, actually. Oh, no, not Fidel. Dead he becomes a symbol working against us. Alive he is an offense to half the world, and a living target, a fine enemy who marshals our people against him. Kill Castro, not at all."

"Then what is this trip for?" Sam said.

Paco answered. "To kill all those innocent American teachers and writers."

"Not me, Paco. Not my men. But a group of fanatical Cuban Communist soldiers will do so. All in the name of Marxist solidarity and purity."

"And so put an end to American-Cuban détente," Paco said.

"Exactly."

Sam said, "That's murder."

"That's war," Welles said, and joined his men for a last briefing.

"He's crazy," Sam rasped to Paco.

"He's a patriot, which may be even worse . . ."

Five minutes later, they came under attack. Two gunboats carrying light cannon and heavy machine guns. They had been lying in wait in the darkness of the channel with all lights extinguished, gunners primed for action. Without warning, they opened fire.

Paco swung the wheel and opened the throttle to full. The first rounds of cannon fire bracketed *La Florida* and the machine gunners, underestimating her speed, fired too low.

Welles's men began shooting back, an effort that would keep them occupied but otherwise have no effect, Paco knew. A backward glance told him the gunboats were closing fast. Welles issued orders to his men, then turned, picking his way forward.

Paco reached into the map drawer and withdrew the automatic pistol he kept there, thrust it into his belt and drew his sweater down to conceal the weapon. At that instant, a shell exploded on the forward deck. *La Florida* bucked. Paco fought for control and the boat picked up speed again.

A second shell landed on Lawrence Grant's favorite fighting chair, killing four of Welles's soldiers. A fifth man fell overboard and disappeared from sight. Welles, a pistol in hand, rushed toward Paco screaming.

"Traitor! You betrayed us!"

Paco flung himself backward and Welles's shot missed. Paco rolled and came over onto his chest, the automatic leaping as he fired. Welles went down, coughing and jerking spasmodically. Then he lay still.

"Oh, my God!" Sam said.

Hector, holding his guts from spilling out of a gaping belly wound, staggered up the canted deck, cursing in Spanish and shooting as he came.

Paco's first shot brought him down; a second round finished him. Paco went back to the wheel. *La Florida* was describing a wide circle, slicing across the lines of fire from the gunboats. A jolt, and then another, slowed the charter boat.

"One of the diesels is gone," he shouted to Sam. "And we're taking water. Get ready to go over. Check the life rafts."

Sam, slipping and sliding on a deck wet with sea water and blood, made his way astern, just in time to take four .50-caliber machine-gun slugs. He was dead before he fell.

"*Dios mío.*" Paco made the sign of the cross without thinking. He kicked off his shoes and shed the pea jacket he wore. One glance at the gunboats told him he had very little time left. He stripped off the rest of his clothes and went over the far side of *La Florida*, using the cabin to protect and shield his departure from the Cubans.

He went underwater and swam until forced to surface. A quick gulp of air and he went down again, repeating the process a number of times. Shock waves tossed him about. *La Florida* had exploded. He felt sad about the loss of his boat, for his future as a fishing captain. But not for long. The gunboats . . .

He surfaced. The gunboats were circling, their powerful searchlights looking for survivors. A finger of light came near and Paco dived.

The game continued for an hour. Finally, convinced there was no survivors, the Cubans left. Paco struck out after them, wondering how far to Cuba. And if the sharks would allow him to make it.

Daylight. The sun put pinpoints of light on the water and Paco swam with his eyes closed. There was nothing to see, would be nothing to see. Worse, should a boat come along, no one would see him. In the choppy waters of the channel, a bobbing head would not be spotted.

He tried not to think of how far he had come. Or how much farther he had to go. Such matters could only weaken his resolve, cause his body to become tense and bring on the killing weariness. Instead he stroked and kicked and forced himself to breathe easily, careful not to swallow water.

It would be good to get back to Cuba. It was his homeland, always would be, and he bore an everlasting affection for it that defied logic and separation, politics and revolution. No matter where he lived, he was a Cuban and once returning for good to his home had been an all-consuming dream. To do so he had connived and plotted and killed, and gone back. To the Bay of Pigs. To defeat. To the death of many of his friends. To the destruction of the dream.

This time would be different. This time he would spend time at home, with Kiki and his mother. She would scold him, of course, for staying away so long. For not being with her in her old age, as a good son should do. She would point to Kiki with pride and say that he had not left his mother. But despite all the scolding, the talk of other sons who did better by their mothers, she would be glad to see him again. He was the first son; that was the difference. A swelling joy took hold of him when he thought about seeing his mother again.

Until he remembered that she was dead.

All his returns ended in violence and death. This time was no different. They never had a chance. Welles was right: they had been betrayed. But not by Paco; Paco was no traitor.

Who then? Welles should never have told his wife what was going on. A secret stopped being a secret when it was shared. Louise had informed Sam Dickey. Who else had she spoken to? Had Sam revealed his suicidal plan to anyone? Paco did not believe it had happened that way. Too many men had died without a chance for it to be the result of idle gossip by an adulterous wife; or the loose tongue of a young man with more ambition than good sense.

There was a traitor; who? His head began to throb and he promised himself to think about it another time.

He swam on. And a vision of *La Florida* sailed into view. The boat had been a tool that allowed him to live a satisfying life and earn a living at it. But he had not loved the boat. No more than he loved his car. Or his gun. They were merely instruments to an end and he invested them with no mystical, mythical qualities.

La Florida had been a good boat and he had paid a great deal of money for it, had worked hard to keep it running and in good condition. The insurance would not cover the loss, for the insurance did not include sinking by Cuban gunboats. When he got back, he would have to work for wages again.

Aieee. It would be difficult in mind and in body to do

so. He was not so young as he had been and was fixed in his ways. Ask anybody. Ask Maribelle. But he had never believed that life was other than difficult. Or should be. Or ever could be.

Maribelle. It had to be Maribelle. There was no one else who knew. Ay, what a woman that one was! That warm sensuous face, Those round heavy breasts, the fine large nipples that fit so perfectly into his mouth. The rest of her, soft and moist and so accepting, so giving. He fit very well with Maribelle. So much beauty, so much spirit, so much life and love. It made him sad to know that he was going to kill her.

He swam on.

Cuba.

It rose out of the blue sea like a magic island. A place of perfect tranquillity and fulfilled promises. He ached to be ashore, to rest, to be among friends and hear only Spanish spoken the way Cubans spoke it. But he held back, careful to in no way alter his stroke. Do not go too fast, he commanded himself. Do not strain or try too hard. That way lay disaster. Cramps, tiredness, and death. He was still miles from shore and so much could go wrong before he reached the beach.

Out of the sea, he stumbled away from the shore to the outskirts of a small fishing village. He crawled into a culvert that ran under the single road that went through the village and went to sleep. Shivering and trapped in a bad dream that later he would not recall, he stirred but slept on. When finally he woke it was daylight and he made his way into the drainage ditch and stayed there until he had been warmed by the sun.

He tracked cautiously around the perimeter of the village. A clothesline gave up a pair of pants and a white shirt that fit reasonably well. At a construction site—a low prefabricated building that would be used as a school—he stole a workman's lunchbox and devoured its contents on his way back to the shore.

He found a boat. A poor boat. Owned by a poor man. An ancient rowboat with only hints of blue paint still clinging to the gunwales. There was a child's pail tied to an oar-lock and Paco took it as a sign that the boat shipped water. The oars were heavy and out of balance, but would do.

Unless he was to stay. Stay in Cuba. It would not be difficult to become part of the country again. He *was* a *cubano* and always would be. He could go to Havana, fade into that urban population. A new identity would come in time. He would find work, something quiet, productive, and live accordingly. An ordinary man spending his days at peace. After a year or two, he would make his presence known to Kiki. Perhaps he would marry one day; he was not yet too old. It could be a good life, and satisfying.

But there was the boat, and ninety miles of sea, and Key West. Only he could do what had to be done. So he took the boat, thinking with regret of the poor fisherman who owned it, but taking it anyway.

It was a long pull to Key West. Too far to go without food and water, or protection from the elements. There was no way he could make it. But he had to try.

He lay face down in the poor fisherman's rowboat and dreamed of Maribelle and the way it was to be with her in bed. Her hands on his flesh were tender and manipulated him with a rare and delicate skill. Her voice in his ear was a distant caress, full of encouragement.

"Take it easy, fella," the little fat man in plaid Bermuda shorts and a captain's hat said. "You're safe now. You're gonna be awright."

The little fat man and another, taller, fat man lifted Paco out of the rowboat and worked him up to two others on the thirty-eight-foot Chris-Craft. They brought him into a cabin and put him into a bunk and bathed his feverish skin with damp, cool towels. The little fat man squeezed drops of water between Paco's cracked lips.

"*Ay, Maribelle, gracias . . .*"

"What's that?" the tall man said. "What's he say?"

"Some women's name, I think . . ."

"Tell him to say it in English," one of the other men said jovially.

"Sure do beat hell, the way these spics are," the tall man said.

"Sonofagun escaped from Cuba, didn't he? Risked his life to get out of that commie Soviet rathole. I tell you, men, what we have got on our hands is a genuine all-American hero."

"Still a spic," one of the others corrected.

The little fat man accepted that. "Guess you're right. All-American spic . . ."

43

The six-o'clock news report out of Miami gave the report. Radio Cuba announced that Cuban naval patrol boats had prevented an American vessel from landing foreign troops on Cuban soil. The adventure had been foiled when the invading craft had been sunk in Cuban territorial waters with all aboard killed.

The Imperialist Adventurers were, Radio Cuba reported, lackeys of the CIA and further proof that it was necessary to remain vigilant against the dastardly attacks of the capitalist enemy. The name of each of the men aboard *La Florida* was read off.

Maribelle, listening carefully, felt immediate relief when she heard Paco's name. Later, much later, she wept. For there had never been another man like Paco Valentín.

There never could be another.

Louise lay in her husband's bed with Marcia, the tiny blond, and heard the same report. She gasped with fear and pleasure when the announcer said Graham's name.

"What is it?" Marcia said.

Then Sam Dickey's name was read off. "The fool," Louise said, sitting up, reaching for a cigaret.

"What is it, honey?" Marcia wanted to know. After a moment, Louise realized that she felt very good about things. Sam and Graham at the same time; she was well

rid of both of them. Graham had been her jailer, and Sam
would eventually have become too heavy a weight for her
to carry. She smiled at Marcia and stroked her small breast.
"Nothing to worry about, lover. Life couldn't be better."

"Oh yes it could," Marcia said, bending over Louise.
And she was right.

Monte Perrin hurried over to Charles's house to tell
him the news. Charles put his face in his hands and wept
and grieved for his son for a very long time.

Jacob Persky phoned Spencer Forester.

"Welles is dead. Fidel's people shot him and his boys
out of the water."

"Any connection to us?"

"Not so's you could notice. I'm careful about such
things."

"I don't intend to let this stop me."

"I agree."

"Can you find someone else?"

"To take Welles's place? No sweat. With the CIA in
an economy drive, there's a hundred ex-case officers looking for work. I'll line up a man by the end of the week."

"This is important, Jake."

"You don't have to tell me, Spence."

"Take care."

"I always do."

44

"They'll kill you, Dutch. You know that they will, no
matter what Iversen said." There were tears in Annie's
eyes.

"They'll try."

"You knew that and you still didn't shoot him? Why, damn you?"

"If I had, I'd've been just like him. No different. I couldn't do that."

"Oh, you fool, come away with me."

"I wish I could. But I'm going to stay and fight them."

"Cop," she snarled. "Stupid cop."

He shrugged. "Some old rabbi once said, 'If I am not for myself, who will be for me?' "

"Smartass rabbi."

He grinned. "If I am only for myself, what am I?"

"But there's nothing you can accomplish. No evidence, no witnesses. They'll harass you, frame you, finally find a way to kill you. Look at poor Paco—they always kill good men."

"He must have had a good reason for being out there, he was that kind of guy. I'm going to miss him."

"And I'll miss you, Dutch. Oh, damn."

"Would you have it any other way?"

"Yes, dammit! Oh, damn, I don't know."

He drew her close and caressed her eyes with his lips, and her cheeks, her ears. "I don't, either."

She clung tightly to him, as if to extract strength and courage from his massive body. "Can't you give it up, Dutch? Let someone else do it."

"There is no one else."

She placed her cheek against his chest. "I love you, Dutch, so very, very much."

"I love you, Annie. I'd given up on love. It didn't seem possible for me to feel that way again. I'd almost forgotten what it meant."

"There is so much love in you, Dutch. So much gentleness and goodness."

"If there is, you brought it back to life."

"Come away with me," she begged.

He searched her face with his fingertips, as if only in touch could a lasting image of her be captured. "Stay with me here."

"Until they kill you?" She disengaged, an abrupt firmness to her movements, as if her mind were made up. "I won't hang around until you're dead. I won't mourn over your body. I'm not strong enough to do that." She avoided his eyes.

He reached for her again and she made no effort to keep away. He kissed her tenderly and she shivered, pushed closer to him.

"I love you too much, Dutch."

"Too much to stay?"

She nodded gravely.

"It isn't easy for me to understand that."

She extracted herself from his embrace and offered up a wistful smile. "I'm not sure I do, either. But it's got to be done, for me if not for you. I have to leave here now. Today."

"Where will you go? That Mexican village?"

"It's a good place to be by yourself. A different way to live. A place without time as we know it. A place to look at yourself, and what your life has become."

He reached out for her and she caught his hand and kissed his wrist, retreated one long step, shaking her head as if refusing herself some precious reward that might corrupt an already corrupted spirit.

"Will you call me?" he said.

"There are no telephones."

"Write me."

"Mail service in Mexico is not very good. In the back country, it's especially bad."

"Will I ever see you again, Annie?"

"If you want to—"

"I do want. When this is over—"

She exhaled. "Yes, when it's over."

"—I'll pay your village a visit."

"I'll be there, Dutch."

"You're important to me, Annie. The best thing ever happened to me. I can't let you out of my life. I don't want you out of my life."

"Ah, that's so very, very nice. Be kind to yourself, Dutch. Take care of yourself."

"Depend on it."

"Promise?"

"Cross my heart and hope to die . . ."

45

Iversen was in a foul mood. He couldn't stop thinking about Hollinger and how he had felt with Dutch's gun against his skin. Never had he been to afraid, so enraged, so helpless. He could forgive Hollinger anything, forget all that happened, overlook the threat that Dutch posed; but there was no way to erase that terrible look at himself Hollinger had forced upon him. No way.

He heaved his jacket against the wall. Kicked his loafers over to the far side of the room. He tore at the buttons of his shirt, tearing one off. He took a can from the six-pack and took a long swallow; the beer was losing its chill.

He hefted his service revolver and examined it as if it were new to him. This weapon, so much a part of him, a dark extension of his most secret self. Using it was natural, inevitable. Killing was easy, a necessary act not to be considered for long afterward. Not to feel bad about. Some men needed to die violently, they courted it assiduously; he was merely the instrument of their desires.

He placed the call to Benny Skaggs. "Send her now," he said.

"I've got a special number lined up, John Roy. A real beauty. Do anything you want without a squawk."

"Don't tell me, dammit. Just get her over here." Skaggs was a dumbass redneck: good enough to run a string of hookers, but nothing beyond that.

"Sure, at once. You hear about Graham Welles, John Roy?"

"I heard."

"Imagine it—him and Paco blown away like that. Wonder what they were doing out there?"

"Dumbness is what it was. Just dumbness." He slammed down the phone. The report out of Cuba had disturbed him more than he cared to admit. He had always considered Graham Welles a shrewd and practical man, a man who trod carefully through life, making no mistakes. Yet he had made the biggest mistake of all, and for what? It made no sense to Iversen and never would.

He went into the bathroom and showered and when he finished felt much calmer. Still naked, he put himself on the bed, propped up with pillows, and went to work on a second beer.

He smoked and drank and thought about Hollinger again. It was over, he told himself with more confidence than was warranted. Hollinger had stirred up the water but had accomplished nothing. There was nothing he could do. No way he could damage John Roy Iversen. Why not leave him alone? Ignore the fool. Let him scratch and dig; he would always come up empty. Any problems he might cause would be insignificant. Why not permit him to live, a daily reminder of Iversen's generosity and humanity?

So deep in thought was he that he almost failed to hear the knock at the door. He considered using a towel to conceal his nakedness; to hell with it. Let the hooker see from the start what a real man was like. Let her get right to work.

Prideful and arrogant, conscious of his rising hostility, he opened the door. The girl was young and beautiful, her face set in that slack sensuousness that went with the trade. One glimpse of Iversen and she uttered a laugh, triumphant and pleased.

He drew away as if in mortal danger.

She stepped inside and closed the door. "Hello, Daddy," Ellen said. She began to unbutton her shirt.

Iversen fell back in confusion and spreading terror, unable to assimilate the facts of his life, unable to make sense out of what was happening to him.

"Look at you, Daddy." She stepped out of her skirt. "Seems like you can hardly wait. Now look at me. Look at me, Daddy. Look at me . . ."

Life is the raw material that every one of us may shape according to his dream. May you see the shining possibilities in ordinary things.

—NORMA INEZ HAYMAN OVERSTREET,
February 22, 1952

ABOUT THE AUTHOR

BURT HIRSCHFELD is best known for his bestselling novel, *Fire Island*. A native New Yorker, Mr. Hirschfeld was born in Manhattan and raised in the Bronx. He left school at the age of seventeen and took a series of menial jobs. Immediately after Pearl Harbor he enlisted, and spent three of his four years in service overseas. After the war, he attended a southern college for several years. For the next fifteen years he worked on and off for movie companies and also did some radio and acting work. Burt Hirschfeld did not write his first novel until he was in his early thirties. He worked on it for three years and, when it only earned $1,500, he abandoned writing for several years. At thirty-seven, he decided to find out for once and all whether he had the makings of a successful writer and began to freelance. He wrote everything—from comic books to movie reviews. He also wrote numerous paperback novels under various pseudonyms and eleven nonfiction books for teenagers which were very well received. *Fire Island* was his first major success. His recent novels include *Aspen, Provincetown* and *Why Not Everything?* Burt Hirschfeld lives in Westport, Connecticut, with his wife and two sons.

BURT HIRSCHFELD

From his first success FIRE ISLAND, to his latest, KEY WEST, this popular novelist has concentrated on bringing famous U.S. resort towns to life. Hirschfeld's engrossing plots are studded with fascinating characters whose hidden secrets are exposed by unexpected situations. WHY NOT EVERYTHING, however, represents a departure for the author, yet this sensitive portrait of a woman shows a new dimension to his writing.

ASPEN

This million-copy bestseller focuses on an ambitious land developer who comes to the skier's paradise with an unscrupulous scheme that will mar Aspen's natural beauty. The plan sets many volatile forces into action, threatening the lives of many people—and ending in murder.

PROVINCETOWN

A blazing novel set against the backdrop of the Cape Cod resort—the haven for artists, hippies and people who flaunt convention. Chosen as the site for a major Hollywood film, the town becomes the magnet for strange events involving an aging actress making her comeback, a tough biker fleeing the law and a handsome actor with a mysterious background.

KEY WEST

The inhabitants of this small Florida resort are stunned by the brutal double killing in the home of a millionaire playboy. A local cop investigating the murders unearths a hornet's nest dealing with greed and corruption—revelations that shake the very foundations of Key West.

WHY NOT EVERYTHING

Libby Pepper is a bright young woman—a wife and mother—who is dissatisfied with her lot. She feels she's out of step with her successful friends. So Libby decides to return to the business world. But in pursuit of her dream she unexpectedly discovers that getting the prize is less important than winning the battle.

(Read these Bantam Books—available wherever paperbacks are sold.)

RELAX!
SIT DOWN
and Catch Up On Your Reading!